DUEL ROLES

William Hatfield

Books by William Hatfield

CAPTIVE AUDIENCE
DUEL ROLES

Dedicated to Karen, my wife and best friend, for sticking with me through all the good and bad times, the trials and tribulations, over twenty-eight years of marriage, and all the other general weirdnesses that have been a regular part of our lives. And yes, I know that weirdnesses is not a word, but it sure fits well.

Thank you to my friends and fellow writers that have always been supportive, even when I was stuck in a huge writer's block that looked insurmountable.

Thank you to the Necronomicon and Oasis science fiction and fantasy conventions that kept inviting me year after year, even when it looked like Captive Audience might be my one-hit wonder. I still don't know how I always end up on the high-tech science panels, when I don't even believe in electricity. And how I'm always on a late Saturday night panel dealing with sex in the science fiction and fantasy genres. I've been married for twenty-eight years, for cripe's sake.

My sincere gratitude to the gnomes and little mice on treadmills that produce that energy we think of as electricity.

I would also like to thank the many people that have come up to me at these conventions, at work and gigs, and said "Well? Where is the sequel?" You kept me aimed in the right direction, even if the momentum was flagging.

My thanks to Jim Baker, a.k.a. JWBaker, for yet another wonderful cover. Wait 'til you hear my plans for the third one, Jim. And no, there will be no wizards. Sorry.

And as always, my thanks to Karen and our two feline kids, Ebbie and Angie.

CHAPTER ONE

Kowloon, China

Groundhog was having trouble concentrating on his work. His right hand slipped slightly, and he adjusted his grip. It was unlike him to have lapses of attention on the job. But the sound of gurgling water in the hot tub reminded him of his first and only professional failure...the Jade Viking.

When he'd gotten the message a month ago, it had seemed like an easy chore. Find out what happened to a missing cruise ship. The Jade Viking set sail from Osaka on July 10th with thirty-five hundred crew and passengers, and was due to arrive in San Francisco, July 14th. The second night out, the ship disappeared.

Groundhog had thought it was a stupid job, but if fools wanted to give him their money, he would take it. The U.S. Coast Guard was already looking and, if it had sunk, there would be traces. If hijacked, it would show up. You couldn't hide a ship that big just anywhere. He would simply follow up while somebody else earned his fee for him.

But he'd been wrong. No traces of wreckage, flotsam, or bodies had been found or washed up on any shore. No ransom message had been delivered. The satellite link connecting Jade Viking to the mainland had abruptly stopped at 1:14 a.m., July 12th.

It was as if the Jade Viking had vanished from the face of the earth.

But of course, that was impossible. Somewhere, there would be a trace. Finding things was one of his specialties. Actually, doing any job for which someone was willing to pay his exorbitant fees was his specialty.

And until now, he never failed to produce.

The Jade Viking disappeared on a high profile cruise, with a lot of important people aboard. The ship was being sold by Viking Lines, a subsidiary of Spencer Corporation, to Sukuru, a giant Japanese conglomerate. The executive vice-president of Sukuru was on board. He was also the heir apparent to the Toshida clan, which controlled Sukuru and a multitude of other Japanese interests. There was also a vice-president of Spencer Corp. supervising the sale, Kimberly Martin.

The captain's name was Jason Lang. The crew was half American, half Japanese, with Japanese Captain Hiroaki Tachibana waiting to assume command upon arrival in San Francisco.

There were several major movie stars, a host of lesser celebrities, the senior class from Chula Vista High, complete with chaperones. Thirty-five hundred people from all walks of life, just vanished.

Groundhog had been hired by Will Spencer, the namesake, chairman of the board, and majority stockholder of Spencer Corporation. He had implied that Ms. Martin was practically his fiancée, but it hadn't taken any time for Groundhog to find out how much an exaggeration that was. They'd dated several times, but by all accounts, she'd been cool to his advances.

Groundhog had tremendous assets for his work, and was very good at what he did. He wasn't a man to get angry, but this simply would not do. His teeth clenched as he tightened his grip with both hands. The obvious first choices, if foul play was to be assumed, were the two corporate players, Spencer Corp and Sukuru. But Will Spencer had hired him weeks ago, and Sukuru had contacted him this morning to do the same. His success rate would have kept either from hiring him if they were involved. He refused the second job on the basis of too many current contracts, but there was still a bitter taste in his mouth from the words. Two contracts for the same work normally would have appealed to him, but not this time.

The fee to Spencer would be returned, but nothing was going to keep him from finding out what happened to the Jade Viking and all the people on board, no matter how long it took.

His burden beneath the bubbling water went slack in his grasp, and he leaned forward to look.

Two faces stared up at him, their eyes bulging. An elderly Chinese man and his young mistress, both nude. Both dead from drowning.

Groundhog looked around for potential witnesses. The view from this cliff-side villa was spectacular. Hong Kong glowed with late night activity across the harbor. He glanced over the low stone wall at the other residences to the sides and below. No sign of life.

He surveyed the scene around the outdoor tub. A tray with lines of cocaine, several empty bottles of expensive liquors, a pipe with the remnants of hashish strewn around was all the evidence needed by the Kowloon police. An accident had been contracted, and one had been delivered.

He stripped off the long plastic gloves and frowned as he noticed the damp cuff of his silk shirt. That meant room service dry cleaning at his hotel in the morning. He would spill some brandy on it to hide the smell of the brominated water.

Groundhog's mind wouldn't leave the Jade Viking. He'd already done preliminary backgrounds on everyone missing. It was time to go deeper. As he carefully locked the gate to the hillside mansion behind him, he decided he would start with the captain.

Just where have you gotten to, Captain Jason Lang?

Space Station Osaka, far from Earth

Kimberly Martin sat down and displayed her best courtroom face as she watched Captains Lang and Tachibana settle back in their seats. The room was reminiscent of a corporate conference room, complete with long, wooden table. It seemed out of place, one door removed from the bridge of a space station, manned primarily by aliens. An open forum for all survivors of the Jade Viking was scheduled in little more than an hour, billed as an initial meeting to decide who was staying on Station Osaka, and who wanted to return to Earth. The captains had asked to see her beforehand.

They were about as different as two men could be. Captain Jason Lang was at least six and a half feet tall, wiry but of solid build, his hair mostly white with just a tinge of the original blond remaining after 63 years. Captain Hiroaki Tachibana was ten years younger, a full foot shorter, without a trace of gray in his jet black hair. Lang could be very boisterous, while Tachibana was reserved and soft spoken.

Yet they had so many things in common. Both men constantly showed consideration and respect, no matter who they were dealing with. And both were true professionals, taking great pride in their competence.

Captain Lang cleared his throat, casting his eyes back and forth between Kimberly and the Japanese captain. "I thought we should discuss several issues before the general assembly."

"A preliminary meeting to plan the preliminary meeting?" Kimberly smiled to show she was kidding. Well, mostly. Their exchange of furtive glances confirmed a suspicion she'd had. "And there's already been a pre-preliminary meeting to plan this preliminary meeting."

"The general meeting is certain to generate some very powerful feelings...and comments." Captain Lang frowned. "We felt cooler heads needed to put some thought into arriving at the best solution to this situation." Captain Tachibana nodded his agreement.

"Isn't this contradicting the concept of open government and total access by citizens?" Kimberly asked, feeling her right eyebrow rise in what she sometimes referred to as her 'Spock" maneuver.

"As it happens, sunshine laws and the like aren't applicable in this, ah, jurisdiction." Lang had the grace to look embarrassed. "In fact, this far from Earth, applicable laws are in rather short supply."

Tachibana spoke for the first time. "I think some people will be very forceful expressing their views, and there are a number of directions people will think we should take."

"It's not like you're going to get everyone to agree to one thing," Kimberly reminded them. "And for the record, I think coordinating in advance is a good idea." She looked at both of them in amusement. "So, why am I here?"

"Captain Tachibana and I feel that you have a singularly focused mind. You are reputedly one of the best corporate lawyers in the business world, and we could benefit from your observations and ideas." Lang looked embarrassed again. "I'm sorry. Is it Ms. Martin or Mrs. Morris, we should be addressing you as?"

Kimberly couldn't fault the question, but still found herself annoyed. She wasn't an indecisive person, but after two weeks of marriage, still couldn't make up her mind. There had been no indecision when she'd agreed to marry Jim less than two weeks after their meeting the first day of the ill-fated final sea cruise of the Jade Viking.

"I haven't taken Jim's name yet. Not sure I will. I'll get around to deciding one of these days." She made herself smile to set the two men at ease. "Kimberly will be fine."

"Well...Kimberly." Lang seemed to struggle a little with the familiarity. "As I was saying, we are going to need people that have leadership abilities, that can dispassionately make decisions, and then act upon them. People like yourself."

Kimberly looked back and forth at the two captains with suspicion. She didn't like being manipulated, and could usually tell when it was happening. Captain Lang blushed a little, but he didn't look away.

Captain Tachibana stared at her, a slight smile causing the corner of his lip to turn upward a bit.

"Ms. Martin, as you mentioned, we've discussed this between ourselves already." He bowed his head slightly. "We are having difficulty coming to an agreement on the best course of action. We both agree that we are not in a situation where an absolute democracy can exist," the Japanese captain continued. "We do not wish to force our plans on anyone, but there are practical considerations."

Kimberly couldn't argue with that. She wasn't a big fan of decision by committee.

"So," she chose her words carefully. "To paraphrase, we need to come up with a plan to let them decide on the course of action we feel they need to take."

"I wouldn't put it quite that way," Lang said with a pained look on his face. Then his innate sense of humor crept into his voice. "But since you have, well, yes."

"Jade Viking will leave for Earth in a week." Tachibana spoke with no inflection revealing his thoughts on the manner. "At this point, there is no consensus on a course of action. On what will happen when it reaches home."

Kimberly looked from one captain to the other. "What is it specifically that you don't agree upon?"

Tachibana shifted in his seat, showing uncharacteristic agitation. "I do not believe that, with all the power and scientific knowledge she represents, Jade Viking should be turned over to the United States government."

"And we should give it to another nation?" Lang's voice deepened in indignation as he frowned at his fellow captain. "Or a corporation? I don't think Sukuru, or Spencer Corp, for that matter, would necessarily have the best interests of the human race at heart." He turned to Kimberly, and a hint of a blush appeared above his crisply creased collar. "No offense intended."

5

"None taken." Kimberly stared from one perturbed man to the other, several times, then leaned back in her chair, the fingers of both hands lightly tapping on her thighs. She once again called on her courtroom face to cover her shock. "Let me get this straight. You're arguing about who to give the ship to when we reach Earth?"

"And under what conditions," Tachibana added fervently. "We can't just land, turn the 'car keys' over, and hope for the best."

"We would need some assurances." Lang did agree with that much, at least. "Some sort of guarantee that all this power would immediately be put to use ensuring the safety of the planet, and everyone on it."

"And how do we extract that sort of promise with any hope they will keep their word?" The normally imperturbable Japanese captain's voice began to rise in volume and pitch.

"And it would be any different with Sukuru?" Lang's voice also began to intensify.

"Gentlemen." Kimberly's voice was barely above a whisper, but it stopped them cold. They turned and stared at her. She deliberately brushed a strand of hair from her face.

"Yes, Ms. Martin?" Tachibana didn't seem to be ready to adopt a casual manner with her. He and Lang exchanged embarrassed looks at their near loss of temper.

"Gentlemen." She repeated herself, keeping her gaze on a space somewhere between them. She waited another moment, then yet another, and as they began to stir, her eyes snapped up, first to Captain Lang, startling him, then flashing over to Captain Tachibana. "Do you really think we dare give this power to anyone...else?"

Immediately, emotions began clouding the two men's faces, suspicion on one, anger on the other.

"I am a loyal American, and..." Lang stopped as Kimberly raised her left hand. The gesture was neither imperious, nor commanding, but it gave him pause.

"Say we return to Earth, land shuttles on the White House lawn, warn the president of dangerous aliens coming our way, and turn the Jade Viking, a captured alien ship with unbelievable power, over to them." She shifted the hand slightly, and Tachibana stopped, mouth open, but not speaking. "Or on government ground in Japan, Sukuru headquarters in Osaka, Will Spencer's back yard in the Hamptons." She deliberately took her time. "Is there any political or business entity on

6

the entire planet that wouldn't first use that power to their own benefit, to settle old scores?"

The last words were bitingly sarcastic. Her expression sardonic, and she considered the two men with a speculating stare. "And what do you think would happen to whoever turned over that power? Would we ever be seen again?"

"So we keep it for ourselves?" Captain Tachibana's stare was cold, calculating. "Use it to our own advantage? Become the most power-ful men..." He nodded to her in contemptuous acquiescence. "...and women, in the world?"

Kimberly could almost feel heat from their glares, and resisted the urge to smile. She'd made her point. Now she needed to repair the trust.

Her hands went back to tapping her thighs, and she let the uncom-fortable moment drag on. Finally, she spoke in a quiet, but firm voice.

"You can believe me when I tell you we could take this power for ourselves? That we could and should seize the day, the potential riches and power?"

Captain Lang's eyes were agonized, the anger gone, replaced by disappointment and, perhaps, a little fear? "I never would have, before now."

Captain Tachibana's eyes narrowed, suspicion showing in them. "Perhaps everything is not quite as it seems." His voice was uncertain.

Kimberly allowed a tiny smile, knowing the honorable Japanese man had been on the verge of a very strong reaction to her words. The smile grew as she leaned back, crossed her fingers over her midrift, and took a deep breath of relief.

"You know me very well, gentlemen. The things we've gone through together have given us all a very clear picture of each other's integrity, honor, and greed. Or lack thereof." Her voice warmed as their postures began to relax, tension slowly seeping away. "You could believe me capable of disregarding everything I hold dear, of betraying the human race?" Her lips pursed. "And yet you would give this gift, this duty we carry, to utter strangers, and hope for the best." It wasn't a question.

Lang gave an audible sigh of relief. "You had me worried for a bit there, Ms. Mart...er, Kimberly."

Tachibana gave an uncharacteristic snort that, for the moment, passed for laughter. "Your husband is supposed to be the actor, but you were quite convincing." His eyes grew serious again. "So, we can not give Jade Viking to anyone. But what can we do, just among ourselves? We would need manpower and resources far beyond what we currently have."

"We need a unified Earth to defend it properly. You've made me see that is highly unlikely." Lang sounded glum, then peered at her with hope. "Unless, of course, you have a plan?"

"Plan? No." Kimberly shook her head in thought. "I didn't come here with any concrete plans or ideas. I hadn't really focused on specifics at all. Just that some of us are staying here on Station Osaka, and some are returning to Earth." She sighed, a little chagrined. "I guess I've been too caught up in my own life to think about the bigger picture."

"Don't cut yourself short, Kimberly." Captain Lang's voice was gentle, his normal grace returned in full force. "In the short time since we seized this station, you've gotten married and inherited a teenage daughter. Most would consider that a full time job."

"Hmm," she murmured, distracted. Her mind flashed from point to point, considering details, resources, the very astronomic geography of the situation. "I do have a couple of thoughts on this."

"We're getting low on time," Tachibana reminded them. "We came here to formulate a plan, but have spent all this time tearing down everything we'd started."

"Well, what needs to be decided before this meeting?" Kimberly asked, and had to remind herself she wasn't cross-examining a witness. "I mean, were we planning on announcing anything more than when Jade Viking would be leaving, and asking people to declare whether they were staying on Station Osaka or returning to Earth?"

"We had intended on giving them details of the return," Captain Lang began, but stopped as Kimberly shook her head.

"They don't need to know that right now." She felt a grin tugging against the corner of her mouth. "If they press you, just tell them that the original destination of Jade Viking was San Francisco, and you aren't in the habit of letting thieving aliens alter scheduled ports of arrival." Her voice mimicked his, and Tachibana turned away to hide his amusement.

Lang had the grace to smile, but he was still serious. "We are going to have a situation when we do get back to Earth. Even before then. We have so many people, and their intentions are splintering in so many directions."

"Some people wish to return and pretend none of this ever happened," Tachibana agreed. "Others will try and sell their story to the tabloids."

"Some will rush to their respective governments to warn them, to tell them what we have, and how to get it." Lang sounded glum. "Once the government catches drift of what has happened, they'll lock us up anyway."

"And I'm sure there will be some spies." The two captains seemed to feed on each other's pessimism.

"We really only have two types of people to deal with." Kimberly spoke slowly as an idea, really a series of ideas began to form a clear pattern in her head. Nodding, she smirked at the two men. "We have people that want to help, and people that don't."

"That seems like a bit of an over-simplification, Kimberly." Lang's voice was kindly, but firm. "We have people staying on the station, manning the ships..."

"...returning to Earth to somehow organize a defense," Kimberly interrupted him without thinking, her mind racing ahead of the conversation. "But it really still comes down to helping, or not. The rest of the issues are simple details."

"How can they be simple details, when..." Lang sounded frustrated, and the Japanese captain didn't help when he too, interrupted him.

"Please explain," Tachibana said, giving her back the stage.

"Okay." Kimberly sat up straight, fighting the urge to chatter in her growing enthusiasm. She'd always had a tendency to speak faster and faster as she got caught up in discussions, arguments, debates, even court cases. This had her on the verge of babbling. "First we find out the true intentions of everyone, whether they are friend or foe. We stagger the return to Earth to give ourselves time to sell our story to the authorities, get released, and scatter before the problem kids get found. By the time their conflicting stories get sorted, we are inserted back into our previous lives, we get legal barriers up to keep the FBI and whoever else from grabbing us. Meanwhile, we have some people return to Earth on the sly, without anyone's knowledge, a kind of fifth column, helping us organize a base for eventually building a planetary defense."

Both captains looked at her, their expressions battling between confusion and hope. Lang ventured a comment.

"Fifth column?"

"Right. We'll have people underground that the government doesn't know about, coordinating between Jade Viking and those of us that are back openly, seeming to be return to their old lives, but really working in dual roles, creating a political and economic entity that can build defenses."

"Duel roles?" Tachibana looked confused, a rare instance of his knowledge of English failing him. "D-u-e-l?"

"No, no," Kimberly laughed. "Dual, d-u-a-l, not d-u-e-l. Well, maybe duel, in Jim's case."

"Indeed." Captain Lang glanced at his watch, and she saw they had less than twenty minutes before the general meeting. "Tell me this, Kimberly." His face held no trace of the humor infecting her. "These ideas of yours sound very fine, at first glance. But how can we separate friend from foe? How can we stagger the return of the evident survivors of the Jade Viking cruise ship when none of the "foes" will agree to it? How can we hold the FBI, the CIA, the corporations, for that matter, at bay?"

"How can we build any kind of credible defense for the Earth under these conditions? We face formidable foes, and the future of the human race is at stake." Tachibana's voice was almost indiscernible, sadness and, for the first time, defeat, showing in his face and posture.

Kimberly leaned back in her chair, folded her legs beneath her and smiled at them.

"Actually, I have a few ideas about that."

❖ ❖ ❖ ❖ ❖

Fifteen minutes later, Kimberly strode out of the room, and Captains Lang and Tachibana stared at each other in awe. Finally, Lang found his voice.

"That woman could be considered...dangerous." Words failed him for a moment. "She may have the most...devious mind the human race has ever seen. Sheer genius," he finished.

Tachibana sighed and turned his head, causing a cracking sound as he relieved tension in his neck. "She and Jim are an imposing combination." A smile tugged at the corner of his mouth. "And they will undoubtably have children combining their traits..."

Lang snorted and pulled himself to his feet. "Time to worry about that later. I'm more concerned with the ideas that were born today." He grew serious for a moment. "And we were the catalyst for their conception. I doubt she even realizes the step she just took."

"I heard it as well. She will realize, and not be happy with us when she does." Captain Tachibana pointed to his watch. "Come. It's time to put this dangerous dance we design into motion."

Captain Lang gave him an appreciative nod of approval as they left the room. "Excellent alliteration, Captain. I didn't know you had it in you."

Tachibana gave a self-deprecating shrug. "I have many hidden skills."

❖ ❖ ❖ ❖ ❖

The Lady Riahi looked into the mirror and liked what she saw. She wore nothing but a long, silk scarf and a tiny thong, both black. The scarf had been wrapped around her chest to hold her ample bosom in place. It also provided the illusion of modesty.

Luxuriously thick, jet-black hair flowed down over her shoulders, contrasting with her pale, almost translucent skin. A thin ribbon, also black, was tied into a headband to hold the hair clear of her face.

Lady Riahi stretched, watching the muscles ripple across her shoulders and arms. She went up on tiptoe and her legs became a study of muscle definition. Very nice cut of the calf, if I do say so myself, she thought smugly. Her stomach was flat, accenting her substantial bust even further as she turned sideways to see her profile. Even on tiptoe, she stood just over five feet tall.

She felt a presence and finished the turn to face her opponent towering in front of her. They both stood motionless for a moment, then bowed, careful not to let their eyes break contact. He also wore black, head to toe. His face, covered by cloth, left only his green eyes visible.

Ninja!

The Lady Riahi began to circle to her left, her hands weaving a pattern that offered defense, but also threatened attack at any moment. They both moved warily over the rocky terrain, avoiding the numerous crevasses that would easily swallow either of them.

Without warning, they leaped at each other. A violent exchange of kicks, blows, and blocks seemed to stretch into an eternity. The villain blocked her every move without pressing his own attack. He seemed content to await his moment, leading her into overextending.

She must not fail. The security of her family and maybe the entire human race rested on this battle. Lady Riahi switched methods without warning, throwing her body into a wild all-or-nothing assault. She leapt high into the air and kicked out, aiming for his head.

The black-clad fiend blocked her, catching her foot with one hand. A fist swept through her defenses and smashed into her stomach. She was unable to recover her balance and crashed heavily to the padded floor of the gym.

"Jesus, Afsaneh! Where is your mind at today?"

The evil ninja, Jim Morris, stood there with hands on hips, glaring down at her. He was just under six feet tall, and his muscles really did ripple with every motion. He had broad shoulders that tapered down to a flat stomach, with narrow hips flaring into powerful sprinter legs. His hair was long, hanging down to his shoulders, framing the light green eyes and closely trimmed beard.

"If you don't pay attention, you can get hurt." Jim made a visible effort to calm down. "We were practicing a specific style. Part of this training depends on you doing the right things at the right times. Don't try those sneaky moves on me. They won't work, and you may walk into a broken nose or worse!" He used the bottom of his sleeveless sweat-shirt to wipe the moisture from his brow.

The motion drew her attention to the partly healed scar that ran from just over his left eye to what remained of the lower tip of his left ear. The same swipe of a Tryr claw that had caused the wound had neatly removed a half inch of his ear lobe. Both the scar and the bottom of the ear glowed bright red from exertion.

"I'm sorry, Jim." Afsaneh Riahi was contrite, her voice husky as she tried to regain her breath. "I guess my mind was on other things."

"I understand, Punkin, but there's a time for everything." Jim looked grim. With that scar, it wasn't hard.

Afsaneh ran a finger under the strap of her sports bra, straighten-ing where it had flipped over during the sparring. Okay, maybe in her imagination, she exaggerated her fitness and writhing muscles a little. But she was slender. The only fat on her body was very well situated, tightly packed into her bra.

Of course, at nearly sixteen years of age, she should be fit, Afsaneh admitted. She rubbed her stomach and winced. She would be feeling that punch for a few days.

She saw Jim watching her, and hurriedly pulled her hand away and began retying her sweat pants. He laughed.

"I told you to wear more clothes," he reminded her. "Padding helps, especially if you aren't going to pay attention. And a little modesty never killed anybody."

She smiled at him sweetly. "I wouldn't know."

"No kidding." As her guardian, Jim had the unenviable chore of acting as the buffer between her and the horde of boys that would soon appear in her life. Even his brutal scar and renown as a martial artist would be hard-pressed to defeat that determined opponent; teenage male hormones.

Afsaneh had no intention of doing anything to make his job any easier, she thought with a smirk.

"What's so funny?" Jim eyed her suspiciously.

"Oh, nothing, nothing."

Afsaneh cocked her head sideways. "Jim, has Kimberly decided to take your name, or keep her own?" She grinned. "God, she didn't do one of those hyphenated things, did she? Kimberly Martin-Morris-san. Hmm, it's got a ring to it."

Jim winced, then shuddered as she continued.

"Or did you take her name?" She felt mischievous. "Jim Morris-Martin. Sounds like a British sports car."

"Afsaneh, can we get back to what we were doing?" Jim looked uncomfortable with the subject.

Afsaneh decided it was still an unresolved issue, and one she could have a lot of fun with.

"Tell you what, Jim. I'll tell her I want to be adopted legally by the two of you and get my name changed to Morris. She'll feel obligated to go along." Jim's lips tightened, and she saw at once she had taken the wrong path on this discussion.

He nodded towards the door.

"We might as well break for the day," he said drily. "Your mind is not on martial arts. And you will not say anything of the sort to Kimberly. She doesn't need any pressure right now. There's nothing wrong with you keeping your name. Down the road, if you want to change it, fine. But you're not going to do it on a whim, or part of some sneaky plan."

"Okay, okay." Afsaneh backpedaled furiously. "I was just kidding you, you know. Sheesh, you can't even joke around here."

Sometimes Jim could be so serious! But it was good to know he was there for her, she had to admit.

Jim and her father, Hakim Riahi, had been college roommates, both had 'dated' her mother. She couldn't remember a time when "Uncle Jim" wasn't around. Her mother had died when she was only two and Jim had stepped right in as her godfather and helped Hakim raise her. In a step still considered unusual, Jim had adopted her. The idea of two fathers in a hetero home was, to say the least, unusual.

Jim and his entire film cast and crew had been aboard the cruise ship Jade Viking, shooting the final scenes for his next film, "Weeping Winds of Fury". On its final voyage under American ownership, it had been hijacked by, of all things, aliens from outer space. Jim and a select group of cast members and crewmen used deception to seize the alien vessel in a bloody battle. When the ship docked at its home base, Station Chaq, they took it by force as well.

There had been a heavy price in lives, though. Her own father had fallen in the final battle for control of the station. Afsaneh was still trying to learn to deal with his death and the whirlwind of activity and events that had followed.

Jim hadn't hesitated a moment. He reconfirmed his commitment to raising her as his own, and proposed to Kimberly, all in one night.

Kimberly accepted his proposal, they married, and Afsaneh not only had a new father, but a stepmother as well. Soon after, that she learned Jim was her actual biological father.

As they left the gym, Afsaneh gasped involuntarily.

Above them the stars blazed gloriously. Only a transparent canopy separated them from the cold vacuum of space. This concourse ran the length of Space Station Osaka and the view was, to say the least, spectacular.

"It never fails to take my breath away," she admitted as Jim glanced at her in surprise. "There are so many more stars visible here than on Earth."

"Earth atmosphere blocks a lot out," Jim agreed. "For that matter, there are just a lot more stars in this part of space. We do come from the sticks, you know."

They both laughed at that.

"Tonight's the big meeting." Afsaneh took Jim's arm impulsively. "Everybody is talking about who is going back, who's staying. At least for us, it was easy."

Jim looked down sideways at her. "Was it? Kimberly has a career, and we all have friends back on Earth. My decision wasn't entirely my own, as I'm some kind of 'figurehead' symbol." His voice sounded a little bitter. "I don't even know what I'm going to do out here."

"Make movies," Afsaneh suggested. "It's what you know, and the special effects would be 'out of this world'!" She laughed.

"My acting days are over." Jim's voice was firm. "I was getting burnt out before we even left on this cruise."

"A three parsec cruise..." Afsaneh sang out in a strong voice. They both laughed, and Jim shook his head and covered her hand with his own.

"Ah, my little 'fairy tale'. What would I do without you to cheer me up." Afsaneh liked it when he used the Persian definition of her name. It made her feel very special.

"Probably spend all your time in bed with your new wife, making little Jimmys and Kimmys." She hoped for a blush, but he was too familiar with her constant teasing to fall easily.

"For a fifteen-year-old schoolgirl, you sure are obsessed with sex." He frowned at her.

"Almost sixteen," she automatically corrected.

"You've been 'almost sixteen' for over ten months, now." Jim reminded her. "I can't wait for you to turn 'almost seventeen'."

"Yeah, then I can date un-chaperoned!" She smirked at him.

"In your dreams, maybe," Jim snorted. "I don't think boys your age are ready for you, yet."

"Who said anything about boys my age," she replied tartly. She smothered a laugh at his expression. Raising a new father had its moments.

She turned his wrist so she could see his watch. "There's a gunnery practice session in twenty minutes. If I hurry, I can just make it."

Jim frowned at her. "Right now? This meeting is important, and I want you to be there."

"It isn't for over an hour." Afsaneh used a pleading voice that had always worked on Hakim. "I'll be back at the apartment long before then." She had found most of the teenagers on board used these "practice sessions" as an excuse to socialize. It did remind her a lot of the arcades in the malls back home. She stepped up on tiptoe and kissed his cheek. "Don't worry, Father. I won't be too late."

Jim got that proud expression adults sometimes get. The few times she called him Father, he was at her mercy. She just had to be careful not to overdo it.

She left him standing, misty eyed, in the concourse. She broke into a trot as she thought about who would be at the practice. All those high school seniors from that class trip!

It was great to be "almost sixteen", going on "almost seventeen"!

A lone figure stood in shadows farther down the corridor. He watched the young girl step close to the actor and kiss him on the cheek. Then he ducked back down a side passage as she turned his way. He hurried to a junction and dodged into it moments before she swept by.

Shinzo Takuan ground his teeth together in fury. That damned little whore! He caught his distorted reflection on polished metal and silently swore vengeance.

The young bitch had broken his nose. He was fortunate she hadn't killed him. The blow she'd struck had been intended to send shards of crushed cartilage into his brain, and had barely missed its mark.

The surviving leader of Sukuru, Security Chief Nagami, had led an attempt to take control of one of the ships captured when the station was seized. Takuan had the dubious distinction of being the only Sukuru survivor of the battle for possession of the bridge of Jade Samurai. A few moments after his nose was broken, he was pinned to the deck by several crewmen, his friend Sado Tarozaemon lay nearby, dead with a broken neck at her hands.

Jim Morris had killed martial artist Naga Furukawa with a blow identical to that which his ward had attempted and, in a fierce and grizzly sword fight, beheaded Nagami.

Gingerly, he touched his nose. The pain was about gone. The Jade Viking would soon be returning to Earth, and he would have a chance to report what had happened. His own dishonor at surviving the battle would have to be ignored until then. His employers at Sukuru were dominated by the Toshida Clan, and they wouldn't take kindly to the death of their executive vice-president, security chief, and champion, most of all at the hands of Jim Morris. And they would have definite ideas about who should profit from this first encounter with aliens.

A pity that doubly-cursed actor hadn't been slaughtered by the alien Tryr along with the father of the little whore.

But his time would come. For now, Takuan would have to wait.

◆ ◆ ◆ ◆ ◆

The planet Hshtah

Commodore Tka despised this entrance hall. First, it was far too large. Tka was not a small Tryr, from his pointed, black, furry ears to the sharp yellowed claws of his toes he stretched over eight charn tall, but the stone walls and ceiling loomed wide to both sides and high above him. And it stretched far before him to the ominous, distant double doors. For all the openness, the lighting was dim, even to his feline eyes. He was sure it was designed to intimidate any non-Hshtahni. He'd made this walk many times, and liked to think it didn't affect him any more.

But he had no inkling of why he'd been summoned, and that made him nervous.

Lord Qatahkh was not one for casual visitors. He, like all other Hshtahni, detested dealing with the "lesser" races any more than necessary.

The massive doors slowly swung inward. Tka forced himself to keep the same pace as he entered the dismal chamber. It also had high ceilings, but many alcoves and offshoots from the central area offered seclusion to the casual eye. He looked around cautiously, trying to see where his lord was waiting.

He knew no one else would be in the chamber but, as always, felt the fur on the back of his neck rise as he sensed eyes upon him. There were legends of invisible guards, assassins, or perhaps even supernatural spirits in Hshtahni palaces. He always discounted them as silly stories by the weak-minded, but every time he came here, he wondered if maybe the tales had some basis of fact.

"Commodore Tka."

The deep guttural voice was soft, but filled the chamber as if it came from all directions at once. Tka finally picked the bulky figure out of a deeply shadowed indentation.

"Lord Qatahkh, how may I serve you?" Tka bowed his head for a moment, then straightened.

Twin amber embers stared out of the gloom. He forced himself to hold eye contact, knowing the Hshtahni would wait, trying to make him fidget or show fear. As always, he had the sense of something else flit-

17

ting about the chamber, sometimes almost touching him, but as usual, he neither saw nor smelled anything.

Finally, the glowing stare blinked.

"I am sending your squadron to assist Lord Machtochk in his sector."

Tka frowned, surprised. Hshtahni lords didn't usually provide each other with battle-hardened troops or ships. They all had their own client races or Tryr clans to protect their areas of influence.

"My lord?"

"Lord Machtochk has had a...development in his sector." By his tone, Tka suspected his lord was annoyed, or even disgusted. "The Ananab have discovered a potential client race but have run into...difficulties. They experienced heavy casualties."

Tka sniffed. What else could happen when the Ananab were involved? But...? He chose his words carefully. "Why would the Ananab have been allowed to initiate the first contact?"

"You do not respect the Ananab?" The tone was ominous in its quietness.

Tka hesitated, recognizing the danger in the moment, then decided frankness was the only alternative to cravenness. His muzzle twitched, but he resisted the urge to scratch it, took a deep breath, and stepped into the void. He was careful to keep his fangs covered as he answered.

"My lord, I have never understood the willingness of the Hshtahni to give so much trust and power to such an incompetent race." He didn't see any obvious reaction, and the two incandescent orbs watched him, unblinking. "They are stupid, undisciplined, and worst of all, cowardly."

"Hmm." The deep rumble was neutral. "Are there not Tryr that serve the Ananab?"

"Lord, the Tcha are the dregs of my race. They are the least intelligent and most incompetent of all the Tryr. Out of their entire clan, they are only able to crew a paw full of ships. They would probably even serve the Srotag for the promise of continued cave and catch." Tka closed his eyes for a moment, berating himself for his carelessness.

"You also have a low opinion of the Srotag, another race that serves the Ananab, which serve the Hshtahni?"

Tka wasn't fooled by the mild tone. He was on a very dangerous trail, fraught with treacherous footing. "My Lord, Clan Tryhk has served your lineage for countless generations, faithfully and competently. Our

18

loyalty can not be questioned. Any opinion I have that offends you is mine alone, not expressed by the clan." He took a deep breath, then hurried on before he lost his nerve. "But I feel that we serve the greatest of the Hshtahni lords, and that is our just deserves, because we are the most capable...by far."

Tka closed his eyes for a moment, strangely calm. Had he just committed suicide?

"Pride is a dangerous thing, in the minds and hearts of subordinates."

His eyes popped open again, and he watched the smoldering eyes darken to scarlet, but never break the gaze that froze him from the shadows.

"If pride leads you to make foolish decisions, or you overestimate your own worth, then yes, it is indeed dangerous. But if it leads you to greater deeds, in the service of your clan or lord, then it can be an inspiration." He forced himself to continue breathing in a measured manner, then had to fight to keep from gasping in dismay.

"Don't you mean...lord or clan?" The tone wasn't as mild as it had been moments before.

Tka scrambled to keep his wits about him. "Lord, I am a warrior, not a politician. I apologize if my wording was chosen poorly. But Clan Tryhk serves you so, in my eyes, one and both are the same."

The silence stretched on for an agonizing length of time. Then the Hshtahni gave a snort that could have been either derision or laughter. Tka couldn't tell which.

"I doubt that."

There was another long pause, then Tka heard the tone change, and thought he could even feel it vibrating through the floor. Was that a sigh?

"Long ago, we found the Ananab, and felt they were pliable enough to raise to a level of sophistication and competency to act as our agents in mundane issues. As a race, they do seem to have a lower ultimate capability than we anticipated. And no, they were not, and never would be authorized to initiate first contact on their own. Someone acted beyond his authority and, I am pleased to say, paid the ultimate price."

That was the longest speech Tka had ever heard Lord Qatahkh make, and he had no idea how to respond. So he kept quiet, trying to read something in the ruby glare that bore into him.

The deep rumble continued, all business now. "Commodore Tka, you will take your squadron and report to Lord Machtochk. He says he has mounted a counterattack, but he is using more of the same fodder that lost him his station in the first place."

The eyes seemed to elevate, and Tka realized the Hshtahni lord was rising to his feet.

"You are there to observe. If this attempt fails, as I think it will, I wish you to go to Station Chaq."

"You wish me to retake the station, my lord?" His mind raced as he began to plan the logistics of quickly acquiring more troops for his ships. If he needed to board a hostile...

"You will take no action, unless an obvious opportunity presents itself."

"My lord?" Tka was startled.

"Station Chaq is uncomfortably close to both Hechktar and Trixmae frontiers, and even the Egelv have been sighted in the region recently. For all we know, this new race of...Humans may be agents, acting secretly on any or all of their behalf. I have more urgent need of intelligence than the immediate return of an Ananab station, however strategically placed."

"Yes, my lord." Tka shifted his feet, impatient to be off. This mission was important, and he had been the one called upon. He realized the Hshtahni could sense his excitement.

"Control your emotions and ambitions, Commodore. As I said, take no action unless you see a quick, easy path to success. Investigate, then report back to me." The tone was more ominous than ever, even in dismissal.

"You may go."

❖ ❖ ❖ ❖ ❖

CHAPTER TWO

Station Osaka

"You have no right to suggest anything of the sort." Howard Prause stood rigid, his head raised in anger. He was arched forward as if he would plant his hands on the table in front of Captain Lang. "Your duty is to get every one of us back to Earth."

"Please sit down, Mr. Prause." Captain Tachibana turned to one of the stewards standing nearby. "Mr. Mahoney, find this gentleman a seat, if you please."

Prause looked as if he wanted to argue further, but allowed himself to be led to the second row where fellow passengers parted to make room for him.

Kimberly surveyed the cavernous hall with resignation. Her time with the two captains had turned out to be very productive, but this general meeting, which included every human not bound by duties, plus representatives of the other races currently residing on Station Osaka, formerly the Ananab Station Chaq, had the potential to be a circus.

Captain Lang had told his purser, Randy Luca, to find a place big enough for the meeting. After conferring with the Hoag, he'd chosen a large storage hanger that felt about the size of Space Mountain to Kimberly. It looked big enough to house a basketball arena, both in floor space and height.

And it was filling up fast.

Kimberly marveled at how innovative the Hoag could be. Not only had they cleared out whatever had originally been stored here, but they'd either found or quickly constructed hundreds of benches as seating.

The Hoag were short, stocky mammals covered with brown fur. They had long, narrow snouts, and tall ears that reminded her of a certain cartoon rabbit. When she had first seen them, Kimberly thought their black eyes beady, sneaky. Now they seemed warm, full of compassion. In this new universe of interlocked alien races, they were service-oriented and seemed to do most of the actual work on the station, as well as the ships.

For hundreds of generations, the Hoag had been the servants, slaves really, of the ruling Hshtahni race, and by extension, the Ananab. No job was too menial, no routine too mundane. At the same time, if there was a logistical problem, or a need to find some resource, there they were, offering the right tool for the job.

The Ananab and their client goons, the Tryr and the Srotag, were contemptuous. Jokes about the flavor and consistency of Hoag meat were common.

When the humans had rebelled, killing the overlords, the Hoag had been in an awkward position. Reluctantly at first, then with growing enthusiasm, they threw in their support.

Kimberly's mind crept back to the meeting she'd just left. One of the key problems with inserting themselves back on Earth would be the fact that the original Jade Viking no longer existed, at least not in ship form. It was going to be hard to look shipwrecked without any wrecked ship.

It took less than four days to seize the P'Tassum from the Ananab and their Srotag and Tryr henchmen. But in that short time, the Hoag completely dismantled the Jade Viking, reducing it to substantial stores of raw material and a large storage area full of odds and ends, mostly personal items that the Hoag hadn't found a use for.

As she'd pointed out, the lack of a ship wasn't as critical as it might seem.

"Gentlemen, as I see it, we have a number of steps in front of us, and that is a mere detail." Kimberly stared above their heads, not really seeing anything in the room. "How many people do you think fully understand Vicki, Sam and Pearl's programming priorities?"

She knew she caught both of them by surprise, and they weren't really seeing where she was headed. But the true capabilities of the station and two ships' computers were essential to her newly hatched plans.

The Ananab ship P'Tassum had a substantially larger computer system than it required. For cycles, for any enhancement or upgrade, new parts had been added, blended with the old. The end result was a computer that was vastly more powerful than a mere cargo-bearing exploration ship warranted.

When Earth was discovered, computer watches were manned by Baerd technicians. The Baerd were a subservient race trained from near birth to construct and operate computers and other complicated machinery. Tall, slender, four armed, nearly hairless, they were a timid race of albinos with pink eyes and skin that projected their every emotion unmercifully.

One technician, Lasty, had a far more curious nature than the average Baerd, and a habit of recording the sexual activities of his masters, the Ananab, as well as the Tryr and Srotag. He'd found there was a lucrative market for such recordings, and had traded several with a Hechktar merchant for an Egelv security program. After examining it, he'd decided it was a palace security code for the Egelv royalty. Once applied, it would use any and all means to achieve its only purpose, which was protect the designated royal family, in particular, the emperor or heir to the throne.

While observing transmissions from Earth, and then the behavior of the captives, he'd become intrigued by the Humans. He'd recognized the potential threat they posed and tried to warn his Ananab Captain, only to be ridiculed and physically disciplined.

While trying to decide if they would try to escape, he'd instructed his computer to reason as a Human would, to better understand their motivations and possible plans. Even as he ascertained that the Humans would attempt a rebellion, it began.

Lasty realized that his and every other Baerd and Hoag's life was now forfeit. Not wanting any word of a revolt to spread, the Ananab would surely kill all witnesses.

On a wild, unexplainable impulse, he downloaded the Egelv security code into the ships' computer while it still was under the parameters he'd introduced, designating the Human ringleader, Jim Morris, as the royal heir.

Jim and his companions seized the bridge, but the computer's assistance was critical in subduing the remainder of the ship with a minimum of casualties. Human casualties, anyway. Eventually, when the dust settled, the Humans controlled the ship, and they had an invaluable ally in its computer. Which turned out to be fortuitous, because they would arrive at Station Chaq in less than a day's time.

Jim, in a light-hearted moment, nicknamed the computer of the newly renamed Jade Viking, Vicki. It turned out that the program was reproducible. Upon docking, Station Chaq and a Tryr warship at a nearby berth were infected, making them involuntary allies. They were eventually renamed the Jade Samurai, or Sam, and Station Osaka, or Pearl. Both played important roles in the final conquest of the station.

Almost no one knew the story of the security code, and Kimberly considered that to be a key to any chance at successfully dividing the passengers and crew between those sincerely wishing to help, and those with ulterior motives.

"Well, the three of us, and Jim, of course." Captain Lang looked lost, but willing to see where she was taking them. "Certainly, Janice and Rick, because they worked so close to the computer, before and after we took the ship."

"If Janice knows, Yvette would as well. As partners, I doubt they keep much from each other," Tachibana pointed out. "And our newly promoted young Captain DelaRosa and Commander Asaya have to recognize the superior capabilities of these computers compared with other ships."

"But that doesn't necessarily mean they understand the complete picture regarding the "heir" issue and such," Kimberly said. "What about Randy and Suyo?"

Captain Lang took a moment to consider it. "Probably to the same extent as Danny and Koro, er, Captain DelaRosa and..."

Kimberly raised a hand, smiling. "I get it. Anyone else?"

'What about Miss Riahi?" Tachibana looked pensive. "She seems to be everywhere at once, and I suspect, is a very intelligent young lady."

"If intelligent means fiendishly clever, you're absolutely right," Kimberly muttered, more to herself than to the captains. "But she does know about them."

"There are a number of Baerd and Hoag that almost certainly know. Lasty, of course, since he introduced the code himself..."

"For this purpose, their knowing doesn't matter," Kimberly interrupted without meaning to. "I'm sorry, I didn't..."

"Do not concern your self," Tachibana reassured her. "We're running low on time. Why does it matter who knows about the computers?"

"They're our ace in the hole." Kimberly felt the grin of victory she always got after cross-examining hostile witnesses. "They know every single thing that happens on this station, and should be able to give us a list, based on what they overhear, of who intends what. We're all wearing the translator earrings or patches, and everything goes through the computers. Pearl?"

"You are correct, Kimberly Martin." Pearl's voice was a strong alto, reminding them all of a mature woman's voice. "Your analysis regarding which Humans are fully aware of my capabilities is also accurate. I've taken the liberty of creating an initial list, dividing between your definition of "with you" or "not", and begun sub-dividing into lists of people staying on Station Chaq or the ships, and those wishing to return to Earth, but intending to help organize defenses against the Ananab."

"Um, good." Kimberly felt a little freaked out by how easily Pearl anticipated her. "Can you create a list of who might be willing to return to Earth secretly, as a fifth column?"

"Yes, and I am also dividing those not with you into categories to help predict their actions upon their return to Earth."

Kimberly eyed both Captains and, seeing how spooked they looked, felt a little better. "Well then, that's step one. Perhaps our next move should be a plan on segregating those not with us to allow a staggered return to Earth, giving our loyal group a day or two head start."

"And do you have some ideas regarding that as well, Ms. Martin?" Captain Tachibana asked, leaning back in his chair without showing any sense of relaxing to his posture.

Kimberly smiled at the memory, reluctantly pulling herself back to "this" meeting, which was about to get under way. Of course she'd had ideas. And they'd both approved. But now, she needed to be paying attention to the present.

Randy Luca, seated at the far left end of the table, stood and called out for attention. The purser was a pleasantly plump man that always seemed to find something funny to laugh about. Outwardly gregarious, Kimberly suspected he was actually quite shy, and self-conscious about his weight. The crowd ignored him and the buzz around the room grew. He tried again, a little louder, with the same lack of results.

Kimberly was seated near the other end of the long table, and saw that most of the people seated between them were getting annoyed with the crowd's lack of manners and attentiveness.

"This is ridiculous," she muttered to herself. "Pearl, lights out, lights on."

The room immediately went black. It lasted less than two seconds, but had the effect Kimberly hoped for. Everyone in the audience stopped in shock and stared in consternation around them.

Before they could start up again, Randy raised his arms high and shouted. "Thank you, thank you for your attention. Let's get this meeting started. I'd like to introduce Captain Lang, who will be chairing this meeting, assisted by Captain Tachibana."

Captain Lang rose enough to wave a hand acknowledging the audience, then sat down and began to thank everyone for coming. He, at least, knew he didn't need to shout. Pearl would amplify his voice as needed to all translators, as well as speakers spread throughout the room.

"Nice job, K.M.," Janice Wooley whispered from two seats to her right. "Of course, there was a fifty-fifty chance they'd all start screaming instead."

"Quiet." Yvette Stephanian shushed them both from her seat between them. She was less than five feet tall, with broad hips that, as she put it, made her perfect for the bearing and delivery of babies. Since she was a lesbian, and Janice's life-companion, it didn't seem likely that theory would ever be tested, although she did have a motherly manner. Janice was a head taller, and thirty pounds lighter. They made a comical sight, but were a delight to be around.

Janice straightened upright, squaring her shoulders, and made a face. Kimberly hid her smile and turned her attention back to the captain.

Social niceties dealt with, Captain Lang addressed the need for the meeting. "I'd like to inform everyone that in a week, we will be sending the Jade Viking back to Earth. We have a table set up near the entrance, and will have several more in the common areas for the next several days, for people to declare their intentions."

The crowd stirred restlessly, and Kimberly saw that several were biting at the bit to interrupt, but respected his authority. She drew her attention back to what Lang was saying.

"...many of us will be staying here on Pearl to act as a buffer for Earth, and we can use any and everyone willing to do the same." He glanced down at his notes and didn't immediately notice the man from earlier stand up.

Howard Prause was a school teacher and the head chaperone for a group of high school graduates on their senior trip. He was probably a good man, but his overbearing protectiveness was beginning to grate on Kimberly's nerves.

"Captain Lang, as I told you before, the students under my charge will not be permitted to make this decision themselves." He was perhaps five feet eight inches in height, and his spine was ramrod straight, thin shoulders squared. "They were released into my care by their parents and the school system, and you are legally required to respect their wishes, which would be the return of the children."

"Old man, you got nothin' to say 'bout this." The young man was tall, lean, very athletic looking, and a wild mass of curly locks framed his face. "I'm eighteen, and I can decide for myself. And I'm stayin'!"

"Got that right!" A black student next to him stood up, dwarfing him. He had to be six and a half feet tall, with broad shoulders so muscular his arms hung wide from his sides. He probably weighed fifty or sixty pounds more than Prause, but not an ounce of it was soft. His head had been shaved at the beginning of the cruise, but now he had a shadowy stubble, both on his skull and face. Kimberly knew he had a football scholarship to play defensive end at Stanford in the fall. Unlike the first student, he portrayed no cockiness. He was firm, but not rude. "We can make our own decisions, sir. And I will be staying to help."

"Both of you shut up and sit down." Prause's face was bright red, and his breathing rapid. Kimberly hoped he wouldn't have a stroke or heart attack on the spot.

"Shut up? Shut up? I'll tell you what you can do with your shut..."

"Mr. Jackson, please." Captain Lang's voice rang out, and Kimberly could hear it both in person and through her translator earring. The volume was definitely cranked up, Pearl's doing. She saw a number of people wince and put a hand to their head, and knew it wasn't just her reception that had been boosted. "Mr. Jackson, please sit down and refrain from belligerency. You will have the opportunity to make your own decision on this..."

"That is unacceptable, Captain Lang." Prause glared at the captain, and his face, if anything, seemed even more flushed. "After these students have been returned to their parents, they can make whatever decision they choose, but until then, they are my charges."

"Mr. Prause, I understand your concern." Lang began in a placating voice. "But you must understand..."

"What I understand is eighty sets of parents giving me the responsibility of watching over their children, and I intend to see them delivered back to where they belong!" His lips were thin lines, stretched tight. "According to California Law..."

"Mr. Prause, we are not in the United States, much less California, and as much as I respect the law, in this jurisdiction, it doesn't necessarily apply."

A small wizened man that looked like he had to be eighty, but seemed to be quite spry from the way he popped to his feet, spoke up.

"Captain Lang, if you do not feel that American laws apply here, what gives you the right to chair this meeting? Or to be in charge of anything, for that matter. Why should any of us respect your authority, or that of Captain Tachibana? Maybe we should hold elections, let the people decide who should be leading us?"

Captain Lang sat still, and Kimberly felt a sudden rush of fear. She knew the Captain would love nothing more than to relinquish his authority.

"Mr. Cowden, there will be elections. Anyone wishing to run for Governor of this station will be welcomed to the process." Lang stood, shoving his chair back as he clasped his hands behind his back, letting his gaze roam the room, finally returning to the old man.

"But..." He let the word hang for a long moment. "That election will be after we have secured this station's safety from attack, and established a line of resupply and contact with Earth. And that will be long after the Jade Viking has returned those of you that so wish, to Earth. The people voting will be the people with the most at stake on this station."

"What gives you the authority to decide even that?" Cowdin obviously wasn't going to let it go that easily. And a few people in the crowd muttered their agreement. "Why should we accept your decisions, or those of any of you at that table? What gives you the right?"

"Expediency." The one word seemed to fill the entire room. Captain Lang turned and gestured to Captain Tachibana and the other officers sitting in a row. "Ladies and gentlemen, when you embarked on this voyage, you put yourself under my authority. We haven't finished that trip yet, and Captain Tachibana and myself are in charge of the infrastructure that is going to return you to Earth. Those of you that wish to."

"So you have the guns, and thereby the power?" Mr Prause was apoplectic with fury.

"I wouldn't put it that way, but if you must, feel free to do so yourself." Captain Lang turned away from him to the rest of the room. He seemed to gain in stature as he spoke. "There is a chain of command with delineated lines of authority. We have a duty to every one of you, and surrendering that authority would not be in your best interests. As I said, we will return those of you that so wish, to Earth. Those of you wanting to stay will be appreciated, and there will be work worthy of your talents and abilities."

He gestured to the far end of the cavernous room. "Again, we have people by the entrances for those of you that have made your decision. This meeting is adjourned."

Several people stood and began clapping. They were quickly joined by hundreds more. The Captain looked startled, then a flush began at his neck. By the time most of the room was on their feet, and the clapping loud and enthusiastic, it had spread to his cheeks.

Captain Tachibana stood next to him and shook hands with him, then began clapping himself. The younger officers immediately followed suit, and Kimberly found herself doing the same, along with everyone else at the table. Any dissenters in the crowd were all but invisible.

Yvette exhaled noisily. "Well, that was...special."

"Coupla jerks," Janice snarled. "I wanted to go over the table after them."

Kimberly couldn't hold back a grin. "Well, I'm glad you didn't."

"Janice, you remember what idiots they both were when we met them." Yvette shook her head. "Prause is overbearing, and completely full of himself. And Cowden is the libertarian anarchist from hell."

Kimberly laughed out loud at the description, then grew serious. "Ladies, can we talk?"

"We all need to talk," Randy Luca leaned close to speak quietly. "Captain Lang respectfully requests your attendance for just one more little meeting." He nodded to Kimberly. "Same room as the last one, in ten minutes?"

"Sure," Kimberly said with resignation. This was getting worse than corporate life. One meeting after another.

Feeling a pull on her arm, she turned and was startled to have Janice shove her face almost against her own.

"Last one?" Janice looked into her eyes intently, and Kimberly could see Yvette's round face peering around her shoulder, also curious.

She sighed in resignation. Just like her old job, secrets were tough to keep.

Glowing Mist, four weeks ago...

Cromar Try sat in comfort, surveying his domain from his command throne. He loved his ship, Glowing Mist, and the bridge was his favorite place. Well, one of his two favorite places. His second officer, Du Brimar, scanned the computer screen intently.

"There it is again." The Egelv lieutenant commander looked up from his viewer, puzzled. "There's no record of established bases, or advanced races in this sector, but there it is!"

"The same primitive transmission?" Cromar was only mildly interested. They were out here in this desolate portion of space for a specific purpose, and it had nothing to do with mysterious transmissions that could have originated almost anywhere.

"Not the exact same thing, but obviously from the same source." Du Brimar brushed back his long white hair with a brown hand. He tucked loose strands behind his high-peaked ears as he spoke. "The computer says it's the same language, and is starting a file for translation."

"Whatever." Cromar Try suspected these transmissions were old ship to ship communications from eons ago, and of little use to anyone. What was more important was finding that traitorous misbegotten son of a squat, Ty Musa.

"Is there any sign that these signals are related to our primary objective?" Du Brimar wilted slightly at the question.

"No," he admitted. "In fact, I'm sure they have nothing to do with him. I am still scanning for any evidence of his passing through this area, though."

Both Egelv officers started as the computer chimed.

"What is it?" Cromar Try hoped it was something related to their mission.

"A ship has been sighted." Du Brimar did a quick check. "It's an Ananab freighter. Ho, it just saw us and went to sheathed stealth mode."

"Don't they know that's a waste of time?" Cromar Try shook his head in mock disbelief. "The Ananab couldn't shield themselves from our sensors if they were immobile, drive engines cold, everyone aboard dead." He turned around and smiled in pleasure as his first officer and mate, Siph Carni entered the bridge.

"I heard the alarm." Her voice was soft, but carried excitement at the idea of something to break up the tedium of the long voyage. "An Ananab ship? Are you going to give it a hard probe?"

Cromar Try laughed and Du Brimar joined him. "A hard probe would probably give the captain of that ship a mess on his bridge deck. You know how weak their bowels are."

"But it would be their Hoag that cleaned it up." Siph Carni's voice held disapproval. "They're nothing more than slaves, whether it's Ananab or even Hstahni in charge."

Du Brimar bent forward to scan his screen again. "That's interesting. That ship seems to be coming directly from the source of those transmissions."

"What transmissions?" Siph Carni looked from one of them to the other, and Cromar Try sighed in resignation. He already knew where this discussion would end. As Du Brimar explained, her eyes lit up.

"Oh please, Captain." She smiled at him, obviously knowing she'd already won. "Let's go see what's making the signals. After all, if you don't know where Ty Musa is, you don't know where he is not! That direction is as good as any, am I not correct?"

"Alright, alright." The captain gave up good-naturedly, and glanced at one of the two Egelv technicians that silently manned the ship's main control console.

"Jo Coran, please triangulate those signals if you have not already." Flinching shoulders answered that question. "Set a course to intercept at the source and proceed."

Cromar Try stood and swept his mate close with one arm. He cocked an eyebrow at Du Brimar.

"I leave you the bridge. Check the records and see if there have been any earlier Egelv excursions in this region. If you need me, I'll be in our suite."

He pretended not to see the envy in his second officer's face as he turned to leave, his arm still around the willowy Siph Carni. He called back over his shoulder.

"Since you're so eager to investigate, I'll stay out of your way until we arrive. The ship is yours. Try not to get lost."

He and Siph Carni smiled at each other as they heard the two techs laugh at Du Brimar. Cromar Try had glanced at the figures on the screen. It would take almost two days to reach the origin of the transmissions. He could certainly think of ways to use that time, and none of them involved going anywhere near the bridge. Time well-spent at his 'other' favorite place.

❖ ❖ ❖ ❖ ❖

CHAPTER THREE

Station Osaka

Lasty felt very out of place. He glanced at his lover, Dutter, sitting beside him on what the Humans called a 'love seat', and saw by her solid hue of pink that she was as nervous as he. Both her left hands grasped his lower right very firmly. In fact, the grip was a little tight for comfort. His upper right arm was around her shoulders, a gesture of affection that a few weeks ago would have been unimaginable.

Well, he might have imagined it, but acting upon the impulse would have been out of the question. The Humans had impacted their lives on so many levels, not the least of which was causing him to risk everything to show his affection for Dutter, forswearing the vow of abstinence all Baerd were required to make before leaving their home world.

Both were from families that had committed them to relationships and eventual marriages of convenience after their years of servitude to the Ananab were at an end. Arranged marriages to complete strangers. But observing, and eventual contact with Humans had taken a heavy toll on tradition.

Lasty was fine with that. Even knowing that neither of them would probably ever return to their families and home world couldn't dampen his happiness.

Well, if the Humans abandoned Station Chaq, or Station Osaka, he corrected himself, that happiness could be fleeting indeed.

He didn't have to look past Dutter to see Gudd and the other Hoag present to know they shared the same worries. He had met Tost, from the Jade Samurai, and Spat, representing the several clans that lived on the station. Gudd was the elder of the clan that served the Jade Viking.

33

Lasty knew very little about him, even though they had both served aboard the same ship for over two primary cycles. Until the Humans had burst into their lives, there had been very little interaction between the various races that served the Ananab.

Now, everything was different. But for how long?

One quick glance confirmed his suspicions regarding the Hoag. He let his gaze continue past them to take quick inventory of the Humans already present. The giant warrior, McGregor perched on a tall stool. Even seated, he towered over most of the rest.

Beyond him, Kimberly Martin, the wife of Jim Morris, sat with her friends, Kiri Oshiba, a warrior in her own right, and the two women lovers, Yvette Stephanian and Janice Wooley. They were called 'lesbians' by some of the other Humans. Same sex relationships were rare in younger Baerd, but after the obligations of family and continuing the bloodline had been met, there were many cases of unions, if not dissolving, being put on hold, as older Baerd were finally allowed to follow their feelings instead of duty. Friendships that grew into sexual liaisons were not uncommon, sometimes same sex, sometimes the more traditional matching.

Lasty had harbored hopes that someday in the distant future, he and Dutter might have that very type of relationship, although they had never discussed it.

Across the room, there was a large desk with two chairs behind it it. Past that, two more open chairs.

Finally, just before the doors, sitting on, rather than at, the table, were the two young officers, Danny DelaRosa, captain of the Jade Samurai, and Koro Asaya, his first officer. Despite the trying times, both men were cheerful, almost to the point of annoying. Nothing seemed to faze them.

Suyo Takashi came in the door to Lasty's left and sat next to the young officers. She was older than the other women, but her hair was still jet black, without a trace of the grey or white Lasty knew was a sign of age among Humans.

Finally, Randy Luca entered, glanced around the room, muttering something Lasty couldn't quite catch. Both captains immediately entered the room, went behind the desk and sat. The portly purser took the last open chair, making Lasty realize how planned this gathering was.

Captain Lang gave a great sigh of relief as he sat, and his eyes swept the room.

"Thank you, everyone. After that last travesty of a meeting, I wouldn't have blamed any of you for skipping this one." He turned to Captain Tachibana, nodded, and leaned back as the other captain began to speak.

"The reason you are here is that we feel all of you are critical in what will be a monumental effort to save the human race from itself, as well as invading aliens." Tachibana smiled with no trace of humor. "I will command the Jade Viking upon her return voyage to Earth. I will remain on board with a crew that will be chosen from those at least temporarily sacrificing their personal lives in the greater interests of ourselves, and loved ones back home."

"Captain Tachibana will not only command the Jade Viking, but will act as Admiral of the rest of the ships as well." Lang coughed and his voice thickened. "Although he'll be able to see Earth with the naked eye, he will not be landing, going home, or even contacting his family."

"You have a wife and children back in Japan," Suyo pointed out. "Surely you wish to inform them that you are alive."

"Initially, there are going to be many questions." Lasty saw the pain in the captain's face. "My past employers, Sukuru, will be watching closely. Eventually, I hope to secret them away. Until then, my wife is strong. She will wait until I can get word to her."

"I will be staying here, and assuming the position of acting Governor of Station Osaka." Lang's face seemed longer, and he sounded sad. Lasty's heart went out to him. Dutter's hands squeezed his, and together they tried to draw his pain away. Beside them, Gudd turned and looked at them, whatever expression he had completely inscrutable. The captain continued to speak.

"Ever since my wife Emily died several years ago, I've been at loose ends. I didn't really want to retire but, with the ship being sold, I seemed to be out of choices." He looked around the room, not really seeing any of them, Lasty suspected. " I was tired and depressed. I hadn't seen my sons since her funeral. And I am past sixty..." He glared now, and Lasty marveled at the vast spectrum of emotions these Humans could attain. "But I am not dead, for Christ's sake. There just wasn't really anything I was needed for. That is no longer the case. This station is our outpost in the wilderness of space. And some of us must stand against the barbarians."

Lasty felt the other humans stir at the older man's words, but felt impelled to ask.

"You are definitely staying here? Not going back to your own world, leaving us to the wrath of the Ananab and the Hshtahni?" He felt rather than saw the excitement of the Hoag.

Lang frowned at him.

"Of course we're staying." He looked in consternation around the room, then back at Lasty. "Did you think we would abandon you, after we've disrupted your lives so?"

"I don't know anyone that would put our interests above their own." Lasty felt his head was wrapped in a thick layer of insulating material, and couldn't seem to catch his breath, but could feel his relief and excitement causing his skin to flame to a brightness that, previously, only being with Dutter could inspire. "Anyone."

"Nor do I." Gudd stood, his diminutive stature hardly making him taller. "We do not fully understand you...Humans, but you have our gratitude and support."

"And we'll need it." Lang seemed to be changing shades a little himself, embarrassed, for some unknown reason. "Understand this, we'd much rather fight this battle here than at home. And we will need the expertise that both your races bring to the table. This is purely good common sense on our part."

"Even so." Gudd surprised Lasty with his emphatic response. It was out of character for a Hoag to show such strong feelings and convictions in front of non-Hoag. "Most would choose a different course."

"It's the right thing to do," Lang muttered, looking around the room for...help? "Um, back to the topic at hand. As far as the rest of you go..."

"I will be staying here." Randy Luca's round face was also red. "Someone has to make sure we don't run out of toilet paper."

Lasty had noticed the purser always seemed to have something to say that, although Lasty might not immediately realize it, was humorous, and tension releasing. This moment was no exception, and everyone laughed.

"I will also stay." Suyo spoke for the first time. "I have no desire to return to Earth and face the Toshida clan. Being executive secretary to the senior vice-president of Sukuru would not save me from their wrath after explaining his death. I will stay with this new 'Jade' clan we have created.

"Nice." Kimberly looked at her with admiration. "I might use that at some point." She turned to the friends next to her on the couch. "What about you ladies?"

Yvette placed her hand over Janice's. "We're going back. Obviously, we'll help any way we can. Jim has already talked about consolidating his various companies and assets, try and free up as much money as possible to finance our efforts. And we have some resources of our own."

"Yeah." Lasty noticed Janice always seemed to have a mocking tone to her smiles. "It's not like we ever have time to spend the money we make. Too busy working." She looked wistful. "Rick Baker said he couldn't leave if he wanted to. There's too much to learn about the computers."

That drew more laughter. Rick and Janice had started an interesting number of rumors and stories about their constant liaisons based on a passionate love. A love for computers. They'd been almost inseparable, trying to learn as much as possible, as fast as possible.

"I'll be staying." McGregor spoke in deep resonating tones. "My wife gave birth to our twins here, and this is where they belong. Mr. Morris has given me the duty of organizing a security force to help defend the station."

"And man the ships, as well," Captain Lang reminded him.

"That would make them Marines, wouldn't it?" Captain DelaRosa grinned at the thickly muscled man that reminded Lasty of nothing so much as a nearly skinless Tryr. He remembered some talk of different divisions of human military groups. He knew that James McGregor had been a member of one in particular, the 'Special Forces'. He also vaguely recalled him calling marines 'candy asses', which evidently meant they were sweet?

The look McGregor gave Danny belied that. Lasty decided there was still plenty he didn't know about humans and their vagaries.

"Jim is staying, and Afsaneh and I as well," Kimberly said, wincing at the thought of Afsaneh, twenty-four/seven, for years to come.

"Needless to say, Commander Asaya and I will be on the Jade Samurai." Danny DelaRosa gave a crooked grin. "Although, at the rate

37

our good friends, the Hoag, are refitting the ships we captured when we took the station, Koro might be getting his first command faster than we would have expected."

"Perish the thought." Kiri snickered, then grew serious. "I'll be going back to Earth, at least for a bit. I've got loose ends to take care of."

"Someone is going to have to lead that cause." Yvette spoke in a flat tone. "Someone that can take charge, get us through the initial confusion and interrogations we'll face."

"You're going back," Kimberly pointed out.

"I can help with logistics and legwork." Yvette was firm. "But I'm not leader material. We need someone with contacts, and knowledge of big business and how governments work."

"Someone who understands corporate mentality," Janice agreed. Lasty couldn't help but notice she kept her face uncharacteristically blank, without jokes or clever remarks.

"It would have to be someone smart and well educated," Randy pondered out loud. "Someone with broad experiences and a background in power manipulation."

"Someone with legal experience." Koro Asaya looked up at the ceiling, his eyes wide and innocent, and Lasty wondered what he was implying. "Someone with leadership skills that can take charge, and make vague ideas into workable plans, and then execute them."

"Well, we don't really..." Kimberly bolted upright in her seat. "Oh no. I just got married. I have a teenage daughter now."

Captain Lang cleared his throat and looked at her, with some trepidation. "At some point, we'll need to cycle just about everyone back into circulation. Especially after we've introduced the reality of this brave new world."

"You could go back, get things started, then return here," Captain Tachibana suggested.

"You'll have to get someone else." Kimberly was firm. "There has to be somebody."

"Who?" Yvette looked sympathetic, but not enough to agree with her. "You're charismatic, smart, you know the law. You've got a business background, extensive experience with the corporate world..."

"I need to stay here with Jim." Kimberly didn't sound like she totally believed it herself. Lasty was impressed with how quickly the entire room had joined forces to convince her. It didn't seem like it had been planned, but she was being bombarded from all sides. If he hadn't been enjoying watching this so much, he would have had sympathy for her. Of course, there was no way she would give in to them. He had seen how strong-willed she was. The idea of someone being able to manipulate her seemed unlikely.

"Well, if you don't think he'll let you go..." Janice sounded more like herself now. She lifted Yvette's hand to her lips, kissed the fingers, then rubbed them against her cheek, and didn't flinch at Kimberly's glare. Lasty kept quiet, not wanting to attract that look by laughing.

"That's not it." Kimberly's tone was quiet now, filled with anger and...resignation?

"Kimberly." Everyone looked at Suyo in surprise. She could be so silent, it was easy to forget she was even there. Now she leaned forward, capturing their attention with her intensity.

"Who could do the job better? Better than you?"

"I just got married," Kimberly said in a small voice, and what Lasty felt, startled him.

Pity.

◆ ◆ ◆ ◆ ◆

"You're what?"

Kimberly winced as Jim Morris stared at her in disbelief. This had the makings of a long discussion.

◆ ◆ ◆ ◆ ◆

Two weeks ago, aboard the cruise ship Odessa, Mediterranean Sea

Matt Stickel was not a happy camper. Well, camper wouldn't exactly apply. Okay, not a happy sailor. A Mediterranean cruise had sounded romantic, exciting.

A lifeboat drill was neither.

He had been sitting in one of the upper deck lounges for almost two hours, hot and uncomfortable in his life jacket. It hadn't occurred to him to bring a book, and he seemed to be surrounded by people that spoke every language in Europe except English.

Idly, he looked at the people sitting packed around the room. One in particular caught his eye. She was small, barely five feet tall, brunette with a boyish figure.

39

Her features weren't boyish, though. He studied her face, careful to hide his interest. Unlike many of the passengers on this ship, she already had a good tan. Her eyes were dark brown and her hair framed her face, bangs almost reaching her eyes.

She looked as bored as he felt, but at least she was sitting with people she could talk to. One older couple looked enough like her that he assumed they were her parents. Several others could be her older siblings, or maybe aunts and uncles.

She sat in an overstuffed chair, arms folded across her life jacketed chest, eyes staring off into space. She looked like she could be anywhere from Matt's own age of nineteen to ten years older.

Matt didn't remember seeing her when they had set sail in Genoa. Of course, just about everyone on board had been out on the decks, waving to the crowd on the dock.

The ship, Odessa, proudly flew the Russian flag. Matt thought it strange that his history seminar class had picked a Russian cruise ship, but she was a flashy sight. A fresh coat of brilliant white paint made her jump out of the crowd of ships leaving port.

He had stood outside with everyone else, even though there was no one to see him off. Of course, there were the other fifty-one people in his group, but he didn't know any of them. He had three roommates, but they were all upper classmen. In fact, they were all graduate students. He was the youngest person in his group by quite a margin. About half the people were retired couples, auditing the class to take advantage of the itinerary and the two knowledgeable professors that were the organizers and color commentators of the trip.

Matt came back to the present with a shock as he realized he'd been blankly staring at her for...how long?

And worse, she was now staring right back at him!

He felt himself blush as he sat upright, tugging at his lifejacket in vain, trying to get more comfortable. She smiled at him, amusement on her face. At least she wasn't mad, or worse, laughing at his obvious interest.

The man he assumed was her father said something and she laughed and shook her head, then smiled in open relief as the announcement finally came, releasing them from the drill.

All announcements were done in six different languages, first Russian, then French, English, German, Italian, and finally Spanish in quick succession. Matt could swear it was the same voice doing all six,

40

but no one was that good at languages, were they?

He watched her leave the lounge, surrounded by family members. Well, this was only day one of fourteen. He would meet her, of that he had no doubt. Of course, he might make an ass of himself doing so, but that wouldn't be anything new.

Matt Stickel was disgusted. He had first seen the young woman Saturday afternoon, and here it was, Sunday night and he hadn't caught a glimpse of her since.

He hadn't made much headway getting to know his group companions, either. The fact that he was a sophomore taking a graduate level course had irritated most of the serious students. The history department at Western Michigan University was so full of itself, anyone operating outside the established rules and routines was heavily frowned upon.

It wasn't his fault the computer had glitched and ignored his age and class level. It had no trouble accepting his credit card.

Well, screw them, anyway! He hated snobs, and pseudo-intellectual snobs were the worst. At least he had this beautiful summer sunset to admire. He had rushed through dinner, as bored with the conversation as his table companions were with him. For a while, at least, he had the starboard stern upper deck to himself.

There was a pleasant breeze and he leaned on the rail, watching the dying sun's last rays reflect on the water. It was amazing how fast the globe actually disappeared once it touched the horizon..

As he watched it sink under the waves, Matt became aware he was no longer alone on the deck.

The girl. Woman, he corrected himself quickly. She watched the last moments of the day, and he watched her. She didn't exactly have a classic beauty, but he found her features fascinating. Her profile accented her nose. It was not too big, but it made its presence known. Her eyes were soft, with long lashes that looked real. She had looked great yesterday afternoon in casual clothes and lifejacket. Tonight, in a long, white, cotton dress with just a little embroidery, she was stunning.

She turned and looked at him. He smiled nervously, and wiped his suddenly sweaty palms on his slacks. She smiled back and he felt giddy. He slid down the rail a few feet to get close enough to speak over the sound of the sea.

"Hi. Do you speak English?"

She shook her head, still smiling. Her smile was captivating. It had a tinge of sadness, as though she had a secret. Or knew more than the people around her.

"No hablo Inglese," she admitted. "Hable Espanol?" When he shook his head and held his fingers close together, she tried again. "Sprechen sie Deutsch?"

"Nein." Matt had taken Spanish in high school, but had hated it. But it looked like it was that or nothing. "Hablo Espanol un poco."

"Bien." Her smile grew wider and he found himself drawn closer along the rail.

Over the next few hours, they discovered a lot about each other. Matt decided he'd learned more than he'd realized in that old crone's Spanish classes. He also discovered even that wasn't enough to converse normally. Every sentence was a drawn out torture, but it was worth it to him.

Her name was Teresa Elizari, and she lived in Madrid. She had a soft, alto voice with a hint of hidden humor. He was disconcerted to discover that she also seemed to have a lisp. She pronounced her last name Eli'th'ari, and her family was from Bar'th'elona. They were Basques, but fortunately, not very politically inclined. Matt knew the Basques were to the Spanish government what the Irish were to the British.

He told her he was a student and asked what she did. She said she was an 'abogado', whatever that was. She tried to explain, but his vocabulary wasn't up to it.

Eventually, she grew cold and they moved into one of the lounges. When that closed, they walked until they found themselves out on the deck again, watching as the ship sailed between Sicily and the Italian mainland.

Mount Etna was flaring and glowed bright red in the dark. It was the highest point in Sicily and awesome. Finally, the coolness drove them back inside and they ended up in the lounge that featured nightly floor shows. It was empty, and they sat and talked for hours.

It was almost four in the morning when he walked her to the junction near her cabin. He was tempted to try and kiss her goodnight, but didn't. He suspected he rose in her eyes as a result.

The next day he was groggy all morning, but by lunch wide awake and excited. They were meeting by the pool in the early afternoon. The minutes dragged by, but when he finally saw her come out onto the deck, it was worth the wait.

Teresa wore a short, white robe and a wide-brimmed straw hat. She carried an Air Espana flight bag and a towel. As she sat down on the lounge chair he'd saved her, she took her sunglasses off and gave him a smile of genuine pleasure. He stuttered out a greeting, and finally lapsed into silence, embarrassed at how transparent his attraction for her was.

That day turned out to be a longer version of the previous night. As he walked her to her cabin at three thirty in the morning, he had one arm around her shoulder. When he released her, he kissed her forehead gently. Her eyes told him he'd guessed right again. His feet didn't touch the deck as he returned to his own room.

The next day they woke to the ship being docked at the Piraeas, the seaport for Athens. Matt had to go with his group on their own chartered bus tour of Athens in the morning, then off on a six hour excursion to the Corinthian Canal.

Normally, Matt would have been intrigued and enthralled by both. The view of Athens from the Parthenon was spectacular, and the deep canal was impressive. Also, there were the numerous temples to various Greek gods they visited along the way. Matt found these ancient ruins brought him a sense of contemplation, and they usually had a calming effect.

Today, they made him think of her.

Teresa went with her family on their own chartered excursion, and he didn't see her until almost midnight. By then, the ship had left port and was winding its way through the Aegean Sea to Istanbul. They would be there by midmorning, and would stay docked overnight.

They reluctantly agreed that they would have to skip meeting the next night. Her family had plans on shore, and he'd already signed up for an excursion to a local establishment that featured belly dancers. She thought that was pretty funny, and kidded him about it off and on throughout the evening.

When they said good night, they hugged and held each other for a long time. He began to hum and dance slowly, and she mirrored his movements. When he finally left, several kisses later, he couldn't quit giggling to himself.

It would be a long forty hours before he saw her again.

Time did pass, as it always does. The belly dancers were entertaining, and the bazaar in Istanbul overwhelming. He had some free time between trips and decided to do a little detective work.

He'd already found out she was twenty-seven years old to his nineteen. That had caused her to roll her eyes in self-deprecation. He wanted to know more, and went to the ships' information desk. That was where all announcements originated, and he'd met the young woman that made them.

It was just one person, an attractive Italian woman. She spoke all six languages fluently, and also had a passable knowledge of Greek and Norwegian. He liked to watch her read notices, bouncing from one language to the next with no pause.

She always answered in the language she was addressed. Once, he watched in awe as she carried on simultaneous conversations with three different people in three different languages.

"Do you know what 'abogado' means in Spanish?" Matt stumbled over the word slightly.

"If your midwestern American accent is as bad as I think, it means 'lawyer'." She smiled brightly, her expression belying the words.

"Lawyer?" Matt frowned. "She doesn't seem to act like a lawyer. And she speaks with a lisp. Wouldn't that make it hard to perform in court?"

"Oh, you mean your little Basque friend?" The Italian woman was tall and busty, with long dark locks flowing over her shoulders. Most women would be small to her. She waited, teasing for a moment, then had mercy on him.

"Her dialect is Castiliano." When Matt showed no sign of comprehension, she continued. "A long time ago, there was a Spanish prince that eventually became king. He was very popular, but had a lisp. It became trendy to speak the same way, to sound just like the king. Eventually, it became the preferred dialect of the royalty." She stopped and gave him a bright smile. "Clear?"

"Yeah." Matt rolled his eyes. "So she doesn't have a lisp, except in Spanish. When she speaks German, it disappears."

"You got it." The woman gave him a sympathetic look. "I know her family. She is a lawyer. I think you call them 'public defendants'."

"Damn, a lawyer." Matt felt out of his depth. After all, he was only a sophomore, and she'd already done law school.

He thanked her and wandered back to his cabin. He would see Teresa later tonight. Did any of this really matter? She seemed as interested in him as he was in her. On the other hand, he hadn't actually had a real conversation with her, ever.

He hadn't been able to find a Spanish-English dictionary. The closest he could get were two pocket dictionaries, one English/Italian, the other Italian/Spanish. It led to some long pauses in their discussions.

Well, he would see if anything had changed in their relationship tonight. And tomorrow, they would dock at Ephesis in Turkey. It had extensive Greek ruins and both her family and his class had plans of spending most of the day there.

It would be good to spend some premium time with Teresa in the daylight for a change.

◆ ◆ ◆ ◆ ◆

Glowing Mist, nine days ago

Cromar Try and Siph Carni entered the bridge, hand in hand. He could see that Du Brimar could barely contain himself, he was so excited. Evidently, the younger commander had been busy while Cromar Try had passed hours of pleasure with his mate.

"Well? Have you found him?" Cromar Try took delight in deflating the others' excitement. Siph Carni pulled her hand free and slapped his shoulder in mock punishment.

"Cromar Try, you are being nasty," she chided him. "Let the young man enjoy his enthusiasm. It hasn't been that long since you showed that kind of passion."

"Over something entirely different." Cromar Try made a point of correcting her, then turned to Du Brimar. "Well?"

Du Brimar rubbed his hands together.

"Sir, I have not found Ty Musa, but what we did find may be even more important."

"I doubt that." Cromar Try frowned and began examining the data showing on the displays. "So you've discovered a race with the ability to broadcast radio waves?"

"Far beyond that." Du Brimar fingered his hair nervously. "Yes, they have a relatively advanced civilization. Nuclear power, limited space travel. They've also fought some major wars, engulfing the entire planet."

"Who did they fight with?" Cromar Try looked at his subordinate in confusion. "Surely, even the Ananab could...?"

"They fought with themselves." All five Egelv on the bridge stared at each other, unsettled by the notion. "Millions of casualties," Du Brimar continued.

45

"So they've depopulated their own planet?" Siph Carni sounded troubled, and she brushed a hand across her eyes. "So sad. Are there many of them left?"

Du Brimar nodded. "You could say that. There are over four billion sentients on that planet."

Cromar Try felt his jaw begin to drop and set it firmly. "Four billion?"

"And that Ananab ship has been here," Jo Coran added. She was the chief engineer/medical officer, and took her job more seriously than Du Brimar. "We found clear signatures of their drive showing they recently orbited the planet for at least several local days." She shrugged. "But it may have been their first visit." She looked uncomfortable.

Cromar Try came to a decision.

"Let's keep stealthed and observe a little more. Then, I think we need to get a few samplings of the population." He glanced towards Jo Coran. "When we get closer, begin looking for a few isolated beings, preferably of both sexes."

He stopped. "Do they have two sexes? What do they look like?" He watched Du Brimar exchange veiled looks with Jo Coran and the other tech, then the young officer turned to his console.

"I think you should see for yourself. They call themselves Humans, but I you'll recognize them for what they really are." He brought a picture of a small group of the humans up to the main viewing screen, and Cromar Try's jaw dropped. Behind him, he heard Siph Carni gasp.

"By the strands of Mesa!" Distantly, he heard the muttered oath, belatedly recognizing his own voice.

This voyage had just gotten more complicated.

CHAPTER FOUR

Jade Viking, en route to Earth

"Gawd, that's hot!"

Kimberly gasped as she slowly lowered herself into the spa. Once she was past her 'delicate' parts, it felt bearable. Kiri Oshiba settled across from her in one of the seats and sighed blissfully. Kiri was, or had been, the star actress for Jim's movie that had been cut short by their abduction. She had a tremendous following in Japan, especially among teenagers.

"I gotta tell you, round eyes." The young Japanese woman grinned at her. "This is why I work out. These jets make it all worthwhile."

Kimberly couldn't argue. Her body felt like it had been stretched and pummeled by the lacrosse team back in college. She had just started taking lessons in self-defense from Kiri and several other members of Jim's movie cast. They were nearly all black belts in their respective styles. It would take most of a week to get to Earth and she intended to take advantage of the time.

Kimberly eyed Kiri enviously. You wouldn't know it to look at her, but she held black belts in Judo and Aikido. Her petite body looked soft and rounded. But that five foot one frame concealed well-toned muscles that sent Kimberly sprawling repeatedly to the mat.

"You're rough on beginners, Kiri." Kimberly smiled to show she wasn't serious. Kiri grinned, stretching her arms above her head, purring like a cat.

"I'm glad the Hoag rigged these locker rooms up for us." Kiri propped her feet next to Kimberly, her chin barely above water. "Wearing a swimsuit takes away half the comfort."

47

Kimberly couldn't argue that. She didn't consider herself a prude, but wasn't a nudist by nature. It didn't bother her to sit here like this. In fact, it reminded her of school days. But co-ed would have been another matter.

"I can't believe we'll be home so soon." Kiri stared off into space. "We need to enjoy this relaxation while we can. Once we're back..." She let the sentence die away.

"I know." Kimberly frowned. "I still can't believe I got talked into this."

"Jim not too happy?" Kiri looked at her shrewdly. Kimberly laughed sardonically.

"Is water wet?"

"And hot!" The Japanese woman feinted splashing at her.

"And hot," she agreed, then turned serious. "I felt like I was betraying him."

"Those puppy eyes." Kiri nodded knowingly.

"You've seen that look?"

"Hey, I've seen all his movies, man." At times, Kiri was impossible to take seriously. For a moment at least, though, her face turned thoughtful. "He didn't say anything at the big meeting, and I hardly saw him the last day before we left."

"Hmm," Kimberly pursed her lips, remembering. "He was still pretty pissed at me."

Kimberly came out of her reverie, hearing voices in the next room. Yvette Stephanian and Janice Wooley came in, towels wrapped around them, both carrying small coolers. They stopped when they saw that the tub was occupied.

"Oh, hi." Yvette glanced back and forth from Kiri to her. "Should we come back? We thought no one was here."

"Come on in," Kiri said lazily as she shifted over next to Kimberly to make room for the two women. "As long as you aren't going to embarrass us and get all romantic."

Janice laughed and splashed water with her hand, testing the temperature. "I think we can control ourselves for at least a few minutes." She pulled a bottle of wine out of a cooler, and four small plastic glasses appeared from somewhere. "Although, under the influence, I can make no promises..."

Kimberly sat up out of her comfortable slouch, and groaned at the stiffness in her neck. Kiri had been careful not to hurt her, but that didn't mean she hadn't hit the mats plenty of times. Belatedly, she realized that sitting upright was not the more modest position.

"Here, let me." The young Japanese began kneading Kimberly's neck and she moaned in pleasure, in spite of herself.

Yvette and Janice both laughed as they dropped their towels and gingerly slid into the tub.

"Oh, hot, hot, hot." Yvette gasped.

That brought back memories of the awful pool band that had played "beach" music the first day of the voyage, so many weeks before, and Kimberly found herself singing along and laughing. Kiri pushed her around sideways so she could use both hands to work the sore neck muscles.

"Me next!" Janice grinned, her hanging breasts swaying as she poured the wine, and Yvette frowned at her in mock anger.

"I better not catch you under the influence of some other woman's hands." She warned, trying to look menacing. It only made her look silly as she accepted a glass.

"Kimberly was just telling me how happy Jim was to hear she was coming back to Earth on the Jade Viking," Kiri said, winking.

"Ouch, I'll bet that was a fun conversation." Yvette gave her a sympathetic smile. "Are you still married?"

"Barely." Kimberly laughed ruefully. "I just have to look at it as giving Jim some premium time with his daughter, Afsaneh."

Both women stared at her, and behind her, Kiri snickered and stopped massaging for a moment. "Ooh, that's rich!"

Kimberly took advantage of the pause to shift back facing forward. This allowed her to sink into the water enough to cover her breasts as Janice passed full glasses to them. She'd gotten to know Yvette and Janice quite well in the past month, and liked them both. She shouldn't feel self-conscious, but, well, she did.

"I hope she keeps out of trouble." Kimberly remembered the high school seniors the young girl had been spending so much time with lately. "She's a handful."

"I think she's going to run Jim ragged." Yvette nodded. "She's always been a handful, but at least Jim and Hakim could gang up on her. Poor Jim..."

Kimberly sobered at the thought of Hakim Riahi, Afsaneh's father.

He'd been killed in the final battle for Osaka. Jim had tried to rescue him, but failed. But he had avenged his oldest friend. Kimberly closed her eyes at the memory.

"I'm going to miss Hakim," Janice said in a solemn voice. Kimberly opened her eyes in surprise. Usually, Janice was irreverent, sometimes brutally humorous. She watched Yvette lay her head on her lover's shoulder, both of them looking lost in memories.

Feeling guilty for bringing the mood down, she searched for a lighter topic.

"You wouldn't believe the scam she ran on me when we first met." Kimberly clenched her teeth in mock frustration. "She implied she was Jim's lover, and had been for years. She told me she was eighteen."

Kiri snorted and the other two women nodded, evidently having no trouble picturing the scene. They didn't laugh, but it did brighten their mood slightly.

Kimberly continued with the story as Janice refilled their glasses. "When Jim and I finally got around to straightening out that misunderstanding, it turns out he thought that I thought he and you were having an affair." This last was directed to Kiri, who snorted.

"Didn't take him long to clear that up, I'll bet." All three women laughed, and Kimberly wasn't quite clear on what the joke was.

"So, you and Jim never...dated?" Kimberly hurried on. "I mean, it doesn't matter who he knew before. Neither of us were virgins, after all."

"I love Jim dearly," Kiri said. "But he's not my type."

"Oh." Kimberly was honest enough to recognize her own bias. Personally, she felt that Jim was probably anyone's type.

She looked across the tub at Janice and Yvette and amended that thought. Almost anyone.

"How about Danny or Koro?" Kimberly nudged Kiri under the water with her elbow. "Both are gorgeous."

"Not my type," Kiri said in a matter-of-fact voice.

"Not your type?" Kimberly thought both men were hunks. Did Kiri like older men or something? "What is your type, then?"

Kiri turned sideways to face Kimberly and smiled sweetly, a mischievous gleam in her eyes.

"Actually, you are."

Kimberly felt her eyes widen and stiffened involuntarily. She looked over at the other two women, who were both looking right back, wide grins on their faces.

"Surprise," Janice managed to say before she began laughing. Yvette nudged her.

"Quit it, you're embarrassing her."

That only made Janice laugh harder. "Too late for that!"

"Didn't see that coming," Kimberly admitted, then jumped as Kiri put a hand on her shoulder. The Japanese woman looked at her intently, studying her reaction.

"Kimberly, I'm not going to rape you."

"Hey, I thought that was the plan..." Janice barely got that out before Yvette punched her in the arm. "Hey, the wine..."

"Stop it, love." Yvette gave Kimberly an apologetic look. "You know her humor..."

Kimberly nodded, and cocked her head, looking at Kiri.

"I didn't know they were going to be here tonight," Kiri assured her. "I thought Jim would have told you by now."

"He knows?" All three women looked at her cynically, and Kimberly rolled her eyes in self-deprecation. "Duh."

"Kimberly, this wasn't a come-on, really." Kiri looked distressed. "I mean, I am attracted to you, but I know you aren't gay. Plus, I really like you as a friend."

This last started Janice off again. "I just want to be friends." She tried to sound sincere, while batting her eyes. "Not again! That arm's still sore!"

The last was at Yvette, who was about to punch her again. The short woman smiled in sympathy at Kimberly.

"Sorry, honey. We really didn't mean to embarrass you."

"That's alright." Kimberly realized she was acting like a school girl. "I mean, it's really a compliment, after all."

All three lesbians looked at her in surprise. Kiri spoke first. "Do you mean that?"

Kimberly smiled at the attractive Japanese woman. They really did have the beginnings of a great friendship, and she didn't want to lose it. "I'll tell you what, you don't try to cop a feel, I won't be paranoid."

The others laughed, relieved. Janice couldn't resist one last dig. "Ya know, she might sneak a peek..." she drawled.

"Hell, I put up with that from you two, why should I treat her any different." Kimberly blushed as Janice let her eyes run down Kimberly's body, partly visible through the water and bubbles. She steeled herself and gave the other woman a laconic expression. "If you're quite finished..." and held up her empty glass.

Janice laughed and sat up, reaching for the bottle. It was empty and she stretched over the edge of the tub to reach the cooler. Yvette pointed at her bare butt rising from the water. "This is definitely her best side."

They laughed.

Kiri hesitantly touched Kimberly on the arm. "I'm glad you're okay with this. I really do want you as a friend. It's not easy keeping secrets from people you like. And once they find out..." She let the sentence fade away.

Kimberly covered Kiri's hand with her own. She looked for appropriate words, but realized she didn't need them. The gesture was enough. They both settled back into comfortable positions, sipping their refilled glasses and enjoying the companionable silence.

For a few moments, the four of them sat, lost in private thoughts. Then Kimberly sat up, startled, as a foot slid up her leg.

"Hey!"

Kimberly splashed at Janice, and the other two quickly joined in. They were all shrieking and laughing when Kimberly suddenly became aware of someone else in the room. They all froze, Kimberly and Kiri standing over Janice as Yvette held her in a headlock.

"Um, hi." Linda Hoffman stood a few feet away, one towel wrapped around her head, another tucked around her body. "Is there room enough for one more? Ah brought a contribution," she said, holding up another bottle of wine.

Kimberly kept a straight face. Linda Hoffman was the wife of a Texas tire tycoon. She was very southern, and probably very conservative. They had met the night before the ship's abduction, and Kimberly hadn't been impressed. Linda had practically thrown herself at Jim, in front of her own husband. And, there was no way those breasts were real.

"Come on in, Linda." Kimberly smiled sweetly, and realized she had the same expression she'd seen too many times on Afsaneh's face. "There's plenty of room. It's just us girls, after all."

Linda Hoffman hesitated. "You don't mind...?"

"Glad to have you, Linda," Kimberly assured her. Janice snickered,

52

then groaned when Yvette punched her again. "We're just lettin' off tension. You know Yvette and Janice?"

"Of course," Mrs. Hoffman looked a little uncertain as she carefully folded her towel on a nearby chair. She followed Janice's pointing and found another glass. "My suit didn't survive the hijacking, but I really wanted to decompress. When I saw you coming in here..."

"Glad ya did, honey." Kimberly wished she knew how Janice could sound like she was chewing gum when she wasn't. Yvette's lover smiled lazily, and patted the seat next to her. "Like our shyster said, it's just us girls."

◆ ◆ ◆ ◆ ◆

Station Osaka

Jim smashed the dummy hard with the inside of his right thigh and his right forearm. Then he did it again, and again. Sergeant McGregor grunted and gave ground under the onslaught. He was trying to brace the large punching bag, but he might as well have tried holding back the sea with his bare hands.

Jim felt the rage sweep through him, exploding outward every time he connected with the bag. He didn't approve of fighting under the influence of anger, but he had to get rid of this negative energy.

Once, several years ago, Afsaneh had come to a workout angry at one of her tutors. She had been sloppy and inconsistent, and Jim had begun lecturing her on anger. She had been quick to give him a very good first-hand display of that emotion, he recalled ruefully.

"Honey, you're swinging haymakers. You're wide open to a counter, and you're wasting energy..."

"I don't care!" Afsaneh snarled at him. She kicked viciously at the bag. "That is Mrs. Bovee's head! And that, and that!"

Jim winced at the fury in her motions, but persisted. "Okay, you're so mad, let's see what you got." He motioned at his stomach. "Go for it."

She was obviously sure he would block and didn't even hesitate. He'd been teaching her since she was five, and she had a pretty good front kick. It caught him full in the stomach, but he didn't budge. She gasped in surprise.

"I'm sorry, Jim. I thought you would counter."

"No problem." Jim just managed to keep his voice at a normal level. Breathe, Jim, breathe. "You wasted energy with that kick. It should have been strong enough to knock the air out of me, but see?"

She nodded thoughtfully. He showed her how she was flailing wildly, and how to put that excess power into the blow, not the motion.

"Okay, one more time."

Again she didn't even hesitate. Jim shuddered inside, but kept his face blank. Her foot caught him perfectly and, even with him prepared, it hurt like hell. He smiled at her to show he was okay.

"Jim, are you all right?" Afsaneh looked at his face with concern. "You're pale. And your lip is twitching."

"Hyi...I'm fine." He managed to get the words out. "That was much better. See how you focused that anger into power by recognizing it and using it, instead of it using you?"

"Yeah, that was better." Afsaneh gave him a shrewd look. "That hurt a little more than you're letting on, didn't it?"

Jim tried to laugh, and almost succeeded. "Now, let's go back to that rage of yours and focus..."

"Hold!"

Jim froze his last assault inches from the bag, held the pose for a moment, then relaxed. The sergeant watched Jim carefully, as if expecting a trick, then reluctantly released his grip. He gave Jim a stiff nod of approval at the effort, although he looked wary.

Jim slowed his breathing, his vision widened as his fury subsided. He was angry because Kimberly was on her way back to Earth, and he was still here, on Station Osaka. So far, recognizing the anger hadn't helped.

"The students are here, Sir." McGregor spoke in a quiet voice that belied his six foot four, two hundred and forty pounds of pure bone and muscle.

Students. Jim scowled as he turned to face the young people waiting just inside the entrance. He recognized all of them, but didn't know the names of the two young men standing next to Afsaneh.

Jim glanced at the others. He knew Suyo Takashi, of course. She was one of the most organized, hardworking people he'd ever met. He was glad she'd wholeheartedly come over from Sukuru. She would be needed in the days to come.

Some faces were very familiar to him. Mariko Iwasaka was a member of his now-defunct movie cast, and Jozen Onoshi had worked on films with Jim twice before. He was a likeable enough kid, and also, Jim suspected, the reason Mariko was here. After all, nothing started off a relationship like a good fight, right? Why wait until you know each other?

The other man was Koro Asaya.

Jim turned his attention back to the two boys he didn't know, and they flinched. The black kid was even bigger than McGregor. Football scholarship, wasn't it? Linebacker, no, defensive end, probably. The other was a little over six feet, and much thinner. He couldn't weigh more than one fifty, max. Jim vaguely remembered seeing both of them around Afsaneh a lot, lately.

"Your names?"

The husky kid stammered and looked pale beneath his coal-black skin. "I-I'm Ellis Jackson, Sir."

"I'm Sean Jackson." The curly-haired kid smirked. "No relation... Sir." He added the honorific as if it were an afterthought. Jim eyed him for a moment. To the younger man's credit, he didn't look away.

This one is going to be trouble, Jim thought. I recognize the type. He'll get carried away for sure. One way or the other...

"Okay, let's get a few things clear. This is not a class. I am not your instructor. This is a workout session for the purpose of staying sharp." Jim sighed and looked at McGregor.

"Sergeant, will you monitor for a few minutes, please?" McGregor nodded. "Fine, let's pair up. And let's not be moving into each other's space, please."

Jim turned to Afsaneh, but she was already squared off with Ellis. The other two women paired, as did Koro and Jozen. This left him the clever kid. Wonderful.

McGregor made a muffled sound. Jim looked at him suspiciously, but the sergeant was busy adjusting Suyo's feet into a more efficient stance.

"Alright, let's go." Jim bowed to the younger man, and it was returned, not quite as deeply. *Already, I don't like this kid.* Jim kept the scowl off his face.

They circled, watching each other.

I'll bet this kid is fast, Jim mused. And limber. He reminds me of someone...

Jackson moved close and snapped a kick at Jim's head, testing him. He shifted slightly to avoid the foot, but made no move to counter.

Another kick came at his head, and when he dodged it the same way, the foot stayed after him, the young man pivoting as he tried to catch Jim napping.

Uh huh, Jim thought. You want to prove something? Your bruises, not mine. He slapped the raised foot enough to upset the other's balance, then fell to the floor, swinging his right foot in a blurring sweep that caught Jackson on the calf of his other leg, knocking him off his feet.

Jim was surprised at how quickly the kid recovered. In a real fight, Jim would have tried to follow up with an attack but, due to the young man's fast reaction, he probably wouldn't have succeeded.

Almost too late, Jim realized his opponent had turned a retreat into an attack. He got his hand up just in time to stop the kick coming at his face. Without coming off the hand he was pivoting on, he snapped a fast return that hit Jackson on his back, just behind the heart.

Jim was back on his feet and moving away, knowing what was next. Sure enough, the kid bounded to his feet and was coming full speed, obviously planning to catch Jim off guard with a fast combination.

Enough of this, Jim thought in disgust. He let Jackson get in close, countering the attacks with his own natural speed. Then he brought his left leg up, hitting Jackson in the side with his knee three times in quick succession, throwing the other's concentration off. Then Jim punched a hard left open hand to the kid's face, following up with a strong right uppercut to the stomach.

Sean Jackson collapsed to the mat, holding his midriff, trying to breathe. Jim stepped in close and touched the young man's nose with his closed fist.

"Crunch, you're dead, hot dog." The youth glared at him, looking game for more. If only he could get some oxygen into his body.

"Jim, what are you doing?" Afsaneh swept by him and knelt next to her friend. "You could have really hurt him!"

Jim looked around. The others were standing, watching with interest what they probably thought was a pretty good match. He could tell Koro and Jozen knew what had happened. He wasn't so sure about the women. Ellis had a thoughtful expression that revealed nothing. Of course, McGregor had no expression whatsoever.

"Let's understand something." Jim said, angry at having to defend himself about this. "We aren't trying to embarrass or kill each other, but we aren't sparring for fun, either. In a fight for your life, you are going to take some damage."

Afsaneh sniffed, obviously bored with an old, familiar message. Well, she could hear it one more time.

"In a fight, you have to be able to take a painful hit, and keep functioning. And I don't mean those fights with people where someone surrenders and it stops." Jim felt his anger from earlier returning. "In the battles we're fighting now, if you're losing and give up, you will die. And so will people depending on you. If you're going to work out with me, expect to get hit sometimes. But don't try to get cute. Because you might be enjoying this, but I'm not."

He looked at Sean Jackson, who was listening as he slowly got to his feet. The young man met his gaze, showing uncertainty for the first time.

"You're just showing off!" Afsaneh had her hands on her hips as she glared at him. "He was doing pretty good, and you just had to show him up!"

"He was being careless, trying to impress me." Jim said in a flat voice. He looked back at Sean. "You're young. Nothing wrong with that, but don't fool yourself. Speed and aggressiveness are great. But until you have the techniques, experience and maturity to go with it, it still leaves you vulnerable."

The younger man looked thoughtful. Afsaneh snorted and shrugged the words off with a wave of her hand. Jim felt depressed now, instead of angry. And tired.

"I"m through for the day," he spoke curtly and, catching up his towel, briskly strode out.

❖ ❖ ❖ ❖ ❖

"I'm really sorry, Sean." Afsaneh was contrite. "He was acting like a bully..."

"Excuse me, Ms. Riahi."

Afsaneh was startled at the cold tone in McGregor's voice. He was always so nice and polite to her.

"Jim Morris could have hurt the young gentleman very badly." He accented the honorific, and Sean blushed angrily. McGregor gave him no chance to interrupt. "Jim could have blocked and countered your attack any number of ways. Most of those would have resulted in your death or serious injury."

"You were pushing him, trying to impress the young ladies and maybe even him," McGregor said. "You're just fast enough and good enough to make him take you seriously. But he could have killed you in the first exchange."

Jackson began to bluster, but one huge hand raised stopped him immediately. McGregor continued as if there'd been no interruption.

"You've got potential. And if you can get Mr. Morris or myself to help you, you'll be very good someday. But he's killed dozens of men and aliens with his bare hands." McGregor picked up his own towel, giving Afsaneh an inscrutable look. "He has to pay very close attention so as to not seriously hurt any of you."

He left, the same way Jim had.

Afsaneh felt a sense of guilt, but anger too. He had no right to lecture them! She looked around at the others. Koro and Jozen shook their heads and went back to their sparring. The two women already had. Ellis was giving her a funny look and she glared at him.

"What?!"

"Damn!" Jim scuffed his feet on the deck as he walked. Two Baerd approaching in the corridor took one look at his face and veered sharply down a side passage. He hardly noticed.

She's going through a phase where she and her friends are always right, he thought miserably. I know this is to be expected, but how do I handle it? What on earth am I doing with a teenage daughter?

And, she's at an age where she can get revenge so easily. God, I do not like this part of being a father. All these teenage boys...

"Pearl..." he began, but stopped. The station computer answered him anyway.

"Yes, Jim Morris?" The computer had a soft, feminine voice that Jim found soothing. Both Jade ships and Pearl had distinctive voices, but produced the same effect. Relaxing, comforting, yet strong and dependable. Pearl's was a bit deeper, more contralto.

The Egelv security program virus made his safety and well-being their primary purpose. At least, he could always count on them being there for him...hmm.

"Pearl, any ideas on how to show Afsaneh I'm right?"

"Does this question apply to when you are wrong, as well?" Did Jim hear irony? No, couldn't be. Pearl was incredibly advanced, sophisticated beyond anything Earth had ever seen. But she was still just a computer.

"Never mind." Jim shook his head at himself and his pace quickened. Raising teenage girls was not in Pearl's job description. On the hand, when Kimberly got back...

Not likely. Kimberly was as lost as he was when it came to rearing children. Anyway, she was probably still mad at him for the way he acted before she left.

"Jim, this was not my idea!" Kimberly threw up her hands in frustration. They had been arguing for hours, with the same results. Jim wasn't being totally fair but, damn it, this hurt!

"Okay, okay." Jim sighed and leaned against the frame of the bathroom door. He looked down at his feet despondently. Kimberly came and put a hand on his arm.

"I really will be back soon." Her voice grew soft. "I quit my job, get things started on the financial front. Eric Miles has a company that delivers supplies to oil rigs. He's got all kinds of contacts and is going to start looking for an island, or some other fairly desolate location for us."

"Balleny Island." Jim looked up at her and smiled, hoping for a truce. Or at least a recess.

Kimberly looked doubtful. "Off Cape Williams?"

Jim shook his head, bemused. "You know Balleny Island?"

"Sure, Antarctica." Her voice sounded nonchalant and Jim realized she was laughing at him. "It's near...uh, Cape Adare."

Jim tried to picture his old atlas. Damn, she was right. He put his arms around her and pulled her close.

"I love you, you know that?" He kissed her forehead and she raised her face to meet him. They kissed and he slid one hand up her back under her shirt. *Hmm, no bra.*

"You think you can distract me with mindless, passionate sex?" Kimberly made no attempt to pull away.

"Actually, I thought I would try conniving, sensual, deliberately taunting sex." He let both his hands slide down, slipping beneath her sweats and panties, cupping her buttocks.

"That would be fine," she said, her own hands doing a little wandering.

"Do you have any idea how long it may be before we can do that again?" Jim sighed as he lay on his back, pleasantly exhausted. Kimberly had her chin resting on his chest, sweaty body draped across him.

"I was hoping maybe twenty minutes, half hour, max." Kimberly put her lips against his stomach and blew as hard as she could, making a sloppy sound.

Jim gasped and curled forward, catching her by the shoulders and rolling over so he was on top. She smiled up at him, letting herself be pinned to the bed.

"Ah, Jim Morris-san is ticklish." She mimicked Kiri's accent. "I am at your mercy, round eyes."

"Oh?" Jim gave her an exaggerated lewd expression and kissed her nose. He began to work his way down to her breasts, making loud sounds of appreciation. "Hmm, salty."

"Hey!" She flipped over, surprising him.

As far as I'm concerned, this side has a certain appeal, too, Jim thought. He began running his tongue down her spine. When he got to her waist, she shrieked in laughter and flipped back over.

"Works for me," Jim said happily.

"Stop, just for a minute." Kimberly gasped, holding his head away from her.

"Well, okay. A minute." They settled back down together, comfortably entwined.

"Will you be okay while I'm gone?" Kimberly finally spoke, breaking a long silence.

"I guess I'll have to be." Jim winced at the bitterness he heard in his voice. "I'm sorry. I didn't mean it that way."

"Yes, you did." Kimberly corrected him. "I know it's not fair." She tried to find a lighter side to the conversation. "At least you won't be dropped off on a deserted island in the middle of nowhere."

"Has it been decided where to leave you?" Jim had been thinking about this.

"Uh huh." Kimberly's voice became playful. "The Aleutians." She swung one leg over his hips, straddling him.

Jim grinned at her and whistled with appreciation. I like what happens when she does that, he thought. Everything moves so...nicely.

"Stop that." She said automatically, and gave him a mock glare. She put her hands on her hips, shifting to sit straighter. They both gasped as the movement made her straddling of him a little more...intimate.

A lot more intimate, Jim thought.

"That's kind of convenient." Kimberly's voice grew husky.

"Yeah...convenient." Jim cleared his throat. He began to move his hips and she moaned.

"Oh, right there." She blushed down at him. "That's a good spot."

"I would have to agree with that." Jim barely managed to get the words out before they stopped talking for some time.

"That was nice."

Jim laughed raggedly as Kimberly made the understatement of the day. Well, night by now.

"I would have to say that ranked pretty high." Jim's breathing began to slow to something between heart attack and normal. "Umm, you do realize we didn't use..."

"I'm back on the pill," Kimberly said. "And if it happens, it happens. I want to start a family when I get back, anyway."

Jim grinned at the words. "Great! Of course, it would help if we practiced diligently..."

"Practice is not an issue here." Kimberly staggered to her feet and groaned. "If I'm going to be able to walk on board Jade Viking tomorrow without limping, we need to slow down."

Jim grew morose at the thought of tomorrow. "Couldn't Suyo do what you're..."

Kimberly disappeared into the bathroom. Her voice wafted back at him. "She's not going this trip. Sukuru would lock her away until they found out everything she knows. And no, she can't do what I can."

Jim climbed wearily out of bed and eyed the sheets with distaste. Where was room service when you needed it. He followed Kimberly into the bathroom. She was in the shower and he gave a wolf whistle. "Are you sure you're not inflating your own value?" He winced. That could have been said a little better. He tried again.

"I mean, Suyo is efficient. So is Frederick, that guy Miles, any number of people...you could stay here."

Kimberly gave him a look of frustration. "Jim, let's not have this conversation again."

"Why not?" Jim leered. "Making up was fun." He began to join her under the water. She pushed him back and frowned at him in irritation.

"Stop it. I said I need a break."

Jim backed off, raising his hands in mock supplication. "Fine, fine. Let me know if you get 'in the mood' again. It's only going to be weeks or months until we get another chance."

Kimberly gave him a sour look. "I'm sure you'll keep matters well in hand." She poured shampoo and began lathering her hair, ignoring him.

Jim glared in disbelief. That was cold! Throwing his arms up his frustration, he left her to her shower. He started to return to the rumpled bed and stopped, remembering the condition they'd left it.

"Damn!" Jim stood still for a moment. He wanted to just walk out, but that wouldn't help any. Resigning himself to a long evening, he began changing the sheets on the bed.

In retrospect, leaving for a little while might have been a good idea, Jim remembered glumly. He'd been a horse's ass, and she hadn't been much better. Some pretty nasty things had been said. By the time they went to bed, both were exhausted from the bickering and tension. She slept on her side of the bed, he slept on his. A cold, barren space separated them.

The next morning Kimberly packed in silence. When it was absolutely necessary to speak, they were coldly polite. Jim wanted to break down the barriers, but didn't know how.

When it was time, they gave each other perfunctory kisses goodbye. She'd looked like she wanted to say something, but then her face hardened and she left without a backward glance.

He sat in their apartment as the Jade Viking cast off. He wondered if she'd watched, expecting him to come down at the last minute and apologize.

Jim wished he had.

Shinzo Takuan tried to conceal his excitement as he boarded the Jade Viking. In one week, he'd be back on Earth. A few days after that, he'd be in Japan.

Then, revenge would only be a matter of time.

CHAPTER FIVE

Glowing Mist, seven days ago

Matt opened his eyes and saw he was lying on a table. He turned his head to the side and groaned. Had he been drinking? It felt like it! He forgot about the headache as he focused on Teresa lying on another table next to his. She was wearing a light blue smock that didn't quite reach her knees.

As Matt looked at her, she opened her eyes and stared around in panic. Seeing him, her brows crinkled in puzzled confusion. She winced and he realized she was suffering the same affliction as he.

"Are you all right?" Matt saw he was wearing the same type of smock and wondered if they were in a Turkish hospital. Had they been in an accident? Teresa was staring at him in confusion. "What is it? Oh, right. Uh...Estas bien?"

"I think I'm okay." He jumped as he heard her voice in perfect English. "When did you learn Spanish?" she said, then stopped and put her hand behind her right ear.

"What do you..." Matt started, confused himself. She had actually spoken in Spanish. He'd heard her. But he'd also heard her in English, from a much closer source. He put a hand behind his own ear and felt a patch adhering to his skin. It felt like some kind of latex or something similar. That was the source of her voice speaking English.

"We have some sort of translators?" There was wonder in her voice. "What happened to us?"

Matt shook his head in bewilderment. "I have no idea," he admitted. He looked at the ceiling. Clean, white acoustic tiles, not a familiar design, but no distinctive design that would give him a clue as to where they were. He sat up and swung his legs over the side of the table.

"Damn." He pulled the hem of his gown down in irritation. This had to be a hospital. Where else would they dress you in these skimpy...these skimpy...these...his thoughts trailed off as he looked over her shoulder.

"Uh...Teresa." He was hoarse and had trouble catching his breath. "Teresa," he began again. She looked at him in puzzlement. Giving up on finding his voice, he
wordlessly pointed behind her.

"What is the matter with you..." She twisted around to see where he was pointing. Her eyes widened, and her jaw dropped. "Oh!"

Matt couldn't blame her for being startled. He could only sit and stare at the four strange beings standing about fifteen feet away. The wall behind them confirmed Matt's suspicions that they were in some sort of medical facility. It was covered with an array of instruments and cabinets.

But it wasn't a Turkish facility, and those were definitely not Turks.

All four beings were well over six feet tall, even the two females. They had long, white hair that contrasted sharply with their light brown skin. They were slender, but not skinny. The two males had thin mustaches and goatees. All four wore slight variations of the same clothing: loose-fitting, vee-necked, short-sleeved tops, and slacks, although the females had shorter legged versions that just covered their knees. Nondescript slippers completed their attire.

What captured Matt's attention the most was their ears. They were long, almost jutting above their heads. Rabbit ears? Or wolves, Matt thought, shivering.

"Are you cold?" One of the females looked directly at him as she spoke.

"No," Matt stammered. "Somebody just walked on my grave, I guess." Damned if he'd admit he was scared.

The four aliens, and they had to be aliens, looked at each other.

"Did the computer foul up the translation?" One of the males spoke to the other.

"No, I don't think so, Captain," the second answered. "It is probably a quaint colloquialism. I think he's just a little frightened is all."

The female that had spoken looked at an instrument she held in one hand.

"They are both reacting rather well, considering the circumstances. I'm surprised they're capable of being rational this quickly."

The second male snorted. "You haven't watched enough of their entertainment broadcasts. I've already seen five different productions that deal with a hypothetical 'first contact' with extraterrestrials. They certainly have active imaginations. By comparison, we probably come across as rather dull."

Matt looked cautiously around the room. This had to be their version of sick bay. They had probably been stunned, which would explain the headaches, then transported to this facility. "Is that a tricorder?" he asked, pointing at the female's instrument.

"A what?" The aliens evidently had similar facial expression to humans, because she looked puzzled to Matt.

"I know what he means." The second male spoke again, laughing. "It's a scanner used on one of those entertainment programs. It's used as a plot device..."

"Yes, yes, Du Brimar." The other male held up one hand and smiled at both of the white-haired women. "He's fascinated with watching their transmissions..."

Matt was beginning to wonder if this was a dream. They were chatting as if he and Teresa weren't even present. Considering the circumstances, they seemed very mild mannered.

"Excuse me."

All four aliens turned their attention to him and Matt tried a friendly smile. They all returned it encouragingly, and he was relieved to see they had normal looking teeth. No obvious vampires here.

"Would you please tell us why we're here?" Matt slid off the table and quickly pulled his gown down. They hadn't even left his underwear! Hey, did that mean...

He turned in time to see Teresa standing, blushing fiercely as she straightened from pulling her own hem down. She glared at him, obviously knowing what was running through his mind. One of the aliens spoke and he swung back around to face them.

"We mean you no harm." The woman who had spoken earlier took a step forward. "My name is Jo Coran. This is the captain of our ship, Cromar Try, First Officer Siph Carni, and Second Officer Du Brimar."

Matt shifted from one foot to another nervously as the man identified as the captain smiled and stepped forward, holding both his hands out, one palm up, the other facing downward.

"I'm pleased to meet you, Matt Stickel. And you, Teresa Elizari."

Matt and Teresa glanced at each other.

"You know our names?" Matt wondered where his wallet was.

"Yes, we did check your identification papers," Cromar Try answered his unspoken question. "We wanted to make sure we had the right languages for your translators. We couldn't believe it when they showed two different ones." He laughed, and Matt was surprised at how disarming a laugh it was. "We almost put you right back..."

"Who undressed me?" Teresa's face was bright red. "Why have you taken us prisoner? Are you going to release us? Where are my clothes?"

"Please, please." Cromar Try didn't even try to disguise his amusement. "We'll answer all your questions, soon enough. Your clothes are freshened and available. We need to find out a few things, then you'll be released, either back where we found you, or anywhere on your planet you would like."

There, it had finally been said. Matt closed his eyes for a moment. He took a deep breath and opened them.

"Our planet?" Beside him, Teresa gasped as she too, picked up the meaning.

Cromar Try glanced back at his companions questioningly.

"Yes." The woman identified as Siph Carni spoke for the first time. Du Brimar reached over and touched a control on one of the panels behind him. What Matt had assumed was wall, flickered, and Earth was floating in space on the screen. It was a picture very similar to many he'd seen transmitted by NASA space shuttles, with one exception. It was partly obscured by a large mass that hung between the camera and planet.

The Moon.

"That was Luna," Teresa whispered fiercely. "We're in outer space. Why aren't we floating?"

Matt shrugged. "Maybe they're spinning the ship to create a sense of gravity. Or maybe they have some kind of gravity generator."

"That would be close." Du Brimar smiled at them as he handed them cups of hot liquid. "Here, try this."

Matt and Teresa skeptically looked at the cups. The aliens had returned their clean clothes and discreetly left them alone for a few moments to change. Jo Coran had then brought them to a lounge where they all sat around a comfortably large table, everyone with his or her cup of...what? There was no reason to suspect intentional foul play, but what about mistakes?

"Go ahead, it's not going to harm you, see?" Du Brimar smiled and took a sip from his own cup. He set it down, and pulled a chair out to sit. Suddenly, he gave a gasping sound and grabbed his throat. Gurgling, the alien slid out of view behind the table.

Teresa stiffened and she snatched her hand away from her cup.

Matt looked around the table at the other aliens and saw a variety of amused and embarrassed expressions. Did he and Teresa look that gullible? He leaned over the edge of the table and looked down at the body on the floor.

Du Brimar lay in a contorted position, his eyes closed. After a moment, one eyelid flew open. Disappointment came to his face when he saw Matt calmly watching him.

"Are you quite finished?" Matt tried to make his tone as bored as possible.

Du Brimar sighed and climbed to his feet. Teresa had recovered her aplomb and glared at him. He meekly sat down.

"Please excuse my 'junior officer'," Cromar Try said, giving a glare of his own. "I'll have to find some way of showing him how much I appreciate his sense of humor."

Du Brimar winced and Siph Carni snickered. At least, it sounded like a snicker.

"I hope you understand we don't plan on keeping you long." Cromar Try smiled reassuringly. "The only reason we did any medical tests on you at all was to make sure we wouldn't inadvertently poison you, or expose you to anything harmful."

"Why did you capture us in the first place?" Matt took a cautious sip and raised his eyebrows in surprise. "It's not bad." He took another sip. "In fact, it's pretty good! Sort of like tea. Um...and a kind of citrus flavoring."

Teresa raised her cup hesitantly, and sniffed. A look of surprise came to her face and she took a tiny sip. She swallowed and waited fearfully for a reaction. "Hmm." She gave a nervous laugh and took another sip. "It is like tea."

"In answer to your question, you two were chosen because you were young, represented both sexes, and were relatively isolated." Cromar Try gave them a sympathetic smile. "No other special considerations or criteria. It was a chance thing. We thought taking you both together would insure just having to research one language." He sounded a little disgusted.

"Why kidnap anyone?" Matt could hear the indignation in his voice. "Was that absolutely necessary?"

"There are some things we needed to find out, and the only way was to ask someone." The captain looked apologetic. "We didn't think just landing somewhere and getting out was such a good idea."

Matt couldn't argue with that. Talk about instant panic. "Did you beam us up here? Or can this ship land on a planet's surface?"

"Beam?" Cromar Try looked confused.

"He means teleport." Du Brimar laughed. He had evidently decided it was safe to come out of seclusion. "One of their futuristic programs uses teleportation to go planet-side."

"Really." The aliens looked at each other and winced. Jo Coran smiled in sympathy. "I guess your technical level hasn't risen high enough to actually try teleporting yet?"

Matt shook his head.

"It's theoretically possible to transport inanimate objects between two points as long as you have reception grids." Siph Carni made a face. "But things don't travel well. Food flavors alter, alloys change, usually weakening, and the process consumes a lot of power. If you don't use a grid, you could end up materializing things six inches off the ground. Or worse yet, six inches underground."

Matt thought he knew what happened then. "Things get fused into the ground?"

Jo Coran laughed harshly. "If everything works out wonderfully, the best you can hope for would be a fusion between your cargo and the ground. That's assuming every single atom materialized between existing atoms with absolutely none of them touching. Do you have any idea of the odds against that happening?"

"Big?" Matt shrugged. "Really big?"

"It can't happen." Jo Coran's voice was brusque. "And when they don't fuse perfectly? You get an explosion. Two things can not occupy the same space at the same time."

"We have discovered and harnessed nuclear energy, you know." Matt didn't like the condescending tone she was taking. A moment later, he liked it even less.

"Yes, you do seem to be doing a good job of using it to kill yourselves, both directly and via pollutant by-products." The woman's voice was acidic as she examined a reading on her ever present scanner. "And you don't even have cold fusion yet."

"Jo Coran, I think we're being a little hard on the young man." Cromar Try gave Matt an apologetic look. "He certainly isn't personally responsible for everything his race does."

"You're right, of course." Jo Coran bowed her head slightly to her captain, then turned back to Matt. "Please accept my apology. Getting back to your first question, transporting people is the last thing we would ever do."

Matt nodded, slightly mollified. Her quick mood changes left him unsettled. "Too dangerous," he agreed.

Du Brimar laughed, cutting in, perhaps, to save Jo Coran from making further deprecating remarks. "Even if we had total control to make every atom appear safely without dropping you on your head or underground, we would never teleport a living, sentient being. The physical portion of your brain is only part of what makes you Matt Stickel. Your brainwave pattern defines your personality and your memories. Teleport someone, you either have a blank slate or an idiot." His voice grew dry. "Neither of which is ideal."

"No beam me up, Scotty?" Matt sighed, feeling a sense of loss.

"And there are more." Du Brimar beamed at him. "For instance..."

"I'm sure you can take this up at another time." Cromar Try silenced his subordinate with a look. "Do you have any more pertinent questions? We want you to feel as comfortable as possible."

Matt wanted to continue with the current discussion, but there was no point in antagonizing these people. He didn't particularly feel like walking home.

"Who are you? Where are you from?"

"I don't know that the answers will help much without reference points." Cromar Try smiled. "We are the Egelv. Our primary star can not be seen from this region of space."

"Egg-elf?" Matt kept his face straight as he took a more detailed look at his hosts. This entire situation was getting more bizarre every moment. They had a superficial resemblance to...but that had to be a coincidence. Didn't it?

"No, no. Egelv." Siph Carni pronounced it as one word.

"Have you been here before?" Matt tried to guess their age.

"No, we have not." Cromar Try's voice grew serious. "When we traced your radio transmissions here, and realized what we'd found, it seemed like a good idea to get some cell samples and take the opportunity to meet some of you, while we still can."

"While you still can?" Matt didn't like the sound of that.

"There will be a strong reaction to finding your people. Certainly, your lives will never be the same again."

"Can't you just...leave?" Teresa said hopefully. "We aren't causing any trouble to anyone."

"It is our duty." Cromar Try sounded grave.

"And it's not as if you can stay hidden out here much longer, in any case." Du Brimar had an uncharacteristically serious tone. "You've been broadcasting unprotected for a hundred years. Transmissions will be intercepted by other ships. They will trace the signals back here, just as we did."

"At least we aren't like the Ananab that were here recently." Siph Carni smiled in sympathy at Matt and Teresa. "When they, or their overlords, the Hshtahni, discover a new race, they sweep in and subjugate the entire planet. We have a much more benevolent attitude."

"Normally," Jo Coran corrected her grimly.

Siph Carni looked at her shipmate and nodded slowly. "Normally."

"What is it?" Teresa spoke and Matt noted with some surprise that she now sounded very much like a lawyer. "What aren't you telling us?"

Cromar Try sighed heavily. "We have had previous contact with your race. We tested cell samples, and there is no question you are genetically related."

"Parallel evolution?" Matt asked. He didn't like where this was going. "Mass seeding of the galaxy long ago?"

"No." The captain sat back and let his first officer explain. "At one time, several millenia ago, our emperor introduced his new palace guard. They were a fierce, warrior race called the Hashir. No one had ever seen any trace of the Hashir before, and no one knew where they'd been found."

Du Brimar gave Matt a cynical look. "I think we now know the answer to that. Anyway, they served twelve generations of Emperors. We were expanding much more aggressively back then, and plots were common. There were also intrigues involving other races, the Hshtahni, the Veng, and more. During that period of time, there was not a single successful assassination or coup. Until the twelfth emperor."

"I don't want to hear this, do I?" Matt asked, looking at Teresa forlornly. Du Brimar continued as if uninterrupted.

"When they fled, they took every member of their race. They didn't have a lot of technical expertise, and the theory is that they never made planetfall anywhere, but I've never been convinced of that."

"They fled?" Teresa spoke up hesitantly.

Cromar Try nodded, taking up where Du Brimar had left off. His eyes seemed to view a scene far away in time and space, and his jaw hardened as his face grew cold. "Yes, they had to."

Matt felt the bright green eyes of the alien captain bore into him.

"Their choices were limited after they assassinated the Emperor and his heir."

◆ ◆ ◆ ◆ ◆

Jade Viking

"Me father was a drinking man, me mither was his wife.
Me father loved that great woman, although they lived in strife.
And if I should live to one hundred and three,
You know what I'd like to be...
As great a man as me father was..."

Kimberly and Kiri paused, looking at each other in askance.

"Freudian slip?" Kiri giggled. Kimberly nodded sagely, and they continued down the corridor, arms about each other's waists.

"...or as great as he told me!"

They laughed and Kiri almost fell as she missed a step.

"Whoa." Kimberly kept a firm grip around the waist of the smaller woman until they got to her cabin door. Kiri straightened and patted her hips, then looked around in bewilderment.

"What is it?" Kimberly asked, concerned.

"I can't find my keys," Kiri muttered, glancing around their feet. "Or my purse..."

Kimberly snickered and opened the door. "Inside, my bleary-eyed beauty..."

"You say the sweetest things." Kiri tried to look nonchalant as she walked, but her feet betrayed her. Kimberly once again steadied her and lowered the oriental girl into a sitting position on her bed.

"Can I get you something? Are you going to be alright?" Kimberly had a flashback to sorority days and drunken sisters.

"Let's order a pizza!" Kiri sat up in enthusiasm.

God, that sounds good! Kimberly closed her eyes, picturing it. She felt herself sway and hurriedly opened them again. *Whoa, Martin. You're not exactly one hundred percent, yourself.*

"You okay?" Kiri looked up at her and Kimberly sank down onto the bed next to her.

"Just a little dizzy, is all." *Don't think of pizza!* "I'm afraid pizza is out of the question." *Arrgh!*

Kiri staggered to her feet and stumbled over to one of her suitcases and began rummaging through it. "Ah ha!"she shouted triumphantly, twirling around and brandishing a carton. She kept twirling, and Kimberly lurched forward in time to catch her just as she lost her footing.

They ended up on the floor, Kimberly on bottom acting as a cushion.

"Ummph!" Kimberly lay on her back and looked up at Kiri, who was half draped over her. "Comfortable?"

Kiri leered at her. "Very! I mean really, Kimberly. You're throwing yourself at me!"

They both laughed as they dragged themselves over to sit on the floor, backs against the bed. Kiri kept her prize hidden until they were both propped up, then pulled it out with a flourish from behind her back.

"Cookies!" Kiri crowed, tearing the package open.

"I don't need to be eating cooki...are those shortbread?" Kimberly groaned in anticipation. "Hurry, get it open!"

Kiri offered her the open package and Kimberly daintily took a single cookie. The young woman sneered as she pulled four out for herself.

They bit into them and simultaneously moaned in ecstasy.

Kimberly blushed, but couldn't refrain as she took a second bite.

"Oh, God! I just love a little flour with my butter." She reached for the package, but Kiri pulled it away.

"Hey, Round-eyes! I thought you only wanted one?"

"Okay, okay. I was wrong." Kimberly stretched, trying to reach across her friend. They froze with their eyes scant inches apart. Neither woman moved for a long moment, then Kiri offered her the cookies, suddenly looking shy.

Kimberly took a handful and settled back into a sitting position. For a while, neither spoke, and the only sound was the crunching of cookies. Okay, Martin, this falls under 'uncomfortable pauses in conversation'. Think of something to say, quick.

"So," she said, her voice artificially casual. "Jim wrote that ditty we were singing?"

Kiri didn't answer at first. She just kept on chewing her cookies, methodically devouring the stack in her hand. Finally Kimberly looked over at her in concern. She looked back with a poker face, dark brown eyes revealing nothing.

"Yep," she finally answered, then took another bite of cookie.

"Oh," Kimberly did the same.

After a few moments, they both broke into laughter. Kiri nudged her with a shoulder and Kimberly nudged back. They sat leaning against each other and the bed, eating their cookies in comfortable companionship.

"Thank God." Kimberly sighed in relief. "This is new for me. At times, I'm not sure what to do."

"You aren't?" Kiri laughed. "How about poor Linda Hoffman?"

At that, they both laughed, remembering earlier in the evening.

"Talk about Daniel and the lions..." Kimberly snickered as she thought about the older woman joining them in the hot tub.

"Ah, we were just a bunch of pussycats..." Kiri said in a demure voice. They both laughed again.

"You know," Kimberly said, remembering. "She's not as bad as we thought."

"You're right," Kiri agreed amiably. "Once she realized we wanted to laugh with her, not at her, she was fine. I think she has some confidence issues."

"Janice had her wondering, I bet." Kimberly giggled and Kiri shook her head vigorously.

"Janice doesn't play the field, she just talks a good time," she said.

"Then I should call her bluff?" Kimberly asked, grinning at the idea of catching Janice off guard.

"Oh, I don't know about that," Kiri smirked. "You might find yourself in bed with both of them before you know it."

"Oh." Kimberly tried to picture the scene and blushed. It was easier than she'd expected. Kiri correctly read her face.

"Uh, oh. Does this mean I can't trust you to behave yourself?" The young woman gave her a gentle elbow to show she was kidding.

"Kiri, if I decide to swing that way, you'll be the first to know...trust me." Kimberly took another bite of cookie and smiled as Kiri got up and pulled a bottle of wine out of her tiny refrigerator.

"You sure we need that?"

Kiri found a corkscrew and waved it at her, leering all the while. "I need something to wash these cookies down. I'm going to have a hangover tomorrow, anyway. No sense worrying about it now. Anyway, I might get lucky."

Kimberly snorted. "Much more of that, you won't know if you got lucky or not."

"Then I'll rely on my imagination." Kiri arched her eyes as she pulled the cork out with a loud pop. "What does that remind you of?"

Kimberly groaned and looked for something to throw. She eyed the pillow on the bed, but decided against it. There was no telling where a pillow fight would take them. Kiri poured them both full glasses and they settled back into their comfortable slouch against each other.

After a bit, the Japanese girl sighed. "I'm kind of envious, you know?"

Kimberly thought about it. "Of Jim, or me?"

Kiri laughed, a little sadly. "No, no, not that. Well, sure. That too. But what I meant was, I'm envious because Yvette and Janice know what they're going to do when we get back, and who with. Linda and Ron have their plans. God, she was so excited about getting back to Earth, I could puke."

Kimberly was surprised. "Aren't you eager to get back?"

"Well, yeah." Kiri downed her drink. She stood and ambled over to the refrigerator and returned with the wine. Topping off Kimberly's glass, she refilled her own and, tucking the bottle between her legs, took a healthy slug. "Kind of, anyway. I mean, you're going to be busy doing business things, then going back to Jim and Afsy. Others are going to go back to their old lives, although I don't see how."

"Afsy." Kimberly tried the name on for size.

"I wouldn't call her that, if I were you," Kiri said in a dry voice. "I don't much, any more. But then, I've known her since she was nine."

I wonder, Kimberly thought. She's cute...hell, she's drop dead gor-

74

geous. Guiltily, she realized Kiri had guessed what she was thinking and sighed in relief when the other woman shook her head with amusement.

"No, no, I don't rob the cradle. And Jim would kill me. Anyway, if anybody in the world, or ship..., or whatever, is boy crazy, it's her." Kimberly had to agree. She thought back to what Kiri had been saying.

"You're worried about what you're going to do?"

"Not just that." Kiri stopped while she finished a cookie. "It's... complicated."

Kimberly set her glass down and took one of Kiri's hands. "Tell me about it." She was gratified to see a tentative smile appear on her friend's face.

"Well, first off, my career." Kiri made a face. "I'm this sex symbol in Japan, see. I'm the young woman that gets all the little boys hot and bothered. Most of my movies, I'm being saved or swooned over. It's like I have two, maybe three moods to portray, and that's it!"

"Can't you get more serious roles?" Kimberly didn't know much about the movie business, but Kiri was so beautiful and talented, surely...

"I'm typecast!" Kiri's voice became anguished. "I'm the young woman from Japan that drives boys and men crazy!"

Kimberly found herself nodding in agreement. She took another sip of wine. "But..."

"Don't you see?" Kiri interrupted her, pulling herself to her feet. She leaned over and looked deep into Kimberly's eyes.

"I'm gay, and I was born in L.A.!"

"You were?" Kimberly frowned, trying to remember the biographies her company had given her on the movie people so long ago. "I thought you were born in...Kyoto?"

"That's how my bio reads," Kiri agreed, a little bitterly. "My family moved back to Japan when I was five. If it got out that I'm American, or gay...I don't know if one would be considered worse than the other in Japan. But either would finish me."

"Are you gay or bi?" Kimberly asked. "In the states, there would be a difference in perception, I think..."

"The only man I've ever been remotely attracted to was Jim." Kiri admitted grimacing. "And even that was more curiosity than anything else." She smiled ruefully at Kimberly. "I like him too much to screw it up by screwing him."

Kimberly nodded and watched as the young woman smoothly opened another bottle. If she didn't know better, she would swear the more Kiri drank, the soberer she was getting.

"I'll be right back." Kiri crossed her legs comically, and scurried into the bathroom.

Kimberly climbed to her feet uncertainly. She should probably leave, but Kiri was opening up to her. Leaving right now would slam the door on any future confidences. And she really did like Kiri. She'd been the first person on board the Jade Viking to go out of her way to be friendly. *God knows, Martin, the way you've let your career rule, you don't have many friends yourself...*

Kiri groaned from the bathroom. "This isn't better than sex, but right now, it feels very, very close. Wine runs right through me."

Kimberly laughed. In for a dime, in for a dollar, she thought in resignation. She emptied her glass in one gulp and, pouring another, she went back to the bed. She sat down with her back against the headboard, sighing at how much softer the mattress was than the floor.

She propped her bare feet up, deliberately not thinking about the lack of modesty this position left her in. Wearing a tee-shirt and short gym shorts, and nothing else, there wasn't much left to the imagination.

After they had gotten out of the hot tub, she had dressed as quickly as possible, tossing her undergarments and workout clothes into a tote-bag. They had gone straight to Yvette and Janice's room to continue "tuning up", as Janice had put it.

Much to her surprise, Linda Hoffman had accompanied them. And even stranger, she seemed to be having a great time. A lot of wine later, Kimberly had volunteered to walk Kiri back to her room. For all she knew, Linda was still there.

Panties would come in handy right about now, Kimberly thought wistfully. These gym shorts...well, next time she would wear bermudas.

Kiri came back into the room, sans sweatpants. As Kimberly well knew, she didn't have any underwear on, either. But, at least her sweatshirt was oversized. Come on Martin, you're obsessing.

Kiri got her glass and the bottle and came over to the bed. "Move over, Round-eyes."

Kimberly slid over, and offered her a cookie. Kiri groaned and shook her head. "Too many, already." She rubbed her stomach. "Those things taste great, but they bloat you up so much..."

Kimberly shrugged. "More for me." She discovered exactly one cookie left. "Oh my God, we ate the whole bag."

Kiri peered at the package. "Not yet."

Kimberly popped the last one in her mouth. "Uh huh! I thwear, ull gum," she said, her mouth full.

They both laughed.

Kimberly washed it down with her wine, and shivered a little. "Strange combination. Not bad, but strange." Kiri nodded sagely.

"Back to what I was saying." Kiri spoke and Kimberly mentally scrambled to remember their last words.

"Right, screwing Jim." She nodded seriously.

"No, no." Kiri looked at her in mock exasperation. "I was talking about not screwing Jim, and how unnatural most people would see that."

"I would find it unnatural to catch someone else screwing Jim." Kimberly realized she was getting a little tipsy. "Okay, I'm sorry. Go on."

"When we get back, we'll be under a microscope. Someone will finally figure out why my bio doesn't always seem to add up right." She sighed. "When people see a discrepancy, they assume I'm hiding the fact that I'm older than I say. That's a very acceptable lie. But gay, and from L.A...."

"Gay, and from L.A.!" Kimberly snapped her fingers in rhythm. "Kind of catchy, you know? Sure you couldn't get a more serious role? One where it wouldn't matter?"

Kiri shook her head. "And, it's not just the roles I'm offered. This whole space thing has changed my outlook. Maybe I need to be more than just an actress..."

"Then do something more," Kimberly said enthusiastically. "What would you like to do?"

"I don't know," Kiri admitted. "But it's not just me. I know Jerry and Frederick have had their heads together a lot. I mean, they were directing and producing a movie that's pretty much toast. I don't know what they'll say to the stockholders and financial backers."

"Weren't they almost done?" Kimberly thought she remembered that the final scenes were being shot on board.

"Sure, but then what?" Kiri refilled their glasses without spilling a drop. "Jim won't be around to promote it, and really, everything is changed now. Movies seem so trite, when you're talking about aliens from outer space."

Kimberly suppressed an urge to laugh. Maybe it wasn't funny, but it sure sounded funny. Then Kiri giggled. "That really sounds stupid."

"Yeah," Kimberly agreed.

"But it's true," Kiri said sadly. "And so many people died. A lot of them were friends. I don't know if I could stand seeing Kogo or Usagi on film without bursting into tears."

And at that point, Kiri did burst into tears. Kimberly held her close as she sobbed, gently brushing her thick, black hair with her fingers. The sobbing only intensified.

"It's okay, it's okay." Kimberly felt useless. It wasn't okay, and it sounded trite, but she didn't know what else to do. So she patted her friend's head, holding her. "Things will work out. Let Jerry and Frederick worry about the movie."

"It's not just that, either," Kiri cried. "You've got Jim, Janice has Yvette, even Linda has a good relationship with her husband!"

"You don't know that," Kimberly said, thinking about the lies and deceptions in her own first marriage.

"But at least there's someone there, even if it's not perfect, or even great. At least there's someone," Kiri sobbed in a broken voice. "I'm so..." She stopped.

"Alone," Kimberly finished it for her. The young girl's renewed weeping confirmed it. *What to do? Come on, Martin, think!*

"Would you want to go with me for a while," Kimberly said hesitantly. "When we get back to the states, I've got to go to New York. It could be fun. We could go shopping."

"I don't want you feeling sorry for me," Kiri sat up, wiping at her tears with her sweatshirt sleeve. "I'll be fine."

"Kiri," Kimberly said, putting one hand on the other's shoulder. "You're not fine. And I don't feel sorry for you. I care about you. There's a difference." She smiled at her, tenderly. "I would like you to travel with me for a few weeks, or whatever. Please."

"Do you really mean that?" Kiri smiled timidly. "I'll quit teasing you..."

"Don't change a bit!" Kimberly was emphatic. "If you did, I wouldn't know who you were." She wiped away a single tear Kiri had missed and rose to her knees. "I mean it. And I also mean this. If I don't use that john right now, there's going to be an accident."

78

They both laughed a little easier, and Kiri made room for Kimberly to slide off the bed.

"I'll be right back," Kimberly promised.

When she came out of the bathroom, Kiri was laying on her side, pillow rolled up under her head. At first she thought she was asleep, but then her voice came.

"Is there anything I could do to help?"

"There'll be plenty to do, and you won't be bored. I can promise you that," Kimberly assured her. "Now try and get some sleep."

"I'm not sleepy," Kiri protested. She hid a yawn behind a hand. "Seriously!"

Kimberly shook her head. Kiri and Afsaneh were more alike than she would have believed. "Tell you what. Lay on your stomach and I'll give you a back-rub. I owe you one from the tub, anyway."

Kiri rolled over to give her room. Kimberly began kneading her shoulders and neck. Kiri gave a sensual moan. "Lower."

"Now you sound like Jim!" Kimberly slapped the other woman's butt. "You just behave yourself, hear?"

"Okay," came the contrite reply. After a moment, she continued. "Will you stay tonight?"

"Maybe," Kimberly hedged. She moved down the spine to the small of Kiri's back. A grateful groan was the response.

As she rubbed, Kimberly thought about what Kiri had said. It had sparked some memory, from back at Station Osaka. But what? Kiri was right. Most of them would never have normal lives again. The movie was a lost cause. Too many dead faces. Too many missing faces!

That was the real worry. When Kimberly and the rest of her group were found in Alaska, they would number a little less than a thousand. The other three hundred would be found a few days later, after Kimberly and her people had been released by the authorities.

That still left almost three thousand people unaccounted for. The police, the FBI, the Coast Guard for that matter, would all want to know where the missing people were. Not to mention the missing ship.

You didn't just hide a cruise ship under an old newspaper.

There would be friends and relatives of the missing and dead asking questions. Insurance companies would be even more persistent. It would be hard to do the work that needed to get done under that kind of scrutiny.

Would it even be possible to organize the support group they would need on Earth? Financing and finding resources had been their biggest initial concern, but in retrospect, meddling, curious people would pose an even greater problem.

Kiri groaned again softly, and Kimberly lightened her touch. At least she was nearly asleep. Tomorrow, she would have the mother of all hangovers. For that matter, Kimberly herself could feel one coming on. But she kept rubbing, lightly caressing Kiri's neck.

So young. She makes me feel so old! No, not old. Grown up? Come on Martin, 'fess up. Around her and Afsaneh, you act younger and more carefree than you ever have, even when you were a kid.

They're good for you, she decided. Just a few days ago, Afsaneh had said...

Kimberly sat up straight.

That was it!

Kiri's voice came to her sleepily. "Wassup? 'ou okay?"

"Go back to sleep, honey." Kimberly quickly leaned over and whispered in her ear. "Everything's fine. You just lay there and let me do this."

Kiri mumbled something unintelligible and moved to her left side, scrunching the pillow up in her arms.

Kimberly kept rubbing gently on her shoulder, reassuring the young girl with her touch. But her mind was racing. Afsaneh had said something to Jim about switching careers. No more action movies. Instead... what was it?

Then Kimberly remembered and felt a smile tug on her tired face. For a long time, she continued soothing the sleeping girl, all the while, thinking furiously.

Who to talk to? Was anyone awake at this hour?

Eventually, she lay down next to Kiri. Five minutes to rest and think this through, she decided.

Just five minutes...

Kiri felt a soft surface pressing against her lips. She gave it a gentle kiss. She was laying in a spoon position around a nude woman, and even in the dark, she could tell that it was Kimberly.

The soft surface was Kimberly's naked shoulder. Kiri ran her hand down the woman's side, moving to her hip. She could feel a response and pulled the woman closer. Her hand slid up to cup Kimberly's breast.

Kiri could feel her breathing growing heavier. Both of them were, now. She rubbed her hand across Kimberly's breasts, searching with fingertips for the nipples.

She lightly bit Kimberly's shoulder and her hand moved downward, to her lover's stomach. Then lower.

Kiri's breathing intensified, and she gasped with excitement.

She crushed Kimberly to her, pressing her entire body against the other's softness.

Then she opened her eyes to see she held her pillow.

Wide eyed, she sat up, looking around. A light shone through the open bathroom door, dimly illuminating the room.

Kimberly was nowhere to be seen.

Frustrated, she punched the pillow, and flopped down to lie on her back. She stared at the ceiling as her breathing slowly returned to normal.

"Damn!"

CHAPTER SIX

Station Osaka

Captain Jason Lang and Jim Morris stood in stunned silence. Numerous Hoag scurried around them in what appeared to be a controlled frenzy. Normally, just watching them was entertaining enough. Time after time, a collision seemed inevitable, but it never happened. The aliens seldom spoke, but each seemed to know its task.

"I told you they were making good time." Rick Baker was almost six feet tall, gangly, short dark hair badly in need of a trim, and he rubbed his hands together in what could only be described as glee. "And as good as the outsides look, it's what they're doing on the inside that will blow you away."

"Uh huh." Jim tore his eyes away from the seemingly endless flow of Hoag guiding antigrav sleds piled high with...stuff, into a series of hatches, while yet more exited with their sleds empty. Despite what Rick said, what they could see outside the observation windows was what had both he and the captain speechless.

"So, these are the three freighters we seized when we took the station?" Captain Lang almost pressed his face against the thick, clear windows before he caught himself. "I don't remember them looking anything like this..."

"The Hoag basically used the ships as raw material. The hull, interior floor plan, engines, everything has been redesigned." Rick waved an arm around enthusiastically, almost clipping a passing Hoag that deftly ducked beneath the gesture, not pausing for a moment. "We're incredibly fortunate that this station was built with the intent of using the lower hub as a shipyard. It has all the tools, relatively good stores of parts and munitions, and this enormous hanger. It can be sealed, or open to space, gravity-free, and when you're done, you drive it right out of the dock."

"Tell me again about the design?" Captain Lang looked past the ship tied up close, to the far side of the expansive hanger. The ship across the way looked almost finished, but not as he'd pictured. He'd thought they were rebuilding one of the captured Tryr freighters to resemble Jade Samurai.

"The Hoag and Baerd pulled up blueprints from Tryr warships, because physically, they're relatively the same size as us." Rick grinned. "Then the computers began playing with the designs, incorporating Egelv, Venn, Hshtahni technology. I'm not sure how they accessed it. None of these races believe in sharing, heh."

The Tryr were giant black panther-like bipeds, almost eight feet tall. Lang wasn't sure he would have said they were comparable in size, but perhaps the difference was nominal to the Hoag.

"We have basic files of most known ship designs stored, and Vicki actually has some detailed Egelv blueprints in the original security code." Pearl joined in the conversation. "Sam is a warship, and has extensive military records, including operation and repair manuals for all Tryr models. With this information, we were able to incorporate the best features for each ship's purpose. These ships will be far more powerful and effective for their size, than anything currently in use...by any race."

"Vicki, and...Sam?" Jim spoke softly, but Lang felt chills up his spine at the implication.

"The less formal address seems more appropriate when speaking with you."

If Lang hadn't known better, he would have sworn he'd heard Pearl pause. Computers didn't pause, did they? He set that thought aside as the station computer continued.

"We consulted with the Baerd and Hoag. Although the design is new and may require some adjustments, confidence is high that the ship you see across the hanger will be able to hold its own against any ship of a comparable class. When these ships are finished, we would like to refit Jade Samurai as well."

"I thought you were just duplicating the Jade Samurai," Jim mused, stepping up next to Lang to stare at the ship. "It almost looks like something we would have built..." He grinned and shrugged. "...in about three hundred years."

"Human aerodynamic design is very efficient. Having to perform in an atmosphere has given birth to concepts that might not have surfaced had you invented anti-gravity technology first."

Pearl sounded like she, er, it, was almost trying to compliment them, Lang thought, annoyed that he'd mentally slipped into the gender trap with Pearl. "When will that ship be finished?"

"The projected date for completion is just under one of your months," Pearl answered. "To complete the other warship of this class will take longer. It will be necessary to find a source for sophisticated computer parts, weaponry, and essential materials for the power system. The framework and outer shell are almost finished, but the remainder of the work will be delayed until we acquire these items."

"That's this one?" Lang asked, pointing at hatches Hoag and the occasional Baerd kept entering and exiting.

"No, you can not see it from this vantage." Pearl almost sounded dismissive. "This is a different design. The other two ships are intended as military vessels comparable to your nautical cruiser, with some cargo capabilities. This ship is much smaller."

"Come inside, take a look." Rick Baker looked like he was ready to bounce of the walls, and Lang had to admit he was curious. "Come down to this hatch. It leads to the bridge."

He led them inside, following a Hoag guiding a raft deftly down a corridor, until the Hoag swung left, and Rick turned right. Then they were in a modest sized room that had what appeared to be two command chairs, and before it, computer stations with seating for four.

The wall in front of the seats had five large windows, or ports, to look outside. Above them were a series of screens that were flashing images almost too fast to view. Five or six Hoag glanced at them as they worked on exposed walls, the cover panels neatly propped against one of the seats. They ignored the human intrusion, working with a speed and confidence that had Lang revising his opinion of Hoag capabilities upward. Two Baerd were equally as hard at work, bent over an open console, taking parts from stacks of loaded trays next to them, inserting them, fastening them with two tools that looked like nothing so much as a pair of screwdrivers.

Screwdrivers that seemed to shift shapes regularly, Lang thought, trying to see how they worked. He'd have to check into that. It looked... fun.

One of the Baerd straightened up, turning to look at them. Lang was surprised to see it was Lasty. He wasn't a bit surprised when the other turned out to be Dutter, his mate.

"Captain...er, Governor Lang." Lasty corrected himself and bowed. "Are you here to inspect? We are not yet finished."

"You don't need to bow, Lasty." Lang was embarrassed. "I'm not royalty."

"Right." Lasty turned to Jim and almost bowed, but correctly interpreted Jim's expression and stopped. "Er, may I help?"

"Relax, Lasty." Rick gave him a thumbs up. "I'm just showing them the ship. This is their first look at any of them."

"This bridge doesn't look very big, compared to Jade Viking, or Samurai, for that matter," Lang said, glancing around, noticing how much lower the ceiling was on this ship. "How big is the ship itself?" He watched Lasty start to answer, then get bogged down trying to put it in terms the humans would recognize.

"This ship is eighty-seven meters long, forty-three meters wide, and thirty-seven meters tall at its highest point. It could fit inside one of your football fields," Pearl answered for him. "The warships are much larger, almost half again as long as one of your largest oil tankers."

"Can they land on a planet's surface?" Jim Morris asked, looking thoughtful. "Jade Viking can't enter the atmosphere."

"Yes, these will not only enter the atmosphere, but will be able to land without any difficulty on relatively rough terrain." A simulation of a completed warship appeared on one of the screens, landing on a hillside, landing gear adjusting to the varied lengths necessary to maintain balance. "Even Jade Samurai can enter a gravity well and land on a planet's surface. But a more level landing site is required, and a dock would be preferred."

"So, this ship will be finished first?" Jim walked around the bridge, looking at everything, coming to a halt before the series of portals. "Aren't windows a little dangerous in space?"

"Humans show a tendency to like to see where they are going, and seem to find viewing the stars enjoyable." Pearl's voice became more businesslike. "The portals can be closed in case of potential hazards or battle."

With no notice, panels snapped down, covering the ports, and immediately began to function as viewing screens, some showing the same thing as could be seen when they were raised, some showing projections, pictures, a schematic of the ship itself.

"Hmm," Lang stepped forward to take a closer look at the last. "What exactly is this ship's purpose? You said it was different."

"Almost eighty percent is dedicated to three functions." Pearl highlighted much of the rear of the display in yellow. "First, speed. This ship will be faster than anything the Ananab have. A ship this size usually has one or two engine nacelles. This one has six."

"It looks dangerous," Lasty volunteered, then blushed at his boldness.

"It should." Pearl might have been discussing color schemes, her voice was so level. Lang mentally kicked himself again for the gender tribute. "A number of different weapon systems have been incorporated into this ship. It contains all the usual defense fields and disruptor projectors. It also carries missiles with a variety of payloads." Red spots showed on the screen, spread throughout the ship. "We've also created a viable projectile weapon, based on your artillery, that fire very rapidly." More red dots appeared.

Lasty leaned forward to look. "I haven't seen this. The weapon placements look strange."

"Every manned station has either four or six of each weapons system under their control. The computer-operated defensive systems are separate and traditionally mounted."

Lasty leaned back in awe. "This is a very aggressive design."

"So you've designed a ship that runs fast and hits hard," Jim drawled and pointed at the uncolored spaces. "This leaves a good portion of the ship unaccounted for. You said three functions?"

"There are two small shuttles, both armed." Two oblong areas, one on either side, turned orange. An oval shape with numerous tentacles glowed green. "This is the twenty percent devoted to crew accommodations and stations."

"And the rest?" Lang could tell that Jim was leading Pearl now. What did the actor see that he couldn't, or hadn't? He guessed it a millisecond before Pearl spoke.

"This is the ship's computer." Blue areas covered nearly as much as the green.

"I see." Lang felt his spine stiffen and he straightened to his full, considerable height. "That is a lot of computer. What exactly did you say the purpose of this ship was?"

"This class ship would be for a small contingent, or even one person's use." Pearl seemed to be choosing her words carefully. "It will have the ability to defend the occupants, flee if necessary, and have a computer able to fully utilize all the capabilities of the Egelv code."

"This class, you say. What about this particular ship?" Lang was tired of Pearl side-stepping his questions, and it showed in his voice.

"This ship will be designated to the protection of Jim Morris, and for his personal use and needs."

Pearl now sounded very businesslike. In fact, a lot like Kimberly had sounded a couple of days ago, Lang mused. He sighed, and resisted the urge to glare at Jim.

"So, Jim needs his own ship?"

"Yes." Thankfully, Pearl didn't leave it there. "Full warships need to be devoted to the protection of the Human race as a whole. As a living symbol of Human strength and resistance, Jim Morris may need to travel between Earth and Station Osaka, or even other places, at some point. To tie up a ship that might be vital to defending this station, or the Earth, would be counter-productive and inefficient."

"Well, we certainly wouldn't want that." Lang let some annoyance creep into his voice. "It seems like those warships might just be a little higher priority, at the moment. And did you discuss this with anyone other than your two 'sisters'?"

"No." Pearl allowed her voice to soften. "Perhaps we misjudged your reaction. But know this. Work on the first warship is going at the same pace it would if this ship had never been started. And we still wouldn't have enough of the proper equipment and fittings to finish the second."

"Uh, Jason, er, Governor Lang, I didn't know about this." Jim sounded embarrassed. "I really don't need my own ship." He brightened. "It could be your flagship. You know, the Governor's ship."

"No." Lang was startled to find Pearl and himself speaking at the same time. He hurried to continue. "I won't be traveling anywhere, anytime soon, and don't need a ship. I don't know that you do either, but it seems to be out of our hands, due to this..." Lang abruptly stopped talking. Giving away the fact that Pearl and both ships' highest priority was Jim Morris' personal safety to every Tom, Dick and Harry that happened to be listening would be stupid. "Well, it's out of our hands now."

"I guess you'll get to pick another name." Lang tried to lighten the mood. As Jim had said, this wasn't his fault, or due to anything he'd done. "So, what will you name this vicious toy of yours?"

Pearl surprised him again.

"Afsaneh Riahi has already named her father's ship."

Jim and Lang looked at each other curiously.

"She said it should reflect your 'alma mater'."

Jim started, glanced around the bridge, then stared at the screen still showing the color-coded ship's layout. He ran a hand down the edge of one of the command chairs absentmindedly.

"Small, vicious, incredibly fast." Jim snorted and shook his head. "She hit that one right on the head." He turned and grinned at Lang, the scar above his left eye making it more sinister than funny. "You know my alma mater?"

Lang tried to remember if he'd ever heard where Jim had gone to school. "Not Tulane, I hope."

Jim laughed. "No, not the Jade Wave." He shuddered in mock horror, then his grin turned to a reflective smile. "University of Michigan."

"Ah," Lang nodded, understanding now. "The Jade Wolverine. Well, I suppose you can still name the shuttles."

"Afsaneh has seen to that as well." Pearl spoke in a grave voice, as a display on a second screen showed the bow of the ship with the name in bold print over a black silhouette of a snarling wolverine's head. The image split to show the bows of the two smaller craft, both with artwork depicting their name under the lettering. One showed a snarling mouth, the other a swiping paw with claws extended.

"Fang and Claw." Lang had to admire the ingenuity. "Did she also take the liberty of naming the computer?" Jim started at his words, his eyebrows rising.

"She did not." Pearl almost sounded regretful. "She said she would leave that to Jim."

Jim's expression cleared. His smile was relaxed, and he looked the happiest he'd been since Kimberly had left on the Jade Viking.

"Well, I'll have to think of a good name for...Irene, then, won't I?" He gestured towards the exit. "Seen enough for one day?"

"Yes, I have." Lang nodded to Lasty and Dutter, and they let Rick lead them off the unfinished bridge. As they left the room, he heard Lasty behind him, asking Dutter, "So, Irene is a female name for Humans? My father's second brother's name is..."

Jade Viking

Kimberly rubbed her eyes wearily. She reached for her coffee cup and discovered it was empty. *I don't need any more anyway. And what time is it?* She'd been sitting around this table for hours now. But then, so had the others.

Captain Tachibana, at the far end of the table, quietly watched Jerry Weinstein and Frederick Farmer gesturing emphatically as they argued. Frederick was the director of the movie "Weeping Winds of Fury" and had final say on most details, but that never kept him and Jerry from going through vast amounts of politicking and posturing.

Watching them, it was hard to believe they were best friends. Next to them, almost unnoticed, Yvette and Janice shuffled through stacks of notes, occasionally setting some papers aside.

They look like I feel, Kimberly thought ruefully. They had just settled in for the night when she called them. When asked about Linda Hoffman, they had both smiled enigmatically and said nothing. *I'll bet that's an interesting story.*

Kimberly had left Kiri sleeping soundly, and power-walked the corridors of the ship for almost an hour. Finally, she had asked Vicki, the ship's computer, to check and see if Frederick and Jerry were still awake. They were, and had been intrigued by what she'd suggested. Vicki had reported that the captain was on the bridge and Yvette and Janice hadn't gone to sleep yet.

"Okay, we know it's possible." Jerry Weinstein stood and put his hands on his hips. "The material is here if we decide to do it. Thoughts?"

"Go for it." Yvette and Janice spoke in unison. They smiled at each other and Janice winked at Kimberly. "Great minds and all that, you know?"

Kimberly grinned tiredly. "I agree. If we change the faces of the casualties, put some of the survivor's features on a few of them, it would be okay."

"So, the next step..." Frederick pushed his glasses up from where they'd slid down the bridge of his nose.

"Now you've decided it's possible." Captain Tachibana broke into the conversation smoothly. "Now, decide how to make this movie without desecrating the memories of the fallen."

Kimberly watched the movie people react to the Japanese captain's words. There were only four of them, but she would swear she could hear at least five voices arguing.

There would be a new Jim Morris movie, and it would not be a simple action/martial arts flick.. And at least they all seemed to agree on that point.

It would be a science-fiction horror movie, and not camp, either. In this film, people died. Relationships were brutally severed, friends and lovers were lost. The villains would be real, the threat believable.

Several Hoag entered, pulling an antigrav sled piled high with video equipment, televisions, monitors and more. The loud discussion broke off as everyone eagerly began sorting through what looked to Kimberly like a pile of junk.

Frederick muttered under his breath in frustration. He looked around, slightly bewildered.

"Damn it, I can't find...Hakim needs to...?" Everyone froze at the director's mental error. Hakim Riahi had been killed in the final battle to secure Osaka. He and Jim had worked together since college, and since Frederick had directed many of the movies that had taken Jim to the top of the action movie genre, he'd known him well. Frederick stuttered, "P-please forgive me..."

Kimberly watched Jerry Weinstein place a hand on his old friend's arm. He seemed to pour reassurance through the contact, because Frederick took a deep breath and nodded his silent thanks. Yvette looked pale and Janice gave her a hug. They missed the Iranian cameraman that had been so much more to all of them.

Captain Tachibana had no triumph in his voice as he spoke. "Now you understand? Do you really want to open these wounds? I'm not saying we shouldn't do this thing, but it's so soon after. Tell me again why this is necessary."

All four movie people turned as one to Kimberly. She felt herself blush at their automatic acquiescence to her leadership.

"There are several reasons to make this movie." Kimberly spoke slowly to allow herself time to organize her thoughts. "We can look at things on the small, personal level first. Quite frankly, some of you need to find a way to salvage something out of 'Weeping Winds'." She looked at Jerry, who shrugged, then nodded grudgingly.

"Second, on the larger scale, this movie can be considered an inoculation. Some day, not that far in the future, we're going to have to expose what's out there." She gestured away from the table. "If people were suddenly told Klingons were real, and proof was produced, they would at least be able to rationally deal with it. They would recognize the threat, be frightened, but not paralyzed with panic."

"At least, not as freaked as they would have been," Janice agreed.

"Right." Frederick Farmer nodded, looking at Kimberly curiously. "I am a bit mystified with the sudden urgency." He hurriedly continued. "Don't get me wrong, it's an excellent idea, but what made you think of it? And why act on your impulse this time of the night?"

They all looked at her, and she felt herself blush. "Uh, I was just walking around, couldn't sleep. Vicki said you were awake..."

"I think it's great that you took the initiative, Kimberly." Yvette smiled and Kimberly felt as if the other woman could see her thoughts. "And she's right. We need to get a solid start on this before we reach Earth. We can always come back up here for a few days if necessary, but every trip with a shuttle increases the chance of discovery."

"That is true," Captain Tachibana confirmed.

"We need to do this." Jerry's voice was firm. He glanced at the two women, then at Kimberly. "If nothing else, we need to do it for their sake." He nodded at the pile of papers on the table. "We can't tell everything that happened when we first get back, but we can show what happened. Even if everyone thinks it's fiction, the truth will come out some day. There were heroes, and their ultimate sacrifice deserves to be recognized."

"Yes." Yvette held Janice's hand, both their faces grim, but determined. "We do it."

Captain Tachibana peered at each of them closely, searching for indecision. Evidently he saw none, because he nodded and spoke to the ship's computer. "Vicki, do you have film footage of all the battles?"

"Yes," came the swift reply. "I also have complete copies of all footage by surveillance cameras throughout both Jade Viking, Samurai, and Station Osaka since the hijacking."

"And you can change some people's features?" Kimberly didn't want this effort to produce an inadvertent snuff film.

"I can replace entire characters with existing people, or make composite fictional ones."

"Good." Jerry looked at his director questioningly. "Frederick, will you be okay? Are you too close to this?"

Farmer sighed and rubbed his eyes tiredly. "Yes to both your questions, Jerry. But, what higher tribute can we give them? And if it helps the cause..." He picked up a video tape and looked at the label. "But I will miss Hakim's input."

"We all will." Jerry agreed solemnly. "But for now, let's try and get this mess set up and get some kind of firm inventory of what we can use."

"I guess 'Weeping Winds of Fury' is out as a title," Janice said, rubbing a thumb across the name printed on most of the equipment. "How about 'Flaming Fists of Fury'?"

Frederick shuddered. "That is an awful title."

"Yes it is." Yvette smiled wryly. "Although, it would have worked for some of the movies we've done in the past. I think we need to get away from the usual genre name style." She glanced back at Janice. "Far away."

"Let's table the search for a working title for now. But I don't know that we want to get too far away from what Jim's fans expect to see. At least not until we have them in the movie theatres." Jerry looked at Kimberly. "Perhaps you and Kiri could...?

"Sure," Kimberly smiled at some of the stupid names that began popping into her head. "When Kiri wakes up..."

"...she finds an empty room and a humongous headache." Kiri had entered unnoticed with some of the Hoag. She was freshly showered and showed no signs of the night before. "What's going on?"

Kimberly looked at the others. "This might be a good test of the reaction we'll get from the rest of the crew."

"Too true," Frederick nodded. "Quite simply, Kiri, we're going to take some of the footage from Weeping Winds and some from the computers logs and rewrite the movie. Instead of an action movie, it'll be a science fiction film with horror aspects."

"Really?" Kiri frowned. "Isn't that a little... creepy?"

"It gives us a chance to show the world what we'll be facing, even though they'll think it's fictional," Jerry said. Kiri caught his somber mood and frowned.

"Familiarity dilutes fear." Kimberly broke in. "Think about it. If you saw a fleshy egg with an opening in the top, you'd start looking for a flame thrower. Recognizing the danger takes away some of the shock."

"Why don't you two discuss this further, somewhere, perhaps over breakfast." Jerry smiled to soften his words. "In the meantime,

Frederick, you and Janice get started helping the Hoag set up what we need to go through the films. Yvette and I will try and come up with a workable script."

"Hrumph." Kiri sniffed in mock disdain. "I guess we can take a hint. Right, Kimberly?"

"Breakfast?" Kimberly suddenly realized she was famished.

"We're out of here." Kiri offered an arm and Kimberly took it on an impulse. They strode out, ignoring the men's surprised expressions. Kimberly noticed that while Janice was grinning at them, Yvette had a thoughtful expression. This would probably require explaining.

After breakfast!

"You said you would stay!" In the corridor, Kiri gave her a mock pinch on the arm. "I was afraid...oh, I don't know. Was I too...?"

"You were fine." Kimberly pinched her back, intentionally a little harder. "I just got this idea, and couldn't sleep."

"You can't edit a film in a few days," Kiri pointed out. "It can take months to go through all the dailies. Frederick and Jerry can be very meticulous."

"Well, this time they'll have to be quicker," Kimberly insisted. "We don't have a lot of time. Vicki is a resource they've never had before, and I think it'll go faster than you think."

"We'll see," Kiri said darkly. "Those two can be the biggest putzers."

"Look at another aspect of this." Kimberly smiled at her friend. "We've got some good footage of you in the battle for the bridge of the 'Viking. This might be the way to broaden your career."

"Maybe," Kiri said doubtfully. "I'm not so sure that's what I want anymore, though."

"Well, at least it may give you a choice," Kimberly reminded her. "Last night you didn't expect to even get a chance to decide for yourself, remember?"

"Yeah." Kiri blushed and Kimberly knew she was thinking about how much of her private self she had revealed the night before. "You had mentioned..."

"Hey, we're still traveling together when we get off this ship, right?" Kimberly helped her out. Kiri sighed in relief, and gave her a shy smile.

"I'm glad." She said simply.

"Me, too." Kimberly squeezed her arm. "Now, we need a name for a science fiction movie with hand-to-hand combat with alien monsters..."

"Kidnapers From the Stars?" Kiri began rattling off titles. "Violators From the Void? Claws From Alpha Centauri?"

"Crabs From Outer Space?" Kimberly returned with a grin. "Crabs, Black Panthers, Rhino-Bears..."

"Oh my!" Kiri finished for her. They both laughed and, hooking arms, began skipping down the corridor. Several Baerd and Hoag stopped and watched, perplexed, as they passed by.

"We-e-e-e're off to see the..."

◆ ◆ ◆ ◆ ◆

Glowing Mist, four days ago

Matt Stickel stood and groaned as stiff muscles complained. He'd been sitting at this computer terminal for hours, helping Du Brimar interpret news articles, rumors, UFO sightings, anything that might relate to a genuine sighting of an Egelv, or his ship.

"I think this is useless." He said flatly. "I don't see how we can tell a quack from a real incident. Even if we decide one story might be true, how does it help? There's no way to follow up!" He grinned at Teresa, who looked as tired as he was. "Uh, sir, sir! Did the alien leave a forwarding address where he might be reached? No? How about direction? Which way did he go, Marshal Dillon?"

"Who?" Teresa gave him a puzzled look.

"Never mind." Matt decided he had to quit using so many old television references. Teresa had obviously not spent a lot of time in front of the boob tube, and the Egelv understood even less.

Du Brimar gave him a skeptical look. "You can tell which news items are lies?"

"Sometimes," Matt admitted. "But you're looking for two things here. First, any sightings of Egelv-like beings that might be this Ty Musa you're looking for. That's not too hard. I would remember seeing a six and a half foot tall brown guy with long white hair. Even better, ears to the top of his head would get noticed."

"He could be disguised..." Du Brimar sounded stubborn.

"He could," Matt agreed. "But would he? Why would he care if people thought he looked strange? But anyway, odds are, he would stand out."

"Probably," The Egelv commander conceded reluctantly.

"But a UFO sighting?" Matt snorted. "There are hundreds, no, probably thousands every year. Some could even be true. But, from the description you give of the universe out there," he gestured upward, "an alien ship wouldn't even bother hiding. Why should they? It's not as though we could do anything about it."

"That's not totally true," Du Brimar countered. "Your planet actually has formidable defenses. It seems like every other nation has nuclear weapons."

"Not quite, but there are a lot of military forces around the world," Matt admitted ruefully.

"Well, we know for a fact that an Ananab ship was here approximately three weeks ago." Du Brimar reminded him. "We passed it on our way here, and we also found trace elements left by their propulsion drive. They orbited your planet at least twice, and expended a lot of energy at least once. Were there any incidents or sightings around that time?"

Matt started to answer, shaking his head, but Teresa interrupted him.

"A cruise ship disappeared," she reminded him. "In the Pacific."

"That's right." Matt remembered reading about it. "What was the name of that ship?"

"The Jade Viking." Teresa smiled at him. "My family was a little bit nervous about going on a cruise so soon after."

"What happened?" Du Brimar demanded.

"It disappeared." Matt closed his eyes, thinking hard. "They never found any trace of the ship or crew. That really had some people going." He opened his eyes and stared at the Egelv. "You don't just lose a cruise ship with three or four thousand people."

"In Spain, the papers sounded like piracy was the most likely answer," Teresa said. "If it had sunk, there would have been debris."

Du Brimar studied his screen and made adjustments. After several moments, he nodded. "Uh, huh. If the Ananab used a stun ray on the ocean vessel, sent three or four, probably four, shuttles down to lift it in one piece with antigrav, it would leave a signature very similar to this. That could very well be what happened."

"What, they just lifted a cruise ship out of the water and into orbit?" Matt was skeptical. "Wouldn't it collapse under its own weight?"

Du Brimar shook his head. "Even the Ananab could easily compensate with the proper use of antigrav...but would they be stupid enough to try and kidnap thousands of beings? Their ship can't have a crew of much more than two hundred." He shrugged, talking more to himself than Matt and Teresa. "Still, with Tryr and Srotag guards, they could probably handle that many humans in shock."

He looked at them with something akin to sympathy. "By now, those people are probably being reeducated as slave labor..." Du Brimar looked back at his screen. "...at Station Chaq."

"Slave labor?" Matt said, horrified. "Aren't the Ananab civilized?"

"Matter of opinion." Du Brimar smirked, then sobered. "I'm sorry, this isn't funny for your people. We don't think that highly of the Ananab, but not necessarily because of this."

"Do your people kidnap and imprison new races when you find them?" Teresa sounded indignant, and that matched Matt's own mood.

Du Brimar shrugged, and they all started as a new voice entered the conversation.

"Not anymore," Cromar Try sounded gruff, and behind him, his mate Siph Carni wore serious expression. "But we would certainly offer a guiding hand to the new race. If we did not, somebody else would lay claim, and their methods would not be as benevolent as ours."

"And if the new race refused the guiding hand?" Matt heard his own voice shaking a little. "What then?"

"I am afraid refusal would not be an option." Cromar Try smiled, as if thinking to lighten the blow his words delivered. "It really would be for their own best interests, in the long run."

"And Earth?" Matt found he was holding his breath.

"That is a little harder to say," the Egelv captain admitted. "This planet is not clearly in anyone's zone of influence. Normally, we would inspect the potential of the new race and decide if the effort necessary to bring your planet into our fold would be cost effective."

"Normally?" Teresa had a look of dread on her face.

"Normally," Cromar Try agreed. "But as it stands now, there is no way we can allow the Ananab, and by extension, the Hstahni, to lay claim to this sector and your people."

"So you come in with a fleet of ships and tell us what we're going to do for the rest of our lives?" Matt asked.

"We can not let the Hstahni claim your world." Cromar's voice grew cold. "We are far from Egelv space, and your people have the emnity of mine for past sins. No, establishing control here would not be practical. As distasteful as it is to us, removing your people from the equation would be more cost effective."

"Where would you take us?" Matt was confused, but Teresa obviously knew exactly what the alien meant.

"They wouldn't take us anywhere!" She stood and faced the Egelv captain with clenched fists. "They would scorch the Earth, killing us all."

"If it came to that, we would certainly be more civilized than 'scorching' the planet," Cromar Try said, defensively. "There are many ways to depopulate a world without resorting to energy weapons. There would really be very little suffering."

"It has been a long time since the death of Emperor Car Vano," Siph Carni pointed out. "Our people might not feel as strongly now as they would have a few hundred years ago."

Captain Cromar Try looked at his mate, his expression unreadable. After a few moments, it softened.

"First Officer Siph Carni is right." He cleared his throat. "It has been a long time. It would depend on the Emperor, of course."

"Right." Matt felt his eyes welling up with tears and forced them back. He would not cry in front of these...these aliens! "The humans that made up your Praetorian Guard were taken from Earth at least twenty-five hundred years ago. They're long dead. No living human being had anything to do with the death of your precious emperor. But what's important is that your 'civilized' race get its vengeance. Get its 'pride' back."

"I'm very tired." Teresa spoke up, her voice dull. "I think I will rest for a while." She looked at him, and Matt found himself agreeing.

"Me, too." He put his arm around her shoulder and they moved to the door. Siph Carni stood in the way, and her eyes showed pity. She stepped aside, evidently trying to think of something to say, and failing. It was just as well. There was nothing Matt wanted to hear right now.

He stopped at the door, his back to the room. Then he turned to face the tall aliens he had liked just a few minutes earlier. He could hear his voice shake, but he didn't care.

"It's funny that you think you're better than the Ananab. From where I stand, I can't see it. They're going to try and enslave our race. You're

98

going to commit genocide. Is this what you become when your race gets 'advanced' enough?" Matt fought the tears, using his anger to build a dam nothing could escape from. "I'll take primitive Humans with a social conscience any day. We're not perfect," he shook his head in disgust, "but unlike you, we have souls."

Matt and Teresa left the room, leaving the Egelv staring at each other in consternation.

CHAPTER SEVEN

Station Osaka

Jim sat down on the bed and leaned forward, resting his forearms on his knees. Kimberly had only been gone two days, and he already missed her. Their apartment seemed deserted, lifeless. Normally, Afsaneh would brighten things up, her irrepressible cheerfulness and enthusiasm combating his natural urge to be introspective. But she'd been aloof since the incident with Sean.

He didn't need to be dwelling on the past. He and Kimberly were going to be fine. She would understand that his boorish behavior had been a natural byproduct of his being upset at their separation.

Right.

He sighed, and it came from his lower gut, noisily blowing through pursed lips.

I've been in love twice in my life.

Almost seventeen years ago, he'd been in love with Afsaneh's mother, Nasri. He, she, and Hakim had shared a suite at school for over a year, and both young men had been desperately in love with her. And very protective. During a weekend Hakim was out of town, a traumatic experience had driven Jim and Nasri to become lovers. News that his parents were returning from Europe to begin divorce proceedings had Jim leaving to meet them in Washington D.C. before Hakim returned.

En route, he found out their plane had crashed, killing everyone aboard. His anger towards them, his betrayal of Hakim's trust, and weakness in giving in to his passion for Nasri filled him with self-loathing.

So he left.

And now, Kimberly has left me. Jim lay back on the bed and stared at the ceiling, wondering what it was that made him self-destruct the moment commitments were made.

Seventeen years ago, he could have turned right around, gone back to Ann Arbor, dealt with the loss of his parents, faced Hakim.

Instead, he'd fled.

◆ ◆ ◆ ◆ ◆

Afsaneh glanced both ways and saw no one. She quickly slipped through a hatch into a vast storage chamber. The ceiling was hundreds of feet high, and as far as she could see, there were stacks of containers, sorted in some indiscernible fashion, some nearly to the ceiling, some barely as tall as herself, creating a maze of small hills and ridges capable of disorienting the most experienced explorer.

She started walking at a normal pace, then couldn't resist, and began to jog. She knew the way, and it only took a couple of minutes to go around a huge pile of...stuff, finding the cul-de-sac entrance almost blocked off by a stack of palettes. She slipped between them and found what she expected to see.

"Hey, girl. You were able to slip away!" Sean and Ellis were sprawled on a couple of crates that to her, resembled coffins. Neither made an effort to get up, but Sean waved to a nearby crate. "Make yourself at home. You know everyone?"

Afsaneh looked around and saw about a dozen kids, mostly from the Chula Vista senior class. There were also a couple of high school girls that had been traveling with their families. She'd watched the way they acted around the senior boys and decided that if they were still virgins, it was a miracle. And if they were, that same miracle had a very short life span in front of it.

One of the boys handed her a small cup and she could tell from the smell that it was wine. After years of mooching sips from Hakim, Jim, and the close-knit group of actors and crewmen that made up her extended family, she could tell it was cheap wine, probably something from the kitchen to be used for cooking only.

Afsaneh thanked the boy, but didn't take a sip. She wandered over to where a boy and a girl were sharing a crate. The girl had a guitar, and the boy small bongos he'd probably bought as a souvenir at one of the stop-overs early in the cruise.

"Hi, Afsaneh." Evie Brown smiled at her, and strummed the strings of the guitar with a flourish. "Joining the party animals?" Next to her, Doyle Franks laughed and did a quick drum roll. Evie and Doyle had been dating since middle school, and had planned on going to a university in Michigan in the fall. Since they'd decided to stay on Station Osaka, those plans were obviously on hold.

She noticed their glasses looked untouched, and it didn't surprise her. They weren't interested in the same things as other kids their age. They loved music, and played most evenings in one of the numerous lounges that had sprung up to cater to the need for a nightlife on Station Osaka. Evie had a phenomenal voice, and Doyle did a good job of backing her up. They tended to sing a lot of songs from the seventies and eighties, but she'd heard them do some current stuff as well. She was a heavy girl, fat even. Next to her, Doyle looked small, even though they were both about five foot nine. She probably out-weighed him by thirty or forty pounds.

"So, the Man let you out?" Sean had come over to stand beside her. "Or did he even notice you leave?"

Afsaneh smiled to herself. Sean was obviously not holding his first glass of wine. He wasn't drunk; they didn't have enough wine to get anyone very buzzed, but it had loosened his tongue a little more than usual, if that was possible.

"Lay off her, Sean." Ellis came to her rescue, nudging his friend. "He was probably our age once." He let a wide grin fill his face. "A long time ago."

They all laughed, Afsaneh a little less enthusiastic than the rest.

"I don't know if he was ever as young as you, Sean," she retorted. "He wasn't but a year or so older than you are now when he killed his first man. Three men, in fact."

As soon as she said it, she regretted it. Before she could make light of the comment, or pretend she'd been joking, some of the other kids began gathering around them.

"Really, he killed three men when he was our age?" Ellis looked disturbed.

She immediately came to Jim's defense. "He caught three men raping a college girl, and killed them," she said flatly, annoyed at herself and her big mouth.

"That is so sad." Evie looked somber.

"More power to him. Rapists are scum," one of the other boys said. A couple more kids agreed with him.

"Did he have to go to court? Was he arrested?" Doyle Franks looked more curious than anything else. She'd noticed he tended to be analytical. "I don't remember reading about that."

"I shouldn't have said anything. Almost no one knows about it." Afsaneh felt the words rush out as she tried to downplay things. "His parents died a couple of days later, and he left town for almost a year."

"Where'd he go?" Doyle asked, and Evie lightly pushed his arm.

"I don't think Afsaneh wants to talk about it, Doyle. Let it go."

"He hitch-hiked to the Florida Keys, then took a ship over to Mexico." Afsaneh closed her eyes. *You are so stupid, Afsaneh.* "It was no big deal."

"He flees the country to hide the fact he's killed three men, and it's no big deal?" Sean dropped several notches in Afsaneh's eyes, but she couldn't leave it hanging like this.

"He didn't flee the country. He traveled on his own passport, wasn't hiding. He just...needed time." Afsaneh remembered the stories that had slowly been pried out of Jim over the years. "And, I think he might have been in shock, a little."

She looked around and saw that she had everyone's attention. They'd circled her, some sitting, some standing, but everyone absolutely focused on her every word.

In that case, she'd better make good use of them, she decided, wondering if she could ever forgive herself for this.

"I think the ship was a freighter..."

Governor Jason Lang sighed and looked at Suyo Takashi and Randy Luca sitting across the table from him. "Should we break it up? Shut it down before she burns any more bridges?"

"I think you should leave them be for the moment." Suyo said, looking thoughtful. "They don't have enough alcohol to get drunk, and it's not like they're driving anywhere."

"But Afsaneh..." Lang hated interfering, and spying even more.

"She's just given up some of Jim's biggest secrets." Suyo shook her head. "If you bust her now, she will never forgive herself, and it will strain her relationship with Jim. Give her a chance. Maybe it will be therapeutic."

Lang looked at Randy, who shrugged. "Don't know what to tell you, guvner."

Lang winced at Randy's humor, but nodded his agreement. His attention dragged back to the story she was beginning to tell.

◆ ◆ ◆ ◆ ◆

Jade Viking

"Ladies, we must quit meeting like this." Janice laughed at her own wit, and Kimberly felt the familiar foot begin creeping up her bare leg again.

"Keep it up and you're going to lose that foot."

Kimberly smiled to show she was kidding, and tried to shift to get the jet behind her lined up with her spine. Despite her hangover, Kiri had no problem throwing and bouncing her around the gym earlier. If anything, Kimberly was stiffer today than she'd been last night.

The five of them agreed that their evening hot tub meeting should become a tradition for what was left of the trip home. She was glad to see that Linda was fitting in, hardly any pretenses, or affected mannerisms.

"I dub us..." Kiri started, then paused for effect. "...the Sisterhood of Naked Ladies."

"Oh, there's something I want batted around the work site," Yvette said, wincing.

"Beats the Sisterhood of Hot Tub Whores..." Janice mused, keeping a straight face.

"Ah kinda like the Bare Butt Babes," Linda said, giggling. "But ah think that might have been used already, some band back in the eighties or nineties."

Kimberly shook her head. "Naked Ladies seems too...formal. Maybe the Nekid Gals?"

"Ah like it," Janice drawled, then looked startled when Linda went to shove her shoulder and pushed her breast instead.

"Oops, sorry." Linda giggled again. "Well, sorta. And there is no way you're from Texas, so where does that drawl come from?"

"Ah'll never tell." Janice glanced over at Yvette. "I think our girl here likes boob grabbin'."

"Don't even start," Yvette warned, and gave Kimberly a weary look. "She wears me out some days. Even Jim..." She looked guilty, then tried to recover. "What I meant was..."

105

"It's okay." Kimberly felt the cheery mood slipping away. "I miss him, he's pissed as hell at me, we'll work it out when I get back."

"Darlin', Jimbo doesn't have a lot of faith when it comes to 'gettin' back'." Janice actually looked sympathetic, then annoyed when Yvette jabbed her arm. "Hey, I'm just sayin' it like it is. People go away, things change. He just has to look to himself for that lesson."

Kimberly stared at them. *What were they referring to? Oh.* "Are you talking about when Jim went walkabout after the death of his parents?"

"Gone walkabout?" Janice looked incredulous. "That what you call it? He was gone almost a year."

"What do you know about that time, Kimberly?" Yvette asked gently.

Kimberly frowned. "Well, I know he was gone for almost nine months. He barely made it back for Afsaneh's birth." She tried to read the other woman's face, and felt a chill. One glance at Kiri's face confirmed her misgivings. What did these women know that she didn't?

"It wasn't exactly one of Jim's finest moments." Kiri said softly and reached to grasp Kimberly's hand under the water. Another time, holding another woman's hand on her bare lap would have made Kimberly uncomfortable, but now she barely even noticed.

"Tell me." Kimberly made her tone firm and tried to invoke her hostile witness voice. "Tell me what you know about that time."

Yvette caught her eye, and shifted her eyes towards Linda, slightly cocking her head.

Kimberly forced a smile. "It's okay. We're the Sisterhood of Nekid Gals, remember? One for all?"

"And all are bare," Janice finished for her.

"Honey, ah can keep a secret." Linda pursed her lips and deliberately folded her arms across her chest. "And I'm probably at least half again as intelligent as y'all give me credit for," she finished dourly.

Kimberly looked around the circle of friends. Kiri to her left, still tightly gripping her hand, Linda looking pissed off, but the folded arms made her boobs stick up and out, and it ruined the effect. Janice looked embarrassed, which had to be a first, and Yvette looked like ...Yvette. Older sister, mothering type, friend you always could confide in, and troubled.

"Tell me what you know." Kimberly turned slightly to the right so she could see Yvette's face better, and leaned back against Kiri.

"Please."

Yvette sighed and leaned over to snuggle against Janice, who wrapped her arms around her for support.

"You know some of the story already." Yvette stared over their heads as she brought back the past. "He hitched to Key West, then took a ship over to Playa Del Carmen. Then he just started walking."

"Walking?" Kimberly blinked. "Walking in Mexico?"

"Oh yeah." Yvette gave a little laugh. "He headed west. Walking and hitching." Her laugh died away. "Of course, when it comes to Jim, nothing is ever that simple..."

◆ ◆ ◆ ◆ ◆

Sidney Australia

Groundhog whistled soundlessly as he inspected the hotel room. He unpacked his toiletries in the bathroom, arranging them exactly as he liked. He set his small suitcase on the bed, turned the television on, and went to look out the window. He could see the billowing sails of the Opera House, and behind it, the busy harbor. Sidney was a bustling city, and there were probably many things one could do to while away the hours.

Groundhog closed the curtains, and began channel surfing. He checked the guide on channel 1, and saw a movie listing for eleven that evening. It sounded familiar, and upon further inspection, it proved to be a Jim Morris film, Ninth Hour of the Ninja.

He made a mental note, and continued his channel surfing.

He did, after all, have time to kill.

◆ ◆ ◆ ◆ ◆

Mexico, sixteen years ago...

Jim glanced down the road leading off to his right. He could see a gate in the distance, with a pickup parked in front of it. He turned his attention back to the road in front of him and sighed. By his estimation, he had at least ten more miles to the next town where he'd be able to refill his water bottles and find a bite to eat, and maybe a place to clean up and spend the night.

He heard the pickup pull onto the road behind him and come alongside, then pass him. It angled over to block his path, and two men with what looked like shotguns grinned at him from the open truck bed. They weren't exactly aiming the weapons at him, but, they weren't pointed away, either.

Two men got out of the cab and came to stand in front of him, the bigger man holding an axe handle, the other with a hand on the pistol holstered high on his hip.

All four men appeared to be Mexican, well groomed and in clean if somewhat dusty, work clothes. The one with the sidearm was tall, slender, with short hair and a thin mustache. He had a cell phone clipped to his belt next to the handgun.

"Who are you? What are you doing on this road?" He spoke in Spanish, and his accent showed he'd had some education. "Answer me, kid."

"I'm just walking, on my way to Guadalajara." Jim answered in Spanish. He didn't like the looks these four were giving him, and each other. "I don't even know where I am. If this is a private road, I'm sorry. Show me which way to go and I'm gone."

"Not going to be that easy, boy." The evident leader of the group smiled, showing even white teeth. "Your accent is interesting. Where'd you learn Spanish?"

"My parents were stationed in Panama," Jim answered truthfully.

"You're American." It wasn't a question. The man glanced at his friends with a half smile playing across his face. Then said in English, "You look very young to be a DEA agent."

"I'm not DEA. I don't even have a job," Jim protested, watching the other two men hop off the back of the truck, holding their weapons loosely. There had to be a way to stop this. "I'm just passing through."

"Right. You're in the middle of fucking cartel farm country, just passing through! Benito!."

The man with the axe handle stepped forward, raising it with a grin that was markedly different from his leader. Shaggy, unkempt hair surrounded a round face with a leering grin that exposed a gap where his upper middle teeth should have been.

Jim didn't hesitate. Stepping inside the swinging axe, he locked his left hand on the big man's right wrist, stomped with his left foot against the inside of his right kneecap, and punched three times, very fast, very hard, with the heel of his right hand, aiming where the sternum met the rib cage. His attacker began to stagger backwards and Jim slid his left hand down to the axe handle, yanking it free.

Jim spun it in his hand as he used the momentum to twirl around, resulting in the satisfying sound of hardwood striking metal and knuckles. As the pistol went flying, he swung again, striking the back of the man's right calf, causing his legs to buckle. Almost as an afterthought, Jim brought his right hand around, open fisted, slapping him with brutal force.

As the leader flew backwards, Jim kept moving. He shifted the axe handle almost without thought to his right hand and slammed it across the shotgun barrel of the closer man. He followed with a backhand that made a sickeningly flat-sounding thud of hardwood against head.

The last man was desperately trying to unsling his shotgun, fear causing him to hurry. The strap caught on his elbow. He finally freed it and tried to get his hands and fingers in the right places but Jim didn't give him a chance, leaping into close quarters, striking the man's left arm so hard, he heard the bone crack. Another blow across the right wrist resulted in a dropped weapon, and the man falling to his knees, sobbing with a crushed wrist as well as the other broken arm.

Jim raised the axe handle and the man sobbed, begging for mercy in a broken voice. Jim hesitated, then gave him a quick crescent kick to the side of the head, knocking him out cold.

Hearing a scraping sound against the baked soil, Jim whirled and threw the axe handle, hitting the leader full in the face as he was trying to raise the pistol to fire. The gun fell to the ground, and so did the man. The original owner of the axe handle was on his hands and knees, groggily trying to get to his feet. Jim stepped forward and used the stiffened edge of his right hand to chop the other across the back of the neck. He slumped forward, unconscious before his face hit the ground.

Jim spun around, arms in a defensive pose, taking in the four men strewn around him. They all appeared to be unconscious. Or worse, Jim thought, feeling despair struggle with an unnerving giddiness. It hadn't taken a moment for him to shift from normal college student to murderous nemesis, with no compunction against crippling or killing an enemy. Or, in this case, enemies. *This is not who I want to be!*

But it's who you are.

The thought struck him harder than any blow an opponent could have delivered.

Jim realized he was hyperventilating, and forced himself to slow his breathing. A quick inspection showed all four were, indeed, unconscious and not dead, although some of the injuries might take months to heal, if ever. They hadn't gotten a shot off, and he couldn't hear any voices or engines showing reaction to the fight.

He gathered his things he'd dropped in the brief battle, and took a step down the road, then stopped, thinking. Inhaling deeply, he went to the truck and checked. Sure enough, the keys were in the ignition. Not stopping to think too much about it, he got in, tossing his pack on the seat beside him, started the engine, continued down the dirt road.

Jim tried to picture the map he'd look at yesterday. This road ended at Road 110, which he could follow to the turnoff to Guadalajara. But the men lying in the road behind him knew that was where he was going. If he continued to the west on 110, then continued on Highway 54, it would take him to Manzanillo.

He'd read that Manzanillo had a thriving harbor, for a Mexican port, and he could probably catch a ship up the coast, losing the pursuit he was sure would begin at any moment.

He drove for several hours, stopping once in Colima for gas. He didn't think anyone paid any attention to him, but at some point, word would be put out to watch for the truck. It was late in the afternoon when he drove slowly along the docks, looking at the ships, trying to decide which ones were about to depart.

Jim made a choice and drove several blocks away, parking at a small mall where he hoped the truck wouldn't be found for a while. It might also cause his pursuers, if there were any, to waste time searching the shops.

He saw a mini-market on the corner across the street from the pier and decided to get some more bottled water and energy bars. He'd been very lucky to not have any intestinal problems to this point, and it was because he choose the local food and drink he consumed very carefully.

Jim walked in the side door, then immediately leaned over to pretend to be looking at some candy bars at a display. Two men, dressed similarly to the four he'd fought, were talking with the clerk. They weren't trying to keep their voices down, so he had no trouble making out the words.

"He's young, light brown hair, long, down to his shoulders, wearing a white tee-shirt and jeans. He has a short beard, like he started growing it a couple weeks ago. Maybe this tall, and American."

"I haven't seen him, but I'll watch for him," the vendor said. "Do you know for sure he's coming to the docks?"

"The truck he stole was spotted at a gas station up the road. He's either coming to the docks or planning on driving up the coast. We're checking both."

Jim crouched as he moved down the aisle to the back of the store. He saw the bathroom door open and an older man come out. Jim slipped inside and carefully closed the door and locked it.

He stared at a cracked mirror, and the person they were describing stared back at him.

Crap.

Twenty minutes later, he cracked the door enough to see that the store was empty, except for the same clerk standing in the front doorway, staring up the road. Jim re-traced his steps back up the aisle, and out the side door, then walked back in, making no attempt to conceal himself.

He chose bottled water and the power bars, taking his time, showing no inclination to hurry, as he felt the scrutinizing inspection by the clerk. He walked up to the counter, and nodded, not smiling, but not showing any sign of anxiety.

The clerk saw a young man, about the right height, wearing jeans. But he had a gauzy cotton long-sleeved button shirt, a bright headband not fully covering his bald head, and a clean shaven countenance. He would remember a man with very bad Spanish, who spoke English with a heavy accent, possibly from the Middle East.

Jim walked directly across the street to the pier leading up to the ship he'd picked out earlier. He could feel the eyes of the clerk still watching him, not suspecting, but still noting where he went. He walked up to a sailor smoking a cigarette, and asked him when the ship would be departing. Eight in the evening, two and a half hours from now.

He thanked the sailor, turning just enough to see the clerk following customers into his store, the bald stranger at least momentarily forgotten.

Jim quickly moved down the docks.

An hour later, he was thanking the purser for a job on board the Cebu. Twenty minutes after that, his gear was stowed, and he was helping pack crates in one of the holds. The air was stifling, but there were no men with guns threatening him, and they departed within the hour. He hadn't planned on going to the Philippines, but, why not?

He found out at least one good reason that evening. The captain and officers of the tramp freighter Cebu loved gambling, and nightly fights between the crew fed their craving.

Jim had no desire to take part, but found out the hard way that pounding the newest crewman to a pulp was a ship's tradition. A tradition he broke that night.

◆ ◆ ◆ ◆ ◆

Kimberly stared at Yvette. Did violence follow Jim as if he were a lightning rod?

"So, let me get this straight." Kimberly almost didn't know how to start. "He catches three guys raping Nasri, kills all three. Making like Caine from Kung Fu, walking across Mexico, he's attacked by four drug cartel thugs, beats them to a pulp. First night on a freighter, he gets forced into fighting...another crewman? The entire crew? The Swedish Bikini Team?"

"That about sums it up," Janice said brightly, displaying her usual sardonic leer. Kimberly wasn't quite sure if it was in response to her own comments, or the fact that Linda Hoffman was now seated in the middle of the hot tub, leaning back between Janice's legs, eyes closed, with a dreamy smile, getting her shoulders massaged.

Kimberly turned to Kiri on her left. "And this all happens in what? A week or so?"

Kiri nodded, her brown eyes sad. "That night, he refused to fight. But his opponent came at him anyway. At first Jim just kinda sparred with him. He didn't have anything against the guy, but he took a couple of hard punches, and just snapped." She rested her right hand on Kimberly's shoulder in understanding. "He did a roundhouse kick that about took the guys head off, and that was that. The next night, as soon as the fight started, he knocked the other guy out, and again the night after." Kiri leaned over and rested her forehead on her hand. "It got so none of the crew would fight him. Pissed the captain off, but he got the last word."

Kimberly wondered what that meant. She turned to Yvette, who was still watching her, looking concerned. She hesitated, then answered Kimberly's unspoken question.

"By the time they landed in Manilla, Jim had retreated into himself. He wasn't the funny, good-natured guy that we know. In his mind, I think he thought it was out of his control. His destiny, and he hated it."

Yvette scooted over close to Janice, who wrapped an arm around her. Linda made a disappointed sound without opening her eyes, and Kimberly laughed despite herself as Yvette made a face and began massaging Linda's left shoulder, where Janice had left off.

"So, what did the captain do in Manila?" Kimberly asked.

"Fight club," Kiri muttered, her lips tickling Kimberly's bare shoulder. Digesting the girl's words, Kimberly grew somber.

"Jim would have hated that."

"After a couple of months, the people behind the fight club took him to Singapore, then Hong Kong." Yvette's voice was stony, and Janice hugged her closer.

"He stayed in Manila, fighting every night for two months?" Kimberly couldn't believe it. This was a man that was willing to be ridiculed to avoid a fight. He cared about people, she knew he did.

"He didn't fight every night." Kiri's voice was muffled by Kimberly's shoulder. "Two, maybe three times a week. Never lost, not even close. Then they took him to Singapore, and finally Hong Kong, and things got bad."

"This wasn't bad?" Kimberly shook her head, disbelieving that she could actually be married to someone and really know so little about him. "Wait a minute, how could this have stayed out of the news. When he got famous, someone would have tracked this story down."

"He had a...stage name." Janice straightened her head, a tinge of humor entering her voice.

"Yeah." Yvette shook her head against Janice's shoulder, smiling despite herself. "With all the hurry to get aboard the ship, when he was asked his name, he got flustered and answered the first thing that came to him."

"Sure glad the radio wasn't playing Purple People Eaters," Kiri snickered, sitting up enough to plop her arm around Kimberly's shoulders.

"Or Amy," Janice added. She glanced around the circle of faces. "Not that there's anything wrong with guys having girl's names..."

"Totally cool with me." Kiri tried and failed to keep a straight face. "I mean, we are twenty-first century women, open minded to a fault..."

"Ah think it would be weird having someone named Amy or Sue with a Barney," Linda spoke up, startling them all. Kimberly had thought she'd dozed off.

"You call men's penises 'Barney'?" Yvette sounded disbelieving. "Barney?"

"Well, ah call one of them Barney," Linda said, a little defensively. "Ah mean, ah don't really talk to the rest. Ah'm a one-Barney kinda gal."

"And yet, here ya are, between the legs of a woman, both of us stark nekid, and more than a little horny..." Janice drawled, lifting her right leg to drape it over Linda's lap.

"Well, yeah." Linda opened her eyes and grinned across at Kiri and Kimberly. "No harm in a little fun, and trust me, if ah get back to the room in the same mood ah was in last night, Ron won't complain a bit." She giggled and put her hands on Janice's leg, tucking it closer to her. "Even little blue pills got their limits. But last night, ah do believe he went to sleep a satisfied man." She giggled again.

"Yeah, we're just having a little fondle..."

Everyone groaned at Kiri's bad pun. Kimberly felt like her emotions were a ping pong ball between the somber stories about Jim, and the hilarious interludes with antics by...just about all of them.

"Okay, enough." Kimberly was tired of watching Linda get an apparently unending massage by Janice, and now by Yvette as well. The sexual innuendos were constant, and she decided it was time to deal with it. She lowered herself to the center of the tub, shifting forward and pulling Kiri over behind her with her left hand.

Kimberly leaned back between the Japanese girl's legs and propped her arms on Kiri's thighs. "In for a penny, in for a pound. My turn to get some serious massage."

She felt Kiri's hands settle on her shoulders, then laughed as Kiri leaned forward to look at her face from the side. "That really you, round-eyes?"

"Yeah, but don't get any ideas. I'm just into this for the decadent massage. But remember, like Linda was saying, some of my parts are for Jim only. Now rub."

Linda smirked at her from a lot closer than Kimberly had realized they would be, and she noticed that technically, she was sort of sitting on Linda's lap, facing her with actually, kind of, well, her feet on either side of Linda's hips.

"Actually, ah was talkin' about Barneys." Linda smiled and pushed Kimberly's nose lightly with her forefinger. "What happens in the girl's locker room, stays in the girl's locker room." She looked puzzled for a moment. "What was that about pennies and pounds?"

Kimberly thought about sliding backwards, but Kiri had dropped down and was snug up against her. She was working on her neck muscles with both hands, and it had that near pain, near ecstasy effect. *I need to not think about what is pressing against my back...and my butt, come to think of it.*

She noticed that Janice and Yvette had slightly stunned looks on their faces, and decided to get things back on track. This was fun, in a very racy, flirtatious way, but there was an unfinished story to be told. And, she reminded herself, it really wasn't a comedy.

"So," she said, turning her neck to give Kiri a better angle. "Tell me how Hong Kong was worse. I already know what he went by, come to think of it."

"Well, Ah don't," Linda complained, to no avail.

Groundhog sipped his bottled water, deep in thought. The movie had been interesting, if somewhat stupid. The plot and the acting left much to be desired, but the martial arts were surprisingly good. Too often, in Groundhog's opinion, martial arts movies used special effects to create fight scenes that were ridiculous. Running on the tips of tree tops, leaping hundreds of feet, striking devastating blows to opponents, only to have them jump back to their feet moments later, apparently unharmed, were only a few of the bad habits of bad movies.

Jim Morris had the reputation of not actually being a martial artist, but using special effects and stunt doubles for fight scenes, but it didn't ring true to Groundhog. He couldn't see any sign of a body double, and he'd seen that fighting style before. He was almost certain he'd seen it in person.

He glanced at his watch. This train of thought would have to wait. It was time to go to work. He'd done all the preliminary tasks earlier in the evening, after darkness had fallen.

An hour and a half later, he watched through his scope as the lights came on in the penthouse suite on the seventy-fourth floor of the Meriton World Towers. Several men entered, carefully inspected every room, then stood off to the side as a couple entered.

They had obviously had an excellent time, and moved in that curiously stilted manner of people who've had one or two drinks more than they can handle. They said something to the two bodyguards, which they definitely were, and the men left.

Groundhog waited as they kissed, giving them that. Then, as they separated, he pressed the button on the remote taped to the stock of his rifle.

Six charges of C4 went off, and the window that was surely bullet-proof against anything Groundhog could bring to bear, was blasted off the building. Earlier in the evening, he'd rappelled down from the roof and attached the packs to all four corners, then in the middle at the top and bottom for good measure. The charges were designed to separate the window from the frame without significant blast inward.

The couple were knocked back on their heels, but didn't fall, which was what Groundhog had counted on. He sighted on the woman first, shot, levered another shell into the chamber, shot again. Then he re-peated the process, aiming at the man. As he fired the fourth shot, he swung back over to watch the woman finish falling to the floor. A quick shift, and he saw the man do the same. He watched for a moment, for any movement, ignoring the two men rushing back into the suite, but he could see where all four shots had gone, and knew he'd succeeded.

He rolled back away from the edge of the roof, then trotted to the door leading inside. He propped the rifle against the door, then took off running for the far side of the roof. He used the ledge as a leaping bar, as if he were doing the long jump. As he left the roof, he pushed the remote in his right gloved hand, and the rifle, well caked with more C4, exploded, setting fire to the shanty-like building that housed the top of the stairwell.

In free fall, he pulled his chute release, and it yanked him upward. He expertly steered clear of the building across the street, then set course for the industrial park over a mile away.

An hour later, his taxi pulled up to the Meriton World Tower, and he looked around in bemusement at all the police cars, fire trucks, emer-gency vehicles surrounding it. A policeman stopped him at the door.

"I'm a guest here. On the forty-third floor. What happened?"

The policeman ignored his question and, after carefully examining his passkey, identification, and consulting a printout, he let him enter. Ten minutes later, Groundhog locked his door, carefully hung up his tuxedo, and fixed himself a short Crown Royal on the rocks.

He sat on his bed, keyed the television to replay the movie, and re-focused on the problem that had dominated his thoughts all evening.

Where have I seen Jim Morris fight?

Hong Kong, almost sixteen years ago...

Jim sat cross-legged, ignoring everyone around him. His hands rested lightly just above his knees, palms up, thumbs and fingers hanging loosely, pointed inwards. His eyes weren't closed. He never closed them, even when he slept, according to some people.

He had no idea how long he'd been here, in Hong Kong, living, eating, and fighting under the same roof. He knew the fight master in Manila had literally sold him to Master Tsang. He didn't consider himself anyone's property, but since he had nothing better to do, going along with the Master's wishes was as good a way to pass time as any.

Jim was intelligent and not under the influence of any drug. He knew what he did was wrong, but as he'd discovered, he was a magnet for violence. Being around the people he cared about only brought them danger. The events that led him here had demonstrated that.

Master Tsang had taken his time bringing Jim into the limelight. His first fight or two had been against lesser foes, and he'd quickly defeated them. Since then, one or two fights a week, he'd worked his way through tougher fighters, winning every fight either with a knockout, or broken limbs or ribs where the opponent couldn't continue.

His popularity had grown, at first very slowly. After all, he was a westerner, an American, if stories were to be believed. Some thought he was European, or possibly even Iranian. One common thread between all the people that theorized his origin, was a desire to see him defeated.

His absolute indifference to everyone, including the few fans he did acquire, his no-nonsense approach to each fight that made most of them very short, thus boring, led to throngs of enthusiastic fans of whoever he happened to be fighting on any particular day.

This month had seen the start of the Kumite. His first two matches had been quick and simple. His first, against a Japanese much smaller, but not faster as most observers had expected, had lasted less than half a minute. Jim had matched him with speed and technique, countering every punch, every attempted kick, until the first burst of energy waned, then Jim counter-punched so hard it lifted the man off his feet, flying backwards, unconscious before he hit the mat.

The second, a Brazilian, hadn't lasted much longer. As big as Jim, and fast for his size, the masters had probably thought this would be a tougher, more drawn out match. It wasn't. The Brazilian tried too hard to get in close, use punishing knees, punches and kicks to wear him down.

Jim let him get within reach, then executed a move he'd seen once at a competition in Detroit. He leaped high, gripped the man with his legs, using the momentum to spin him to the floor. But the man fought the hold, and didn't take defensive precautions, landing hard on the back of his head. Jim rolled free, and sat a few feet away, watching the referee check him, then summon the medical team. At first, he was feared to be dead, but it was not the case. As of this morning, they were still examining him to see if he had permanent spinal or brain damage.

"Cisco Kid."

The call brought him out of his self-induced trance. He smoothly rolled to his feet, and walked to the arena. Then the call for his opponent came.

It was a woman. She was German, and as large as he was, maybe a little bigger. Jim frowned and looked at the judges, then at the referee. They stared back at him impassively. He shook his head and bowed to his opponent. She returned the courtesy and smiled at him. It wasn't really a friendly smile, but it wasn't a sneer either.

Jim had never fought a woman, and had no desire to do so now. He was here as penance for his sins, and beating up a woman wasn't going to make up any moral ground. He considered withdrawing, but before he could decide, the referee motioned and the match began. He circled, buying time, considering how he could beat her without actually hurting her.

Perhaps close in, get a strangle hold, cause her to pass out...he snapped back to the present in time to block her initial attack. She had an aggressive fighting style, and Jim had to give ground. Distantly, he could hear a raised murmur among the audience. He never retreated, simply matched, blow for blow, countering most if not all, until an opening would occur. Then the fight would be over.

She was very good, and several of her blows landed. *She kicks hard.*

Hits hard, too. Jim knew he was pulling his own punches, not wanting to physically punish a woman. He decided to get in close, get her in a judo hold, force her surrender.

It didn't go as planned. He was not responding to her blows fast enough with counter-punches, wasn't using most of his arsenal because he didn't want to risk hurting her badly. He tried to grapple with her, but she slid away, countering with a punch to the side of his head, miraculously not bursting his eardrum.

In pain, he reacted without thought, whirling to kick her in the kidneys. She came right back with a kick to his exposed crotch.

He staggered backward, trying to get a moment's respite, but she was relentless. She bombarded him with a barrage of punches and kicks. He tried to block and counterpunch, then without even thinking about it, he leaped into the air, spinning, bringing his foot around in what should have been an impossible attempt, kicking her hard in the back of the head. She pitched forward to the floor and didn't move. The referee moved in, signaled Jim to retreat, and then went to inspect the woman. After a moment, he raised his head to the judges and shook it.

They stood, motionless for a moment, then nodded to him, then the fallen body, and finally to the referee, who signaled a victory for Jim.

The crowds were dead silent for a moment, but then they went crazy, some cheering, some screaming epitaphs at him. Several fights started in the stands.

Jim didn't even think of the traditional bow, but just staggered back to his place with the other fighters. They moved over, giving him plenty of space. Deaths were not unheard of, but this was the first of this years' competition, and first time anyone had heard of a woman dying in competition.

Jim sat staring at nothing during the rest of the day's matches. Then he went back to his room, ignoring the usual offers of sex by women, lay down on his cot and slept for twelve hours.

The next day, Jim was matched against an enormous Chinese man. He was huge, but he knew how to fight, and he was good. And very strong.

Jim pulled out every style, every move he could think of, or do without thinking, and the Chinaman blocked, absorbed, ducked, and closed every chance he got. And there were several. Jim was bruised, his left ankle was sore, and it felt like he was getting a black eye. The large Asian kept coming at him, shaking off every attack, until he finally got

Jim in a close hold, and began squeezing, all the time hitting Jim with any part of his body he could bring to bear.

Jim tried to break free, but couldn't. He head-butted the Chinese, and almost knocked himself unconscious. It hurt his adversary as well, but not enough to break the grip. Jim could only get a little leverage with his right hand, and slammed it against the larger man's ribcage as hard as he could. Then again, and again. Breathing was getting difficult, his vision foggy, and he couldn't get more than about an inch and a half of space to strike, but he kept hitting, over and over again, until he felt he was about to pass out, the grip loosened ever so slightly.

Jim renewed his punching, and was able to push forward with his feet, driving them both backwards, until the Chinaman stumbled. As they fell, the grip broke, and Jim tumbled over the other man, hooking his left arm around the thick neck as he went. His right foot got planted, and his left knee spread out to keep him balanced. He tried to punch the side of the man's head to disorient him, but as he did, the Chinaman twisted his head to the left, trying to break the stranglehold. Jim simultaneously tightened his grip and struck. There was a loud cracking sound, and the huge man went limp in his grasp.

Jim couldn't see or hear anything. The fog in his eyes wouldn't clear. He felt hands pulling him away from the fallen foe, and almost struck at them, but didn't. He recognized the referee and two other officials holding him, and quit struggling. They immediately let go, and he slowly rose to his feet, turned, and walked into the tunnel that led back to his quarters.

That night, Jim sat on his bunk, staring at the blank wall. At some point, someone knocked on the door. He ignored it, but the knocking continued. He paid it no attention, and eventually, the door opened.

Master Tsang entered, with two men behind him. He stood looking at Jim, as if waiting to be acknowledged. Jim sat without moving, his eyes focused either somewhere deep within, or far, far away. The Master watched him for a few moments, then gestured. One of the men stepped forward and tried to slap Jim's face.

Jim caught the man's wrist, stopping the blow less than two inches from contact. His eyes shifted to the man, then to Master Tsang. He didn't let go, and the man tried to pull free, but couldn't. With an angry oath, he started to punch with his other hand.

A simple twist, and Jim broke the man's wrist, then, letting go, one punch to the chest sent him crashing into the wall. Jim had risen several inches to complete the punch. He sank back onto his bunk, but looked at Master Tsang.

"I am finished." Jim spoke with no inflection in his voice. "I have to leave this place."

"You leave when I say." Master Tsang folded his arms. "One more fight tomorrow, then you can quit, leave, do anything you wish."

"Tomorrow is the semi-final." Jim looked at him with a glimmer of life, of curiosity. "Who do I fight, and why do you think I won't have to fight the next day?"

"Tomorrow you fight Chang, and lose."

Jim thought about that. "Chang is good, and very popular, but I can beat him."

"But you won't." Master Tsang watched the injured man be helped from the room by the other. "You will fight, it will last several minutes, then Chang will defeat you."

"How can you be sure."

Master Tsang stepped close and looked down at him, his expression unreadable. "You will make sure it happens."

Jim shook his head. "I don't wish to continue, but it isn't in me to throw a fight. It won't happen."

"It will happen, or you won't live the day out."

Jim laughed, without a trace of humor. "You actually think death frightens me?" He lowered his gaze. "I'm already dead."

"There are many ways to die."

Jim closed his eyes, shaking his head. "You'd do better betting on me. If you want, I'll fight these last two fights, but I won't lose either of them."

"You will do as you are told." Master Tsang and his men left.

Jim sat for a while, then heard movement in the corridor outside his room. He sighed, opened his eyes, looked around the room to see if there was anything he couldn't leave behind, and decided there wasn't.

Standing, he did several quick stretching motions, then the door flew open.

Just after dawn, Jim approached the Marine sentry at the entrance to the U.S. Consulate on Garden Road. His shirt was torn, what remained of it was bloody, and he had a slight limp. He bent over, pulled his left shoe off, yanked the sole free and pulled out a battered passport.

"I'm a U.S. citizen. I need to speak to the Consulate General..."

Kimberly sighed, and it seemed to come from her very heels. She couldn't think of anything to say. Across from her, Janice was uncharacteristically quiet, her right arm hanging over Linda's shoulder, across a breast, holding hands on her stomach with Yvette, who sat sideways, her head in the crook of Janice's left arm. Yvette had a dejected look on her face, and Janice bent forward and kissed her head, whispering something quietly in her ear.

Linda looked shell-shocked. Her head was back against Janice's chest, but there was no amorous intent. Her hands rested on Kimberly's knees, and didn't even seem to notice it.

At some point, Kimberly's massage had stopped, because Kiri's arms were now wrapped tightly around her, their four hands tightly entwined.

"That poor man," Linda said slowly. "He's fought everybody in world, practically, and just wants to be left alone, and now, we need him to fight everybody out of this world."

Kimberly stared at her.

"Sorry we ruined the mood, darlin'." Janice reluctantly let go of Yvette's hands as Linda began to stir, as if to get up. Kimberly realized she was still straddling her, but Kiri was hugging her tight, making it difficult to move. She solved it by grasping Kiri's arms with one hand, pushing against the floor of the tub with the other, using the water's buoyancy to bring the two women up to the seat level. Kimberly got them both perched on it, giving Linda room to rise.

"That's alright. Ah think ah'll let Ron get some sleep tonight. At his age, three nights in a row might just kill 'em." She gave Kimberly an amused look, and she realized that she and Kiri must look silly, like she was giving the Japanese girl a piggy-back ride. Then as Linda's eyes sank slightly, she realized what the woman was really amused by. Sitting there with her legs braced to hold them both in place, she was, well, kind of...exposed.

"Well, I feel vulnerable," Kimberly muttered. Kiri hugged her tighter, if that was possible, and whispered.

"I'll protect you."

That lightened the mood a little, and Linda sat for a moment, half in, half out of the hot tub. "Gals, tomorrow night, let's talk about something a little lighter, maybe a little more fun. How about Texas Longhorn football?"

"We'll tackle that subject just for you, honey," Janice drawled right back at her.

"Don't think ah didn't notice those sneaky-pete fingers of yours, tonight," Linda said, tweaking one of Janice's nipples as she began an insincere apology. "Ah didn't say ah minded. Ah jess wanted to make sure you know ah noticed."

With that, she threw her towel over one shoulder, stepped into her sandals, picked up her cooler and left, singing "back in the stirrups, again."

Janice looked at Kimberly, then they both looked after Linda., but it Kiri that said it.

"She does know there's other people on this ship, and that she's naked, right?"

"And isn't it, 'back in the saddle, again'?" Janice asked in all innocence.

Kimberly sighed.

"On that note I'm heading to bed," Yvette said, rousing herself to climb out of the tub. They all followed suit.

Within moments, Janice and Yvette were gone, towels wrapped as sarongs. As Kiri and Kimberly retrieved their robes and covered the tub, Kiri spoke.

"You okay?"

Kimberly sighed. "Yeah, it's just, I've heard part of this story from Jim, but finding out the details..." She sighed again and looked at Kiri. "Would you be up for a sleep over?"

Kiri laughed softly. "Round-eyes, that is probably the stupidest question you've ever asked anyone in your life."

"But I'm talking sleep, snugglin' maybe, but no naughty hands." Kimberly put an arm around her friend as they left the room. "I mean it."

"Of course." Kiri reciprocated the gesture. "You can trust me."

"R-i-ight."

123

"...so Jim fought his way across Hong Kong to the Consulate. It took them three days to get him out of China."

"So he fought in arena combat for, like, months?" Alicia was one of the Chula Vista seniors. "Do you think he killed anyone?"

"I don't know, maybe." Afsaneh was already regretting her indiscretion. She'd watered down the story significantly even from what she'd been told. And she knew she'd gotten the 'M' rated version, at best.

"I can't decide if this makes him a hypocrite or not." Sean looked troubled, which was out of character for him.

"It made him human, struggling within himself," Ellis answered, and most of the kids stopped and stared at him. "What? I'm majoring in psychology at Stanford in the fall. Well, I was," he amended.

"I gotta think about this." Sean shook his head, then tried to recover his attitude. "And you were gonna major in defense and quarterback mutilation at Stanford."

Jason Lang sat back and looked at Suyo and Randy in amazement. "I actually think this may have been a positive experience for the group. They're thinking about ethical behavior, right and wrong, not drinking rotgut wine," he finished with a satisfied nod of his head.

"You think that was the whole story?" Randy asked, frowning. "She skimmed through some parts of it."

"If I know Jim, and what I knew of Hakim in the little time I knew him, she got an edited version." Jason sat back in his chair and squared his shoulders. "I'm sure we'll never know what really happened."

Groundhog woke to the sound of the coffee timer going off, and gathered his thoughts. And just like that, he remembered. It had been at least fifteen years ago. Then he remembered more details, and knew it had been almost exactly sixteen years. As he lay waiting for the coffee to finish, he replayed that momentous week in his mind.

He and his mentor had been in Hong Kong for the Kumite. The first few days had been less exciting than he'd anticipated, boring even. They'd picked several fighters of interest to watch, and bet on their progress, but so far, there had been no upsets, no brilliant play. Only one injury of any consequence. That fight had brought Cisco Kid to their attention.

It was obviously not his real name. Both Groundhog and the man he knew only as "The Frenchman" felt the shaved head and face weren't his normal grooming, and that he must either be in hiding, or escaping from a life he could no longer bear.

But none of that had kept the Kid from marching through some very good fighters. A quick check on past fights had shown a rather astounding rise to the upper echelon of fighters from...nowhere. His fights traced back to Manila, and before that, as far as anyone curious enough to pry could tell, Cisco Kid hadn't fought any sort of professional fight, or even existed.

"We should research him." The Frenchman felt Groundhog could use the practice, but before they could continue, the Kid was called upon to fight.

When they saw it was a woman, Groundhog grunted, feeling it would be a wasted fight.

"I've seen her fight. She's exceptional. She has to be, to successfully compete at this level as a woman." The Frenchman scolded Groundhog for his immediate assumption. "And I think this Cisco Kid will have a problem striking a woman. Look at his face."

Groundhog saw he was right, and the fight did turn out to be exceptional. Later that night, over drinks in their suite, the Frenchman predicted the Kid was broken, desolate after killing a woman. Tomorrow, he would lose.

Groundhog demurred. "This may have been the event to put him over, give him the killing edge he obviously was lacking."

"Well, tomorrow we'll find out. A little wager to spice things up. The loser can buy dinner after my meeting."

Groundhog's interest perked up. "What do you think the job is?"

"Too soon to tell. Could be simple industrial espionage, could be a kill, anything between." The Frenchman wasn't one for speculating. "We'll know, soon enough.

The next day, Cisco Kid didn't disappoint them. After he left without bowing to the judges or referee, they exchanged speculative looks. The last fight of the day was almost anticlimactic, Chang easily besting his South African opponent.

The Frenchman gone to his meeting, Groundhog had a drink in the lounge of their hotel, brooding. The fights of the day had left him curiously unsettled. That, and he'd sensed something in the Frenchman's demeanor that he couldn't define. This meeting, of which Groundhog knew no details whatsoever, was troubling his mentor. Their arrangement was going on four years, and Groundhog had never seen him quite like this.

His cell phone rang, and he saw it was the Frenchman. "Meet me outside. I'm in the Citroen."

Twenty minutes later, they were parking in an alley near the waterfront. "Come, we have to check something." He led the way, walking briskly. Groundhog followed more cautiously, scanning the surrounding buildings and streets for potential threats. He caught up to the Frenchman as they reached an area dominated by private yachts. The older man had binoculars out, focused on one near the end of a pier. He slowly lowered them, and Groundhog saw doubt in his eyes.

"We will pass on this one." The Frenchmen's tone left no room for discussion, shaking his head even as Groundhog began to question him. "This job was presented as one thing, but the identity of the owner of that ship changes everything. The difficulties, dangers, complexities of working with certain people in the future, make this too costly, no matter what we charge." He turned, and Groundhog saw his true age show for the first time. "We walk away. I'll show you some of the details when we're safely gone."

"Away?" Groundhog asked as they walked back to the car.

"Yes, we leave for Zurich tonight. I'll return the retainer." The Frenchman tried to recover his usual aplomb. "I would have liked to stay and seen the matches tomorrow. Cisco Kid would have beaten Chang."

Groundhog shook his head, taking part in the conversation, but his mind racing ahead. "Chang is too good. He would have beaten the Kid, even before he lost his spirit today." He took it a step further, to keep the conversation going. "I could beat the Cisco Kid."

"You could kill him, certainly," the Frenchman acceded. "But in the arena, under those conditions, you could never beat that boy in a fight."

They reached the car, and the Frenchman had his keys out, as Groundhog disagreed. "I would win."

As his mentor shook his head in friendly dissent, Groundhog stepped in close and stabbed him in the back, aiming to sever the spine. Even distracted and off his game, the older man almost avoided the attack, causing the blade to nearly miss its target. But Groundhog was relentless, even as he twisted the blade to finish the job, his left hand came up, an identical small blade, barely two inches long, but almost as wide, thrusting up under the chin. He left the blades in place to keep blood from spurting as he lowered the body to the ground.

He pulled the first squat knife out, and used it to gouge both eyes, destroying them, making a retinal identification impossible. He pulled the keys free of the dead man's grasp and opened the trunk and went to work on the body. Twenty minutes later, he abandoned the vehicle, knowing that no identification could be made without any fingers to print, or eyes to scan.

Not that the Frenchman could be identified in any case. Both of them had destroyed traces of their past long ago. And there was no more chance of anyone tying him to the body left in the trunk, than of the car itself being connected to the two men sharing a suite at the Conrad Hong Kong.

Groundhog poured a cup of coffee and sipped it, ignoring the near boiling temperature. That had been a significant time in his life, and now he knew a significant fact, although he hadn't yet considered if, or how, to use it.

Jim Morris, the actor that reputedly couldn't fight, was the Cisco Kid.

◆ ◆ ◆ ◆ ◆

CHAPTER EIGHT

Aleutian Islands, Alaska

Kimberly and Kiri stood and watched the shuttle disappear into the early morning sky. It rapidly shrank to the size of a dot, then was gone.

"Well, that's that," Kiri said brightly, then rubbed her arms. "Brr, I wish I'd put more clothes on."

It was chilly, Kimberly admitted to herself. This remote island in the Aleutian chain that extended from Alaska nearly to Siberia was perfect for their purposes. Relatively near where the Jade Viking vanished, it was remote enough to land without much danger of being observed.

But all in all, she'd rather be in Florida, where the beaches were warm.

Calling this shore a beach was a stretch. It consisted of stones as small as fine gravel all the way up to rocks too big to be moved without heavy machinery.

Currently, it was strewn with people and their luggage. Most were digging into their suitcases for heavier clothing. A few lugged their things to higher ground to avoid the fine spray of salt water caused by waves crashing into huge boulders.

Kimberly was glad she'd packed jeans and a sweatshirt. In any case, the sun would be up soon, and two of the sailors were already walking to the tiny settlement on the far side of the island.

"Gosh, I just can't wait to get rescued!" Kiri and Kimberly grinned at each other, happy to be back on Earth!

Heck, Martin, you're almost home. Kimberly knew it would take hours for the authorities to react, and there would be questioning for a day or two. But then, home to her apartment in Manhattan.

Her own bathroom again. Her own bed!

Yvette and Janice stood a few feet away, tightly embraced with a blanket around them, and still looked like they were freezing. "M-m-man, this damp cold'll kill you every time," Janice managed to say, her teeth chattering.

"Are you okay?" Kimberly frowned. Janice couldn't seem to stop shivering and her lips looked blue. It didn't seem that cold, but then again, Janice was so thin, the brisk breeze off the water probably went right through her. "Aren't you from Michigan?"

"Different kind of cold," Janice snarled, then looked startled as Eric Miles put his heavy jacket around Janice's shoulders over the blanket.

"Here, this will help." She looked grateful as she pulled the collar of the denim jacket close around her neck. Yvette smiled her thanks.

Kimberly had talked to Miles several times on Station Chaq, and then again on the return voyage. He was quiet, but not afraid to speak his mind, and she'd grown to like him. She also suspected he would be invaluable in the months to come. He was a financial planner, and very methodical in the way he identified and attacked problems.

Linda and Ron Hoffman stood nearby, and she happily accepted her husband's jacket as he took the other man's cue. The Hoffmans hugged, and Kimberly smiled as she glanced from them to Yvette and Janice. Loving couples tended to have a lot in common, regardless of their sexual preference, she decided.

That thought reminded her of the unsettled state of her own marriage, and she felt her smile slip a little.

"Let me guess. Your thoughts are millions of miles away..., literally." Eric Miles said, startling her out of her reminiscing.

"Something like that," she admitted ruefully. "I'll see him again, soon enough."

"Yes, you will," he agreed in a firm voice. "In the meantime, there's work to do, and I would imagine a few loose ends from your old life to deal with."

"That's putting it mildly." Kimberly felt a smile tug at one corner of her mouth.

"Don't hesitate to call me if you need anything." He flinched as a wave crashed higher than usual, giving both of them a fine mist rinse. He gingerly moved farther from the sea. "I mean that. It doesn't have to be about work, either." He eyed her with a shrewd, but friendly smile.

"Sometimes, it helps to talk to someone removed from your daily routine."

Kimberly met his gaze. *Is he trying to pick me up?* "Thank you. I'll keep that in mind."

"You'll need to delegate, you know." His smile broadened. "Keep Kiri busy."

"I'll uh, do that." Kimberly stumbled on the words. "I guess you know she's traveling with me for a few weeks..." Her voice trailed off.

"Oh? I hadn't heard, but you two are obviously close." His voice held no recriminations. In fact, he seemed amused.

"Do I hear my name being taken in vain?" Kiri appeared at her side, and Kimberly felt her face redden. She was saved from having to reply.

"Coast Guard boat!" One of the sailors had been standing on a high rock watching the sea. He was jumping up and down excitedly, pointing to the south at a smudge coming around the island. How on earth could he tell it was the Coast Guard?

"Plane!" Another voice yelled out. As one, everyone strained their necks to see. Sure enough, a small dot quickly grew into a twin engine Cessna that dipped its wings and began to circle overhead.

Kiri had a huge grin and they laughed and hugged each other. Around them bedlam reigned, people laughing and crying at the same time, waving and cheering in excitement and relief.

Eric Miles stood alone, watching the impromptu celebration with a wistful expression. He had no one to share the moment with. Kiri reached over, pulled on his arm, and the two women hugged him.

"Thank you," he said quietly, his smile reappearing.

"Our pleasure," Kiri patted his arm.

"We're going home!"

❖ ❖ ❖ ❖ ❖

Jade Viking

There it was again!

Shinzo Takuan looked down at the deck, half expecting to see movement. The tremor had been slight, almost undetectable. No one else seemed to notice, so he said nothing.

Takuan was in one of the newly converted lounges, big enough to allow fifty or sixty people to sit and read, play board games, or even watch movies. At the moment, it was almost at capacity.

He began to rub his nose thoughtfully, but stopped himself in time. His nose was almost better, but still sensitive, as he noticed every time he sneezed, or forgot and rubbed it.

He looked around for familiar faces. There were a few Sukuru employees that studiously ignored him. He could care less. They would pay for their lack of loyalty when he finished his report to the home office.

A middle-aged man with a grim look on his face, happened to make eye contact with him. They stared at each other. On a hunch, Takuan nodded in a friendly manner. The other man stiffened, then relaxed and nodded back.

This American was the one that had spoken out against the plan to stay at the station, arguing bitterly with the captain.

Perhaps this man could be of use. Takuan looked around to see if any of the people clearly loyal to the captains were watching. He didn't see any, and rose to speak to the teacher.

Then he stopped, confused. None appeared to be present. When was the last time he'd seen anyone he was sure was an enemy?

Takuan wasn't sure what this meant, but it had to be important.

❖ ❖ ❖ ❖ ❖

"All shuttles back aboard, sir."

Captain Tachibana took one last look at the screen. Earth hung in space, agonizingly close. He gave a mighty sigh.

"Take us out to the far side of the moon. Slow and easy. Maintain stealth cloaking."

❖ ❖ ❖ ❖ ❖

Sasama Sakakibara looked across the calm waters of Lake Tahoe. The sun to his left was just high enough to make the water glow in rich, golden hues. A few ambitious early morning risers tried to encourage their sails to catch what little breeze there was at this hour. They would never know how close they had come to seeing their first UFO.

One of the shuttles for Jade Viking had dropped him and Iori Kojiro here at Jim's cabin. Three stories tall, built into the side of the hill that rose steeply from the water on the eastern shores of the lake, it had eight bedrooms and four full bathrooms.

Cabin, indeed.

He'd been here last winter for one of Jim's parties. It had impressed him then, and it impressed him now. The key was right where he'd been told it would be, cars were in the garage.

Sasama smirked. Of the four teams secretly dropped off in addition to the main party, Iori and he definitely had the best assignment. They would stay here, watch the news, decide on a course of action after they saw what kind of reception the survivors of the Jade Viking received.

In the meanwhile, a beer sounded pretty good.

◆ ◆ ◆ ◆ ◆

"You don't remember anything?"

Kimberly pretended to concentrate, then shrugged her shoulders in defeat.

"I'm sorry, but I can't." She allowed a little frustration to enter her voice. "The last thing I remember was after the cocktail party, on my way back to my cabin." She tried to look perplexed. "I don't remember getting there, though."

The FBI agent was named Karl Costa. Call me KC, he'd said when they met.

He and a large contingent of agents had arrived in force almost as quickly as Kimberly's group had been transferred across the island. A number of tents had been erected near the tiny cluster of small houses that constituted the entire population of Semisopochno Island. It was in one of these that Kimberly now found herself with Agent Costa.

His initial friendly manner had deteriorated to one of disbelief and poorly masked suspicion. "Ms. Martin, there are almost two months during which you claim you can't remember a single thing. That seems... unlikely."

"Are you calling me a liar?" Kimberly asked in a frosty voice. "What about the others? What do they remember?"

"Nothing." Costa leaned back in his folding chair and eyed her thoughtfully. "Not a blessed thing."

"Well, there you are," Kimberly said, giving one of her 'dumb blonde' smiles. "I really don't know what else I can tell you, Mr. Costa."

The government agent picked up a clipboard and gestured with it.

"These are search reports. Planes, boats, people on foot all searched this island weeks ago. You know what they found?"

Kimberly shook her head.

"Not a damn thing!" Costa visibly calmed himself, then continued. "You weren't there four weeks ago. This morning we find, not just the nine hundred and eighty-three of you, but your luggage as well." He waved the clipboard again.

"Maybe they weren't very thorough in their search," Kimberly said in a helpful voice.

"You're saying they just missed you?" Costa stared at her. "You were there the whole time?"

"What I'm saying is, I don't know, Mr. Costa." Kimberly put a little steel into her tone. "I've either been kidnapped, or the victim of some catastrophic, unexplainable event."

"Not just you," he countered. "There are still over two thousand people missing. Not to mention the ship itself!"

"I don't have it, Mr. Costa." Kimberly opened her purse and angled the opening so he could see inside. He pointedly ignored it "And I don't know where it is. Or the unfortunate people still missing. I wish I could help you, but I can't."

"Can't?" Costa almost snarled as he stood and leaned over table. "Or won't?"

Kimberly stood to meet him on a more level plane. "I believe we are finished here."

"We're finished when I say we are, Ms. Martin." His face began to turn a bright shade of red. "The FBI has a lot of flexibility when it comes to missing persons."

"Does it have the flexibility to change the constitution?" She spoke in clipped words, painstakingly enunciating each syllable. "Unless you are going to charge me with something, we are finished for the moment. You have a case you're trying to solve. I have six weeks missing from my life. Pardon me if I seem a little selfish."

He looked at her in silence for close to a minute, then nodded.

"You've been through a lot, Ms. Martin." Costa didn't sound sympathetic. "We may need to ask you some questions in a followup interview..."

"No problem," Kimberly smiled sweetly. "I believe you have my

Manhattan address."

She left the tent.

◆ ◆ ◆ ◆ ◆

Agent Costa sat back down and gazed thoughtfully after her. She was a beautiful woman, five foot four inches, blonde hair kept short and styled, a firm body that showed she probably played a lot of tennis. And she was a liar.

"You believe her, sir?" His junior agent sounded skeptical.

"She's a lawyer. She wouldn't know the truth if it came up and slapped her silly."

"I don't know what she knows," Costa finally admitted. "She's hiding something. The luggage found matches the people on the beach. Do you have any idea the odds against that if there was a ship wreck, or a..."

"Or a what, sir?" His young assistant had an annoying habit of asking tough questions.

"I have no fucking idea," he muttered, louder than he'd intended. Sighing, he came to a decision. "Patch me through to the Sacramento office. This is way out of my pay scale."

◆ ◆ ◆ ◆ ◆

Glowing Mist

Matt and Teresa paused at the entrance to the bridge. Captain Cromar Try and Siph Carni sat at the command module, talking. Her hand rested lightly on his leg. Off to the left, Du Brimar sat at his work station, deeply engrossed in some task. Jo Coran stood next to him, looking over his shoulder. Matt cleared his throat.

"May we come on the bridge?"

Jo Coran straightened and looked at her captain, who nodded. Matt and Teresa approached Cromar Try.

"We wanted to ask you something." Matt's voice sounded hoarse to him, and it was with difficulty that he resisted clearing his throat again. The captain regarded him with a impassive expression. "Uh, sir."

135

Cromar Try smiled mirthlessly. "You want to know if we're going to kill you?"

Teresa took a quick little breath, and Matt felt his spine stiffen, but refused to show fear. He nodded. "Yes, something like that."

Cromar stared at him and Matt resisted the urge to shift back and forth on his feet. He returned the stare, trying to keep any hint of emotion from showing. Finally, Siph Carni pushed on the captain's leg reprovingly. "Cromar..."

The alien, and for the first time since he'd awakened on this ship they <u>seemed</u> like aliens to Matt, patted her hand in an absentminded manner.

"We aren't going to kill you," Cromar Try admitted. "I considered if it would help to take you back with us. But I don't think it would change anything."

Matt felt his head spin at the thought of traveling to another planet. To be the first human...but then he remembered, he wouldn't be the first human to set foot on another planet.

"When we've finished our search, we'll drop you off wherever you would like." Cromar Try smiled, obviously trying to lighten the mood. "It might be a good opportunity for you to see some part of the world you haven't been to yet."

"Aren't you afraid we'll tell the authorities about our abduction?" Teresa sounded skeptical.

Du Brimar chuckled at her words. "Who would believe you?"

"And what if they did?" Siph Carni asked in a gentle voice. "Whatever action the Emperor decides to take, there won't be much your people can do about it. You would never know if we actually returned or not." She paused. "Until it was too late."

Matt looked at her with wide eyes. Gradually she became a blur as he stared beyond her, beyond Cromar Try, the screen on the wall, past the planet shining on the screen, to the future. He was distantly aware that he was nodding, and that the Egelv were looking at him with concern.

"How long?" It took a moment to realize that the voice asking the question was his own.

"How long until we let you go? A few days at most." Cromar Try nodded in sudden comprehension. "Oh, that." He looked at Siph Carni questioningly.

"Three or four days to Station Chaq, see what the situation is, return to Egelv, another twelve to fifteen days..." She shrugged. "Anywhere between one and three months to return to Earth in force." She looked at Du Brimar. "We'd probably have to do something about Station Chaq..."

"We could take care of that when we leave here." Du Brimar answered her unasked question. "That way, there's less chance of any of the hijacked prisoners being moved already."

"That's true," Siph Carni agreed, oblivious to the disbelieving stares she was getting from Matt and Teresa.

"Hold on there, varmint," Du Brimar spoke suddenly. He cocked his head, evidently listening to some report with his personal link to the computer. "They just found some survivors to the Jade Viking."

Matt and Teresa looked at each other in sudden hope. Cromar Try saw their faces and raised a hand. "This doesn't change anything. The Ananab know about your planet, even if they didn't take the ship. And this is still the world that bred the Hashir."

Du Brimar looked at his screen and frowned. "I'm almost certain I looked there..." He touched the controls lightly and mumbled under his breath. Then he nodded in triumph.

"I thought so." He looked around the room at his impatient audience. "Yesterday I did a quick search of surrounding islands and such, trying to see if there was any sign of survivors."

"And..." Cromar Try looked impatient.

Du Brimar looked at his captain apologetically. "I thought maybe we were not thorough enough, and premature in our conclusions. Maybe if the Ananab didn't have any hard data on the Humans..."

Cromar Try gave him a contemplative look, and he hastened to continue. "And nothing. I scanned every island in the Aleutians. Absolutely no sign of survivors. We'll be in direct line in about twenty minutes. I'll check again."

"Well." Cromar Try leaned back in his seat and cupped his hands behind his head. He stared up at the ceiling thoughtfully.

Siph Carni watched her mate and groaned. "He's got that look."

"Yeah," Du Brimar said, wincing. "And that usually means more work for me."

"May you live in interesting times." Matt was sick of this supercilious piece of shit . The Second Officer looked at him, not understanding the reference. He mumbled for a moment, then his look of uncertainty deepened.

"Chinese proverb, early..." He cocked his head, looking at Matt. "Is that good or bad?"

Matt smiled, a thin parody of the real thing, to be sure, but a smile, nonetheless.

"Yes."

◆ ◆ ◆ ◆ ◆

CHAPTER NINE

Station Osaka

Governor Lang gave Lasty a dark look. I'm sunk, he thought with disgust. He's got it, and he's going to give it to me. And there's not a blasted thing I can do about it.

Across the table, Randy Luca gave him a sardonic smile. The ex-purser made a show of looking at his hand, then laid a card face up on the table with a flourish.

Ten of spades.

Lang winced. I'm right. Definitely sunk.

To his right, Lasty groaned as he peered at his hand. The Baerd was terrible at disguising his feelings. Of course, a racial tendency to turn bright red at any hint of excitement or emotion didn't help. His skin was albino white, and when he blushed, it was spectacular.

Lasty shifted his cards from lower left hand to lower right, all the while scratching his head with his upper left forefinger. Reluctantly, he laid the queen of spades on top of the ten. In the game of Hearts, the queen of spades was worth thirteen points. And, of course, the idea was to keep the score down. Low man wins.

Lang looked at Randy, who returned his stare with the serene smile of a man who knew he was in full control.

"Problem, Sir?" The purser's voice was so innocent sounding, both Lasty and James McGregor, the fourth member of their "friendly" little game looked at him in surprise. Then, as one, they swung back around to their Captain.

"Problem? No, no problem," Lang said dryly. "Though I believe I said I could use a few pointers, not points." He tossed his last spade, the king, onto the table.

It didn't help any when Lasty gave a big sigh of relief.

McGregor grunted in exasperation and scooped the loose cards up, using his ace of spades as a shovel.

"I think someone at this table has played a little more than he let on," McGregor spoke accusingly. "I thought we sent all the riverboat gamblers back to Earth, sir?"

Lang laughed, relieved at not getting stuck with the queen. "I think you might have something there, Sergeant. Randy, you're not thinking to turn these wagers into hard cash at some point, are you?"

They had started recording the scores after each game, joking that each point represented a dollar. At the rate they were going, the captain and Lasty would owe the other two men new cars if they ever got back to Earth.

"By the way, Captain," Randy spoke without looking up. "Both Jade Wolverine and the new warship are finished. The Hoag finished installing the last weapons pods this morning."

Lang grimaced. "And we can't finish the second warship until we get more computers and munitions.

"We have everything we need at this station to manufacture anything from a hand weapon up to and including, a moderate sized ship," Lasty said. "As long as we have sufficient raw materials and the necessary components for intricate machinery."

"Easier said than done." Randy frowned. "We're going to have to come up with something of value to use as trade goods."

"The defense grid is about as good as it can be made, considering whoever designed this station didn't know squat about fortifications." Understandably, with his background as an Army sergeant, James McGregor was focused more on the military issues than the economic. He laid a three of hearts.

Excellent, Lang thought. My five should be good unless the distribution is perfectly even. Randy just smiled at them as he slipped a deuce under the three. Lasty groaned and played his four. Muttering to himself, Lang flipped his five on top of the little pile. That was dumb, he realized. He should have thrown his highest heart if he was taking the trick anyway.

Four points, Lang sighed. At least he could get rid of the lead now.

There was only one heart left lower than his seven. He laid the card, and leaned back in his chair to watch the others try and scramble to avoid taking the hand.

McGregor casually tossed out a queen of diamonds.

"No hearts?" Lang said, feeling a sinking sensation. McGregor silently shook his head. The sensation grew as Randy played a six of hearts. One look at Lasty, and Lang couldn't resist a groan. The Baerd threw another diamond and answered for both himself and McGregor.

"No more hearts."

"Lang looked at his hand and sighed. He suspected he was stuck, and it was quickly confirmed as Luca answered his nine of hearts with an eight. "I believe I have the rest."

The others made a show of checking their cards for points. Luca's voice was deadpan as he recorded their scores.

"Let's see, Lasty, nothing for you? Uh huh. James, me boyo, I believe you had just the one card? Thirteen for you. And I had...none. Let's see Captain, that would give you..."

"All right, all right," Captain Lang grumbled. "I had thirteen. Your deal, Lasty."

As the Baerd began carefully shuffling the deck, Lang looked over at Luca. "You're killing me, Randy."

"Just be thankful we're not letting that little Riahi girl in this game. Talk about card shark..." The purser gave a mock shudder.

"Amen to that." McGregor's voice was forceful and Lang looked at him in surprise.

"Sergeant, I'm shocked." He smiled to show he wasn't really. "I thought you liked her."

"After watching the way she manipulates Jim and those teenage boys, the last thing I want to do is play a gambling game with her. I know my limitations."

They all laughed, Lasty a little hesitantly.

"So you do not like the daughter of Jim Morris?" he asked, looking puzzled.

"It's not that at all, Lasty." Lang smiled and the Baerd looked reassured. "I don't know how your race deals with sexuality, but we generally make a complete mess of it. And that 'little girl' embodies everything that leads normal men into acts of insanity."

Lasty blushed bright red. "My race...ah...abstains while in space.

Um, usually." He busied himself dealing the next hand. "This hand is... pass three cards to the right."

The three humans looked at each other in amusement. Then, as one, their attention swung back to the dealer.

"Usually?" Randy had a perfect poker face.

"Um...yes, usually." Lasty's blush began working its way down over his chest and shoulders. Lang watched in fascination.

"Tell us more, Lasty," Randy purred. "Tell us about the...unusual."

"Hmmm?" Lasty finished dealing and picked up his cards. He made a show of looking at them and shifting them around with his lower hands. "Oh, it's...unusual when we don't do the... usual thing." He smiled a bright red smile around the table without focusing on anyone. "Which is, of course, nothing at all," he finished in a hurried tone.

His blush deepened and continued to spread downward. Captain Lang decided to have mercy on him, but before he could say anything, Randy got another question in.

"And in your case...?" The purser had a pretty good poker face of his own.

"That would be the...unusual choice." Lasty counted out three cards and slid them over to Luca. He kept his eyes on his hand. "Two of clubs leads."

Lang and the other two men belatedly picked up their cards and began sorting through them. He gave Luca a stern stare and the purser looked embarrassed. "Whenever I play cards, my aggressive side pushes through. Sorry, Lasty."

The Baerd's blush began to recede up his chest. He shrugged. "It is easier to speak of these things with you than it is with my own people. You don't disapprove, you're just curious."

"Nosy would be more like it," Lang muttered, and McGregor nodded his agreement. He decided to change the subject. "Lasty, have you thought about returning to your home world?"

"I would like to," Lasty admitted. "Dutter and I are in an awkward position, and nothing will be settled until we go back and face our families."

"You don't think they'll accept your union?" Captain Lang asked.

"It's not a feud like the Hatfield and McCoys, or Romeo and Juliet, is it?" Randy leaned forward in anticipation. Almost as an afterthought, he placed three cards in front of McGregor, who frowned at them.

"Chief..." Lang began in exasperation.

"No, that is okay," Lasty spoke almost eagerly. "Dutter and I have been unable to discuss this with any of our own people. Our families hardly even know each other, but we were both betrothed before we left Baerd."

"But not to each other..." Randy quipped, then quickly tossed out the two of clubs as Lang glared at him.

"That is true," Lasty admitted. Lang watched in fascination as the blush stopped retreating. *I'm surprised these people don't wear long robes with high collars, instead of their usual vest and baggy shorts.* Lasty followed suit with the king of clubs.

"Is it because you didn't wait and ask for permission?" Lang hoped he wasn't prying.

"That is not an option." The Baerd projected his frustration as he scooped up the four clubs and played a jack of spades. "Unions are decided early, by elder decisions. When we return to Baerd, the first thing that will happen is we'll be separated, brought up on charges..."

"Excuse me?" McGregor sat upright. He had just taken the last trick of cards, but forgot about that as he stared at Lasty. The sergeant's face reddened. "Charges? For falling in love?"

Lasty flinched even though he knew the anger wasn't directed at him. "Yes, it is forbidden to partake in any sexual activity while in service of the Ananab, or any other race."

"No nookie?" This came from Randy. Lang and McGregor both glared at him. "I'm sorry! Sorry! Poor choice of words on my part."

"I should say so." Lang transfixed him with a steely gaze. McGregor nodded his agreement.

"I know what it's like to have a relationship that isn't approved. My wife is Korean." His deep voice was bitter, and Lang glanced at him, shocked. He'd never heard McGregor speak of this. Everything was always business, or tactics in their conversations. The 'gentle giant', as people called him, looked anything but gentle, at the moment.

"When I met Eun Joo Sung, her family hated me at first sight." McGregor selected a card and tossed it on the table. Lang wouldn't have bet one way or the other whether the huge man even knew what it was. Randy hurried to follow suit. "They forbade us to see each other, accused her of being pregnant."

He stopped and visibly pulled himself back into tight control. He gave a mirthless grin around the table. "At that point, we'd never done more than kiss. I told my family about her. Their first thoughts were that she had trapped me."

McGregor scooped another trick and led again. Lang started as he realized he had no idea what card he had just played.

"Uh, James..." he hesitantly began, not wanting to interrupt.

"You played the seven of clubs," McGregor read his mind and continued his story without a miss in the beat. "They were sure she was pregnant." He gave a harsh laugh. "They never bothered to ask if we'd even slept together..."

McGregor had led a spade, and Lang smiled inside as he watched Randy and Lasty play harmless small cards. With a sigh of relief, he played his ace of spades.

"But we have slept together!" Lasty cried out, revealing his inner pain. "Baerd don't do that..."

"Bull!" Randy was blunt. "When the attraction is there, it will happen. Maybe not when or where you expect it, but it will happen."

"That's absolutely correct," Lang agreed. "James, you defied the prejudices of both your families. Lasty, you ignored a social rule to follow a stronger calling." He smiled in sympathy at the anguished alien.

"You fell in love." He played a low diamond.

"There are very good reasons we don't procreate in space." Lasty rubbed his eyes, and Lang realized Humans and Baerd had at least one more thing in common, crying.

"What reasons?" McGregor demanded.

Lang started to protest, but Lasty answered the sergeant. "As you've noticed, we have a very difficult time hiding our feelings. Our passions run strong." As if on cue, the red began creeping back down over his shoulders.

McGregor played another low diamond and Randy followed suit with the ace.

Lasty suddenly smiled at the purser, then put the queen of spades on Randy's ace.

Lang snorted, and McGregor twisted his lips, then released a snicker of his own.

"Go on," Lang encouraged Lasty as Randy brooded over his cards.

"When we were first taken by the Hstahni, they stole a number of our young. A decree was passed secretly. There would be no off planet births. The only way to insure that is abstinence." He shrugged his shoulders weakly. "We seem to be a very fertile race."

"Is Dutter...?" Lang stopped, at a loss for a comfortable way to ask the question.

"No, and probably the only good luck I've had since we found your race," Lasty admitted.

"But, you've got a unique position in the history of your people," Randy protested as he laid the six of hearts. "You set your people free. You found the, the...Chammorz!"

"Or, I set the Ananab, Tryr, Srotag, and the Hstahni on my people by being part of this rebellion." Resignation showed in Lasty's face as he lay a smaller heart, the two.

"Lasty, our experience in the universe is limited." Lang played his four. "But one thing I'm sure of. The drive to safeguard one's race through procreation is a strong one, maybe the strongest. You were following the instincts of millions of years of evolution."

"Do you think so?" Lasty didn't sound convinced.

"Listen to the Captain, Lasty." McGregor smiled, and the bitterness of moments ago was gone. "My wife and I are starting a new life here at Station Osaka, and so can you." He tossed a five of hearts down. Randy scooped the four points up and led the eight of diamonds.

"My parents weren't going to give us a very warm welcome when we got home. Eun Joo's family cast her out." McGregor's face was stony and expressionless, but his voice was impassioned. "Be the first in your race to embrace freedom. Lead your people by example."

"Do you really think so?" Lasty looked encouraged by McGregor as he played a heart on Randy's diamond lead. The purser grimaced.

"Absolutely!" McGregor bent forward over the table. "We have a home here. Four hundred years ago, my people would have embraced this cause with bagpipes."

Lang stared, open mouthed. This was a new side of James McGregor. He spoke as he also threw a heart, having no diamonds. "James, I've never heard you like this."

McGregor proceeded to show the Baerd weren't the only ones capable of blushing. "Ah, Sir. I'm sorry I spouted off like that..."

"Don't be ridiculous," Lang protested. "Your beliefs are part of your strength. And believe me, we'll need that strength in the days to come."

"That's right," agreed Randy. "We can't expect to have Jim carry us all. We have to be our own pillars."

Captain Lang didn't begrudge any admiration for the actor, or belittle anything Jim had done but, by damn, there was more to this than kicking the crap out of aliens and traitors.

It wasn't just battle. They were building something here, too. Something very precious.

He realized the table was very still, and he started. "Is it my play?" But the cards on the table were the same ones that had been there a moment ago.

"Captain, I didn't mean that exactly the way it came out..." Randy began.

"Nonsense," Lang hid his feelings. "Jim saved us a dozen times over the last few months. I'd be an idiot not to see that."

"That's not what he means." McGregor's voice was gentle. "I know when I said a leader, I meant you. Jim's more like a..." The sergeant stopped, at a loss for the right word.

"Almost more like a warlord, or a shogun," Randy chipped in.

"That's it!" McGregor nodded his head furiously. "You are our spiritual and social leader. That includes politics, no matter how unspiritual or social they might be. But he's our center of focus on the war front. The Romans had their equivalent, as did the Japanese, the Chinese..."

"I know you don't believe in the legend, but he is the Chammorz," Lasty spoke almost apologetically. "For my people, he will be a spiritual center..."

"That's fine," agreed Mcgregor as he sat back down and selected a card from his hand. "He can be the rallying call for your entire race, and still be just a man. There are great men throughout history who inspired greatness in others. But they never quite fit in day-to-day life. We still need the leaders that can keep the trains running." Lang winced and McGregor shook his head disparagingly.

"I'm sorry, sir. A very bad example. Damn!"

They all started at his explosive expletive. He was staring at the seven of diamonds he had just laid. He looked at Lasty and Lang in consternation. "You're both short-suited in diamonds?"

"Oh, no!" Lasty moaned.

The three of them turned to look at Randy. He smiled benignly at them as he lay down his hand of solid diamonds. "Nobody has any? Oh, dear! I guess that means I shoot the moon. I think I'll take twenty-six points off my score. No, wait."

Randy pinched his lips together in mock-concentration as he added the scores. "If I add twenty-six to each of you instead...Lasty has one hundred and twelve. The Captain...has one hundred and four, and Mac has seventy-three." He paused for dramatic effect.

Lang shook his head in bemusement. No matter the topic of conversation, Randy had never veered from his path in the game. He scowled at the purser. "And...?"

"I have four," Randy beamed at them. "I win."

"Damn." McGregor shook his head in disgust. "While we were talking, he was scheming. He wins, again."

Randy flipped his notebook to the last page with a flourish. He leaned over it as he wrote, blocking their view of the figures.

"He's more devious than the Trixmae," Lasty complained.

McGregor stood up and put his hands on his hips. "Chief Purser Luca, I have serious questions regarding the integrity of our knowledge of your sordid past in regards to cards."

Lang looked at the tall sergeant in admiration. McGregor was letting loose tonight. That sentence would have been a tongue-twister for anyone."

Randy smirked again. "I may have played a little in college..."

"A little?" Lang protested. "Did you ever actually study?"

"I studied life," Randy blew on his fingers, rubbing them against his chest. "Okay, let's see..."

"We don't have to have a recap right now..." Lang began hurriedly.

"Sure we do," Randy argued. "Chief Technician Lasty, social and religious groundbreaker for the Baerd...has thirteen hundred and sixty-nine."

"I don't understand," Lasty looked at Lang. "How does he do it?" Lang shrugged.

"Not the best choice for advice, Lasty." Randy squinted at the numbers. "Governor Jason Lang has nine hundred and eighty-six."

"Still holding under a thousand," Lang tried to sound optimistic. McGregor snickered, drawing the pursers attention.

"Ah, yes. Staff Sergeant, Security Chief, Father, Husband, James McGregor, has six hundred and ninety-eight. Watch it big guy, You're crowding the big seven oh oh."

Lang rolled his eyes. Randy did love to ham it up. "We don't need to know your..."

"And..." Randy paused for dramatic effect. And to gloat, Lang thought. "I have...uh...sixty-four."

"Shaddap," McGregor glowered at him, then looked around the table down at the other two men. "I don't know why we put up with this."

"It is hard to explain," Lang agreed, then experimentally raised one eyebrow as he gazed across the table at Luca. The purser just smiled back enigmatically, then picked up the cards.

"Another game?"

"Sure," McGregor sat back down. "But it's the Governor's deal, not yours."

"I knew that," Randy hastened to say. "I was just keeping the cards warm."

"This game is not good for my self-image." Lasty shook his head as he shifted in his seat. "Do we pass across this time?"

Lang nodded as he began to shuffle. Randy grinned at them, then turned to Lasty.

"Now, about this...usual and unusual..."

The sound of a piano and voice wafted down the corridor, and Afsaneh cocked her head to listen. It had to be Daddy, uh, Jim.

She smiled to herself as she walked towards the music. Once she found out Pearl could tell her who her natural father was, it had only taken a week for her to give in to the temptation.

When she'd been a young girl, she'd fantasized that she would take Jim as a lover. Other times, when she was angry at Hakim, she had thought of Jim as a substitute father, never considering he actually was. He had always been an uncle in everything but fact.

And her only uncle. Her mother and most of her family had been killed in a bomb blast when Afsaneh was just an infant. Because of this, Hakim's family, still living in Iran had shied away from any contact, fearful of further retaliation by the terrorists responsible for the blast.

Afsaneh didn't find out about her mother's murder until she was ten. After much coaxing, Hakim had reluctantly told her the truth. She had been both furious and sorrowful to hear how the mother she couldn't really remember had died. Those...scum, had taken away any chance of her ever really knowing the woman that had brought her into the world.

Hakim and Jim had looked distraught as she ranted and raved about revenge. Finally, Hakim, without looking at Jim, had said it was taken care of.

Jim's face could have been carved from granite. Unmoving, expressionless, harder than the toughest steel. No amount of demanding or pleading would sway either of them. They just said that the people responsible for the bomb were dead, and that was that.

She still wasn't sure what Hakim had meant. But knowing more about the days of her conception and birth, she had a few ideas. One day, she would drag it out of Jim.

Afsaneh peered into the darkened room. Jim sat with his back to the door, playing one of the pianos salvaged from the original Jade Viking. He sang softly, and she could barely make out the words and melody.

She leaned against the doorframe, enjoying the old Elton John tune from the early seventies. It ended and she held her breath, hoping he wouldn't turn around. She hadn't heard him play since the last time they'd been in San Francisco, some months ago.

Jim ran his fingers up and down the keyboard, obviously improvising as he went. Finally, he settled into another old song by Cat Stevens. She drew closer to try and hear the words.

Afsaneh tried to remember what he had told her about silent movement. She moved without a discernable pattern, trying to stay out of his peripheral vision, listening all the while.

The song was about conflict between father and son, neither really seeing the others' point of view. Her eyes began to mist, and she stopped about eight feet behind him. The volume increased as he reached the final verse.

Afsaneh knew she was a handful, and not the kind Sean implied. She didn't always play fair with Jim, and hadn't with Hakim, either. A little twinge of guilt entered her mind.

"Hi Afsaneh."

With a start, she realized the song had ended. "How did you know?" she demanded.

Jim turned around in his seat and gave her a sardonic smile, raising the usual eyebrow. "Rhetorical question, I presume?"

"I suppose," Afsaneh came to sit next to him on the piano bench. Some of her earliest memories had been of sitting like this as he sang strange, beautiful songs to her. Of course, the other earliest memories of Jim were him teaching her to kick, box, and roll. She leaned her head against his shoulder, watching his hands as they rambled around the keys.

"I bought you that perfume, you'll recall," he said, giving away his detecting methods. "How did classes go today?"

Afsaneh made a face. "Boring, very boring. I mean, how crucial is English Literature? And government class? Oh, and chemistry has got me so excited I won't sleep tonight."

Jim smiled, his eyes never leaving the keyboard. The melody became whimsical, much lighter than when she'd found him.

"That one of yours?" she asked curiously.

He shook his head. "No, there was a guy that used to play all the smaller clubs in southern Michigan when Hakim and I were in school. I always wished I could write like him..."

Afsaneh was astonished. It had never occurred to her that Jim could be envious of anyone. "Did he ever make it big?"

"No, I don't think so," Jim answered. "I don't what happened ever to him. Probably moved to Florida..."

Afsaneh laughed. Growing up with Hakim and Jim, moving to Florida had always been the symbol of retirement, fading from sight. Where the average age was between fifty and death, as Jim put it. Of course, spring break in Pensacola would be okay...

"What's your day like tomorrow?" Jim surprised her with the question.

"School all afternoon," Afsaneh answered, then brightened. "Gunnery class at eleven."

"I hear you're getting pretty good..." Jim nudged her with an elbow.

Afsaneh blushed. It wasn't often she got praise for her efforts. Usually, it was just criticism. "Thanks," she said. "Why did you want to know about tomorrow?"

"Governor Lang and I are meeting in the morning." Jim stopped playing and put his arm around her shoulders. "It's time to decide on a the crew for Jade Wolverine."

"Really?" She sat up in excitement. "Can I be on it? What about Sean and Ellis? And Janey?"

"Whoa, slow down," Jim laughed. "Yes, you'll be registered as a gunner and assistant computer technician."

"Computer tech?" Afsaneh wrinkled up her nose. "Booorrrring."

"The ship is no good to anyone if we don't know how to use it," Jim reminded her. "That's why you take classes. Science to help understand the ship and universe around us, literature and social studies to understand ourselves. There's more to life than just war and boys."

"That's a crock," Afsaneh muttered, then repeated. "What about my friends?"

"Some of them might end up as crew," Jim said carefully. "Not necessarily all of them."

"They're some of the best gunners in training," Afsaneh pointed out. "You just don't like some of them. You don't like Sean."

"He's pretty brash," Jim admitted. "But it's not that I don't like him... it's, well, he's..." He seemed at a loss for words.

"Too much like you?" Afsaneh teased.

"Too much like me at one point in my life," Jim agreed. "He's still got a lot of growing up to do, and so do you. I hate having you grow up too fast. I know what I was looking for at his age..." Jim's face reddened.

Afsaneh kept the smile off her face. Jim had so much self-confidence and poise, he hardly ever blushed. Things that would get Hakim bright red would have Jim roaring in laughter.

"I"m not interested in Sean," she said coyly.

Jim looked relieved. "Really?"

"Really." Afsaneh giggled. "It's Ellis I'm really interested in. Sean's just a friend."

"Ellis?" Jim looked startled. "He's...a nice kid," he finished lamely.

"He's not a kid," Afsaneh reminded him.

"To me, he is," Jim shot back. "And so are you. It doesn't mean you aren't growing up, very fast. But he's a kid that would have gone to college last week. And you're fifteen, with a couple of years of high school to go."

He stopped and took a deep breath, then continued in a softer tone.

"Look, I do like Ellis. I just ask that you don't let anything get out of control. Don't hurry things. Believe me, life will zip by fast enough." Jim frowned. "Uh, maybe you should ask...damn! Every blasted female we know is back on Earth, or on the way."

Afsaneh put her hand on his arm. "Father, don't worry. I've read the book, I know about the birds and bees, and I'll be careful. I really don't want to settle for just one boy, right now, anyway."

Jim whipped his head around, then smiled in relief when he saw she was grinning at him.

"That's supposed to make me feel better?," he grumbled, his inherent good humor showing through. "You're driving me crazy!"

"Short trip," she advised him, then shrieked in laughter as he began tickling her. "No, stop, stop, please?" She grabbed his arm and held on, trying to keep his fingers from her sensitive ribs.

With a grin, he stood up and held his arm out to the side. She hung on for dear life, giggling all the while. He used to do this all the time when she was young, but it had been years.

"Okay, okay, enough," she gasped. "Put me down."

He lowered his arm until her feet touched the deck. She immediately let go and slugged him in the gut.

Afsaneh backed away from him warily. With a sniff, she straightened her clothes. "That's no way to treat a lady."

"Uh huh," Jim snorted. "No comment."

"Are you done playing piano?" Afsaneh asked. "If so, I have a little free time and wouldn't mind beating you at a few games of ping pong."

Jim cocked his head at her. "You are either kidding or delusional."

Afsaneh knew that there were going to be more conversations like this. But, if only for the moment, they were at peace. She hooked her arm in his.

"Vee shall zee, daddy-o. Vee shall zee."

CHAPTER TEN

San Francisco, California

The sound of the jet engines increased in pitch, signifying the eminent departure of the flight. A few people scurried to the gate, but most passengers were already aboard. One straggling group hung back, trying to cram more time into last minute goodbyes.

Kimberly stood talking with Ron Hoffman while a few feet away, Kiri, Yvette, Janice, and Linda all seemed to be speaking simultaneously. The two of them watched with amusement.

"Well, Linda seems to have made some new friends," Ron said dryly. "That's never been one of her strong points."

"We all like her," Kimberly said honestly.

"Even after her first impression?" Ron asked shrewdly.

Kimberly blushed. Hoffman obviously knew his wife well. "It wasn't that bad..." she began, but stopped at his broad, knowing smile. "Okay, maybe a little. But when we got to know her, she fit right in."

"It seems that way." The man looked at the four gabbing women and shook his head. "Not in a million years..." He stopped in embarrassment.

"What?" Kimberly asked, and immediately regretted it.

"Well, I, uh, don't know exactly how to say this." He searched for words. "The last few evenings, she's been going to the gym to ride the bike, then hit the hot tub, and doesn't come back to our room for hours. And when she does, she's been more than a little drunk."

"Oh?" Kimberly stalled, trying to decide what to say.

"Now, don't get me wrong, I'm not complaining," he continued.

"Oh?" Kimberly couldn't think of anything else to say.

Ron blushed. "At our age, getting us on the same page, in the mood and physically, isn't always easy. Linda hasn't been as...eager, or interested, the past few years. That's changed."

"Oh?" Kimberly felt like a broken record.

Ron shook his head. "She was..." He stopped and gave her a wry smile. "She says that you ladies get together in the gym, and that y'all've made her feel right at home." His expression became shrewd. "She doesn't usually get along all that well with other women, you know."

"Oh?" Kimberly said weakly.

"I doubt I'll ever know exactly what..." he began, than looked at her expectantly.

"No." Kimberly didn't give him the slightest opening.

He held up one hand and grinned. "Don't worry, I'm not pumping you. Well, not too much. I guess you know those two are a couple in every sense of the word?" He pointed at Yvette and Janice.

"Well, yeah." Kimberly's mind raced. "It's no secret..."

"It doesn't matter," Ron smiled as he bent over to pick up his briefcase. "The important thing is, my wife is happy, and it hasn't taken a thing away from our relationship." He beamed. "In fact, it's added quite a bit." He winked. "Know what I mean?"

Kimberly laughed nervously, and nodded. She started as he leaned forward to whisper to her.

"By the by, you might wanna watch out." He pointed at Kiri with his head. "I think that little filly's got her eyes on you...and this is San Francisco, you know."

Kimberly watched open mouthed as Hoffman collected his wife and they boarded their plane. After a moment, Yvette and Janice joined her and she gave them a final hug. "We'll see you in a week or so." Yvette had tears in her eyes as she spoke.

"That'll be great," Kimberly said, meaning it. "Janice, get your hand off my butt."

The four of them broke into laughter, then it was just Kiri and Kimberly watching their friends board their plane.

"Let's get a taxi and get to Jim's condo," Kiri sighed.

"Sounds like a plan," Kimberly agreed fervently.

"Ron and you seemed to be in a deep conversation," Kiri said. "What was that all about?"

"I'll tell you over a drink and a hot meal," Kimberly said, thinking of all the things she'd missed for the last few months. "And a bath."

"A hot bath," Kiri grinned. "I'll wash yours if you'll wash mine?"

Kimberly groaned, both at the thought of the bath, and Kiri's persistence.

"We'll see."

Lake Tahoe, Nevada

This is the life, Sasama marveled. He sat in a recliner lounge chair on Jim's screened porch, his feet propped up. Next to him, in a rocking chair, Iori snored softly. A radio could faintly be heard from inside.

He knew it wouldn't last, but they were making the most of the situation while they could. They were leaving tonight, heading for either San Francisco or Seattle, depending on the ladies.

Sasama eyed the empty blender with regret. Another frozen daquiri would be delicious, but if he was driving, out of the question. Plus, he would have to get out of the recliner.

"Sasama, can you hear this transmission?" Jade Viking's computer spoke into his ear via earring transceiver. "Please answer if you can."

"Jade Viking, this is Sasama," he said, sitting up and shaking Iori awake. "Go ahead."

"Mr. Sakakibara." Captain Tachibana's voice replaced the computer's. "Ms. Martin and Ms. Oshiba are on their way to Jim's condo in San Francisco. Do you know the address?"

Sasama nodded, then realized his mistake and spoke out loud. "Yes, and there's a small hotel nearby we can get a room at."

"Very good, Mr. Sakakibara. You will probably be visited by Mr. Soshami." The captain's voice warmed a little. "Please be careful. And do try and be inconspicuous."

Sasama smiled. "You can count on it, Sir."

"Very good." Tachibana was all business now. "Jade Viking out."

Sasama turned to Iori, who was watching intently. "San Francisco, Jim's condo."

"Okay," Iori nodded, getting stiffly to his feet. "Which vehicle we taking?"

Sasama looked at him gravely. "Captain Tachibana told us to be discreet."

Iori nodded, equally grave. "So, our choice is a silver and blue four-

155

wheel drive Jeep Cherokee with all the extras." He paused for effect. "Or, a candy-red 1997 Dodge Viper GTS."

They looked at each other for a moment, then grinned and spoke in unison.

"The Viper."

Jade Viking

Shinzo Takuan set his empty bowl down. That was exceptional soup, he thought. It's amazing what you can do with tofu and a little imagination.

He watched an older couple sitting at the next table. They had already finished their meal and were relaxing, sipping their iced teas. The man's head was bobbing slightly, and he yawned. The woman, presumably his wife, elbowed him, then yawned herself.

Takuan suppressed the urge to do the same, grimacing. More addictive or suggestive than the strongest drug, his mother used to say.

He noticed a young girl nearby actually sleeping with her head on the table. Her parents were shaking her gently. There was no response and the mother made a joke to her husband, then put her own head down.

A waiter passing by stopped in time to catch the old man at the next table as he tried to rise to his feet. The young waiter gently lay him on the floor, then hurried to another drowsy diner.

Belatedly, Takuan realized that people were collapsing all around the room. Waiters and sailors were spread out, presumably to keep anyone from being hurt by a fall. He looked at his empty soup bowl in chagrin.

Drugged!

They'd been dru...

San Francisco, California

Kiri grinned from across the vast expanses of the bathtub. Soap bubbles covered her clear up to her chin. Her wet, black hair clung to her skull, the ends disappearing into the thick layer of bubbles that floated on the water.

Kimberly gasped. "Oh, right there! That's the spot. Harder!"

"Will power of Jello," Kiri snickered, obeying. "How's that?"

Kimberly answered her with a low moan. God, that felt great! Kiri knew every button to push, she conceded. I've got to quit putting myself into these situations. I should make her stop, this very moment...

Without warning, Kiri changed from a strong, deliberate stroke to a feathery light touch, and Kimberly shuddered at the sensation overload.

"Oh, my God!" Her voice was barely below a scream. "Stop, stop, oh please?"

With a gasp, Kimberly pulled her foot away. Kiri giggled as she reluctantly released her grasp. "What'sa matta, round-eyes? You ticklish?"

"On the bottom of my feet?" Kimberly gave her an incredulous look. "Isn't everybody?" She pulled her feet up beneath her so Kiri couldn't reach them.

"Wait, did you hear that?" Kiri sat up straight, soap suds providing very little cover.

"Quit it," Kimberly scoffed. Kiri was clever, no doubt about it. But no way was she going to fall for that old trick.

"No, I mean it," Kiri insisted. "Listen."

Kimberly looked at her friend skeptically, then started. She did hear someone or thing in the next room. Their eyes met, and without a word, both carefully rose, trying not to splash the bath water.

They quickly pulled their robes on and began to move to the door. As they did, there was a thump, and the sound of a voice quietly cursing.

Kiri pointed and Kimberly nodded. She took hold of the doorknob and, as Kiri signaled, pulled the door inward, stepping behind it out of Kiri's way. The young Japanese woman launched herself forward into the person standing just outside.

The man grunted and fell backwards, Kiri knocking him to the ground. She ended up straddling him in the hallway, her right fist poised to strike. Kimberly rushed forward to see the intruder's identity.

Kabu Soshami smiled weakly up at them. Kimberly and Kiri gaped. "Kabu, what the hell are you doing here?" Kiri asked for both of them.

"Ah, good to see you again, too," he joked, then smiled wryly. "Kiri, don't think I'm not enjoying this, but we both know it wouldn't work. Plus, you're getting me all wet."

Kiri blushed and hurriedly stood, releasing him. Kabu looked down at himself, ruefully. His entire crotch and midsection were soaking wet from where she had sat. Kiri pulled her robe back into the proper position, muttering to herself.

"Don't you believe in knocking?" Kimberly demanded. "The FBI might be watching us, you know."

"They might," Kabu agreed. "But they aren't right now. And, as for what I'm doing here, I believe you might need these at some point." He handed her a sheathe of papers. "Your marriage certificate, papers granting you power of attorney for Jim, Captain Lang, others. And a bunch of other legal stuff, equally interesting, I'm sure."

"Thanks," Kimberly said, feeling his curious gaze as he surveyed their state of dress and the full tub visible through the open door. She blushed as she thought about what was probably going through his head. She heard Kiri snicker and sighed. No point in even trying to correct his interpretation of the situation.

"Any other news?" she asked, glancing towards the door meaningfully. He took the cue.

"Ah, no, that about does it." He appeared to be struggling inside about whether to make any comment or not. "I guess I'm off to connect up with Eric Miles in San Diego. Oh, I'll be taking Jim's mini RV." He grinned a crooked grin at them. "That'll leave you the sports car."

He left and they looked at each other, bemused, dripping water on the carpet in the hall.

Kiri grinned. "Tub's still hot and waiting."

Kimberly frowned unconvincingly, then gave her friend a questioning look.

"Do I have a sports car?"

Aleutian Islands, Alaska

Howard Prause groaned and tried to turn onto his side. Something hard stuck into his hip, and he opened his eyes.

He was laying on a rocky shore, one of his suitcases acting as a pillow. Bewildered, he sat up and looked around. Hundreds of people were awakening up and down the beach.

He saw what looked like pine trees nearby and felt a sense of relief. They had to be on Earth, but why had he been unconscious? The last thing he remembered was eating dinner.

He glanced at the luggage piled next to him. It appeared that all of his stuff was here and, from the piles of suitcases littering the ground around them, so was everyone else's.

Twenty yards down the shoreline, a Japanese man climbed to his feet, staring around wildly. He began to scream in his native language, whirling around in a complete circle.

Howard didn't know Japanese, but that sounded like cursing. Perhaps he should say something to the man. After all, there were women and children present.

Howard Prause stiffened in shock, and staggered to his feet, staring around furiously.

"Seniors from Vista Chula! Sound off! Seniors..." He stopped, beaten.

Tricked.

CHAPTER ELEVEN

Glowing Mist

Cromar Try sat brooding, staring at the multiple screens in front of him. He hadn't moved in several hours.

Earlier, Du Brimar had brought hard copy printouts of the Aleutian Islands, but Cromar Try barely glanced at them. Du Brimar hastily retreated to his work station and became engrossed in some task.

Matt stretched wearily. They had been on the bridge for hours. Teresa was scanning a computer screen Siph Carni had reluctantly allowed her access to. The Egelv woman had pointedly locked her out of all files except an educational series she had assured Teresa all Egelv children received at a very early age.

Du Brimar snorted and slapped his hand on the armrest of his seat. "We have definite signs of Ananab activity. It had to be the P'Tassum, but since when does anybody throw back the prisoners they don't want? Why didn't they just dispose of them?"

Matt stiffened. He had a good idea of what the Egelv commander meant by "dispose of".

"But how does an Ananab ship just breeze right past us undetected and make a drop planetside?" Siph Carni made a face. "Even if we weren't watching for them, we should have noticed."

"Maybe they've improved their stealth capabilities." Du Brimar didn't sound very convinced. "But it still doesn't answer the question of why bother to bring those survivors back?"

"I don't know," Siph Carni admitted. "Nothing about this feels right."

"Maybe the humans took the ship, and those are all that survived," Matt said hesitantly."

"Nonsense." Du Brimar looked at him, not without pity. "No offense, but it just isn't going to happen. Anyway, if that was the case, where's the ship?"

"The ship is halfway back to Station Chaq by now," Siph Carni agreed. "The only way we're going to get any answers is by asking some of the survivors."

"They all say they can't remember," Matt reminded her. "Do you guys have some kind of 'forget all details' gas or ray, or something?"

Both of the Egelv laughed, glancing at their captain. When he didn't join them, they quieted down. Siph Carni shook her head.

"We could possibly reprogram a Human's memories, but it would be tricky, given the different physiology." She smiled wryly. "For an Ananab, or even a Hstahni to be able to do that with a race so unlike themselves, both physically and psychologically...absolutely not."

"The ship is still nearby." Captain Cromar Try spoke for the first time in hours.

"What?" Du Brimar spoke incredulously. "There's no way an Ananab ship could be nearby without our knowing."

"Just the same, it's out there," the captain said flatly. "Somehow, they've improved their stealth technology. And, they aren't doing anything to show up on our screens."

"Can't you do anything to make them visible?" Teresa asked, looking around the room at all the impressive technology.

"We could do a hard scan, and nothing they have would prevent our finding them, if they're out there," Du Brimar admitted. "But then we would be visible, too. Inversely, if they do a hard scan, we might not show up on their screens, but we would certainly see them."

"Since when do the Ananab have the patience to sit under stealth, or sheathed, as they call it?" Siph Carni was very skeptical. "And so what if they see us? They're just one ship."

"How do you know that?" Cromar Try asked softly.

All the Egelv became perfectly still. That hadn't occurred to any of them aside from the captain. Then Du Brimar shook his head. "I still don't believe it. They just aren't that good to sneak by us with one ship, much less a fleet."

All three Egelv froze. In fact, Matt noticed, the two techs that had been so quiet all this time also stiffened in what looked like shock. Then

162

Du Brimar strode purposefully to the Captain's station and picked up the printouts he had left there so long ago.

"Don't bother," Cromar Try said dryly. "They weren't there."

"What's going on?" Matt asked, confused. "Who wasn't where?"

The Egelv exchanged meaningful looks, then the captain shrugged and Siph Carni spoke.

"Another group of survivors have turned up on an island further out the Aleutian chain. We orbited over that spot hours ago and have visual proof they weren't there." She glanced at the other Egelvs grimly. "So where were they?"

"They couldn't have been dropped without our noticing," Du Brimar insisted. "We would have picked up emissions from their engines!"

"Maybe, maybe not," Cromar Try made several adjustments to his panel. "If they dropped while we were on the opposite side of the planet, it would have been more difficult to see them. Especially if they coasted."

"Then the shuttles must still be there," Siph Carni pointed out. "They sure aren't going to coast upward out of a gravity well."

"What if they used their antigrav?" Du Brimar spoke in a wondering voice.

"That's expensive in power," Siph Carni protested. "And why would they? Do you think they know we're here, and are trying to stay out of our sight?"

"Impossible," Du Brimar exploded. "Nobody could have detected us, not even another Egelv ship."

"Maybe they don't want my people to see them," Matt thought out loud. "Engine exhaust is more visible to the naked eye than this 'antigrav', isn't it?"

The three aliens looked at each other, nonplussed. Then Du Brimar shrugged. "I'll accept that. Even if I can't think of a reason for them to bother."

Cromar Try stood and paced back and forth in the small space near his seat. Both his mate and junior officer stared. That obviously wasn't a normal habit of his.

He finally seemed to come to a decision.

"We need more data that we can't get up here." He spoke in a flat voice. "We'll use the same methods they seem to be doing. We'll use one of the shuttles and coast down, using antigrav for brakes and propulsion. Du Brimar and Jo Coran will go to the surface and find one of these 'survivors'. Matt will accompany you." This last was directed at Du Brimar, who immediately began to protest.

Cromar Try raised his hand to stop the him. "We need fast answers. It would take too long for the two of you to learn your way around. His presence should also soften the blow of our appearances and very existence."

Du Brimar nodded slowly. Matt had to admit, it seemed to make sense if the Egelv were assuming he and Teresa would be helpful little servants.

For all their smarts, there was a lot the Egelv didn't know about humans. And he and Teresa would be happy to help in their education.

◆ ◆ ◆ ◆ ◆

Aleutian Islands, Alaska

Special Agent Costa stared at the man across the table. Why did he get all the crazy ones? The last interview had been simple. Shinzo Takuan's story had been very similar to the first survivors found. No explanations for anything, including the fact that his group had miraculously appeared in an area that had been intensely scrutinized just yesterday.

These people are nothing if not consistent, he had thought, watching Takuan be wisked away by representatives from his employer, Sukuru. They had arrived hours too late to catch any of the earlier survivors before they were transported, first to Seattle, then on to San Francisco, which hadn't made them happy. Costa had found himself on the defensive with them. After all, those people were victims, not criminals. He couldn't very well hold them indefinitely, just so some corporate types could interrogate them.

But this?

The man seated across from him was Howard Prause, a school teacher from southern California.

"I'd like to be sure I understand you, Mr. Prause," he began again. "You were in your cabin reading...?"

"Ulysses, by James Joyce," Prause helped him. "The next thing I know, I'm in a large hold of a spaceship with all the other passengers and the crew."

"And you were carried there by...?"

"There was a servant race, called the Hoag. They did all the menial labor." Prause shuddered. "The guards were awful. The Tryr are giant black panthers that walk on their hind legs, and the Srotag are bald bears with armorlike skin. Incredibly ugly, too. We called them rhino-bears."

"Rhino-bears." Costa wondered if his face revealed his thoughts. "Well, Mr. Prause, uh, you've gotten back to Earth somehow..."

"We revolted." Prause leaned forward in excitement. "Jim Morris and his cast were aboard. You know, martial artists, and all that. They overpowered the guards and took the bridge in a bloody battle, killing the officers, which were the Ananab race."

"Ah, yes, the...Ananab." Costa sighed. "And what did they look like?" I will regret asking that, he thought. A moment later, he was proven right.

"Giant lobsters, or crabs. They had to be close to twelve feet tall, with huge eyes on the end of long stalks."

His agent began coughing, and Costa glared at him until he stopped.

"So, Jim Morris died killing all these bad aliens?" I'm an idiot.

"Oh, no!" Howard Prause exclaimed. "He was cut up a little, but we won. Another race, the Baerd, helped him gain control of the ship. Then, when we arrived at the space station, they helped take that over, too."

"Space station?" Costa closed his eyes for a moment. "Is this station orbiting Earth?"

"No, no. It's about a week's travel away."

"By spaceship." Costa's man chipped in, grinning. Costa glared until the other dropped his eyes.

"I see you don't believe me." Prause stood up indignantly, flushing. "Perhaps the news media will!"

"Sit down, Mr. Prause." Karl Costa put a little steel into his voice. "I said, sit down."

The teacher settled back into his chair uneasily. "This isn't doing anything to help the situation."

"The situation?" Costa was baffled. Should he take notes? Or just shoot the guy?

"I had almost a hundred high school seniors that I was responsible for, and most of them stayed at the station. I insisted they return, but Captain Lang and that lawyer woman overrode me."

165

"Lawyer woman?" Costa sat up straight again. "Which one was that?"

"That Martin woman, or Morris, or whatever she's going by now." Mr. Prause was obviously not enthralled with Kimberly Martin, Costa noted with interest.

"What do you mean, Morris or whatever..." he let the sentence dangle.

"There was a big ceremony, and she married Jim Morris," Prause frowned. "After that, she seemed to be a part of every decision that was made. Between you and me, I think she had that old captain wrapped around her finger."

"Kimberly Martin married Jim Morris, the actor?" Costa shook himself, giving up. "Mr. Prause, this man is going to go over everything, once more with you. Please give him as much detail as you can." He smiled sourly at his agent. "I need to make a call."

Prause also rose to his feet. "You will do something about the children, won't you? They were my responsibility, and less than ten of them made it back with me."

"I'm going to have that Martin woman picked up and questioned again." Costa promised, outwardly sincere. "We'll get answers, I promise you. Then we'll take whatever course of action seems appropriate."

Like having you locked up in an asylum for the rest of your life, he thought dourly. Bug-eyed giant crabs, for Christ's sake. Still, it gave him an excuse to have another go at the Martin woman. He had thought before that she was hiding something, and now he was sure of it.

Kimberly Martin might think she was clever, but he would show her what happened when you played with the FBI.

San Francisco, California

"My name is Kiri Oshiba," Kiri said, flirting with the harried young man behind the United Airlines counter.. Kimberly looked over at her, and she smiled back serenely. "Window seat, please."

"I guess she leaves me the middle seat," Kimberly said, smiling at him as she handed over her driver's license.

"Too bad you aren't going to Atlanta with us," Kiri flirted with him. "You could be in the middle."

Beads of sweat popped out on the flustered man's brow. He stammered as he took their cash and gave them their tickets and boarding passes, returning their I.D.s. They both thanked him warmly, and Kiri's hand lingered on his as she took her ticket.

"What are you doing?" Kimberly whispered as they walked up to the security checkpoint.

"Cheapest thrill he'll get today," Kiri grinned.

"That would be true," Kimberly agreed. "Of course, it means he'll remember us now."

"I would like to think so. He can't be getting too much attention with all those zits?"

"Christ, you're impossible," Kimberly grumbled. "I can't take you anyplace."

"You know what they say." Kiri had a mischievous look on her face.

"Do I want to know?" Kimberly asked warily.

"You can undress 'em," Kiri laughed. "But then you can't take 'em out."

"I would like to see you go one day without obsessing about sex," Kimberly said.

"Do you have any idea how long it's been since I got any?" Kiri asked.

"A while?" Kimberly ventured.

"A very, long while," Kiri corrected.

They walked up to a gate with an American Airlines flight to New York leaving in a few minutes and presented their tickets.

"Thank you, Mrs. Grotsky, Ms. Chen," the airline attendant smiled as she took their tickets, barely glancing at their fake I.D.s. They barely nodded, not quite rude, but not warm and friendly, either.

Twenty minutes later, they were airborne to New York.

"That should slow down anyone trying to find us," Kimberly said, satisfied.

"Just long enough for us to get to New York and out of the airport," Kiri nodded. She glanced over at Kimberly. "It won't take long to realize we never boarded that plane to Atlanta."

"That's okay. They won't know for sure if we boarded another plane, or just left the airport for hours." Kimberly looked at her fake driver's license, impressed with Vicki's work.

Kiri looked out the window. "I wish we could have taken Jim's car to New York. A burnished silver Ferrari, all the fixings." She smiled lazily. "We could have really given the engine a test, traveling across country. We could have been...oh..."

"Like Thelma and Louise," Kimberly retorted dryly, then reclined her seat back. "Wake me east of the Mississippi."

Karl Costa retreated to the privacy of one of the smaller tents and began going through other agents reports. The second one made him sit up straight. He read a little further, set it aside and began skimming through the stack.

This can't be happening. I'm a good agent. I don't deserve a weird case like this.

Some kind of mass hysteria. It had to be. Either that, or one hundred and forty-six of these people were willing to swear under oath that they'd been kidnaped by aliens.

The stories and descriptions of the aliens matched almost perfectly.

He started to reach for his cellular phone, then carefully took his hand away.

Call upstairs, then be relieved of duty, immediately.

Perhaps a little discreet investigation of his own, he decided as he reached for the phone again.

◆ ◆ ◆ ◆ ◆

CHAPTER TWELVE

Station Osaka

"Thank you, gentlemen. That will be all." Jim gently, but firmly, escorted the Hoag workers out the door. Their leader, Hung, took one last glance around the room and the six place settings at the dinner table. Then Jim was closing the door, with them on the outside.

"I thought they'd never leave," Afsaneh joked as she deftly opened a bottle of red wine. She's very good at that, Jim mused.

Lasty and Dutter were invited to dinner, along with James McGregor and his wife, Eun Joo. Tonight would hopefully be a celebration.

He looked at his daughter's oversized robe. One of Hakim's, he realized with a pang of depression. He missed his old friend.

"Time for you to get dressed, young lady?" he asked, hiding his sadness. He must not have done a very good job, because she gave him a searching look. Jim forced a smile. "Move it. Our guests will be here in a minute."

Afsaneh disappeared into her bedroom.

Jim walked into the little kitchenette. There was what looked for all the world like a crock pot on the counter. He lifted the lid and sniffed.

Not bad, he conceded.

Jim had wanted to prepare the meal himself, but when the Hoag modified this suite for him, it had never occurred to them to supply it with a functional kitchen. It only had a microwave, and a tiny refrigerator.

Jim bowed to the necessity of having the Hoag prepare and deliver the food, ready to eat. But he'd drawn the line at serving and cleanup. Afsaneh and he would handle that.

He saw a bag on the counter and snooping, found a bottle of champagne and six glasses.

At least they hadn't "helped" by opening it for him, Jim thought ruefully as he found space for the bottle in the refrigerator's tiny freezer.

"I hate being the host and not knowing what we're serving, or if it's any good," he muttered out loud.

"I'm sure it'll be fine, Father," Afsaneh's voice came from the open door to her bedroom. "Would you relax?"

"I am relaxed," Jim protested. "Aren't you ready, yet?"

"Almost," she promised.

Yeah, when have I heard that before? But then she surprised him, making her entrance.

"How's this?" she asked, and he looked at her with appreciation.

Once again Afsaneh had proven unpredictable. A sweater only marginally too tight, a pleated skirt, and sandals gave her a very school girlish look. Well, maybe a very mature school girl, he admitted, eyeing the sweater. She correctly interpreted his look.

"Father, almost anything I wear is going to be a little tight there," she pointed out. "Unless I go for the sloppy oversized look all the time."

"You're fine," he assured her.

"You have guests at your door." Pearl spoke to both of them.

"Thank you, Pearl," Jim said as he went to greet them.

"Come in." Jim smiled as he opened the door. "Welcome."

"Thank you, Sir," McGregor spoke in a low tone. As always, he seemed ill at ease in a social setting. "Good evening, Ms. Riahi. I believe you both have met Eun Joo."

"Of course." Jim watched with amusement as Afsaneh smoothly took over hostess duty. "But please, call me Afsaneh."

Jim and McGregor shook hands, and he nodded to Eun Joo. Then he turned his attention to the Baerd.

"Lasty, Dutter, welcome to my home." Lasty only hesitated a moment before shaking hands. He was still getting used to human customs.

Jim blinked as he took in the Baerd garb. *Where are my sunglasses?*

Lasty wore baggy slacks, and Dutter had clinging tights. Both wore loose fitting tunics and slippers. Certainly nothing special in style.

But the color combinations!

Incomplete patterns of paisley, or camouflage, but with boldly contrasting, multiple shades of pink and orange, competed with a strong theme of seemingly random neon green.

Lasty noticed Jim's interest and a rosy blush started in his cheeks. He glanced at Dutter, then spoke shyly.

"We are, as you would say, living on the wild side," he admitted. "Many of our people would disapprove our decision to announce our relationship by coordinating and subduing our color patterns in our dress."

Jim kept a straight face. *Did he say subdued? Some one could have made a killing selling those tunics at Woodstock.*

"Please, come in and sit down." Afsaneh gestured to the chairs and sofas surrounding a low table that held refreshments.

McGregor and Eun Joo settled into one sofa, and after a moment of hesitation, the two Baerd sat gingerly together on a loveseat. When Lasty saw McGregor put his arm around his wife, he gingerly took Dutter's lower left hand in his lower right. She started, and a pink hue appeared on her neck and cheeks. But she made no attempt to pull her hand away.

"Would anyone like a drink?" Jim asked, scanning his guests. "We have beer and wine and, of course, soft drinks."

"Is it our new locally brewed beer?" McGregor asked cautiously. When Jim nodded, the sergeant winced. "Actually, wine sounds pretty good to me. Eun?"

"I'd best have fruit juice, if you have," Eun Joo said in a tiny voice that showed infinite regret. "I'm still...breast-feeding. But, I would rather have...seven and sevens?"

Jim laughed. "I know what you mean. Real booze is going to be in short demand for a while. But I hear the 'beastie beer' is improving."

"Have you tried it?" McGregor asked shrewdly.

"Not likely," Jim grinned. "I think they need to keep looking for local equivalents to barley and hops."

"These are alcoholic drinks, are they not?" Dutter asked, her face showing disapproval. "Don't they do brain damage?"

"Dutter!" Lasty sounded horrified. Her red tinge darkened perceptibly, but she looked stubborn.

"No, that's okay," Jim raised a hand. "There's a lot we don't know about each other."

Afsaneh handed the McGregors their drinks and stood waiting. McGregor took a sip of his wine, appearing very self-conscious. He raised his eyebrows in surprise.

"That's a Shiraz from Australia. It's a lighter red than you'd expect," Jim said, looking at Afsaneh. She got the point, gave a sniff, and went to pour him a glass.

He turned back to Dutter. "In answer to your question, drinking is like most things that are enjoyable. Too much of it can hurt you,. But it can taste delicious, and there is a school of thought out there that a glass or two a day is actually healthy."

Afsaneh gave him his wine, and then presented Dutter with a tall glass of fruit juice. The fruit was a native of the Baerd homeworld. Jim had tried it and liked it. The flavor was a cross between grapefruit and pineapple.

She sniffed her drink carefully, then smiled her thanks. Jim looked at Lasty quizzically. "The same for you, Lasty?"

The Baerd glanced with some trepidation at Dutter, then spoke carefully. "I must confess to some curiosity in this matter." Dutter looked at him in astonishment.

Jim suppressed a smile. "Pearl, how would the Baerd body react to alcoholic beverages? Compared to a Human?"

"Your physiology is similar enough that they would experience the same symptoms," Pearl answered. "Their tolerance would be considerably less."

"May I just have a taste?" Lasty said, sounding a little fearful.

"Afsaneh?" Jim sat in one of the chairs. "Would you pour Lasty a small glass of wine, please? Oh, and make yours the same as his."

Afsaneh gave Lasty his drink. He sniffed it cautiously. Dutter watched apprehensively.

"Well," Jim said, raising his glass. "To long friendships and overcoming obstacles."

"To long friendships," the others echoed, and they all drank. Jim watched over the lip of his glass as Lasty worked up the courage and took a minuscule sip. His head tilted slightly, and he looked over at Dutter.

"This is...interesting," he finally said. Jim held his smile in check as he watched a healthy pink glow fill Lasty's face.

"Is it good?" Dutter asked, a look of dread on her face.

"I can't decide," Lasty admitted, his lips twisting a little. He took another sip. "The flavor is...I think I like it."

"Let me try a little bit," Dutter said, reaching for his glass.

Dutter took a tiny taste and made a face. Then she took another. Reluctantly, she gave him back his glass, then turned to Afsaneh, handing back the fruit juice.

"May I change my mind, please?"

Jim and McGregor exchanged amused looks. "I may have created a monster," Jim admitted.

"How are the twins doing?" Afsaneh asked Eun Joo. The tiny Korean woman beamed.

"They grow so fast..." she laughed, shaking her head. "This time next year, they'll be bigger than I am..." She got a wicked expression on her face. "Tonight we have...babysitter. First time we both get break." She nudged her husband. "And privacy for few hours."

Jim saw both Lasty and Dutter zoom into the red zone, and grinned. For that matter, he noticed, McGregor was doing a pretty good imitation of a Baerd as well. He decided it was time to change the subject.

"Lasty, Dutter, have you definitely decided against returning to Baerd?"

"I don't think that would be wise at this time," Lasty admitted.

"Returning home is not a good idea, right now," Dutter said firmly. "It will be the end of our careers."

"And our life together," Lasty added, looking depressed.

"I might have something else to offer," Jim began carefully.

Both Baerd perked up and looked at him expectantly.

"Jade Wolverine is finished," Jim said. "Most of the crew will be human. I'll need some Hoag, maybe a dozen..."

"Sixteen," Lasty corrected him automatically, then blushed. "I mean, they work in units, that is, four per shift..."

Jim held up a hand, laughing. "Sixteen is fine. This illustrates an important point. My experience commanding a ship is, well, non-existent."

Jim leaned forward, elbows on his knees. "The thing is, I think I should have a couple of Baerd on board. Would you and Dutter be interested?"

Lasty and Dutter looked at each other with a curious mix of excitement and relief. After a moment, he turned back to Jim. "I think it would be safe to say we're...interested."

"It's not a free ride," Jim warned. "I would expect you to help train the rest of my crew, which will be mostly young humans."

"So we would be...in a teaching capacity?" Dutter said carefully. Was she hiding disappointment? "That would be our primary jobs?"

"Not at all," Jim grinned at her. "Lasty would be head pilot, second in command. You would be co-pilot and purser. The two of you would divide the technical duties between you. But I do believe that a major part in any leadership role is teaching and training."

"I would be second in command?" Lasty was shocked. "Of a Human ship?"

"Who is more qualified?" Jim smiled at him. "I need people I can trust."

Lasty and Dutter stared at each other, dumbfounded. They hugged in excitement, then hurriedly pulled apart. Their skin was bright scarlet.

"Lasty would be pilot...and second in command?" Dutter sounded dazed. Jim nodded and kept the grin off his face.

"And third?" Lasty looked at McGregor, obviously making an assumption.

"No, it won't be Mac," Jim said, genuine disappointment in his voice. "He's too valuable here at Osaka. And he has a family to raise. No, I've got somebody else in mind for head of security and defense."

"So who will be third in command?" Dutter asked. Afsaneh leaned forward in obvious anticipation. Jim winced inside. He knew she wouldn't be happy with this answer.

"Angela Dawson." He sat back and watched their reaction. Afsaneh, as was to be expected, looked disappointed.

Angela Dawson was an experienced police woman from Los Angeles, and she was tough. She had grown up through the gangs, and could just as easily have turned out bad. Instead, she was an excellent cop with no tolerance for excuses. She was black, and she'd made it out of the ghetto. As far as she was concerned, anybody could, if they were willing to work hard.

"Who's her second?" Afsaneh asked softly.

Now that's what I call a trick question, Jim thought. Time to tread carefully. "You will be," he admitted. "And Ellis, and everyone else in the weapon stations. It'll be up to you to prove you deserve second. There're no hereditary jobs on board my ship."

"As long as I get a chance at it," Afsaneh said in a sullen tone. She got a glint in her eyes. Uh, oh, Jim thought. Watch out! "What about Sean? Will he be part of the crew?"

"Afsaneh, I can't just put all your friends on board." Jim gave her an exasperated look. "This isn't high school, or a popularity contest."

"He's good," Afsaneh pointed out. "He deserves a chance. And Evie, too."

Jim blinked at that. Evie was an overweight high school senior that got along with everyone. He couldn't fault her personality, but hadn't noticed that she was part of the crowd Afsaneh hung around with.

She has an angle, of course, he thought dourly. When doesn't she?

"We'll see," he hedged. When she raised her chin and straightened her back, he knew he was going to lose this battle. "We'll see," he repeated.

She smiled, obviously recognizing victory.

"Thanks, Daddy," she cooed.

"Oh quit it." Jim shuddered. He'd rather she was angry.

"Has Captain Lang had any problem with you getting a ship?" McGregor asked.

Jim winced, then shrugged.

"I don't think he was too thrilled that Pearl unilaterally decided to build me one," he admitted. "And I'm not sure he thinks I really need one..."

"You do," McGregor said firmly. "You're in a unique position, and you'll need autonomy."

"For what?" Jim asked curiously.

"I don't know," McGregor admitted. "But the chain of command is squirrelly enough already. It's better to acknowledge the situation and find ways of dealing with it."

"What do you mean?" Lasty asked, looking confused.

"First of all, we have this station with Governor Lang in command." McGregor went slow, obviously choosing his words carefully. "His only authority is that he was in command of a cruise ship that got hijacked. And he has Jade Samurai, with Captain DelaRosa under his command. So now he's not just a captain, or even a governor. Now he's also a fleet commander."

"Fleet?" His wife grinned at him. "One ship?"

"Two," McGregor corrected her, gesturing outward. "Jade Viking is still supposedly under his flag. But 'Viking is on Earth, almost a week away. And then there's the new ship they're just finishing."

"And there is Captain Tachibana to consider," Afsaneh pointed out. McGregor gave her an approving nod.

"Exactly." He didn't look the least bit shy as he warmed to the subject. "Captain Tachibana willingly agreed to place himself under Captain Lang's authority, but he is a senior officer, and as we said, he's at Earth. We're very spread out, at this point."

"And I don't see that changing," Jim pointed out. "But, go on."

McGregor nodded. "He's pretty autonomous. And then, of course, there are the people back on Earth working with Ms. Martin. We have people spread all over the place with no clear line of authority, or process of selection."

"True," Jim agreed. "And although we're from a democracy, I don't see us holding elections any time soon."

"Or separating civil from military functions," Afsaneh chipped in and both men looked at her with surprise.

She shrugged. "Not enough of us to form a really good bureaucracy."

Everyone laughed.

"That does bring up another good point," McGregor said, growing serious. "If uh, Mrs. Morris recruits a few thousand new people, we could have an election that could be controlled by the newcomers."

"I don't think that would be wise...," Lasty began.

"You got that right," Afsaneh said darkly. "They'd have no idea what we're up against."

"We need to come up with some kind of structure," McGregor said. "Even the U.S. constitution wouldn't do the job under these circumstances."

"I know some people we could get to help us with the framework of a viable constitution," Jim said. "They're back on Earth, but I'm bound to get back there..." His voice trailed off as the discussion reminded him of his best reason to return to Earth." He saw that everyone knew what he was thinking, and decided to shelve his self-pity until later. He gestured to the dining table.

"Anyone hungry?"

Osaka, Japan

Shinzo Takuan nervously wiped the palms of his hands with a handkerchief. He patted his brow to remove the beads of sweat that flowed freely down his forehead. There was nothing he could do about the wetness under his arms and collar.

How long would they keep him waiting? It was hotter than dragon's breath in this tiny cubicle. He tried to sit perfectly still, but it didn't help. He was wearing a dark suit and tie over a long-sleeved white shirt which was probably turning dingy grey by now. But it was the only appropriate wear when you were seeing the Obayun.

And what kind of waiting room was this, anyway? The walls were bare of any adornment, broken only by the door he'd entered through, and another door on the opposite side. The furniture consisted of exactly one bench. One bare light bulb hung from the ceiling.

The room seemed inconsistent with where he was.

Sukuru Castle was a tremendous high-rise complex on the side of one of the many hills that surrounded Osaka. Pagoda styled roofs topped multiple towers, some stone and concrete modeled to resemble castle walls, and others of dark-tinted glass. Low, featureless buildings surrounded the compound.

Something that couldn't be discerned from the outside was the extent of the sprawling underground facilities. As Shinzo well knew, no building permit or public blueprint showed even a tiny percentage of the hidden construction. He had worked for Sukuru for almost ten years, mostly out of this facility, and still wasn't sure of his way around outside the west wing.

The door, not the one he'd entered by, opened, and a security guard motioned for him to follow. They walked down a short corridor and, at the end the guard held the door open. Shinzo hesitated for only a moment, then entered, taking a deep breath as he did.

The door closing behind him sounded ominous and final.

He was in a bath house. Several pools filled most of the space. There were a number of low benches and seats, some occupied by men wearing towels. A few scrubbed themselves, but most had female attendants to do the scrubbing. The young, attractive attendants were nude.

Shinzo felt the blood leave his face despite the heat. This was the most dangerous room he had ever entered in his life. He had never been privy to the inner circle of power at Sukuru, and would have been perfectly happy staying that way.

He saw the Obayun, or president, as the corporate structure would have read, in the shallow end of one of the pools. Injo Toshida didn't look like a powerful man. In fact, he resembled nothing so much as an elderly scholar.

But Shinzo knew better than to be deceived by appearances. This man ran the international conglomerate known as Sukuru with an iron hand. The few times he made public appearances, he would look at people kindly through round, wire-rimmed glasses that had slid part ways down his nose. His younger brother, Yoshi, was the one viewed as the taskmaster.

And, Shinzo thought desperately, it was the death of that very brother he was here to explain.

I am dead, he thought, resigned. They will hear my story, then torture me to find the "truth", which I will have just told them. Then they will kill me, slowly and painfully.

He ignored the guards spaced seemingly at random throughout the room, and approached the pool Toshida stood in. He stopped about six paces away and bowed as deeply as he could without falling over.

The Obayun let him stay in that position. His back began to ache and his calves burned with the tension of holding the uncomfortable position. He began to feel lightheaded and prayed to the gods not to let him faint.

"Come." The voice was so quiet and calm, he almost missed it. Holding his sigh of relief inside, he quickly stepped forward and knelt at the edge of the pool, hands folded on his lap, head still bowed.

And he waited.

After what seemed like an eternity, the Obayun spoke again.

"You can tell me what happened to my brother and my ship." It was not a question. "And also, my chief of security and Naga Furukawa."

"Yes, master," Shinzo began, then winced as a cynical voice came from next to the Obayun.

"Yes Uncle, and maybe he can tell us why he is still alive."

Shinzo risked a glance upward and blanched. Sho Toshida, son of Yoshi Toshida, and nephew to the Obayun, leaned lazily against the side of the pool. Shinzo had never met the young man, but had seen him in business meetings.

Fully dressed, of course. Dark suit and tie, white shirt, black shoes, the company uniform. In fact, the uniform of the Japanese business world.

Sho Toshida was wearing a suit of sorts. A complex series of tattoos covered him from neck downward, disappearing into the water, presumably to his ankles.

Yakuza!

Shinzo averted his eyes, thinking furiously. There had always been rumors that Sukuru had ties to the Yakuza, the Japanese mafia. Everyone had heard them, of course. Any time a corporation grew as powerful as Sukuru, stories would appear. But he had never seen any proof.

But here was Sho Toshida, heir apparent to the Sukuru financial empire, wearing the tattoos of a major player for the Yakuza. As he glanced around the room, he saw that many others in the room also wore the sign of the Yakuza.

I am dead, he thought numbly.

◆ ◆ ◆ ◆ ◆

Seattle, Washington

"You're dead," Agent Costa promised into his phone. "If you can't find where they went, your career is dead. Patrick, if you can't keep track of two drop dead, beautiful women, you're going to find yourself wearing long underwear every day for the rest of your life. It gets very cold on the northern coast of Alaska."

He closed his phone, then started as it rang. What could young Beatty want now?

"Well?"

"Is that how you answer the phone?"

"Groundhog, it's about time you called in." Costa pulled himself together. This man required special treatment, and was too valuable a resource to irritate. "Did you read the package?"

"No," the voice said derisively. "I read your note. I browsed the package. Backgrounds on thirty-five hundred people and over a thousand interviews fill a lot of pages. I'll work my way through whatever I need."

"I just talked to one of my agents in San Francisco." Costa hesitated, then continued. "They lost the Martin woman at the airport."

"Why does that not surprise me?"

"Okay, okay. Lay off my men." Costa took a deep breath. "Can you pick up her trail?"

"Not with your men all over the place." Groundhog paused. "She still with the Japanese actress?"

"Last we knew," Costa agreed.

"Neither of them have residences in northern California. Didn't that

179

teacher say she married Jim Morris?"

"Yeah..." Costa drew the word out, stalling as his mind raced. What had the other man already seen? He frantically leafed through the pages piled on his desk. "Hey, Morris has a condo near Chinatown!"

"Your men can check that out."

"What are you going to do?" Costa asked, then winced and bit his lip.

"Check a few other leads."

"Yeah, whatever." Costa belatedly realized the other man had hung up and carefully replaced the receiver. Then he began to swear steadily.

He hated dealing with this guy. He knew him only by his codename, and every time he swore he'd never use the man again.

But you couldn't argue with success, and Groundhog always produced.

Costa had first come in contact with him about ten years ago, in a joint project with the NSA. It had been a mess from the start, and Groundhog had finally been brought in to resolve the situation.

Ever since, if Costa had a particularly sensitive problem, or a mystery he couldn't even get started on, he would leave a message at the number Groundhog gave him. He always produced.

If anyone could make sense of this mess, Groundhog could. He charged an arm and a leg, but was worth every penny.

That lawyer Martin might think she was clever. But if she was harboring any secrets about the Jade Viking, he would have them soon enough.

With a sigh, Costa opened his phone. He would have Beatty check out the Morris condo, try and pick up the trail again. God help him if he screwed up again. Or, maybe he liked snowshoes.

Somewhere in the United States

Was it worth going to the Aleutians to check out the two sites personally? Groundhog leaned back and closed his eyes. He hadn't been entirely honest with the good agent Costa, but then, he seldom was.

He'd given the interviews a quick read, skimming most of the details, looking for significant facts or coincidences. He had a photographic memory, so it only took one time through. And, of course, he'd already read the personal files on everyone.

Kimberly Martin and Kiri Oshiba.

Martin was an attractive woman, an excellent lawyer with a keen ability to work within the confines of the corporate world. Viking Cruises was just one division of the parent company, Spencer Corporation.

Kiri Oshiba was a popular actress in Japan. By Western standards she was, at best, barely competent. On the other hand, it could be the roles she kept getting. More important, she had ties with Jim Morris. They worked together often, most recently on the ill-fated Jade Viking.

Howard Prause said Kimberly Martin married Jim Morris, who worked with Kiri Oshiba, who was traveling with Kimberly Martin.

Groundhog opened his eyes. The Japanese woman had her home U.S. residence listed near Malibu. That was a possibility. But Martin was a lawyer. She would want to re-establish herself as soon as was feasible.

He glanced at his watch. Almost nine a.m. They had probably caught a red-eye flight last night, or first thing this morning.

No point in going to San Francisco. He would catch the next flight east and find them in New York.

◆ ◆ ◆ ◆ ◆

Northern California

"We're going to New York?" Iori's voice revealed his excitement.

Sasama grinned at him, then returned his eyes to the road. He was driving thirty miles over the speed limit, but the car gave such a smooth ride it was impossible to tell without looking at the speedometer.

"Yes we are!" The exhilaration from driving was addictive. "If you're really nice to me, I might let you drive, later on."

"I trust it will be at a more reserved speed," Captain Tachibana's voice spoke into his ear. Both Sasama and Iori jumped in their seats. "I'm speaking to both of you so there will be no confusion or misunder-standing."

"Yes, sir?" Sasama asked, foot was already lifting, allowing the sports car to slow a bit.

"You are traveling at an extremely high rate of speed, Mr. Sakakibara." The captain's voice was soft, but there was no missing the iron in his tone. "What would you tell a state trooper if you got pulled over for doing over a hundred in a seventy mile an hour zone? And when he asked to see your drivers license? Aren't you considered dead or missing?"

"Yes, sir," Sasama mumbled, allowing the Viper to slow under eighty. "We'll keep a good watch out."

"Better yet," Tachibana's voice changed abruptly. "Drive with the traffic flow."

"Yes, sir," they both responded meekly.

Iori looked upward out his window. "Can they really see us from way up in orbit?" he asked plaintively.

"No, but they can track our transceivers," Sasama said, then hurried to continue as Iori opened his mouth to speak. "And they can hear us, too." He tapped his ear meaningfully, and Iori's mouth snapped shut.

Sasama had a thought and grinned. He gave a backhand slap to his friend's arm and winked. "On three."

"What?" Iori asked, confused.

Sasama began to sing. Iori laughed out loud and quickly joined in.

"Five thousand bottles of beer on the wall, five thou..."

New York City, New York

"You know," Kiri said.. "There's one thing you can not get in outer space."

"Oh?" Kimberly poured Italian dressing on her salad. "What's that?"

"A good cheeseburger," Kiri assured her, then took a huge bite. Kimberly used the motion of setting the salad dressing bottle down to steal one of her friend's french fries. "I saw that."

Kimberly smiled as she gazed out the window, chewing thoughtfully. They were in a restaurant in downtown Manhattan. Their table gave a good view of the busy rush hour traffic.

"What are you thinking about?" Kiri gave her a knowing smile.

Kimberly reached over and stole another fry and dipped it in her salad dressing. She felt serene, and wondered if it was the calm before the storm.

"I was just thinking about how much I miss Jim. I wish he were here," she answered.

Kiri nodded, understanding. "Instead of me."

"No, in addition to you," Kimberly assured her, and realized it was the truth.

Station Osaka

Millions of miles away, Pearl did her usual periodic check on the Heir-Prime, Jim Morris. His welfare was her absolute primary concern, even above the safety of the station or herself. She would check on him at regular intervals throughout the night.

Jim Morris had rolled over in his sleep. Beyond that, there were no changes, except one.

He was smiling.

CHAPTER THIRTEEN

Aboard the Jade Wolverine

"Deploy grapples."

Jim clenched the armrests on his captain's perch tightly.

"We are docked with Station Osaka," Dutter reported in a crisp, confident tone.

"Confirmed." The voice of Irene, Jade Wolverine's computer, was higher pitched than either Pearl or Vicki. Jim could almost swear it had a slight accent, but he couldn't place it.

In any case, at least the maiden flight was now history. Jim gave a sigh of relief and sagged in his seat. "Report."

To his left, Lasty stirred. "Engineering is secured and shutting down. Skeleton maintenance crew in place."

"All umbilicals with Osaka connected and functioning," Dutter said. She turned to face them, smiling in excitement. A slight pink hue covered her face and shoulders. "Sensor watches set, main bridge staff dismissed."

"All weapons stations secured, sentries set at the main hatch, Sir." Angela Dawson had a strong contralto no nonsense voice. She stood and pivoted, facing Jim and placed her hands behind her back. Jim suppressed the urge to salute.

She was an imposing sight. Jim had seen her bio that had been prepared when they were still prisoners of the Ananab. It said she was five foot nine inches and one hundred and sixty pounds. As far as he could tell, it was all muscle and bone. She had obviously pumped iron regularly back on Earth.

Jim smiled as he watched Lasty finish closing down most of the ship. Choosing the Baerd to be his second had been a good decision. He stood and stretched lazily, hiding his amusement at Lasty and Dutter as they fought the urge to hug each other.

They never knew their ambitions and abilities until there was an outlet for them, Jim thought. Life under the Ananab had been harsh, and opportunities limited. Now they were officers on a ship with a captain and crew that appreciated and liked them.

More importantly at this point, they could acknowledge their feelings for each other. Lasty and Dutter had gasped when he told them they could share a suite on the Jade Wolverine, if they so chose. After the usual shift to bright scarlet, and a brief whispering session, they had agreed.

The two Baerd and Angela Dawson were the only people that would initially be living on board. Eventually the rest of the crew, including the Hoag, would establish residency. For the moment, Jim preferred to keep his crew list fluid until he was sure he had a good mix. It would be much easier to make changes if people weren't settled in with all their personal belongings.

Afsaneh had already suggested she move on board, along with Ellis and Sean, but he had quickly squelched that idea. Angela wouldn't appreciate having babysitter added to her duties.

Jim whistled tunelessly as he strode down the corridors to the main hatch. Ellis Jackson was stationed just inside the ship, armed with an AK-47. He saw Jim and snapped to attention.

"Uh, Captain leaving the ship," he called out in a nervous voice. He stood ramrod stiff as Jim passed, then gave a start as Jim turned back and whispered softly.

"Ease up, son," Jim told him in a not-unkindly voice. "We're in a safe harbor."

"Yes, sir," he amended, looking embarrassed.

Jim laughed and slapped him on the shoulder as he departed. There was another sentry stationed dockside, with monitor screens set to see up and down the main corridor this gantry passage was attached to. He bit his lip as he watched his daughter pivot to put her back against the wall as he passed. Her assault rifle, which looked like a toy in Ellis' hands, seemed almost as big as she was.

"As you were, soldier," Jim said with a straight face.

She stuck her tongue out at him. "Thank you, sir! All clear station-side, sir!"

Jim glanced at his watch. She and Ellis had sentry duty until all non-duty personnel cleared off the ship. Then Irene would assume all security duties until their next scheduled drill. "See you at dinner?" he asked.

"Yes, Sir!" Afsaneh answered. "I'll be famished, Sir!" A low whistle came from Ellis. It was obviously a signal and she waved goodbye as she picked up a clipboard to check off the approaching departures. Jim waved back and left.

He would have to speak to Angela about coming up with some kind of dress code or uniform. Two piece leotards that showed bare midriff left a lot to be desired, as uniforms went.

"Jim Morris, Governor Lang would like to speak to you," Pearl spoke through his transceiver.

"Fine," Jim said. "I'll be at the bridge in a few minutes."

"Actually, I was wondering if you could check something out on your way here." Lang's voice surprised Jim. And there was something in his tone.

"What's wrong?" Jim frowned.

"Maybe nothing, maybe something," Lang answered. "I just received a request from the Trixmae ship. They want to depart immediately."

"Why?" Jim began walking at a brisk pace down the long corridor to the hub of the station. The Trixmae ship was in the next spoke, almost a mile away.

"They wouldn't say." Lang did sound worried now. Jim thought about it as he walked. Since the Humans had seized the station, there had been a continuous Trixmae presence. Sometimes the ship visits would overlap by a few days, but Jim suspected the main reason they kept a ship nearby was to watch and see what developed between the Humans and the Ananab.

That's it, Jim thought with a sinking feeling in his gut. Either that or... "Pearl, is there another Trixmae ship approaching Osaka?"

"No."

"Are there any ships approaching?" Jim asked, speeding up even more. "Can you scan for ships running under stealth?"

"I detect no sheathed ships within scanning range." Pearl's voice sounded confident.

"Well, there has to be some reason they want to leave so quickly," Jim muttered and then a thought occurred to him. "Do the Trixmae have better scanning equipment than we do?"

"Doubtful." Jim rolled his eyes. Great, a computer with attitude.

"Well, take another look around and try and extrapolate some reason they want to beat it," Jim said, trying not to show his irritation. "Something's not kosher."

"Kosher?" Pearl asked.

Jim sighed. "Just check, will you?"

Osaka, Japan

Sho Toshida sat and watched his uncle. Injo Toshida had been the Obayun for as long as he could remember. In fact, his father occasionally complained about how, even with twenty years difference in age, the older brother would probably never die, just to frustrate him.

He could understand how his father had felt, since he'd had the same thoughts. Eventually Injo would die, and Yoshi would rule for decades, while Sho grew older and older.

But Yoshi Toshida was dead, at the hands of alien invaders from outer space, if that fool Takuan was to be believed. Sho wasn't sure he was ready to accept that story quite yet.

But more important, Yoshi Toshida was dead, leaving Sho as heir to the family leadership and, by extension, the powerful Sukuru organization.

And Injo Toshida grew older every day.

Sho would turn thirty in February, and his chance would come. All that was called for was patience and obedience, and Sho would provide both for as long as it took.

And so he sat here waiting for his uncle to open his eyes. Was he sleeping, or...? Sho's head snapped up to see the old man watching him with knowing eyes.

"I'm not dead yet," the Obayun said in a dry voice.

"I apologize, Uncle," Sho answered smoothly. "I found myself immersed in this puzzle and lost track of time for a moment."

"Of course." The old man's eyes bore into him, his expression unreadable. "You're very ambitious, aren't you, nephew?"

"Yes, I am," Sho answered truthfully. He bowed his head. "But I am also loyal. And very patient. I have much to learn from you."

The Obayun snorted. "If only you really believed that." He shook his head. "No matter. At the very least, you are pragmatic. You will need to fly to San Francisco and confer with Takeda Nagashino."

Sho blinked his eyes at the sudden change in topic, but quickly recovered. Takeda Nagashino was the new temporary head of security for Sukuru. With the report of Nagami's death, it seemed likely that position would be made permanent. "Of course."

"You will then proceed to New York and meet with William Spencer. I wish to know what compensation he has in mind."

Sho suppressed a shiver at the sudden cold tone of his uncle's voice. "And your instructions?" he asked cautiously.

"Use Takeda wisely." The old man gave him a shrewd look. "If nothing else, cultivate him for the day you replace me. He is a strong force and a useful ally."

The Obayun carefully rose to his feet. Sho gave an inward sigh of relief as he recognized the end of the interview. But the old man wasn't quite finished yet.

"According to the man Takuan, this gaijin woman, Kimberly Martin, is part of this conspiracy." The eyes of Miyazaki Toshida grew tiny and black as the darkest night. "Obtain her and deliver her to our new facility in San Francisco. I will make arrangements to have her brought back here. I did not like her manners when she met with Sukuru representatives in the matter of the Jade Viking. It will be a pleasure watching her learn her appropriate place in the universe as she tells us everything."

"Yes, sir." Sho stood and bowed deeply. "I will oversee her 'acquisition' myself."

"Good," the Obayun agreed. "Be wary of her."

Sho looked at his uncle in surprise. The old man snorted and shook his head.

"You will see."

Seattle, Washington

"You're sure they were there?" Karl Costa held the phone away from his ear and thought for a moment. "Did they leave any luggage? Check for their specific bags. No? They're probably back at the airport. Go."

He hung up and leaned back in his chair, thinking. There were questions to be answered. He straightened and grabbed the phone again.

"Margaret, I need airline bookings, from San Francisco to the east coast and as far west as...Chicago." He winced and hurried to continue. "I know, I know. It's a lot of flights. We're looking for two women, flying between eight o'clock last night and...now. One Caucasian, one Japanese, both attractive. The Japanese is in her early twenties, the other, her early thirties. Yeah, let me know."

He started to hang up, then reconsidered. "Margaret, you still there? Book me next available, to San Francisco. I better get closer on this one."

His wife wasn't going to like such short notice, but what else was new?

Somewhere in the air over the United States

Groundhog signaled for service. After a moment, an attractive young black woman came to his seat.

"Yes sir?" Her smile revealed perfectly even teeth, bright white against her ebony skin.

"Are we still on schedule?" The Captain hadn't update their progress in over an hour.

"Oh yes, sir." She continued smiling. "In fact, with the tail winds we're experiencing, we've actually picked up a few minutes. We'll be in New York just before seven o'clock tonight."

"Thank you. May I have a scotch, please?"

"Certainly. Will Glenfidditch be okay?"

"That will be fine." He opened his laptop.

Somewhere in the middle of Nebraska, miles below the aircraft, two Japanese men argued loudly about which fast food drive-thru to use for dinner.

Their red sports car ate away the miles at a steady rate. The thrill of driving it had worn off somewhere in the Rocky Mountains. Now driving was a chore, only slightly less boring than riding as a passenger.

New York City couldn't come soon enough for either of them.

Jade Viking

Captain Tachibana muttered under his breath. His first officer, Craig Randall looked at him questioningly.

"Excuse me, Sir. Did you say something?"

"Those two are driving me crazy," Tachibana said dryly. "Vicki, take me off the monitor feed for Sakakibara and Kojiro."

"Certainly, Captain Tachibana."

Randall laughed. "You've lasted longer than any of us. Are they really best friends?"

"Supposedly." Tachibana decided he had complained enough. "Can you give me an update on each team's progress?"

"Of course." The younger officer was all business again. "Mr. Farmer and Mr. Weinstein think they should be done with the editing of their movie no later than tomorrow. Vicki says the only things holding them up at the moment are...artistic differences between the two of them and her."

"Between a Hollywood producer, director, and an alien computer?" Tachibana felt his lip trying to twitch. "That's... interesting. What else?"

"Ron Hoffman has ordered twelve dozen pump-action shotguns. He doesn't expect there to be any holdups." Commander Randall grinned in apology at the unintended pun. "For Christmas gifts to his management personnel. It's amazing what you can order from a catalog."

Tachibana stared at his first officer. "He mail ordered one hundred and forty-four shotguns? Just like that?"

"And enough ammunition to...well, shoot them a lot." Randall laughed. "He lives in Texas, remember? Gun control? Bah, we don't need no stinking gun control..."

Tachibana cleared his throat and the younger man quickly returned to the facts. "Um, let's see. He's also started sending out advertisements for a new company that provides security in obscure locations. The ad says it's looking for well-adjusted people with military or police backgrounds willing to relocate to exotic settings for long periods of time. Families are encouraged. No crazies or militia fanatics."

Randall looked up from the sheet, awe in his face. "This guy is good! He hasn't even been home two days and he's got four or five balls rolling. Setting up accounts for people to try our 'new and improved' flash drives and backup hard drives. Putting out feelers on buying a couple of old oil tankers in Galveston, a junkyard in Houston."

"It just goes to show what a good staff can accomplish," Captain Tachibana said, hiding his own amazement. "How about Ms. Stephanian and her friend? And Mr. Miles?"

"Not much yet," Randall admitted. "Ms. Stephanian has initiated steps to start up an international corporation, for the moment, based out of Nassau. But they're also busy starting the early publicity advances for Alien Death Grip, which thankfully, is still just a working title.

Tachibana winced. "And Miles?"

"He's found a possibility well off the coast of Columbia," Randall admitted. "He's working on a couple of corrupt officials."

"Excuse me, Sir." One of the Baerd technicians spoke up from her station. Inam was the head of the contingent of Baerd that ran the bridge functions. "That Egelv ship was definitely here. We've found trace emissions to confirm. What we can't seem to settle on is, when."

"When?" Captain Tachibana frowned.

"We have conflicting data, ranging from almost a month ago up to as recently as...yesterday," Inam admitted.

"What does that mean?" Randall asked. "Could our instruments be off?"

"No," came Vicki's curt reply. "Either something is distorting the data, or our interpretations are correct."

Captain Tachibana sat up straight as he saw the Baerd on duty flinch. Oh. He turned to face Inam. "What about it, Ma'am? Could these... Egelv, still be here?"

Inam exchanged glances with her second, Irle. He shrugged, and Inam rubbed both sets of hands together nervously. "It's...possible," she admitted. "We'll start a passive search. But it might not be conclusive," she warned.

"Why not?" Tachibana was curt.

"If we do a hard search, it will reveal our location." Inam looked at Irle for support. He nodded his agreement.

"It's true," Irle picked up where Inam left off. "The Egelv are more advanced than the Ananab. A hard search might not even find them. But it will most certainly show our location. And so far, there is at least a chance they don't know we're here."

"With all the shuttle trips we've been running?" Randall sounded skeptical. "Jade Viking herself has been in close orbit several times. Wouldn't we have shown up on their instruments?"

"Not necessarily," Irle disagreed, then blushed at his boldness. Tachibana motioned for him to continue. "The shuttles have been running on antigrav, at your insistence. That's not a common method, for a number of reasons. They may not have been looking for the right signs."

"And Jade Viking was on an elliptical, non-powered orbit when we did get close to the planet," Inam pointed out.

"So, do we change anything?" Captain Tachibana didn't like this nebulous state. Either there was an enemy out there, or there wasn't. But which?

"Our choices are very limited," Randall pointed out, and both Baerd nodded their agreement. "I think we have to continue what we're doing, but cut down on shuttle runs, and be very, very quiet."

He beamed at Captain Tachibana. "We're hunting Egelvs."

Glowing Mist's pinnace

Du Brimar hummed as he brought the pinnace into Earth's atmosphere. Seated to his left, Jo Coran ignored him and studied her screen, looking over the accumulated data related to the missing cruise ship.

Matt Stickel, seated on the pilot's other side, was not so calm. As far as he could tell, they were falling in an uncontrolled drop. The planet grew swiftly to lose its spherical shape and take up the entire screen.

"Look, we're a meteor," Du Brimar said cheerfully.

"Meteors burn up in entry," Matt said through tightly clenched teeth. "Do you always fly like this?"

"Technically we aren't flying," the Egelv pointed out.

Matt looked at him. "Oh?" was all he could manage.

"Well, yes." Du Brimar's eyes twinkled. "Technically, we're falling."

"Du Brimar, quit that," Jo Coran said in exasperation. "Quit tormenting him. It's cruel."

Matt stiffened. When he could trust his voice, he spoke. "Like pulling wings off a fly."

"Pardon me?" Du Brimar looked at him in puzzlement. "I didn't catch that."

"Never mind," Matt said, watching the planet take form and become the Earth he was used to. They were now over the Pacific Ocean, coming in fast, and Du Brimar concentrated on his flying. Within moments, they were streaking mere feet above the water. "How long before we reach land?"

Even as he spoke, the light grew dimmer, and they moved into nighttime. He looked up and saw the stars, his stars, and tears grew in his eyes.

He was home again, sort of.

Teresa was still aboard the Egelv ship, in orbit high above them. An insurance policy, Du Brimar had suggested dispassionately. It had been decided that the teacher, Howard Prause, would be a good place to start investigating.

So, they were on a mission to torment a high school teacher who had already endured so much. Matt was along to help Du Brimar find Prause, back in his recently recovered life.

Evidently they thought Teresa would be enough to keep him from messing things up, or trying to escape, Matt thought dourly.

Matt sighed silently. They were right.

New York City, New York

Kimberly moaned with pleasure at the sensuous caresses that engulfed her body. The feather light touches against her skin brought a dreamy smile to her face.

"Kiri, this is great," she breathed. "I had no idea how..."

"How much you missed your silk sheets?" Kiri teased. "You lay there much longer, we won't be discussing how to spend the evening, but what to have for breakfast."

"Are you hungry?" Kimberly asked as she reluctantly slid to the side of the bed.

"Not at all," Kiri said, shaking her head. "I'm still stuffed from lunch. You have any watering holes in this neighborhood?"

"Yes-s-s..." Kimberly said. "I'm not sure I really feel like bar hopping tonight."

"Not bar hopping," Kiri argued. "We could just..." She stopped as the telephone rang. They both waited to hear if any message was left.

Kimberly winced as she recognized the voice.

"Kimberly, this is Will. Pick up if you're there." She made a face and glanced over at Kiri. The young Japanese woman grinned and made as if to pick up the receiver. Kimberly glared at her and Kiri raised her hands in mock submission.

"I know you're back, because the phone rang four times, which means you've cleared your messages. Pick up the phone." Kimberly wasn't in the mood to deal with Will right now. Probably wouldn't be tomorrow, either, for that matter.

"Okay, I'll come over." Kimberly frowned in consternation. Kiri grinned at her and winked. "We need to talk. I'll see you soon."

The machine went silent. Neither woman spoke for a moment, then Kiri giggled.

"Boy, is he in a hurry to see you," Kiri said suggestively. "This is his fourth call. Were you two an item?"

"No." Kimberly said firmly. "Not that he didn't try."

"Uh huh," Kiri said, straight-faced. "Is he cute?"

"Don't you start." Kimberly glared at her. "Cute or not, I didn't think it was appropriate to get involved with my boss. Or a client, for that matter. And technically, he's both. But he kept trying. It was getting a little awkward towards the end."

"I can't wait to see you explain being married to Jim," Kiri smirked. Kimberly nodded glumly. "You'll have your chance soon. He's on his way over."

Kimberly groaned and made up her mind. "Not tonight. I'm not ready to deal with him just yet. Come on, let's get out of here. I know a place nearby. It's kind of a hole in the wall, but that's good. It means he'll never have heard of it and won't find us."

"Hole in the wall." Kiri nodded in approval. "You spend a lot of time there?"

"No." Kimberly tried to stare the younger woman down. Kiri just grinned at her. "Come on, let's go. He doesn't live that far from here."

Twenty minutes later, Kimberly stopped in front of a rough wooden door. A wrought iron dragon wrapped from the upper left corner of the door around the top and down the side, the tail bent outwards to provide a door handle.

Above the door, a simple sign read Dragon's Breath Saloon. The two o's in saloon were the closed eyes of a sleeping dragon's head. There were no windows.

"This is your favorite hangout?" Kiri asked skeptically, looking up and down the street. "Do we need bodyguards?"

"Why?" Kimberly felt mischievous. "We have each other for protection, don't we?" She gestured to the door. "After you, brave adventurer."

Kiri gave one last look around the darkened street and made a face. "Well, okay. But I've got a bad feeling about this..."

Kimberly watched with anticipation as her friend pulled on the door handle. Kiri gave a startled cry as the two eyes in the sign popped open. Bloodshot, venomous orbs glared at them for a moment, then the eyes closed as Kiri leaped backwards. Kimberly broke into laughter.

"Bitch!" Kiri snarled as she straightened out of her defensive stance. Kimberly started coughing as the laughter made her throat scratchy. The Japanese woman cautiously tried the handle again. The eyes appeared, and she glanced over her shoulder at Kimberly rubbing her throat. "Serves you right."

"Come on," Kimberly said hoarsely. "I'll buy you a drink or three."

"I'll have to change my panties first," Kiri muttered darkly. She blinked in surprise at the cosy, pub atmosphere. The left wall was dominated by a long well-stocked bar. Hardwood booths lined the right side and small tables filled the center, with two pool tables towards the back.. The room was about half full of patrons, mostly well dressed, in their twenties or thirties.

Kiri looked at Kimberly and grinned. "Hole in the wall? Yuppie pub is more like it. You hang out here a lot?"

"Once in a while," Kimberly admitted, wincing inside.

Kiri nodded and looked around. "Living on the edge," she agreed.

"Okay, okay, how about that drink?" Kimberly had never felt self-conscious about this place before. She led the way to a booth in the back. "I know I'm ready for it."

"This is very nice," Kiri assured her, looking over Kimberly's shoulder. "Very nice."

"Sarcasm is..." Kimberly began, then stopped as a tall, buxom blonde waitress appeared at their tableside.

"Hi, can I get you anything to drink?" She was drop dead gorgeous. "We're on the light eaters menu tonight."

"I'd like a glass of Chardonnay." Kimberly watched as Kiri turned on the charm. "Do you have a house brand? Or perhaps something you would recommend?"

Several minutes of animated chatter later, she had their drink orders. She started to leave, then turned back. "Oh, if you need anything else, my name is Britney."

"Of course it is," Kiri said in a de soto voice, too low for the waitress to hear. She smiled at Kimberly serenely, leaned forward and spoke in a stage whisper. "Her name is Britney."

"Shaddap." Kimberly sighed. It was going to be a long night.

◆ ◆ ◆ ◆ ◆

Groundhog stood watching the entrance into the Dragon's Breath Saloon. A thirty-something couple came out, and he watched them get their bearings, then strike off towards Broadway.

It looked like a young professionals hangout. It was a good thing they'd clowned around at the entrance, or he might have lost them. He'd actually walked this street before, and didn't remember ever noticing the bar.

Blending into the crowd might be a problem. An idea occurred to him. He pulled out his phone and dialed.

◆ ◆ ◆ ◆ ◆

"Damn, can't you go straight!" Kimberly snarled. Disgruntled, she took a gulp of her wine. "Your turn."

"Thank you," Kiri smiled brightly as she lined a shot at one of the striped balls. "And no, I can't. Nine in the corner pocket."

"Enough with the sexual innuendos, already," Kimberly groaned.

"Sorry," Kiri muttered and began furiously chalking her cue. She moved stiffly to the far end of the table. "Fifteen in the side. Damn!"

Now I've done it, Kimberly thought, and followed her around the table and gently lifted the other's chin so their eyes met. The unexpected intimacy of the movement startled them both and they stared at each other. "Kiri, I'm sorry. I didn't mean to snap at you. I'm just not used to fighting off advances by gorgeous ladies."

Kiri's expression was like pictures Kimberly had seen of deer surprised in the wild, eyes soft and widened. And cautious. "It's your play," she finally said.

Kimberly nodded and looked down at the table, then back at Kiri suspiciously. Was that an intentional pun? Kiri mouth twitched, providing the answer.

Before either of them could speak, a new voice broke into their conversation. Two young men stood scross the table.

"How would you girls like to play...doubles," the taller one spoke. He was clean shaven, sandy haired, a little over six feet tall. His friend was a couple inches shorter, and very Italian.

Kimberly and Kiri grinned at each other. The two men mistook the expressions for acquiescence and Kimberly groaned inwardly as one of them began motioning for a waitress.

"Excuse me," she heard herself say. "We'd really rather play with ourselves." Beside her, Kiri snorted, spilling her drink. *Good one, Martin.*

The taller man glanced at his friend. "You girls wouldn't like some company?"

"Yeah," said the other. "Playing with us would be a lot more fun."

"No," Kimberly kept her voice level, but firm. "We just want a little private time to ourselves."

"We have so much catching up to do...," Kiri said in her brightest, most irritating voice."

"You guys have a nice evening." Kimberly could have been dismissing a witness from the stand.

The two men shrugged and returned to the bar.

Kimberly impulsively gave Kiri a hug. "Sorry I was so bitchy," Kimberly whispered in her ear. Embarrassed, she stepped to the pool table and looked for a shot.

"Hey, it's okay," Kiri said in a quiet voice. Then her inevitable humor returned. "It's what we are. It's what we do."

They played for a while, and Kimberly was glad when she saw the two men finally leave. She sunk the eightball, winning the game. "That's two out of three. Wanna go best out of five?"

"Can't." Kiri shook her head. "Someone put some quarters down. He's got winner."

"Who?" Kimberly hadn't seen anyone come near the table. She glanced around the room and saw a guy at the bar pick up his drink and stroll over.

"Got a winner?" the big man said in a friendly voice.

"We're both winners," Kiri quipped.

"I can see that," the man grinned broadly.

Kimberly found herself smiling and was surprised. Normally, she wasn't so congenial to strangers in bars, but he had a disarming manner. He also reminded her of somebody, but she couldn't put her finger on who.

"Eddie Little." He was big, and not just tall. But more of a soft big, instead of Sergeant McGregor, hard as nails, big. He had to be, oh, six foot three, and probably over two hundred and fifty pounds. Big baby face, reddened by exposure to the sun. I'll bet he burns easy, Kimberly mused.

"Kimberly Martin," she said, belatedly responding. "And this is my friend, Kiri Oshiba." *Way to go, Martin. Keep up the incognito.* From Kiri's expression, she knew the same thoughts were passing through her friend's head.

"Really, Kiri Oshiba?" Eddie Little grinned down at her. "Not the actress?" He squinted at her. "I can't believe it. I've seen a bunch of your movies."

"Thanks," Kiri said, and Kimberly stared. Was she...blushing? She watched the two of them chatter away as he racked the balls for the next game. Kimberly thought he was really young at first, but the more she looked, the less certain she was. He just has a baby face, she decided. I'll bet he couldn't grow a beard to save his life.

"Your break, Miss Martin," he said.

"Mrs.," she corrected, then winced. Now why did I do that?

A few shots later he excused himself to go to the restroom. Kiri sidled up next to Kimberly on the cushioned bench that ran along the back wall.

"Aren't we the babble-on sister, tonight," she teased. "A little be-guiled, are we?"

"No, he's just really easy to talk to. I don't know what it is," Kimberly confessed. " He reminds me of someone."

"Me, too," Kiri agreed. Then she straightened. "I know..."

"John..." Kimberly had it. They both finished the name together.

"Belushi," Kiri said.

"Candy," she said.

They started to argue, then stopped and thought about it.

"I can see it," Kiri said finally. "He's a cross between them. And a pretty good one, too. He's funny."

"Like a big puppy," Kimberly nodded. "Watch it, here he comes."

"Well, which was it?" Little asked in an amused tone.

"Which was what." Kiri stalled in her dense chick voice.

"John Candy, or Belushi," he asked dryly. "Don't bother denying it. Literally everybody I meet notices at some point.

"Um, notices?" Kimberly felt her face redden.

"I saw you ladies talking when I came out." He grinned. "I recognized the subject."

"We might have noticed some resemblance," Kiri admitted.

"Personally, I can't see it." He beamed. "I've always thought I looked more like...well, John Wayne."

Both women looked at him. In his dreams, maybe, Kimberly thought with amusement.

"Hey, are we playing pool, or what?" She pointed her cue at him. "Your shot, 'Duke'."

He stood up straight.

"That's, 'The Duke', to you, non-believer."

He then preceded to clear the table.

Two hours later, Kimberly covered a yawn and glanced over at Kiri. They had given up trying to beat Eddie an hour ago, and had retreated to a table. The three of them talked about a wide variety of things, and Kimberly had to admit, the man was charming, in a little boyish way.

And funny, very funny.

But it was getting late, and tomorrow was going to be tough. She caught Kiri's eye.

"You ready, Kiri-sama? Long day tomorrow." Kiri nodded reluctantly and Kimberly caught the waitress' attention. "I got it."

"Let me," Eddie smiled, reaching for his wallet.

"No." Kimberly and Kiri answered together, then grinned tiredly at each other.

"Okay, okay." Eddie laughed, raising his hands in surrender. He watched silently as Kimberly paid the bill, tipping generously. "You two sisters or something? You're almost always on the same track."

"Sisters in soul," Kiri slurred, groaning as she stood. She raised an eyebrow at him. "Two peas in a pod, and all that."

"All right, 'pea-pod'," Kimberly said good-naturedly. "Let's hit the road."

"Before we hit the commode," Kiri agreed solemnly.

Eddie snickered. "Are you okay to get home?"

"We're fine," Kimberly assured him. "I'm in decent shape and I'll watch her."

"Always in control." Eddie nodded his agreement. "I noticed that. Well, be careful."

"I will," Kimberly assured him.

"Yes, we will," Kiri corrected as she slipped an arm around Kimberly's waist. "Good night, noble sir."

When they reached the sidewalk, the cool night air seemed to refresh Kiri. Her walk straightened out, and she grew quiet.

"You okay?" Kimberly asked, a little concerned.

"I'm fine," Kiri said. She sighed. "You know, if all guys were like Eddie, I might regret being gay a little more."

"Do you have a choice?" Kimberly asked, doubting.

"No, I guess not," she admitted, her voice sounding sad. "But it does make it easier to accept this lifestyle having ninety-nine per cent of all guys be jerks."

"So if it was something you could choose..." Kimberly gave her the lead.

Kiri snorted. "You think anybody in their right mind would choose to be gay? It's not choice. It's more like..." She stared up at the sky as they walked. "...like a decision to accept the inevitable. To admit the unthinkable."

"You don't want to be gay?"

"Hell no! Oh, I don't know." Kiri walked a little closer so she could take Kimberly's arm. "I mean, I like women. Hell, I love women. But, would I have chosen to love women? Probably not."

"Why not?" Kimberly asked, trying to draw Kiri out farther.

"Gays are the last acceptable bigotry," Kiri said bluntly.

"Excuse me?" Kimberly asked, startled.

"If you call a Latino a spick, he'll slice you up, or shoot you. Call a black man a nigger, he'll kill you. And everyone will agree, at least publicly, you deserved it." She raised a hand to stop Kimberly's protest. "I know. There are still lots of bigots for race and sex and all that other stuff, but they don't express it outside their own circles of friends that feel the same way."

Kiri stopped and turned to face her. "But if you call somebody queer, or faggot, or dyke, people just nod or keep their mouths shut. It's the last acceptable prejudice in America. Or the world, for that matter."

Kimberly nodded, but before she could speak, another voice broke in.

"Well, isn't that a shame?"

Kimberly and Kiri both whirled, then froze as two men moved out of the alley they had just passed. One, a tall, slender black man, sported a knife, and moved to stand in front of Kiri. He grinned at her, showing a gap where two front teeth were missing.

"Ooh, exotic stuff." He waved the knife and took a step closer, as did the other man, a chunky, short white guy.

"In the alley 'ladies'." The white man leered. "We want your purses, and...heh, maybe some of your 'other' valuables, too."

Kimberly felt, rather than saw Kiri tense up, and knew what was going to happen. *Oh, no! Martin, you're not ready for this!*

As one, they reacted when the men moved in closer. Kimberly tried the only kick she really felt comfortable with. Using her right foot as a feint, she kicked straight up, hitting the white man in the face with her left foot as hard as she could.

To her amazement, his head snapped back and he dropped to the ground, groaning, holding his face. In horror, she watched blood seep between his fingers.

With a start, she turned in time to see Kiri twisting the arm of the black man as he lay on the ground. She yanked it hard and he shrieked in agony as his shoulder dislocated. For good measure, she kicked him in the ribs.

The sound of someone running made them turn, both dropping into stances, as Eddie Little rushed up to them. He looked at the two men on the ground in amazement, then at them.

"Uh, do you need my help?" he asked uncertainly.

"I think we've about taken care of things, thank you," Kimberly said, feeling a little dazed. "But thank you anyway. What are you doing here?"

"I was headed back to my car." He pointed farther down the street. "Are you sure you don't want a lift?"

"No thanks, I live just around the corner." Kimberly shook her head, bewildered. "What do we do about them?" she asked, pointing at the two men on the ground. She looked at her hand. It was shaking. She had never been in an actual fight before, not even as a child.

"Well, we could call the police," Eddie began. Kimberly looked at Kiri, who made a face. That idea didn't appeal to her, either.

"Can we just leave?" Kimberly looked uncertain. "Are their injuries life-threatening?"

"Not likely." The big man glanced at the two groaning men, leaning over to pick up the knife in a gloved hand. "Anyone making that much noise isn't about to die." He grinned. "Except maybe of embarrassment. I would just go home and avoid having to answer a bunch of questions by the cops. Plus, that way, these creeps will never know who you are, or where you live. The last thing you want is them showing up on your doorstep."

"You got that right," Kiri agreed fervently.

She and Kimberly glanced at each other, a little self-consciously. Finally, Kimberly spoke. "Well, thanks for trying to help. It's the thought that counts."

"Believe me, it's my pleasure." Eddie said, his round, ruddy face breaking into its' habitual grin. "Maybe I'll see you two again some-time."

"Good night," they both chorused and, with one last glance at the two fallen, would-be muggers, hurried back to Kimberly's building.

As they entered the elevator, Kiri gave Kimberly a wink.

"I like your hangout, but the neighborhood...?"

"It's full of career criminals," Kimberly said with a straight face.

"Really?" Kiri sounded surprised. Kimberly nodded.

"Yeah. Lawyers, mostly."

❖ ❖ ❖ ❖ ❖

Groundhog watched the two women disappear around the corner, then grabbed both men by the scruffs of their necks and dragged them into the alley. They stared at him, having no idea who he was.

"I paid you to do a particular chore. You failed."

"You didn't say anything about their being able to fight." The man's voice sounded muffled by the hem of his shirt he was holding to his bleeding nose.

"Hey, you'll still pay us, right?" His voice full of pain, the black man with the dislocated shoulder tried to leverage himself to his knees. "I'm gonna need to see a doctor..."

"No you won't." Groundhog's voice was barely perceptible, he spoke so softly. He quickly stepped forward and neither man had a chance to react. He thrust the knife into the white man's sternum so hard, the hilt itself was partially embedded in his chest. With no pause in motion he grasped the head of the black man, and with a sharp twist, snapped his neck. The first man was lying on his back, still gasping, and Groundhog slung his friends body across his face, letting the weight of the body finish the suffocating process.

Straightening his jacket, he made sure no blood had splashed on him, then, without a backward glance, left the alley.

Station Osaka

Jim took a deep breath. It didn't matter how many times you saw the Trixmae. When they first came on the screen, it was...disturbing. What he saw was either one Trixmae, sex unknown, composed of a bunch of oily looking, black cables and ropes, writhing constantly, or a whole bunch of ropelike creatures twisting and turning around each other.

Having sex, maybe?

Were they a group entity? Was there a body or trunk inside that mass of spagetti? Was the camera too high, only showing Trixmae greasy kidstuff hair?

"Hello, my name is Jim Morris. I am the...uh, Shogun of the humans on Station Osaka." *Shogun? Was that the best he could come up with?* "Whom do I have the pleasure of addressing?"

"The Trixmae."

I should have seen that coming, Jim thought ruefully. He tried again.

"I've been told you requested permission to depart?"

"No."

"Oh." Jim felt relieved. "You don't wish to leave?"

"Yes."

Jim blinked. "Yes? Uh, yes, what?"

"Yes, Shogun?"

"No, no." Jim closed his eyes briefly. "I mean, yes, you don't wish to leave, or yes, you do wish to leave."

"The intention is to leave, not to ask permission."

"Oh." Jim got it. "Why do you wish to leave."

"That is not important."

"Well, actually, it kind of is." Jim tried to be polite, but firm. "You have maintained a ship at this station since we took over. Your habit has been to give plenty of notice before departure. Now you wish to leave immediately. There must be some reason."

"There is."

"What is it?"

For the first time, Jim thought he detected a moment of indecision.

"The time is appropriate," the reply finally came.

"Have you sighted approaching ships?" Jim tensed.

"Have you?" came the swift counter.

"No-o-o..." Jim admitted slowly. "But I suspect your sensors may be better than Ananab."

"They are."

"Okay." Jim was getting tired of this. "So, have you sighted something we haven't?"

"There are many things you do not see." Did the alien sound chiding?

"I'm sure," Jim said drily. "I'm more interested in any enemy ships out there."

"The Trixmae can not become involved in a dispute between Ananab and Human. This ship will disconnect from the station in five of your minutes."

"I'd rather you didn't."

"May good fortune be yours, Shogun of the Humans." The connection ended.

Jim sighed, then started as Pearl spoke. "Long range sensors have been modified, based on observation of Trixmae and Hstahni systems." Pearl sounded...excited?

"How did you get that data?"

"It was stored in my memory."

Jim grinned. "Why didn't you ever try and update your sensors before?"

"No one asked me to."

Jim laughed outright. "From now on, use initiative to make any self-improvements you think will be helpful."

"That will be...useful."

So that's the sound of an excited computer, Jim thought, amused. The mood didn't last.

"I have sighted six anomalies that appear to be sheathed ships, moving slowly towards this station to avoid detection. At their current rate, they will be within effective firing range in approximately twelve hours."

"Whose ships are they?"

"Inconclusive, but it appears there are three Ananab and three Tryr ships. This data is subject to revision, as they close on the station."

"Close enough." Jim was grim. "Irene, recall the crews for Jade Wolverine and Jade Samurai. Pearl, patch me in to Governor Lang."

He began walking briskly to his ship.

CHAPTER FOURTEEN

Jade Wolverine

Lasty risked a glance at the Jim Morris. The Human sat slouched in his Captain's Perch, a scowl on his face. It was definitely not a time for idle chatter.

Everyone else on the bridge seemed to share his opinion. Rick Baker and Dutter had their heads bowed over their screens, murmuring observations and exchanging data. They kept their voices low and, every now and then, would glance surreptitiously at the Captain.

Angela Dawson sat at her security post off to the left and frowned at her screen. At intervals, she would raise her eyes to glare at the Jim Morris. Lasty was no expert at judging human expressions, but it looked to him like she was struggling internally with some decision.

Lasty started as she abruptly rose and approached the Jim Morris, who transferred his scowl to her, as if daring her to speak.

"Captain, I must protest your removing my best gunner from her post. If we are going into battle, I need my best men at battle stations."

"She's not a man." Lasty blanched at the cold tone. Angela Dawson didn't flinch. "She's a fifteen going on sixteen year old girl." Jim Morris eyed his security chief in open skepticism. "And she's not your best gunner."

"Yes, she is." Angela Dawson glared back at him, and Lasty wished that he were elsewhere. "Irene, your analysis, please?"

"I concur with Security Chief Dawson," Irene said. "Afsaneh Riahi has consistently graded out higher than any of the other humans, including the crews of the other ships, and Station Osaka. She has a very good mind for tactics, she anticipates her opponent's movements, her reflexes are faster, and her aim is better."

"She's just a child." Lasty felt sympathy for the Jim Morris. He was trying to protect his daughter, but the safety of remaining at Station Osaka was illusionary. The Humans were sending three ships, two untested, against six, all experienced. Should they lose this battle, the ships might withdraw and flee, but the station would remain at the mercy of the Ananab.

The Ananab didn't even have a word for mercy in their language.

"In times of war, children have to grow up fast." Angela Dawson's voice had a softer tone now. "And you don't need me to tell you how fast she's growing up."

"Yeah." The Jim Morris looked depressed. "I know." He slapped the arm of his chair in obvious frustration. "I just want to keep her safe!"

"There is not a place she would feel safer, than near you." Lasty felt himself blush at his words. "I-I mean no disrespect, Jim Morris, but there probably is no safer place."

"That is true." The computer's voice was blunt. "Although Pearl would take any and all measures to safeguard her, this ship provides a means to escape, if it comes to that."

The Jim Morris stood up and raised his arms, hands balled into tight fists. He looked grim, but determined.

"Broadcast this ship-wide, Irene," he said, his voice strong and firm. "I would like to clarify things, in case there is any doubt in anyone's minds."

Lasty adjusted his screen to split into eight separate windows to show the crew at their various stations. The younger gunners looked sullen, but the rest of the crew listened attentively.

"We are currently riding in Jade Samurai's exhaust, in stealth mode. The only external power is in our tractor beam, which Irene has assured me is undetectable by the ships we are approaching." He paused. "This does not mean we have the option of flight. When we reach the optimum range, we will power up and attack. The first sign our enemy will have of us, will be when we attack."

Lasty realized he was holding his breath, and cautiously let air out, trying not to attract any attention. The Jim Morris continued.

"The Ananab think they are six ships against one. They expect to dock at Osaka in hours, and retake the station with minimal effort."

Jim smashed his right fist into his open left palm and Lasty jumped in his seat, his heart racing. He saw Afsaneh's friends were perched on the edge of their seats, not feigning boredom.

"They will not have an easy space battle. And the only way they'll ever dock at Station Osaka..." Lasty felt shivers up and down all four arms, what the humans called 'goose-bumps'. "...is as prisoners!"

Lasty watched humans on the screens jump to their feet, shouting in exultation. The tall, black youth, Ellis Jackson exchanged handslaps with the other Jackson, Sean. Height fives, was it? Hind fives?

"Damn straight!" He was surprised to see Angela Dawson nodding her head vigorously. "We show them whose house it is, now!"

Lasty gasped and sagged in his seat, exhausted. If there had been any doubt in his mind, this scene erased it. Even though the Jim Morris was the Chammorz, even if the Humans were his best chance of personal happiness and a fulfilling life, and yes, he counted many of them among his personal friends now, there was one absolute truth.

In their own words, they scared the hell out of him.

Chula Vista, California

"Now remember, Matt, just let us do the talking." Du Brimar had a wide grin on his face. "You just confirm whatever we say, or Jo Coran will be very angry. She has faith in you, and you know the saying about 'Hell hath no fury...', right?"

"That saying doesn't apply to this situation."

"You'd better believe it applies to how she'll feel," Du Brimar advised coolly.

"Let's just get this over with, okay?" Matt stepped up to the door of the small ranch-style house and rang the bell. The two Egelv moved to the side, out of the view through the peephole.

Howard Prause opened the door.

"Yes?" The teacher blinked at him, obviously not recognizing him. And why should he? They'd never met. "Can I help you?"

"Yes, Mr. Prause, you can," Matt began, but Du Brimar smoothly stepped into view and reached forward to touch the teacher on his temple, the tiny translator adhering to his skin.

"Howard Prause, we need to ask you a few questions," he began, ignoring the teacher's gaping stare. "Could we please step inside?"

"Uh, uh." Prause began hyperventilating. His face went completely white with fear. "You're, I, I mean...oh, my God!"

"Yes, quite," Du Brimar agreed amicably, stepping forward, causing the high school teacher to back-pedal in panic. Jo Coran motioned to Matt to enter before her, and she closed the door and, after a moment's examination, locked and bolted it.

Howard Prause didn't even notice. He couldn't tear his eyes off Du Brimar. "You're..." he began.

"Aliens." Du Brimar completed the thought, nodding his head sympathetically. "I know this must be quite a shock, but we need your help."

"My help?" Prause's voice squeaked on the first word.

"Yes, your help." Du Brimar beamed and nodded again. "Is there some place we can talk, perhaps a little more comfortably?"

"Talk?" Prause looked around wildly. "The living room..."

"...would be perfect," Du Brimar agreed. He guided the confused teacher into the adjacent room, giving Matt a warning look before he continued. "My name is Du Brimar, and my associate here is Jo Coran. This is Matthew Stickel. He is our human liaison in this matter."

"Matter?" Prause said weakly.

"Well, yes." Du Brimar grew serious. "The matter of the hijacking of the Jade Viking? You were on board when it was taken, were you not?"

Prause just looked at him, dumfounded.

Du Brimar worked his lips, probably trying to keep from laughing, Matt thought.

"Perhaps I should clarify our position." Du Brimar took a seat in an overstuffed easy chair, looking slightly ridiculous, Matt thought.

Prause hesitantly sat at one end of a couch and openly flinched as Jo Coran sat at the other end. She didn't crack a smile, just stared at him.

"Mr. Prause...may I call you Robert?" Jo Coran rolled her eyes. "Robert, our race is called the Egelv. We are also officers of what you would call...an intergalactic police force."

Matt made a strangled sound and Jo Coran shot him a warning look. It didn't help to see that she was also having trouble keeping from laughing. Du Brimar continued smoothly.

"We've been chasing certain Ananab fugitives for years now, trying to find their hideout. We're almost certain your kidnappers are the same criminals we've been searching for." Du Brimar leaned forward and Prause automatically leaned back in his seat. "We need to question others that made it back to Earth, find out everything we can, and bring these villains to justice!"

"Justice?" Prause's voice was weak.

"Yes, by God. Justice!" Du Brimar's voice was filled with emotion. "I've heard about the plight of the children in your group, of your struggle to bring them all back, safe and sound."

"You have?" Prause sounded confused. "How?"

"Letterman," Du Brimar said smoothly.

"Oh." Prause looked around at them. "We were told there was no interstellar police force, no governing body of authority..."

"Of course you were." Du Brimar laughed. "Do you think the Ananab want you to know the truth, to give you hope of rescue?" He grew solemn. "They know full well, the rules and laws against taking advantage of less developed races, of interfering, the..."

"Prime directive?" Prause asked hopefully.

"Uh, yes, exactly so." Matt made a sound in his throat and Du Brimar turned to him, transfixing him with a stare. "We, of course, call it something different. But, in essence, it's the same. We must..." He looked like he was searching for words. "...nourish these young races, of which yours is only one! Allow them to grow naturally, to mature."

"What can I do?" Prause looked awestruck.

"Well, I know you've already told your own authorities once, but if you could..." Du Brimar let the sentence die away.

"Of course!" Prause sat up straight in his seat in excitement. "At least, I know you'll believe me! Those FBI idiots..."

"Understandable, under the circumstances," Du Brimar said graciously. I think I'm going to be sick, Matt thought. "Please, start wherever you wish..."

"Well..." Prause rubbed his hands together, obviously relishing the chance of an understanding audience.

"...and the next thing I knew, I was lying on a stony beach." Prause sat back, looking tired from the long tale.

"Amazing!" Du Brimar gave him a sympathetic look. "And you say this 'Kimberly Martin' is one of the ringleaders in this plot to keep the truth hidden?"

"That's right." Prause's eyes had a triumphant gleam. "She would know all their plans."

"Tell me." Jo Coran spoke for the first time. "Is the captured Ananab ship still in orbit, or did it return to the space station?"

"I don't know," he admitted. "I think as soon as they figured out who felt what way, they began plotting in secrecy. I never heard any of them discuss what was going to happen after we were returned."

"This Martin woman can tell us what we need to know about that," Du Brimar assured him. "We're going to follow up on these leads. May we call on you again, should we need to?"

"Oh, please!" Prause was practically vibrating, he was so excited. "If I can be of any assistance..."

"We'll let you know." Du Brimar stood and extended a hand. After a moment, Prause shook it. Encouraged when nothing bad happened, he proceeded to vigorously shake first Matt's, then Jo Coran's hand. She allowed it, almost hiding her distain.

It took almost ten more minutes for them to escape the enthusiastic teacher, but finally they were outside, with Du Brimar giving one last solemn wave.

"Don't worry, Robert. We'll save the children. You can count on it." His voice grew thick. "It's chances to make things right like this that made me go into the service in the first place. We'll bring your children home!"

There were tears in the teachers eyes as the door closed. No one spoke until they were down the sidewalk to the edge of the road. Then Du Brimar gave a little sniff of his nose and dabbed at the corners of his eyes.

Matt looked at him suspiciously, not buying it for a moment. Du Brimar stopped and looked back at the small house. "That man...that poor man..."

He put a hand over his face as he turned towards them. It didn't cover the escaping grin as he fingered a small control that caused the teacher's translator patch to dissolve.

"I should have been in the movies."

San Francisco, California

Karl Costa nursed his Wild Turkey. He wanted to slug it down and have another, but he'd given in to that urge too often lately. He swirled the ice shards and watered down bourbon in the bottom of the glass, watching the ice slowly disappear.

"Sir, I think we've got it right, this time."

He didn't look up. Patrick Beatty was a good kid. Very loyal, hard working, clean-cut, attentive to details. He would probably have to kill the poor bastard someday. He sighed and carefully took a minuscule sip.

"Go on, Patrick," he said finally.

"Well, Sir, after the lead to Atlanta didn't pan out..." The young man hesitated. "We broadened the search to include all Asiatic woman for starters, in particular those with a female companion."

"What I thought you were going to say was that you'd found out where they went." Costa narrowed his eyes and frowned at his agent. "Cut to the chase, Pat."

"Uh, I prefer Patrick, sir."

Costa glared at him. "I know."

"Oh." Beatty hurried to continue. "New York, Sir. They flew to New York. The Oshiba woman was disguised as a Chinese."

"Disguised?" Costa closed his eyes. "What kind of disguise, University of Beijing t-shirt? Never mind." He came to a decision.

"Book four tickets to New York, next available. Bump passengers, if necessary. I want the two of us, Gonzalez, and Roosevelt in the air within the hour." Beatty nodded, concentrating as he listened. "Call the office in New York, have somebody make arrangements for us to have rooms somewhere near Central park, on the...west side. That's where her condo and workplace are. "Oh, and have someone meet us at the airport."

"Yes, Sir."

"Oh, and Patrick..."

"Yes Sir?" Beatty looked at him, obviously expecting a compliment.

"Call my wife and explain to her that I've been called to the east coast, and will be gone a few days."

Beatty blanched, and Costa chided himself. It was too easy to bait the boy. And cruel.

"Just kidding, Beatty. Call New York."

Costa noticed he'd finished his drink at some point. He resisted the urge to order another one. He had to call his wife, and somehow, she would be able to tell.

Somewhere near Chicago, Illinois

Sasama swore and veered into the next lane. These people drove like maniacs. Beside him, Iori alternated between inspecting his map, and glancing fearfully at the cars swerving from lane to lane all around them.

"Well? Which turnoff do I take?"

"Um, the next right, I think." Iori frowned and traced a line on the map with his index finger.

"You think?" Sasama fumed. "We didn't even need to go near Chicago. This...loop is crazy, and so are all the drivers on it. Now find how we get back on the right path to New York!"

"Okay, okay, sorry!" Iori pointed. "Take the next right. It takes us back to I-90."

"You're sure."

"Yes, I sure." Iori glared at him. "I've had about enough of your complaining. I know how to read a map. Turn here!"

Sasama did so, cutting off a pickup truck that immediately sounded its horn. As they left the irate driver behind, Sasama sighed in relief and looked at the sign overhead as they passed.

Downtown Chicago, these four lanes.

◆ ◆ ◆ ◆ ◆

New York City, New York

"This is where you work?" Kiri leaned back and looked up at the tall office building in awe. "Your company uses this whole building?"

"No." Kimberly laughed. "Only the top eight floors. Spencer Corp leases the rest."

"So your company does own the whole thing." Kiri shook her head, as if trying to figure how much a building with sixty something floors in downtown Manhattan would cost.

"Not my company," Kimberly reminded her. "Although my boss, William Spencer, is the majority stockholder."

"You own any shares?"

"A few," Kimberly admitted. "Not much really, on the grand scheme of things."

They rode the speed elevator in silence. Kimberly was lost in thought, and Kiri seemed subdued by the surroundings. The door opened and they were confronted by a wall bearing the corporate logo, a slashing S resembling a lightning bolt.

"Catchy," Kiri said, giving it a thorough investigation. "It kind of looks like the Sukuru emblem when they use American lettering."

"American?"

Kiri grinned. "You know, not the Japanese squiggles and slashes, the letter 'S'."

Kimberly laughed. "I'm glad to see you're in touch with your roots. Where is everybody?"

They walked down a hallway to a corner office. Kimberly tried her keycard. She raised her eyebrows when it worked.

"I would have bet money he'd have changed the combination by now," she muttered.

"Who?"

"My boss, Will."

"Good looking." Kiri inspected an autographed picture on the wall. Kimberly watched her friend furtively snoop around, trying to get a feel for Kimberly's work atmosphere.

"Good looking, but also very possessive." Kimberly turned her computer on and saw she had a message. I wonder who left it, Kimberly thought sardonically. She played it.

A video picture came on her monitor, and Will Spencer looked out at her from his office. Kiri jumped in surprise.

"Hey, Kitten." Kimberly winced, feeling rather than seeing Kiri glance sideways at her. She concentrated on his words.

"I missed you last night. I'm glad you're back." He smiled, as if waiting for a response. "In case you're wondering, the company picnic is today. We're all down at the Park. The usual place. Come join us. I'm sure everyone would like to see that you're okay." He gave her a knowing smile. "I know I would." His expression changed subtlety. "Seriously, we need to talk. I'll expect you."

The picture ended.

Kiri whistled softly under her breath. She inspected the hardwood of Kimberly's desk and cabinets, then opened the refrigerator. Her eyebrows shot up. "Well, well! A bottle of Dom. Not your usual diet sodas, frozen lunches, and yogurt, that's for sure."

"That's not mine," Kimberly protested. Kiri just smiled at her.

"Does that mean we can't take it to the park with us?"

Kimberly considered. Did she really want to answer a bunch of questions right now? On the other hand, an informal setting might be just the thing. And Will had been rather firm about her coming.

"Why not?" Kimberly shrugged, and gave Kiri a smile. "Give me a minute or two, to reacquaint myself and we'll be off."

"We'll need glasses," Kiri reminded her, raising the bottle.

"Got 'em," Kimberly reassured her. "Go powder your nose or something."

Thirty minutes later they were on the street, Kiri with an insulated bag containing the champagne and two glasses hung over her left shoulder. They had stopped back at Kimberly's place to change to more casual clothes. Both wore sweatshirts, jeans, and athletic shoes, and carried lightweight jackets. It was a beautiful October afternoon, but when the sun started setting, the temperature would drop.

"One thing I can't figure out." Kiri sounded hesitant.

"Shoot." Kimberly smiled at her.

"If Spencer Corp is so big and powerful, so rich, how did we just walk right in?"

Kimberly grinned.

"On the weekends, access to that particular bank of elevators is restricted. Security was watching us from the moment we entered the building, until the point we entered the Spencer offices. Then internal security took over to my doorway."

"And inside your office?" Kiri teased.

"If I ever find out there are any surveillance cameras in my office, someone will be pulling them out of their ass."

Kiri shrugged. "In Japan, it's not uncommon for companies to videotape their employees for any number of reasons, anywhere on the work site."

Kimberly shuddered. "Thank God I don't work in Japan, then." She decided to change the subject. "Have you ever been to New York before?"

"Sure," Kiri said. "But usually, it's for a purpose, and on a tight schedule. I've never actually come as a tourist. Or a guest."

Kimberly impulsively put an arm around her friend's shoulders. "Well, you can be my guest, any time, for as long as you like."

"Thanks," Kiri said shyly, slipping her own arm around Kimberly's waist. They walked for a few blocks until the park began coming into sight. Then, by unspoken agreement, they pulled apart, a little self-consciously.

They had barely entered the park when a voice called out in excitement.

"Kimberly! Kimberly Martin!"

A young man waved to her, pointing for the benefit of the two women flanking him.

"Tom Adams!" Kimberly waved back. She nudged Kiri. "He's one of the nice ones, if you know what I mean."

"I can't knock his taste in women," Kiri said mischievously. One was blond, the other brunette. Both were about the same size as Kimberly, both extremely attractive. "Which one do you think he's with?"

"Knowing Tom? Both." Kimberly grinned. "But not the same night."

"Tom, how are you?" Kimberly allowed herself to be hugged. She took a closer look at the two women. "Jill, is it?" she asked the blonde, who nodded.

"I'm Carol," the other woman told her. "I just started at Spencer a few weeks ago."

"Watch out," Kimberly confided. "There's sharks in them there offices. And Tom is one of the hungriest."

"Hey," Tom protested good-naturedly. Kimberly raised an eyebrow and he laughed. "Oh, it's true," he admitted. "I just don't want her to find out yet."

"How's the turnout this year?" Kimberly looked over to where the Spencer pavilion stood.

"Record numbers." Tom squeezed her arm. "Mr. Spencer put the word out you'd be here."

"Really? Did he now?" Kimberly began a slow burn.

"Kimberly, you're back."

"Will! So good to see you." Kimberly pulled away when the hug showed no signs of stopping..

Will Spencer was a lean six-footer with short, jet-black hair and aquiline features. He was dressed casually in polo and shorts. The wide grin he flashed featured perfect white teeth.

"Kimberly, thank God you're safe, and home where you belong." He turned to face Kiri, while slipping his arm around Kimberly's waist.

"So who's your friend?"

"Kiri Oshiba, Will Spencer," Kimberly said automatically. "We met on the cruise. We've become very good friends."

"So, you're the Spencer in Spencer Corp, eh?" Kimberly watched in fascination as Kiri shifted into her clever, jet-set, charismatic mode. "I like your building. It's so...big."

"Uh, yes." Will cleared his throat, then shook a finger as if suddenly realizing something. "Wait a minute. You're Kiri Oshiba, the actress!"

"Guilty as charged."

"Tom, did you know who this was?" Within moments, Will had Kiri surrounded with admirers. He skillfully drew Kimberly off to the side. "You didn't answer my messages."

"I just got in yesterday." Kimberly had been expecting this, but it still irritated her. She didn't like having to explain herself to anyone. "I knew I'd see you today."

"You were found days ago." Will's voice had a slight edge. "We live in the age of cell phones and computers. You should have contacted me at once."

"I was being questioned by the FBI," Kimberly reminded him. "By the time I got them off my back for a moment, I wanted nothing more than to catch my breath for a day or two."

"Well, you still should have called me." Will was mollified, but only slightly. "You know how much you mean to me. I've been worried sick."

"Sorry." Kimberly glanced around, not wanting the conversation she knew was coming.

"You wouldn't believe what the tabloids have been saying about you and the ship. By the way, what did happen to my ship?"

"As I told the FBI, I was up late at a series of parties. The next thing I knew, I was waking up on a cold, rocky beach in Alaska."

"What really happened?" Will wasn't buying it, she could see. *No surprise there, Martin.*

"What I just told you." Kimberly kept her face impassive. "Do you think I would lie to the FBI?"

"What I think is, you're the best lawyer I've ever worked with. You could convince the FBI they were the CIA."

"Well, I must be slipping," Kimberly said. "I don't think they believed me."

"So where's my ship?" Will repeated.

"I don't know." It's true, Kimberly thought. It's been broken down into pieces, I don't know where they are. "All I know is what I told the feds."

"Look, I have to see Sho Toshida tomorrow, and I'm going to need answers."

Kimberly felt a chill run down her spine. Another Toshida! Yoshi Toshida had been a royal son of a bitch. The last thing she wanted to do was meet another one. Her mind raced. "Maybe you should be asking him questions," she parried. "After all, none of his high-ranking people have showed up. Maybe they're with the ship, wherever it is."

She held her breath as he contemplated that idea.

"Hmm, interesting thought." Will looked at her suspiciously. "That still doesn't explain why you can't remember almost two months of your life."

Kimberly shrugged. "I couldn't possibly imagine what happened during that time." *Not in my wildest dreams would I have ever imagined the past two months. Wait, what was he saying now?*

"...so I want you to see this...specialist," he finished.

"What? A shrink?" Kimberly frowned at him. "I'm not going to have a bunch of doctors and quacks poking at me, both physically and mentally. No way."

"Kimberly, this is something I want you to do." Will looked at her meaningfully. "For me, if not for yourself."

"No." Kimberly was blunt. "I'm not going to do it."

"Yes, you are." Will showed some of the steel she knew was hidden just under that congenial surface. "I'm still the head of this corporate family, and you'll do as I say." He grew earnest. "Do this for us, Kimberly. You know how I feel about you, care about you. Let me help solve this mystery."

"Will, there is no us." Kimberly'd known even before the cruise this day would come, but she still wasn't prepared for it.

"Kimberly, you're still confused from whatever ordeal you've been through. We're good for each other, can't you see that?"

"What I see is, you're not listening. I don't love you, I work for you."

She watched his face grow dark with fury, then subside until, if she hadn't seen his expression a moment before, it would have been impossible to tell how angry he was.

"If we have to do it this way, we will." He placed his hands on his

219

hips. "You do work for me, and you'll do as you're told. Monday morning, you're going to see the doctors I tell you to. I won't stand for any more insubordination."

"Damn it, Will. You don't own me." Kimberly became uncomfortably aware of the nearby people, listening in fascination. Kiri winked at her. It helped. "But you have helped me with one decision. I quit, effective immediately."

"The hell you do." Will was flabbergasted, then furious. "We have a contract. You can't walk out in the middle of all this!"

"Can, and have." The moment she'd quit, a load seemed to float away, and she felt calm and in total control. "You'll have it in writing by the time you get back to the office. As of this moment, I no longer work for you."

She started to turn away, and he grabbed her arm. She froze and looked at his hand pointedly. Her face was a mask as she raised her eyes to meet his, and he flinched. "Let go."

"You can't simply walk away like nothing has happened." Will blustered, but let go. "You're the one who lost a cruise ship worth millions! I'll have you declared mentally incompetent!" His eyes narrowed. "Think about it, Kimberly. You don't want to go down this road. We could still have the kind of relationship I've always pictured us working towards."

The hell with it, Kimberly decided wearily. "I doubt it, Will. I don't think my husband would approve. And you don't want to piss him off."

"Husband?" Will Spencer was rigid with fury. "Those stupid tabloids are right? You really did marry Jim Morris?"

"Yes, she did," Kiri called out from where she stood. "And you betta watch it, huh? He kick you ass, boy!"

"He's still missing." Will watched her face closely, and Kimberly kept her features calm.

"I turned up, he will too." She couldn't resist a jab. "He's quite a man."

"I hear he can't do half the things his movies show," Will sneered. "I hear he's a fake!"

Kimberly and Kiri broke into laughter. The people around them separated to allow them to come together. Kimberly took Kiri's hand and as they turned away, she tossed back one last comment.

"Don't believe everything you hear."

They walked for a while, and Kimberly realized she was holding Kiri's hand very tight.

"You still got the bottle and glasses?" she asked huskily. It was just hitting her what she'd done. For years, her career had been everything to her. And she'd just thrown it away. She felt...great.

Kiri patted her bag still slung over her shoulder, and it clinked. Kimberly steered them towards an empty picnic table under a huge oak tree.

"Let's celebrate!" Kimberly felt tears welling up in her eyes, but ignored them.

"I'm unemployed!"

◆ ◆ ◆ ◆ ◆

Chula Vista, California

Robert Prause stopped and ran a fingertip over the bookshelf and looked at it closely. Not a speck of dust. He checked an end table and found the same to be true.

With a sigh, he went to the kitchen and replaced the furniture polish under the sink. He looked at the paper toweling critically. Not worth using again, he decided, and threw it in the trash bag hanging on the inside of the cabinet door.

The doorbell rang.

Now who could that be, on a Saturday? He grew excited as he thought of his earlier visitors. Maybe the Egelv Patrol had returned for more help!

He hurried to answer the door, and was disappointed when it turned out to be three oriental gentlemen, all dressed in black suits.

"Good afternoon, Mr. Prause." The one in the middle spoke and they all bowed slightly. He did an awkward bow in response.

"Yes? May I help you?"

"We represent the Japanese government, Mr. Prause. May we ask you a few questions?"

"The Japa...uh, certainly. Come in, come in." He stepped aside to allow them to pass. They turned into the same living room that had contained the Egelv mere hours before. One of them stopped just inside to look at an art print he had bought years ago.

That picture was one of his favorites. A rich mixture of reds and oranges, it featured Chinese junks in a glorious sunset.

As he walked by the Japanese he felt a stinging on the back of his neck. He turned in time to see the man holding up a long needle.

"You stabbed me..." Robert Prause kept turning, and turning, and hardly felt the hands that caught him moments before he hit the floor.

Then he felt nothing.

New York City, New York

Will Spencer stood and glowered at the people having a good time around him. They kept a clear distance away from him, knowing he was angry. What they didn't know was how angry he was.

No was not a word he accepted very often. Never, in fact. And certainly not from some bitch who was lucky to have her job in the first place. Promoting her to such a high position had been a gamble in some of his peer's eyes. But he hadn't cared. From the moment he met her, he knew he would have her, eventually. And who would have thought, she turned out to be a brilliant lawyer.

He considered his options and kept his distaste off his features. He would get Addison in legal after her first thing in the morning. Sunday or not, he would have a court order by noon.

"Pekkar!" He snapped his fingers, and his personal assistant appeared immediately "Phone." He was handed his cellular. He thought for a moment, then dialed.

To his surprise, he didn't get the usual answering machine. He actually got a person.

"Hello," said a male voice.

"You don't usually answer in person."

"Mr. Spencer, what can I do for you?"

"You read the papers." It wasn't a question, and the man at the other end of the line didn't bother to answer. "One of my employees, Kimberly Martin,, has just turned up sans Jade Viking. I want you to find out everything you can about the survivors. In particular, the Martin woman. She just quit, and I think she's involved in all this somehow."

"Anything else?"

"Keep track of her." Spencer came to a conclusion. "I think she might try and disappear soon. A deposit will be made to your account before five o'clock today. The usual, I presume?"

"That will do, for now," the voice agreed.

"Thank you..." Spencer realized the other man had hung up.

Groundhog pushed the button to sever the connection and lowered his binoculars. That man had entirely too much power at his fingertips. But, his money was good.

He lifted his glasses to continue watching the two women sitting at their picnic table, laughing and drinking wine. One would think they didn't have a care in the world.

CHAPTER FIFTEEN

Station Osaka

"I'm bored," Afsaneh said to the empty room. "Pearl, please hook me into Jade Wolverine's internal surveillance system?"

"I can not do that, Afsaneh Riahi." Was that a reproving tone she heard? "Any transmission between Jade Wolverine and Osaka could reveal their position to the approaching enemy ships."

"Okay." Afsaneh had to admit that was a valid point. "So patch me into Jade Samurai's."

"That would not be wise at this point. Instead you should be concentrating on the pending battle, or running simulations."

"I've done so many simulations that I dream them," Afsaneh retorted. "Anyway, I'm the royal heir and you have to do what I say." She grinned triumphantly, then frowned at the computer's next words.

"Actually, you are the heir to the Heir. In any case, my primary duty is not to obey you, but to protect you. Since you are considered a minor in your own culture's eyes, my program allows me discretionary decisions. You need to be alert, not distracted."

"That sucks!" Afsaneh sullenly inspected her fingernails.

It wasn't fair! Most of her friends were on board Jade Wolverine! Hell, she'd gotten them their postings! At least they were about to go into battle, and their stations were grouped in twos, to allow one person to cover both stations in case of injury, or whatever.

This stupid space station had defensive and offensive weaponry stations spread all over the place. All the manned stations were very close to the actual weapons. This gave the personnel added incentive, she had once heard Lasty tell McGregor. And since no one had instructed otherwise, when the Hoag had built the extra weapons stations, they had continued that practice.

Which meant that she was stuck way out here at one of the extremities all alone. The nearest living human was probably a quarter of a mile away, tucked into his or her private purgatory.

She glared at the screen. All she could see was Jade Samurai closing on the six blips that represented the enemy. The Ananab force was still running under stealth mode, even though they had been identified and hailed by 'Samurai. Captain Asaya had warned them to turn away or face annihilation.

So far, no response.

"Well, can you show me 'Wolverine's position on my screen?"

"Certainly." A faint, glowing green blip appeared just above the wake of 'Samurai. The two ships were attached by thin lightblue strands that represented tractor beams. And more thin lightblue strands stretched from the back of the her ship to a third green blip.

"Hrumph." Afsaneh tossed her head, sending her long black strands flowing around her face. She brushed them back with one hand absentmindedly. "I should be there."

"I agree."

Afsaneh gaped. "Really?"

"Yes. There is a...the Ananab have answered." Pearl's voice grew businesslike, the words clipped and to the point.

"Put it on my speakers!" Afsaneh was surprised when she got no argument.

"...is the Ananab Command ship P'Funct. You are ordered to power down all weapons. The stolen Tryr ship approaching will stop all engines and prepare to be boarded. The captured Station Chaq will do the same. Any act of defense or aggression will be met with overwhelming force, and the guilty parties will be destroyed."

"I think not." Afsaneh suppressed a laugh at Captain Asaya's dry tone. "You are within range of our weapons, and no further warning will be given. Turn back or be destroyed."

The Ananab answered by coming out of stealth mode. They were spread out in a relatively straight line, the three Ananab ships on the right, the Tryr to the left. One of the Ananab ships fired at Jade Samurai.

They were still far enough apart that it looked relatively easy for

Jade Samurai to avoid the volley of missiles and energy beams.

Afsaneh gave a little gasp as the thin blue lines holding the human ships together dissolved. Jade Samurai looped down and to its left. Jade Wolverine and the green blip behind it continued towards the enemy, still not revealing her existence.

Afsaneh leaned forward, unable to tear her eyes off the screen. Jade Samurai swung back towards the attacking ships, concentrating it's fire on two of the Ananab ships.

The two green blips were almost on top of the Ananab when Jim's ship fired. Jade Wolverine immediately uncloaked to save power. The damaging assault had already taken it's toll on the enemy ships.

It was obvious that the second ship was a total surprise. One of the Tryr, and one of the Ananab ships staggered as their defenses reacted too late.

"Oh!" Afsaneh gasped as the Ananab ship exploded into a bright expanding cloud of debris. A moment later, the Tryr ship followed suit. "Yeah!" Afsaneh grinned in excitement as she watched Jim's ship, her ship, pound the other Tryr.

Jade Samurai wasn't faring as well.

Several shots had gotten through to one of the Ananab ships and it was drifting on it's original course towards the station. The third Tryr and the remaining Ananab ship were pounding away at 'Samurai.

So far, she hadn't taken any direct hits, although Pearl confirmed over the loudspeakers that several near misses had done some damage and there were casualties.

Jade Samurai gave ground stubbornly as the space between her and her two attackers was alive with energy fire and masses of missile exchanges. As Afsaneh watched, the Ananab ship took a hit near it's stern. It didn't seem to have much effect , though.

The third green blip finally uncloaked and Afsaneh got her first glimpse of the newly commissioned Jade Conquistador. She heard Captain Dela Rosa over the intercom. "Fire!"

The Tryr ship 'Wolverine had been battled abruptly flashed brilliantly and was gone.

Jim's ship immediately moved to aid 'Samurai. Another missile hit the Ananab ship in nearly the same spot as the first, and the ship wobbled as it's drive ceased operating smoothly. Jade Conquistador concentrated its fire on the last Tryr ship.

"Pearl, they've done it!" Afsaneh practically screamed in excitement. "We've won!"

"The battle is not yet concluded," the computer reminded her. "Both ships are still capable of inflicting damage, and the Ananab ship is still functional, if somewhat damaged."

"Ananab?" Afsaneh remembered the ship damaged in the initial exchange of fire. It was still drifting towards Osaka. In fact, it seemed to Afsaneh, it was drifting awfully fast!

"Pearl, give me a close-up on that Ananab ship, and let's do a hard scan on their power emissions." She bit her lip as the data appeared. "I don't think that ship is disabled at all. I think it's giving seemingly random bursts of power that are all aimed at increasing its speed as it approaches."

"That is possible." Pearl grudgingly agreed. "It would be a highly unlikely maneuver for an Ananab ship under these circumstances."

"Hmmm..." Afsaneh thought hard. "Didn't Lasty say the Ananab would consider this a vendetta, their earlier defeats a disgrace and insult to their entire race?"

"That is true." Pearl sounded less skeptical now. "I am sounding condition 'red' while I consider this theory."

Afsaneh tore her eyes away from the approaching ship in time to see the last Tryr ship explode. The Ananab ship was being battered by all three ships now.

To her surprise, the Ananab Captain came on-screen and called for a cease fire.

"Do you surrender?" Captain DelaRosa's voice was cold and merciless. Reluctantly, the Ananab agreed. Jade Wolverine suddenly gave a burst of speed and made a sharp sweeping turn back towards the station.

Afsaneh's heart quickened and she sighed in relief as she recognized Jim's voice broadcasting. At least he didn't seem to be hurt!

"Ananab ship, brake to a halt and stop all engines at once. Answer or we will destroy you!"

Afsaneh gave a start as she realized the damaged enemy ship was running directly towards the station at full speed.

"How long will it take to get here?" Afsaneh's voice sounded weak, even to herself.

"It appears that the Ananab ship is powering up to go to interstellar speed. If they continue their current course, they will pass this station in less than ten minutes."

"They're not passing anything," Afsaneh said through gritted teeth. "Sound an alarm. Inform Governor Lang that they're on a collision course."

"They, as well as the station, would be destroyed, and all on board both would die."

"Exactomundo." Afsaneh began tracking the ship with her weapons systems. At this rate, they would be in range in just over five minutes. "Do you think humans would, or could ram us, under the same circumstances?"

Pearl didn't answer, but alarms began going off all over the station.

"Afsaneh Riahi, at their present course, they will impact very close to your station. Please go to Sector A, immediately. I am summoning someone to take your place at these controls. Afsaneh Riahi, do you hear me? Please go to Sector A, at once!"

"Negatory, good buddy." Afsaneh tried to sound confident, but her voice felt weak. "This is my job, and....uh, I'm the best there is at what I do."

"Your safety is paramount. You must go to Sector A at once."

"Pearl, work with me on this." Afsaneh could hear her voice strengthening. "This is where I'm supposed to be, and this is where I stay. End of subject." She hoped the computer couldn't see her shivering.

"You are frightened. You must retreat while you still can."

"No. Now concentrate on saving this station, and my safety will go hand in hand."

"Not necessarily. You are in an exposed position. Please retreat."

"I'm done arguing with you, Pearl." Afsaneh's voice rose in pitch and volume. "Now let's bag us an enemy ship."

To accent her words, she fired a salvo of missiles, even though she knew it was too early. The Ananab began returning fire with what had to be everything that was still operational.

Quick flashes died just as quickly on the screen as small defensive rockets intercepted the first assault. Afsaneh was dimly aware that Jade Wolverine was closing from behind the Ananab ship. She was also aware that the help that represented wouldn't arrive in time to be a factor in this battle.

"Prepare for collision!" Lang's voice thundered through every speaker in Station Osaka. "Impact in less than three minutes. Everyone get to a secure position, now!"

"And where would that be?" Afsaneh asked out loud, her tone sarcastic. "Pittsburgh?"

She jumped as the Governor addressed her personally.

"Afsaneh, you've got to get out of there. You're too close to where the impact will be."

"Will people just leave me alone, and let me do my job?" Afsaneh fought the panic that was threatening to take hold of her. She shot a random series of missiles and energy beams at the looming ship, cussing as most of them were blocked or deflected.

Pearl seemed to be dealing with the incoming fire. Nothing much was getting through. It was the one big missile that had Afsaneh worried.

She cheered as one of her shots got through and the Ananab ship staggered. But it wasn't nearly enough to stop it, she knew. She tried another volley, but she was even less successful with this batch.

It was as if the enemy was learning her style. Afsaneh slapped herself on the forehead. That was it! The ship's computer was finding a rhythm to her attack.

Her eyes grew bigger and felt like they were glazing over as she tried to change her methods. Then she quit thinking about it consciously. All that mattered was that she penetrate her opponent's defenses.

Her hands flew across the controls, and she began humming, first a calypso beat, then a funky soul staccato. She lost track of everything except the screen before her eyes and the controls beneath her flashing fingertips.

She was vaguely aware that Lang was shouting at her, and that Pearl was saying something insistently, but she ignored them both and kept concentrating on her task.

The Ananab ship grew in size until it dominated the screen, nearly filling it. It had ceased firing, most of it's weapons systems evidently destroyed, except for defensive ones.

But it still had one weapon left.

Itself.

Afsaneh was half-standing in her seat, trying everything she could think of. Someone in the room was screaming, and she had just enough time to realize it was herself before the ship completely filled the screen.

Then it was too late to scream, and the world ended in thunder and lightning.

Jade Wolverine

"No!"

Jim stood, his hands gripping the rail in front of him tightly. He stared in horror as the Ananab ship exploded and Station Chaq shuddered with the impact.

The bright flash subsided and streams of escaping gases appeared from a dozen or more places at once. An indent was visible where the ship had seemed to plow into the station.

"Did...?" Jim started and stopped. His throat was too dry to speak. He swallowed and tried again. "Did it hit? Irene, what about casualties?"

"The Ananab ship exploded approximately one thousand meters from Station Osaka. Damage from the debris is considerable. Casualties are unknown at this time."

"Call Pearl, find out what you can." Jim couldn't tear his eyes away from the leaking station. "Reduce speed and swing us around as soon as you can."

"Jade Wolverine, this is DelaRosa. We can't raise Pearl. How bad is it?"

"I don't know yet, Danny." Jim tore his eyes away from the grim sight and checked on 'Samurai in another screen. "Have you got things under control with the P'Funct?"

"Oh, they're behaving just fine. Koro and I have them bracketed. One move and we'll blow them to hell, and they know it." Jim nodded his approval at the other man's cold tone. Danny didn't sound like he would hesitate a moment.

"I hope everybody's okay at the station," DelaRosa continued. "Where did you have Afsaneh put during all this?"

Jim's blood ran cold. "Uh, I don't know. I just turned her over to Mac. Irene, do you know where she was stationed?"

He swayed unevenly on his feet as there was no immediate response. "Irene, do you know? Tell me!"

"She was assigned to gun station Eagle. I do not know if she was there when the Ananab ship exploded. She...may have been moved when collision seemed obvious."

"Where..." Jim hung on to the rail as if to save his life. It was the only thing that kept him on his feet when Irene highlighted the location of gun station Eagle.

It was almost exactly in the middle of the indent that marred the once smooth surface of Station Osaka.

Jade Viking

"And this."

Captain Tachibana inspected the displays his Baerd Chief Technician was bringing up on his screen. Arrows pointed at the telltale signs.

"And this means...?" Hiroaki Tachibana didn't want to admit he had no idea what he was being shown, so he nodded knowingly as he prodded Inam for details.

"There is definitely an Egelv ship somewhere in this system, probably in some kind of orbit around Earth." She paused, then continued. "And I'm very sure they've sent shuttles to the surface. More than once."

"And they could be aware that we are here, too?"

"In light of the interviews the released passengers have been giving, it must have occurred to them, even if they haven't found physical proof yet." She sounds confident of her data, Hiroaki thought gloomily. He resigned himself to the conclusion that there was a good chance he would be meeting a representative of the Egelv in the near future.

"What is the status of our own shuttles?" He didn't want one of them getting picked off, or even picked up by a potential enemy.

"All are on board at this point." Inam checked a schedule. "Mr. Soshama was supposed to leave in one hour, with a load of external hard drives for Mr. Miles, and to pick up supplies for Osaka."

Tachibana came to a decision. "Tell Kabu his flight is canceled until further notice. Have him talk to me if he gives you any arguments."

"Yes, Sir." Inam returned to her station.

Captain Tachibana stared at his screen moodily, not seeing a thing.

He'd read up on the Egelv. He couldn't think of a single reason for Humans and Egelv not to be able to get along.

Hiroaki Tachibana, you're a paranoid old man. You're flinching at shadows.

He rubbed his eyes wearily. For the first time since they had captured Station Osaka, he was glad his wife and children weren't with him. He missed them more than he could admit, but at least on Earth, they were safe.

He shifted in his seat, and reluctantly came to a decision.

"Vicki, I've got a chore for you," he began.

Newark, New Jersey

"Iori, are you asleep?" Sasama shook his friend's shoulder.

"Not any more," the younger man groused, yawning. "What is it?"

"Look."

Iori peered ahead and inhaled sharply. "Ah-h-h..." was all he said.

New York loomed before them, and behind it, a bright red sun was just appearing over the horizon. At first just a sliver, it quickly grew to a perfect glowing circle. Brilliant colors flashed off windows in tall buildings in the distance, threatening to blind both of them.

Iori turned to Sasama and bowed his head. "Thank you for allowing me to see this glorious sight. You are a true friend."

"You're welcome, Iori, my best friend. Ah, what a morning. Nothing could go wrong on a day that begins like this. I'm going to sleep for two days, while you watch out for Kimberly and Kiri." Iori just smiled, yawning again.

"Good thing it's Sunday morning. Traffic is light." Iori sat back and closed his eyes. "And now, even though the sunrise is magnificent, I'm going to try and get a little more sleep."

"Good morning, boys." A cheerful voice sounded in both of their transceivers. Sasama groaned.

"Good morning, Kabu." He tried to sound optimistic. "Are you calling with our reservation confirmation for a luxurious hotel suite?"

"Not exactly," Kabu admitted, not quite concealing a chuckle. "I'm afraid Kimberly and Kiri are going for a ride."

"A short trip to the park for a long day of relaxation?" Sasama asked hopefully.

"They're headed to Kimberly's new home."

"She just buy a house, or something?" Iori sounded puzzled, and Sasama himself was confused.

"No-o-o..." Kabu snickered. "She's married to Jim now, remember? His house is her house."

Sasama and Iori exchanged horrified looks.

"That's right, boys." Kabu was disgustingly cheerful. "You're on your way to Ann Arbor, Michigan. Have a nice day!"

Highway 80, somewhere in Pennsylvania

Kimberly took a cautious sip of her coffee. Still too hot! She blew on it and winced.

Martin, you've got the mother of all hangovers. You know better. Champagne is not your usual choice of substance abuse.

Beside her, Kiri snored noisily. *God, if I only had a tape recorder,* she giggled, then groaned.

Just drive, Martin. Just drive.

Groundhog took a deep swig of coffee. It was too hot. He took another.

When the alarms went off, he couldn't believe it. He'd rigged an electric eye to monitor Kimberly's door, and it went off promptly at six A.M.

He'd hoped one of them was going for bagels or newspapers, but no, they were carrying suitcases, and the Martin woman was pushing a cart piled high with more.

It was a good thing he'd had the foresight to bug her car. By the time he got his things together, she'd been almost to the New Jersey tunnel.

It took him thirty miles to catch up to them, but eventually he caught sight of her gold BMW ahead, cruising along at a steady twelve miles over the speed limit.

He noticed a red Viper ahead, keeping a steady distance between it and the Beamer.

He closed in enough to see two young Japanese in the front seat. They were talking and gesturing at the women's car.

Another tail, and not a very good one. Not that the two sleepy women would notice.

Groundhog lifted his foot from the accelerator slightly, and allowed himself to drop back a hundred yards.

He flipped up his laptop and began typing. He had his answer in less than a minute. The red Viper was registered to James Morris, Lake Tahoe, California residence. From its dirty appearance, they must have just driven it across the country. He sincerely hoped they weren't about to drive it all the way back.

He settled in for a long drive, following the red car that followed the gold car.

◆ ◆ ◆ ◆ ◆

New York City, New York

Matt Stickel backed around the corner, holding one arm out to slow down his two companions.

"Wait," he hissed.

"Whatever is it?" Du Brimar asked mildly. Jo Coran just watched, silent as always.

"I think those were FBI agents. I saw them flash their ID's at the doorman."

"And, that means...?" Du Brimar gave him a questioning look.

"We really don't need to have a confrontation with local authorities at this point." Jo Coran spoke up, her voice firm.

All three of them backed into the alley across the street from Kimberly Martin's apartment building. A moment later, a figure appeared on one of the balconies high above.

"Is that one of your 'FBI' agents?" Jo Coran asked, pulling a small tube from the pouch she carried.

"I think so," Matt said, squinting as he peered upward.

"We'll know in a moment," she said, peering through a tiny sight mounted on the tube. "Got it."

Matt started as human voices began speaking through his translator.

"Sir, all their suitcases are gone..."

"...suitcases are gone. We've found items that they had in their possession when we questioned them, so we know they've been here..."

Karl Costa half-listened to Beatty drone on as he pondered things.

Of course they had been here. The two freshly rinsed wine glasses in the drain board in the kitchen and the two empty champagne bottles in the trash attested to that! The real question of the moment was, where were they headed now?

He looked at his watch, even though he didn't need to. Just before noon. How long had they been gone, and where were they going now?

Costa could have the airports checked, but he'd already found how slow that could be.

What had they come to New York for? It had to be for more than just clean socks and underwear. There had to be some clue in here.

He turned away from the rail of the balcony and returned to the living room. His eyes came to rest on the telephone.

Matt listened with fascination and a sense of dread. After all, this was the FBI they were snooping on. He listened to the senior agent give quick concise orders, and snickered at the obvious irritation in the man's voice. He couldn't blame him. That Beatty guy sounded dead above the neck.

Two agents stayed in the apartment to do a more thorough search. The rest left.

"Here they come," Matt hissed.

"Fine." Jo Coran sighted the senior FBI man with what looked like a tiny flare gun. She clicked something. As far as Matt could tell, nothing happened.

"Uh, I don't think your gadget worked," he began, but stopped when

236

he saw their smirks. Jo Coran casually aimed the 'flare gun' in the general direction of the departing agents and fired it.

This time, he could see results. Something flared and shot out of the mouth of the device. He immediately lost sight of it.

Jo Coran flipped up a tiny screen and a ghostly image of the area across the street appeared. The walking men were tiny dots, one of them a slightly different shade than the others. Yet another blip moved in close and slowed to the same speed as the men. It attached itself to the singularly shaded dot.

"And that, as they say, is that." Du Brimar grinned at him. "Audio range up to seventeen of your miles. Tracking range..." He looked upward, as if looking for their ship. "...anywhere on the planet."

Matt watched as she packed the device away. Just like that, and the FBI was now being monitored by aliens from outer space...and him. He was starting to enjoy this, and realized something with dismay. The FBI agents weren't the bad guys. He was with the bad guys, and he was helping them.

Glowing Mist

"Finally!" Cromar Try looked up at his mate with interest as she slapped her console triumphantly.

"What have you got?" he asked.

The image she was watching appeared on his own screen.

"Ah."

A blip was moving outward at an ever-increasing pace. Within a few minutes it would be at interstellar speeds, many times faster than the speed of light. It was already almost past the orbits of the outer planets of this system.

"What is it?"

Siph Carni's eyes narrowed. "It's an unmanned probe. It was probably launched via some sort of slingshot effect under stealth mode."

"Can we catch it?"

Siph Carni made a face. "Yes, but not very quickly. Whoever sent it obviously programmed it to have the engines kick into high speed just far enough away to make it inconvenient for us to chase. We could overhaul it, but it could take several days round trip." She tossed her head, long white hair flowing smoothly around her shoulders. "And we would probably be detected in the process, which might be the whole point."

Cromar Try frowned. "Can we extrapolate back to the source."

Siph Carni sniffed. "Of course we can."

"Then let's see who is hiding, and where."

"Without Du Brimar and Jo Coran, we're a little shorthanded," Siph Carni warned.

Cromar Try snorted. "Glowing Mist may not be the newest thing off the assembly line on Egelv, but it more than a match for anything this system can throw at it, Ananab ships or no. Even shorthanded."

"Yes, Sir!" Siph Carni didn't hide her amusement from him, and he tried to frown at her, but failed. He did sound pompous, he admitted to himself.

Several minutes passed as he watched her search, check data, check it again, then clap her hands in excitement.

"This is priceless!" she exclaimed. "Some one has a sense of imagination!"

"What?" he asked apprehensively. He didn't always share the same appreciation she did. She could admire ingenuity for it's own sake. Personally, a clever opponent wasn't high on his list of favorite things.

"They've actually launched two probes." There was respect in her voice now. "The one we see disappearing in the general direction of Station Chaq, and another, which is in orbit around Earth."

"What's it doing?" Cromar Try slaved his screen to hers so he could watch as she demonstrated.

"What it is doing, is producing emissions very similar to what an Ananab freighter operating in sheathed mode would." She stood and came over to lean against his shoulder, giving his left ear a nip in the process. He started to reprove her, then reconsidered. After all, there wasn't anyone else on the bridge at the moment.

"So where are they, then?" He felt her right hand begin to slide down his spine. How she could become so aroused by intellectual stimulation was beyond him, but he wasn't complaining.

She leaned forward to point, one breast brushing against his now ultra sensitive ear. Her right hand came back up to rest on his shoulder, just a fraction of an inch from his other ear.

"They are..." she whispered hoarsely. "...holding position on the far side of the moon, at a very shallow altitude." Her lips touched his ear again and he almost went through the ceiling. "Very clever, if you ask me."

"Yes-s-s," Cromar Try managed to get the word out with great difficulty. "My dear, I think we need to postpone this, this..."

"Discussion?" she asked sweetly.

"No." That was the hardest word he'd spoken in a very long time. "I think we need to postpone this...enthusiasm, until later."

She stood up and stared at him in astonishment. "You're not serious?"

Cromar Try knew he would be pay dearly for this, but he had a curious misgiving about that ship hidden behind the solitary moon of this planet.

"I'm afraid I am. In fact, I think you're right. We'll recall Du Brimar and Jo Coran. They can pick up where they left off later." He looked up at her hopefully. "Perhaps we could take this up a little later, too?"

"Perhaps," was all she said as she returned stiffly to her post.

Or perhaps not, Cromar Try sighed in sincere disappointment.

CHAPTER SIXTEEN

Station Osaka

Jim sat slouched in his chair, stony faced. He was only half-listening to Governor Lang address the Ananab prisoners.

"...remain under lock and key until such time that we arrange transportation to return you home. Any attempt to escape or cause trouble will be severely dealt with."

The Ananab captain rose to his full height and raised one claw high above his head. The human guards stirred uneasily, and their weapons came up in anticipation. On either side of Lang, neither Jim nor McGregor moved a muscle.

"We give you one more chance to surrender your weapons and our station. If you do so now, we will spare anyone not directly involved in the revolt. Of course, all ringleaders will be executed immediately, but it will save the lives of the rest of your people."

Governor Lang shook his head. "You are a piece of work. This chamber will be your prison until you are shipped out." He stood, and Jim and McGregor followed suit. Their chairs and the folding table they sat behind were quickly removed by Hoag workers that studiously ignored their previous rulers.

"Wait!" The Ananab Captain gestured with a claw at the several dozen Srotag and Tryr guards that huddled near them. "You will need more chambers for these other species."

"You can all share the same facilities," Lang said shortly.

"Impossible!" All the Ananab were waving their claws in agitation now, and several started to surge forward. They came to an abrupt halt as over a dozen weapons came to bear on them.

"That will be quite enough of that." There was unmistakable steel in the governor's tone. "You will do as you're told. Get used to it."

When they were outside and the hatch bolted, Lang noisily breathed out in relief. "Well," he admitted. "I don't care to do that again any time soon."

"Hmm," Jim said, his mind only partly observing the scene around him. "Pearl?"

"The doctor is finished and is cleaning up. He would like to see you as soon as possible."

"Is she...?" He couldn't finish the sentence. A part of him noticed that both the governor and McGregor were hurrying after him as he strode briskly down the corridor.

"Her condition is unchanged. The doctor would rather he told you any details in person."

"What do you think, Pearl?"

"My assessment is that Dr. Gonzalez is very competent, and would rather speak to you in person."

Any further discussion was cut off as Jim reached the medical center. He went straight to the doctor's office. Dr. Gonzalez was just getting there himself.

"How is she, Doctor?" Jim asked, dreading the answer.

"Come in, Jim." The doctor was about Jim's own height, clean-shaven and looked very trim. He gestured for Jim to precede him into the office. When Jim just stood and glared at him, he shrugged and went in himself.

Do not hit the doctor, Jim, he told himself firmly. He was dimly aware that the Lang and McGregor followed him into the office. Dr. Gonzalez was already seated behind his desk, and Jim reluctantly slid into a chair facing him. The other two men did the same.

"Now, Doctor," Jim's voice was dangerously soft. "Would you please tell me Afsaneh's condition?"

"She's still unconscious." The doctor folded his hands on the desk in front of him. "She has a broken left arm, and right leg. Neither are serious, and should heal completely. Her head injury is another matter entirely."

"Go on," Jim said, struggling to get those few words out.

"She's lost a fair amount of blood. That's not the real problem, although we will need donors. You're her father?"

Jim tried to answer, but couldn't. He mutely nodded his head. He tried again to speak.

"How did you know?"

Dr. Gonzalez smiled. "I've seen you both walk. Can you donate?"

"Of course." Jim closed his eyes for a moment, then opened them and looked at the doctor calmly. "You mentioned a problem?"

"She received a blow to the head that is hemorrhaging internally. She needs surgery to relieve the pressure, and soon. Further, she's in a coma. That could last an hour, or a year. But I don't see her coming out of it at all without surgery."

"Can...can you do it?" Jim wasn't breathing.

"No." The doctor was blunt. "I'm not a surgeon. Certainly not on that level. She needs the kind of care she can only receive on Earth. She needs to get home, fast."

"Home." To Jim it sounded like an epitaph. "That's at least five days away."

"Jade Wolverine can make it in under four days." Pearl was blunt. Jim looked at Captain Lang, who hesitated, then nodded.

"By all means, take the ship and go."

"What if the Ananab attack again?" Jim asked quietly. "I'm taking a third of your defenses."

"The hell you are." McGregor vigorously shook his head. "With the Ananab ship we just captured, we can scavenge what we need to finish the other warship. And you'll recall, it was the stations own defenses that nailed that last ship, even if it was one of your ship's gunners."

They all sat in uncomfortable silence, remembering who the gunner was.

Jim felt his eyes mist over. By the time his ship had landed, she had been pulled from the rubble, but looked pitifully tiny. Pearl had probably saved her life by flooding her compartment with fire retardant hardening foam. To some extent, it had cushioned her from the debris.

But only partially.

"Irene, how long before we can depart for Earth?" His voice sounded desolate, hopeless even.

"It will take about six hours to get provisioned and get the crew moved on board."

"Get started." Jim rose to his feet. "I'll be right there. We might be able to trim some time off that."

"There is nothing you need to do," Irene answered quickly. "The time would be better spent resting."

243

"I agree." Captain Lang spoke forcefully, also standing.

"If you're going to donate blood, you'll need the time." Dr. Gonzalez said, a tinge of steel entering his voice. "And, for what it's worth, you could use some rest."

"Later." Jim turned to leave, but stopped when McGregor placed a hand on his arm. He looked up startled. The younger man had never shown such familiarity before.

"Jim." The giant's voice was gentle. "You have good people. Let them do their job. Give the blood, get a good meal and some rest."

Jim could feel the exhaustion that was in part, reaction setting in. As tired as he was, he knew he couldn't sleep. But they weren't going to leave him alone until he gave in.

"I'll try." But he couldn't get the image of that tiny little girl, looking so limp and fragile out of his mind. "Can I see her?"

"Of course." The doctor stood. "We can take the blood in her room so you can spend some time with her, maybe get a nap," he added pointedly.

"Maybe," Jim said in a vague voice.

Sean Jackson straightened to attention in surprise. He listened for a moment, then grinned at his friend, Ellis.

"You hear that? Earth! We're headed for Earth!"

Ellis nodded soberly, his expression somber.

"You know why, don't you? Afsaneh." The big black man looked worried.

Sean grew serious. Ellis was right. She'd been busted up pretty bad. In fact, it was a miracle she was alive. He liked the young girl, liked her spunk.

"She'll be all right, bud." He slapped the other on the back in sympathy, then looked around in irritation. *Where was their relief?*

Standing guard in front of a deserted ship was even more boring than regular guard duty. After all, the ship had been searched, and the crew taken prisoner. It wasn't as if any of the Hoag going in and out were going to steal it.

He felt something and turned in surprise, but there was no one there. But he could have sworn...

"What is it?" Ellis asked, unstrapping his AK-47. Sean waved a hand to relax him.

"Just a breeze, I guess. See?" He gestured around. There was a pause in the Hoag activity. In fact, there was just one in sight, passing in the nearby corridor.

His eyes narrowed as the Hoag froze. A startled look quickly changed to one of terror.

"What is it, little buddy?" He decided the minute alien had been frightened by Sean bringing his gun to bear. "It's okay, we're the good guys here."

The Hoag ignored him and slowly backed up to the wall of the corridor. Then he was sliding down it, moving as fast as his short legs would carry him.

Sean looked around again, but saw nothing except their relief walking towards them farther down the passage.

"Peculiar little buggers, aren't they?" He grinned at Ellis, who didn't lose his worried look. "Here comes our replacements. Let's go get packed."

"Should we report this...?" Ellis glanced at his watch, obviously begrudging the time it would take.

"Yeah, right." Sean snapped to attention. "Sergeant McGregor, Sir! Ghosts in 'D' Concourse, Sir!" He relaxed his posture and pointed at the two approaching guards. "There's our ticket out of here. Let's not blow it."

After a moment's hesitation, Ellis followed him.

New York City, New York

Sho Toshida wanted to reach across the table and strangle the American, but he did nothing. Behind him, two of his men stirred. The little finger on his right hand twitched, and the movement stopped.

"So you see, our interests coincide," Will Spencer said, doodling on a piece of paper as he spoke. "The FBI were just here. They think she returned to California. I'm not so certain."

"And why is that?" Sho kept his voice bland.

"She took her car." The American sat back in his chair as if that explained everything. Sho waited, and Spencer grew impatient. "There is no way she'll leave her 'beamer in an airport parking lot. She's not flying anywhere."

"It is possible to drive to San Francisco," Sho pointed out.

"Not Kimberly." Spencer was firm. "She hates long road trips."

"How far would she drive?"

Sho watched as the American jumped up and went to one of the many bookcases that lined his office. After a moment's deliberation, he chose a book, an atlas. He came back to his seat and opened the book to show the continental United States spread over both pages.

"I can't see her going any farther than, oh, Atlanta. Or maybe Nashville."

At Sho's inquiring look, he explained. "She went to school at Vanderbilt." He smiled, then rolled his eyes and continued. "That's in Nashville."

"You think she went back to school?" Sho's voice was very quiet.

"Hell, no!" He laughed. "But maybe she went to visit old school friends."

A few minutes later, Sho and his men were riding down the elevator. They didn't speak until they were on the sidewalk and half a block away.

"That man is not as stupid as he would have us believe," one of his men, Omi Gonnosuke finally said.

"No, he is not." Sho was careful not to show his pleasure. He was grooming the young man to be his personal assistant, and was pleased at his progress. "We need more information. She is supposedly married to Jim Morris. Find out if he has any east coast residences."

"Hai!" Omi began speaking into his phone as they walked. It was a beautiful fall evening, even in New York. And walking helped clear Sho's head of extraneous details.

It gave him a chance to deliberate over the teachers words. The man was an obvious idiot, and it was difficult to believe anything he said. But if he was telling the truth, incredible as it seemed, aliens from space walked the streets of this nation.

Just as he now did.

He suddenly laughed out loud, and his men looked at him inquiringly.

"I think stupidity is contagious," he announced.

"Then we should leave this country very soon, before we catch it," Omi said.

"Omi, I think you're right." Sho felt a familiar pang in his stomach. "I'm hungry."

They came to a stop in front of a restaurant, a Japanese steakhouse. Sho shook his head.

"Not that hungry."

They continued walking.

Jade Viking

"Holy shi...Captain, we're being hailed!" Commander Randall's voice rose, both in pitch, and in volume. Captain Tachibana stared at him in shock.

"Control yourself, Mr. Randall. Hailed by whom?" Captain Tachibana motioned to Inam who signaled a ship-wide alert.

"I'm not quite sure," his first officer admitted. "You want me to..."

"Captain Tachibana, we are being approached by an Egelv ship." Vicki sounded...apprehensive? "I would like to suggest that you wait a few moments before opening any direct channel between their ship and ours."

"Why?" Captain Tachibana frowned. "Is there something you haven't told me?"

"Many things, but specific to this moment, remember my programming is of Egelv origins. Precautions need to be taken. And, done. Do you wish to respond to their hail?"

Tachibana's frown deepened. "Open a channel to the Egelv ship."

"This is the Earth Ship Jade Viking. Please identify yourselves, and your intentions."

He wasn't particularly surprised when the answer came back in English. But the words he heard shocked him just the same.

"Jade Viking? Don't you mean the pirated Ananab ship P'tassum? You realize that you're perilously close to the surface of your moon?"

Captain Tachibana scowled and cut off contact. Their stealth shielding obviously wasn't hiding them. He gestured to Randall. "Bring us up out of orbit on a heading away from Earth."

Inam turned to him from her screen. "Captain, I think I've located their ship. Their shielding is excellent, but there is a discernable energy wake."

"Good. Alert our defenses, just in case." Tachibana re-established the contact. "We are very aware of our ship's capabilities, and you need not be concerned. You haven't answered my question."

Glowing Mist

Du Brimar muttered to himself, and Cromar Try looked at him questioningly.

"I've been scanning them. No Ananab, no Tryr, no Srotag. I find twelve Baerd, thirty-six Hoag, and some sixty-six Humans."

Cromar Try shrugged. None of that was particularly startling. "And...?"

"That's all fine," Du Brimar admitted. "But I can't gain access to their computer. "Hstahni, Trixmae, H'eckhtarr...I could understand not being able to get in. But an Ananab ship? Impossible. The Baerd are clever and have potential, but it's unlikely they could improve this ships capabilities to that degree."

"What about the Humans?" Cromar Try asked.

Du Brimar snorted. "Oh, please. You've seen their broadcasts, the level of technology." He laughed. "You've even seen live specimens. Do you think they could improve even Ananab technology exponentially?"

Cromar Try glanced at his mate. She studiously ignored him. Mentally sighing, he moved his gaze to Jo Coran, who shrugged.

At first glance, it was hard to disagree with Du Brimar's assessment. Earth was primitive. They were certainly clever, but they weren't even close to the technical level required to fine-tune even primitive Ananab systems.

But here was an Ananab ship, recently acquired by the Humans, resisting Egelv probes even other Egelv ships would have trouble blocking. Du Brimar could be irritating, but he was very good.

It didn't make sense.

"Keep trying." He came to a decision. "Re-open audios, and establish visuals."

◆ ◆ ◆ ◆ ◆

"They are trying to probe me."

Did Vicki sound a little panicked? Tachibana didn't want to think about the concept of frightened computers.

"Can you keep them out?"

"I believe so. But that in itself is going to present a problem. An Ananab ship shouldn't be able to resist at this close proximity."

Tachibana's mind raced. "Can we block any possible access so the question of your abilities doesn't arise?"

"If we do that, we will be deaf and blind. It's our sensors they're trying to use to gain access. And I must admit, their system is very powerful."

"Is that a note of admiration, Vicki?" Tachibana had to smile.

"If I was capable of emotions, it would be fear."

Tachibana winced. If Vicki felt so threatened... He dragged his attention back to the bridge. Inam gestured she was receiving another transmission from the Egelv ship.

A brown face appeared on his screen.

The Egelv was male, with long narrow features that included ears that rose nearly even with the top of his head. The brown could be either natural, or deep tan. It was impossible to tell. It seemed incongruous with the long pure white hair that framed the face and fell over his shoulders. He wore some sort of casual shirt or jacket with no collar that was a rich royal blue color. It ended at the base of his neck, not unlike a tee-shirt or sweatshirt would.

"I am Cromar Try."

He's almost human, Hiroaki mused. The look of sudden interest that suddenly appeared in the Egelv's face confirmed that their facial expressions were similar to his own.

It also confirmed that his ship was now transmitting his own likeness. A quick glance at his screen verified it. Either Inam or Vicki had split his screen so that he could see both, the Egelv, and how the alien saw him.

"I am Captain Hiroaki Tachibana."

Matt stood with his back against the wall on the bridge, watching the screen. It was really true! That ship was manned by Earthlings, people like himself.

Humans could finally reach the stars!

He saw Jo Coran watching him, and modified that thought. The stars had finally reached them.

With a start, he realized Jo Coran was speaking to him through his translator patch. "You will not speak or move into the camera's range. If you attempt anything whatsoever, you will be rendered unconscious and removed from the bridge. This would make me very angry."

Matt opened his mouth to agree, then snapped it shut and carefully nodded his head. Jo Coran relaxed her hand which had hovered at a control on her console.

So what does that button do? Bridge defense, or something built into his translator?

For the first time, he began deliberately planning his escape.

"Captain Tachibana. We've heard so much about you."

Hiroaki kept a frown from appearing on his face. "You've heard of me? From whom?"

The Egelv gave a very human smile. "I don't think I'm going to tell you that, yet. But don't worry. We have no hostile intentions for you or your ship. We're more curious than anything else."

"Is that why you're trying to probe my computer?"

Cromar Try kept the surprise off his face.

"Well, we did initially try a probe, just for security sake." He tried to look sincere. "You may or may not know it, but we aren't exactly best friends with the Ananab. And we're very interested in knowing precisely how you managed to capture that ship and, if it is to be believed, Station Chaq."

❖ ❖ ❖ ❖ ❖

Hiroaki suddenly felt cold.

How could they know about Osaka? Somehow, they must have talked with someone that had already landed.

If they had gotten the information via probe, then they would know about Vicki. He didn't think they did, but the alien seemed cocky, confident he was in control of the situation.

What made him think he could openly probe another ship's computer without it being considered a provocation?

❖ ❖ ❖ ❖ ❖

"Uh, oh."

Cromar Try didn't look at his second officer. Du Brimar was being careful to not allow his voice to be transmitted. He turned his palm over questioningly, out of the viewers range.

"He just figured out something he doesn't like." Du Brimar spoke inside his throat so that only his own communication implant would pick his words up. "And it scares him."

"He doesn't look like he frightens easily." Siph Carni entered the subvocal conversation. "I think it's more a feeling of dread."

"He said computer," Jo Coran said suddenly.

Cromar Try felt his brow wrinkle and saw the Human catch it. He tried to salvage the moment. "If you've been monitoring Earth transmissions, some of your passengers have been quite vocal about your 'three day cruise'. It makes for interesting reading. Did one of you really defeat both Tryr and Srotag guards barehanded?"

"What do you mean computer?" he asked sub-vocally.

"With their present technology, it takes many computers to do major tasks. Whenever they refer to computers, it's almost always in the plural."

"That's right!" Du Brimar sounded so excited, he must have very nearly gone vocal.

"Calm down," Cromar Try admonished.

Du Brimar went back to his console. "I think I understand. It would explain..."

"Explain what? Cromar Try risked turning to look, but Du Brimar was oblivious. He kept working, his hands flashing across the controls.

"They must have a stronger computer system from some other source." Jo Coran sounded hesitant. "But from where, or who?"

"They are probing me again." Vicki sounded...strained? Hiroaki wet his lips, then spoke.

"Please desist from your probe. It could be considered an act of hostility."

"We must break off contact!" For Vicki, this was almost shouting. "I can't keep them out much longer."

"Now see here..." Hiroaki began to bluster, hoping to derail their attention. The Egelv interrupted him.

"Where did you get it?" The brown face was emotionless, except for what might be...fury? "From Ty Musa?"

"I don't know what..." Hiroaki stalled, sweat breaking out on his forehead.

"We must break off and flee. Now!"

But even before Vicki finished the word now, the Egelv snapped out words that didn't translate into English.

"What the hell?" Hiroaki started to ask, but never finished the oath.

Because at that moment, the lights went out.

A moment later, gravity followed.

My ship is dead, he realized.

"It's not the computer!" Cromar Try could see that Du Brimar wasn't going to stay sub-vocal for much longer so he inserted a sound buffer in front of his pickup.

"What do you mean, not the computer?" he asked, staying sub-vocal.

"Well, it is the computer," Du Brimar corrected himself. But it's not the hardware. It's the software!"

Cromar Try didn't get it at first, but his mate obviously did.

"They've got it?" she asked incredulously. "How?"

"Who knows, but they do." Du Brimar was positively gloating. Belatedly, and with growing anger, Cromar Try understood.

He turned back to the Human on his screen and dropped the sound buffer. "Where did you get it? From Ty Musa?" The Human blustered, and tried to stall.

"They're going to flee," Jo Coran warned.

Oh no, they aren't, Cromar Try vowed, and quickly spoke the self-destruct sequence, knowing even hearing it would be enough to cause the program to crash.

The Human on the screen vanished, and was replaced with an external view of the 'Jade Viking', as they called it.

Every exterior light on the ship was out. It was just barely visible, outlined against the stars in the background.

"What have you done?" The human, Matt stickel cried out.

Jo Coran was moving, and cut the young Human off as he tried to reach Cromar Try."

What have you done?" he repeated weakly, his eyes never leaving the sight of the now-listless ship on the screen.

"They had the royal security program." Siph Carni sounded gentle as she explained it to him. "Somehow or other, they acquired the program that was stolen from us."

"And, like Humans seem fond of doing, they showed no regard for the ownership, or practicality of installing that program on a ship they know hardly anything about." Du Brimar didn't have his usual humor in his voice. "The fictional stories of Frankenstein, Pandora's Box, and a multitude of others are obviously based on a clear understanding of the Human tendency to...meddle!"

"What? How?" Matt Stickel looked confused and lost. "What are you talking about?"

"That program was never designed to be installed on such a large computer. It was far too powerful to be given that kind of autonomy." Cromar spoke softly, as if to ease Matt's pain.

"I thought you said the Ananab computers were inferior?"

"They are," Siph Carni agreed. "But that ship has probably added newer updated computers as least three times in its life-span. And they wouldn't have bothered replacing them. They just added on, making the overall system far bigger than the program was ever intended for."

Du Brimar continued for her. "All the program was ever intended to do was run palace security systems, or perhaps a small personal ship's defenses, at the most."

Matt looked at Cromar Try. "But what did you do to the ship?"

Cromar Try had sympathy for the young Human. His race showed so much potential, but it would never get the chance to achieve it.

"I fed the computer the self-destruct command to shut the program down, permanently."

"What about the ship?" Matt Stickel had a wild look in his eyes, perhaps desperate hope.

Cromar Try decided false hopes were crueler than the truth, and the look turned to horror as he spoke.

"I killed the ship. And everyone on it."

CHAPTER SEVENTEEN

Northern Ohio

"Hello, Yvette? Yes, it's me." Kimberly fought the urge to yawn and lost. "Sorry, we've been on the road since dawn."

"Where are you?" Yvette asked.

"We've just left I-90 onto U.S. 23, going around Toledo." Kimberly said. "I think that puts us about an hour away. You guys up to anything?"

"You could say that," Yvette said, mischief in her voice. "Jerry and Frederick are here."

"Oh?" Kimberly looked over at Kiri, who was listening to her side of the conversation. Kimberly grinned and Kiri raised an eyebrow questioningly. "What are Jerry and Frederick doing at your place?"

"We're about to head over to the Marriot." Yvette paused for so long, Kimberly was about to prompt her when she finally spoke. "I think you two might want to join us there. We'll be up in the penthouse suite."

"Ooh, what's the occasion?" Kimberly turned to Kiri. "They're all going to the Marriot and want us there, too."

Kiri made a face and lifted one arm and sniffed suggestively. Kimberly snickered, then stiffened as Yvette's words sank in.

"We're meeting Entertainment Tonight for a camera interview."

"You're kidding!" Kimberly exclaimed and repeated the news to Kiri. The Japanese woman looked indecisive, obviously torn. Kimberly switched over to speaker phone so Kiri could hear and speak for herself. "What's going on?"

"They want to do a piece on the film. That, and Jim's disappearance."

"I can't be on camera!" Kiri moaned. "Look at my hair. And I've got bags under my eyes..."

"We don't have time to go to Jim's first to get cleaned up?" Kimberly asked hopefully.

"That would kill another hour or more, with traffic the way it is. Jim's house is quite a ways from here." Yvette laughed. "Don't worry, Kiri. The cameras don't pick up scents."

"We'll be there." Kimberly said firmly. "It's too good a chance to pass up. But we should be careful what we talk about."

"Heya, gals." Janice spoke for the first time. It was almost possible to see her expression, the drawl was so pronounced. "How 'bout you, Kimberly? Don't you think ET would be interested in your recent marriage?"

"I don't think ET even knows who I am, and we'll keep it that way for a while," Kimberly said firmly. "There will be enough unanswerable questions, as it is."

"We'll see," Yvette answered vaguely. "When you get to the hotel, just go to the main desk. We'll leave directions for you."

"Okay. See you in a little bit."

"Bye guys," Kiri chipped in just before the connection was broken. She stretched and moaned in delight. "Gawd, it'll be good to walk around. Pull over at the next rest stop."

"What? Why?" Kimberly looked at her, perplexed. "You heard them. We're on a deadline here."

"I am not appearing on ET looking like this." Kiri's voice discouraged any dissent. "I need my make-up bag from the trunk. And a change of clothes."

"What? No shower?" Kimberly teased. She immediately regretted it when Kiri got a thoughtful expression on her face.

"No way! You're not going to drip water all over my leather upholstery..."

The argument continued unabated all twelve miles to the next rest area.

◆ ◆ ◆ ◆ ◆

Again? Groundhog watched the gold 'Beamer signal an exit at the approaching rest area.

Those women drink too much coffee. He reached for the phone.

"Thank God," Iori sighed heavily. "I don't think I could have waited five more minutes."

Sasama just shook his head and drove.

◆ ◆ ◆ ◆ ◆

New York City, New York

"Ann Arbor? Why the hell would they be going to Ann Arbor?" Will Spencer wondered out loud as he cradled his phone.

◆ ◆ ◆ ◆ ◆

Sho Toshida smiled.

It had been worth the bother to bug his office, after all. He took another sip of green tea, savoring it.

Takeda Nagashino sat across the table from him. He also sipped his tea, but no sign of pleasure or displeasure showed in his face.

Sho had the same slender build of his father. At five foot ten inches, he was just a little taller. Takeda, on the other hand, was one of the biggest Japanese men he had ever seen outside the Sumi ring.

He would look more natural if he were bald, Sho decided. That was not an observation he planned on sharing with the other man any time soon. A full head taller, and probably over a hundred pounds heavier, Takeda Nagashino was an imposing sight.

"So," Sho finally said. "The two women have gone to Michigan. I noticed Jim Morris has an address there. I think you should take some of the men and acquire them both."

Nagashino nodded silently.

Sho took another sip, then stared out the window as one of his men refilled his cup. No one spoke. His men knew better, and Nagashino had nothing to say.

New York is an interesting city, he decided. It would be worthwhile to stay a few days and see what else could be learned from the American idiot, Spencer.

"I will meet you in San Francisco," he said, watching Nagashino for any reaction. As he expected, there was none. "Take them to our offices at the docks."

The big man rose to his feet.

"And Takeda?"

The big man looked at him questioningly.

"My uncle wants them in Japan in one piece."

At the mention of the Obayun, a flicker of some unreadable emotion crossed the giant's face for a moment, then was gone. He nodded and left.

Sho didn't allow his men to see his relief. Some day, he too, would generate that respect, that fear.

Jade Viking

"Quiet!"

Hiroaki Tachibana waited as the fearful cries slowly died down. He could see nothing and, as he could tell by the queasy feeling in his stomach, there was no gravity. Someone across the room was retching.

"Everyone remain calm. Inam? Where are you?"

He heard someone speaking unintelligibly and sighed in relief as dim bands of red appeared around the bridge. Inam closed a panel under her terminal and turned to face him.

She spoke and he couldn't understand a word she was saying. Of course, the computer did all the translating.

"I'm afraid the humans on board aren't going to be much good until they get over their panic." He felt himself starting to drift out of his seat and firmly gripped an armrest. "And until they get used to not having any gravity. But this language thing may be the worse."

Inam stared at him in growing comprehension. She looked thoughtful for a moment, then mimed the acts of choking and shivering.

"Although suffocation and freezing to death could be a bigger issue," Hiroaki said slowly.

She looked at him, puzzled.

Right. He made a motion on the side of his terminal as if to crank up the computer by hand, then gave her a questioning look.

She shrugged, then looked around as if searching. She put a hand on top of her head, then lowered it until it was barely above her waist.

"The Hoag?" Hiroaki looked around the bridge. The glowing beams made it look like a scene from of Dante's Inferno. "We need everyone calmed down, and to make sure no one is trapped anywhere. I'll make an anouncem...no, I won't." He smiled sheepishly, and the Baerd woman nodded, not understanding, but obviously sharing his frustration.

"It's hard to keep things in perspective," he admitted. "I suggest we send Hoag runners to retrieve everyone. They're the most familiar with the ship."

She just looked at him. He motioned all around to signify the ship, then pointed at a few of the people on the bridge. He then made a gathering in motion. It was quickly followed by a frantic motion to regain his grip on his chair.

He looked at her quizzically. "Well? Do you understand?"

It was hard to read her expression in the dim reddish glow, but he thought he saw a glimmer of humor. She nodded and spoke to Erle. He began calling out and was soon gesturing wildly to a couple of Hoag. They left, followed by Erle and a couple of other Baerd.

It took more than an hour to get everyone rounded up from all over the ship. Far too long, Hiroaki thought. The air wasn't too bad yet, but it did seem to be colder already.

Inam had labored nonstop, trying to get the computer back online. With no success. Without power, there were precious few options, and they were quickly eliminated.

The Hoag spent long minutes trying to tell him that there weren't enough batteries on board to power up hardly anything.

"We may have to abandon ship," he said glumly. "We have four shuttles. I wonder if the Eglev are still out there?"

Inam looked at him, trying to piece together what he was muttering about. He pointed at a dark screen and gestured to extend his ears to an absurd height. She shook her head.

He waved all around to mean the ship and she nodded. He extended his arms, then brought them together to form a little ball with his hands. He then raised four fingers on one hand and had them separate from the other hand.

Inam slapped a wall panel in excitement. Then she was frantically trying to grab something as the reaction from the impact sent her spiralling across the room. She hooked an arm around a seat. She raised four fingers of her own and did the same cranking motion he had done earlier, then pointed at the screen.

"If we jury rig all four together, it might be enough to turn the computer on!" Hiroaki spoke excitedly. She nodded her head hesitantly.

"Then what?" he asked. "Will the computer be able to bring everything else back online?" He waved a hand expansively to represent the entire ship.

She shrugged. Then she spoke to the screen and cupped her ear, as if waiting for an answer.

"Good!" Hiroaki grinned, nodding his head vigorously. "We'll ask Vicki what to do."

Inam motioned to the people around them. She then held up the same four fingers and pointed at them, then at the people.

"Good idea." Hiroaki said. "Pass the word around. We'll head for Alpha Hanger. Then we can send some of us on to Beta Hanger, so we don't overwhelm the resources of the two shuttles docked in Alpha." He held up four fingers and walked towards them with the fingers of his other hand, then held the first two fingers with the motioning hand.

She actually laughed at the walking fingers. A few minutes later, he saw her showing another Baerd, and both were laughing.

It seemed to take much too long to get everyone moving, but eventually they were all headed for the shuttle hangers. They were almost there when Hiroaki heard excited shouting from ahead.

"What's going on up there." Hiroaki froze as a horrifying thought occurred to him. "The Egelv didn't dock and board us, did they?"

"I hope they did," Kabu said grimly. The lithe Japanese and his fellow security people had joined up with him a few minutes earlier. He checked the load in his AK-47. Hiroaki had thought it silly when he saw many of the men were carrying their weapons, but now he felt relief.

"Captain, you need to see this." One of the original Jade Viking sailors from the American crew spoke from the hatchway to the docking hanger.

"What?" Hiroaki followed the silent man to the nearest shuttle. The lights were on low inside and he watched his step as they made their way to the control deck.

Inside, every single screen showed exactly the same thing.

He'd never seen what kind of written language the Baerd and Hoag had, but he would bet he could read at least one word in each of their languages.

The screens all showed three lines of letters, or symbols.

260

The first was in English, and it was just one word.
Wait!

Station Osaka

"How long have we got?" Sean asked as he lifted a duffle bag to his shoulder and picked up a suitcase with his other hand.

"We're supposed to be aboard in thirty minutes." Ellis took one last look around their bunk area, then snapped his single suitcase shut. He picked it up with his left hand, his right holding his AK-47. Sean's was strapped over the same shoulder as his duffle bag.

"Wanna swing by the brig? See who's guarding the crayfish and kitties?"

Ellis frowned. "I don't want to be late."

"Look, it's hardly out of our way. We'll just see who's there, give them a hard time, and split, okay?"

It only took them a minute to get to the corridor leading to the make-shift brig holding the alien prisoners. A few twists and turns and they could see the four men guarding the hatch.

Sean nudged Ellis.

"Look, there's Louie. What a dweeb he is." Ellis made a noncommittal sound. Sean knew his friend didn't like talking trash about people. But Louie Portano? C'mon!

"Hey, Louie!" he called out. "Louie, Louie, whoa, whoa!"

Jason Lang frowned at his ex-first officer. Danny DelaRosa was captain of his own ship, the newly christened Jade Conquistador, and had a right to dress as he saw fit, but...still. He still wore slacks, shirt and tie, but had abandoned the jacket and traded his brilliantly polished black shoes for sneakers.

And no cap.

Jason knew he was old school, and the old ways were changing faster than he ever would.

But really, Danny was overdoing it.

Admitted, there were alien prisoners aboard. And he would be the last to say he felt comfortable with the situation. They were dangerous. But, this was over the top!

A .45 caliber automatic rode on Danny's right hip, a large gutting knife on his other. To top it off, he had his sawed-off shotgun strapped in a quiver on his back, handle up, Jason supposed, to allow an easy draw.

"You look like a damn pirate," he muttered, wondering if there were chambered shells in those weapons. "You're going to shoot your foot off. Or your butt. And on my bridge."

Danny grinned, albeit the humor didn't quite reach his eyes. He'd just been perusing the casualty reports, and it made for grim reading.

All things considered, they'd been incredibly lucky. 'Samurai had only one human and two Hoag dead. 'Wolverine, and Danny's own 'Conquistador had been even more fortunate, and suffered no major injuries.

Osaka hadn't done nearly so well. Two humans, one Baerd, and seven Hoag had died, all due to damage caused by the exploding Ananab ship. Countless other minor injuries.

Lang had buried crew before. But it had been decades since the cause of death was combat. Many years of work aboard commercial vessels had dimmed the memories, but they were still there, and these last few months had brought them back with a rush.

Danny wasn't so experienced. The only military background he had was being in the reserve National Guard. To him, being an officer meant clean white uniforms, entertaining pretty daughters of rich people, giving more attention to passenger comfort than serious duty.

None of that had prepared him for seeing people die under his command. Jason missed the irrepressible young man that had come aboard to serve under him just a few short years ago.

But would any of them ever really be the same again?

If anyone would, it would be Randy Luca. His ex-purser somehow rolled with the punches, making jokes that would be considered inappropriate if uttered by anyone else.

"He looks more like a road warrior in one of those post-holocaust films." Luca's wide face split into a grin. "You should quit shaving and grow a beard, or something."

Jason covered his mouth with his hand, hiding a smile. Danny had started growing a Van Dyke beard several weeks earlier. Actually, it was

262

growing in nicely, but the young captain had taken a lot of kidding about it.

The three of them were sitting on the bridge, watching reports come in from all over the station. Jade Wolverine would be fully stocked and ready to depart in a little over an hour. It had been fortunate the ship hadn't received any significant damage.

Osaka and 'Samurai would take longer. Luckily, none of the damage to the ship had affected its battle worthiness. Osaka, on the other hand, had two weapon emplacements totally destroyed, and two others out of commission for at least a week.

And dead to bury.

He sighed and glanced at his watch. Forty minutes until the memorial service. It was quick, but Jim had requested it be held before 'Wolverine's departure so he could attend.

A disturbance near the main hatch caught his attention. A Hoag crewman was waving his arms frantically in a heated discussion with Spat, the senior Hoag aboard Osaka. Two other Hoag bridge crew stood nearby, looking nervous.

"What's going on?" he asked Randy Luca. The heavy-set man shrugged.

"I'll go find out."

Before he even rose from his chair, Spat turned around and marched over to them. He stopped directly in front of Lang and nodded his head in deference.

"What seems to be the problem, Mr. Spat?" Jason kept his voice mild. These Hoag spooked easily. Jason watched him weigh his words carefully.

"Sir, this crewman comes to me with a report that seems wildly ridiculous. I would not even bother you, but he is usually so reliable, and is so insistent, I thought you should hear it."

"What did he say?" Jason watched as Spat turned and waved his arm at the Hoag standing, fidgeting nervously by the hatch. "What is your name?"

The Hoag stared at him, his crisis momentarily forgotten. He finally spoke, his head ducking in embarrassment. "My name is Wim, Sir."

"Well, Wim." Jason frowned, as on either side of him, Randy and Danny both stirred in their seats. "What seems to be the problem?"

"Sir, I have felt the...Demons...aboard this station!" He seemed to have trouble settling on a word for his fears.

"Demons?" Jason glanced quickly at Spat. The other Hoag shook his small head.

"They are but a legend to keep us in fear. Stories say they were created, not evolved."

"Created by whom?" Jason felt like he was playing a jigsaw puzzle minus half a dozen pieces. "And for what purpose?"

"By the Hshtahni, to assassinate their enemies. They are reputed to be invisible to all races and scanning devices."

"Then how do you know they exist, if no one can see them?" Randy Luca asked. He had his best poker face on.

"They don't," Spat said firmly.

"They do!" Wim insisted. He was shaking, whether from fear or indignation, Jason couldn't tell. "They were used several times against the Hechktar, and once in a squabble between Hshtahni factions over succession of power. My great grandfather was there. He saw!"

"He saw the demons?" Danny asked quickly. "How?"

"He didn't actually see the demons," Wim admitted. "They're invisible. But he saw the Hshtahni, and their guards dropping dead, horrendous wounds appearing with no apparent cause." He hesitated, then continued. "He also said you could sense the invisible demons, if they passed close to you. And they passed very close to my great grandfather."

Jason frowned. "Sense them? How?" He interrupted the Hoag before he even had a chance to answer. "Pearl, what can you tell us about these...demons?"

"There is no substantiation to their existence, only rumors," Pearl said. "There have been incidences that could be explained by invisible assassins. There is no confirmation, however."

"Is the technology available for personal stealth shields?" Jason shivered at a sudden thought. "Or, for that matter, is there any record of an invisible race? Is such a thing possible?"

"There are several directions research could take towards developing individual stealth fields. However, I know of no serious efforts that have achieved, or even come close to success." Pearl took what was for her, a long time to continue. "I have no record of any invisible race ever being discovered, but the very nature of such a race would make it difficult to be conclusive."

So that's what a computer sounds like when it waffles, Jason thought dourly. "Well, think about it, Pearl. See what you come up with."

Spat bowed his head. "I am sorry to have bothered you with this, sir."

"No, no, you did the right thing. And so did Wim." Randy Luca cleared his throat, and Danny seemed inordinately interested in inspecting his fingernails. He ignored them both. "We're new at all this, and your input is extremely valuable."

It took several minutes, but finally the Hoag retreated. Danny stretched lazily, faking an enormous yawn.

"Before you say a word," Jason said. "The first person to make an obvious pun in poor taste, based on any aliens name will be doing laps around the perimeter corridors of the station." He looked at Randy's vast stomach.

"Lots of laps."

Randy rubbed his jaw with one hand, then did an elaborate pantomime of zipping his lips shut. Danny wet his lips.

"Don't do it, Mister," Jason warned. His ex-first officer got a pained look on his face.

"Okay," he sighed. "You whim."

❖ ❖ ❖ ❖ ❖

Jim played hard and fast. His fingers flew across the keyboard of the piano as he pounded out a heavy rhythm and blues tune.

Without pausing, he switched to an instrumental song from the late sixties. Normally, the song required multiple guitars with an orchestra backing them. Covering most of those elements of the song with one piano was challenging, but Jim welcomed the diversion.

He knew without looking, he only had a few more minutes before he needed to leave. There was going to be a memorial service for the casualties of the battle that had raged only hours earlier. Jim tried not to begrudge the precious time slowing his departure.

He felt like he was on a high precipice, his back to a stone wall, standing on a narrow ledge. For most of his adult life he'd practiced martial arts as a form of discipline and exercise, to be used only when all else failed.

A few friends had pointed out that he made a living making action movies that featured frequent violence. His response had been that he made movies for entertainment, not to press his moral opinions on others.

Growing up, he'd been taught not to use his natural talent and skills to bully others, and by and large, he'd followed that course. Until his nineteenth year, when he caught three men raping Afsaneh's mother, Nasria. That was the first time he'd ever used his training under the influence of an anger so strong it completely submerged his conscience.

It was also the first time he killed a man. Three, actually.

That night began the roller coaster ride that included the death of his parents, fighting the illegal bouts, first in the Philippines, then Hong Kong.

He returned to Ann Arbor, where he found Nasria married to his best friend, Hakim, about to give birth to a beautiful baby girl. That baby was Afsaneh. It would be years before what he always suspected was proven true. She was his daughter, not Hakim's, or the rapists.

He thought he'd healed when Nasria flew to London to reconcile with her family. She hadn't spoken to any of them since her pregnancy was discovered. Even marrying Hakim hadn't cooled their wrath. But finally, after almost two years, they had made overtures. A last minute ear infection kept Afsaneh from accompanying her.

It saved her life. A terrorist bomb killed every member of her family in that restaurant.

To Jim, it was as if he'd snapped right back two years to the Far East. It had taken months, but eventually he tracked down the men responsible for the bomb.

Until this trip, those were the last men he'd ever killed.

Violence begets violence. He always believed that, but knowing it and stopping it were two different things. The past reached out to claim him.

You are, and always will be, a killer. Accept it.

Jim hit the keyboard with a closed fist and winced. He hated people that abused things because they were angry. It was petty, and weak. He was no better than a common bully.

I will not let these failings, or feelings, consume me, he swore to himself. Taking a couple of deep breaths to calm down, he felt eyes watching him.

"Yes?" he said, turning around on the piano bench.

To his surprise, the room was empty.

He sat there for a few moments, feeling strange. I'm not wrong about something like that very often, he reflected. He closed his eyes and listened.

Nothing. What had made him turn? Shrugging, he went back to his piano.

◆ ◆ ◆ ◆ ◆

"Captain Lang, upon consideration, I believe the matter of 'demons' warrants further investigation."

"Oh?" Lang said in a guarded tone. He had hoped Pearl would come back with an assurance that there were no ghosts aboard his space station. "What kind of investigation?"

"To begin with, I would like to instruct the Baerd to hook up a direct link between myself and the captured Ananab ship."

"For what purpose?" He was a little hesitant to risk Pearl to an unknown. "Why don't we just make a copy of the program and infect it indirectly?"

"Time, for the most part. This is faster, and, I can scan the memory lodes. If there were any unusual passengers aboard, the ship's computer will have record of it."

"As long as you're sure the ship can't corrupt your system," Lang said. "Go ahead."

"Actually, I've already sent Baerd technicians to make the connections," Pearl admitted. "In the meanwhile, I've begun an unscheduled atmospheric scan of the entire station."

"Why?" Lang hated to show his ignorance about the station but, there were more important things than his pride these days.

"That's a good idea," Randy nodded enthusiastically. He grinned at Lang and explained. "I've been trying to learn the maintenance and re-supply procedures, and I remember that one. It's to show contamination or leaks...and, uh..." He grimaced as some of the details obviously escaped him.

"It can show any contamination, change in breathable air, any natural buildup of toxins, any number of other useful purposes," Pearl agreed. "I am comparing this scan to the last one made before the captured ship docked. Any stealth capacity, or unknown alien race might emit unusual levels of ozone, or perhaps some by-product of their breathing."

"How long will this take?" Danny squirmed in his seat. "If there's a real chance of intruders, we need to alert the station."

"The scan is complete, as is the comparison."

"Show-off," Randy muttered under his breath. Lang smiled. If she had found anything, she wouldn't be playing coy.

"And?" Lang asked.

"And there is no conclusive difference. There are some variations, but they are minuscule and scattered widely about the ship. The subversion of the captured ship's computer will be completed in less than two minutes."

"You say there are some variances," Lang mused. "Can you show where they are on the ship? Is there any pattern?"

"Show us on the screen," Danny urged.

The large screens showing the surrounding space changed to show a three dimensional schematic of the station. A large number of light blue spots appeared. They seemed to be spread throughout the main body of the station, but were in only one of the many concourses that stretched out away from the core.

"Show the Ananab ship." Lang stirred uneasily. It was on the same concourse. His attention switched over to the main body. Many corridors had the dots, but most compartments and rooms were clean. Except a few. One compartment at nearly the opposite end of the station from the contaminated concourse show signs.

In fact, Lang realized, you could almost draw a line..."Pearl, try and follow the signs from that compartment near F Concourse. See if it can connect back to C Concourse and the Ananab ship."

"Just like the maze drawings," Randy chuckled. "Connect the dots."

"This is no game," Danny retorted, standing up and taking a step closer to the screen. Even as he spoke, a faint green line ran from the compartment in question clear back to the hatch of the captured vessel. "Show where the prisoners are."

A large room glowed yellow. There were dots near the only entrance.

"The bridge?" Lang spoke softly, thumbing the cover of his holster open, trying not to be obvious. "And what's in that one compartment?"

A klaxon began ringing and Pearl's voice carried above, thundering in a tone he'd never heard from any of the computers before.

"Intruder alert! Intruder alert!"

Then all hell broke loose.

268

CHAPTER EIGHTEEN

Station Osaka

Jim stopped playing abruptly in the middle of a phrase. He didn't turn, he just listened. He heard the tiniest shuffle and threw himself to the left. Almost simultaneously, alarms began going off, and Pearl's voice spoke urgently through his transmitter.

"Jim Morris, there are sheathed intruders aboard the station."

He heard something hit the piano and felt air move very close to him. He reversed his direction and spun kicking. He felt his foot hit something with a satisfying thud. Something screamed and he kicked again. The sound ended in a muted groan.

"Pearl," he gasped. "Stop all noise in this room, and put the lights out. Now!"

She immediately complied. He came to a rest against the wall and froze. He strained to hear something, anything.

He sensed more than heard movement directly in front of him. Not hesitating, he leaped forward, doing a front kick as hard as he could. There was a sharp cracking sound, and then something hit the floor.

Jim carefully stepped to the side. Whatever was in here with him, had two less members now. How many did that leave?

A sudden thought sent a chill down his spine. What if they could see in the dark? An almost imperceptible rustling sound answered his question and he dropped to the ground, feeling something clip a lock of flying hair from his head. He landed pivoting on one hand and swept-kicked across.

He felt rather than heard the creature leap over his foot and he reversed his pivot and came back with the other foot just in time to catch his opponent squarely.

There was a startled squeak, then something landed right beside him. He came over with his arm and felt the back of his hand crush something. There was suddenly static and visible flashing of some power source shorting out.

He came down squarely in the middle of the buzzing sparks with the heel of his right foot. He felt something give way.

Jim silently crawled a few feet away from the body and listened. He couldn't hear a thing except an occasional crackle or buzz from the fallen foes.

He waited.

"Uh, oh." Sean heard Ellis's groan just before he saw the cause of it.

"Gentlemen, this is not a very direct route to your ship, and you are due there in...seventeen minutes."

"Sir!" Both young snapped to attention. Sean smiled at McGregor weakly. "Chief, we were just, uh, going to say goodbye to our good friend, Louie."

"Your good friend Louie is busy right now. He's doing something important, something helpful. He is at his station keeping enemy prisoners where they belong. He doesn't need distractions in the form of goof-offs such as yourselves."

Sean nodded, and started to answer, then stopped. He felt a shiver and saw that, much to his surprise, he had goose bumps on his arms. *When and where had he felt that?*

Guarding the enemy ship.

He strained his eyes to see any kind of threat in the corridor, but there was nothing. McGregor noticed his tension.

"What is it?"

"I don't know, Sir." Sean felt frustrated. "I could swear..." He stopped, not knowing what was bothering him.

"You'll have me swearing," McGregor warned, but took a careful look at the four sentries less than twenty yards away.

"You felt this earlier, when we were getting off duty, didn't you?" Growing comprehension appeared in Ellis' eyes. He turned towards McGregor and stiffened.

The security chief wasn't moving a muscle. His eyes were narrowed and he was staring intently towards the other group of men.

"It doesn't help to stare," Sean advised him. "Try looking off to the side, so you're using your peripheral vision."

McGregor nodded, and began to turn his head, but then it snapped back to the posted sentries. Sean turned just in time to see all four men start to fall, blood silently gushing from wounds that appeared almost magically.

Sean about jumped out of his pants as McGregor and Ellis both began firing waist high, above the fallen men. He struggled to get his duffel bag off his shoulder so he could get to his weapon.

Then the hatch popped open, and Tryr started pouring out. He saw some flee the other way. Then all he could see was a wall of Tryr and Srotag charging them.

◆ ◆ ◆ ◆ ◆

Lang leaped to his feet, then sprawled to the deck. Bridge personnel were rushing around, trying to get to their duty stations. Swearing, he pulled his revolver out of its holster and peered around the room.

He saw one Hoag, running at full steam, come to a complete halt, then fall backwards, blood streaming from a vicious looking wound.

Lang didn't hesitate. He fired at the spot the Hoag had collided with something. There was a bright flash and a small grey body went flying backwards. It lay where it landed, unmoving. Sparks flew all around it, and dark blood poured from it's mid-section.

Behind him, he heard the explosive roar of Danny's shotgun fire, then again, and again.

A security man ran towards him, gun drawn. He suddenly veered off to the side, his throat torn out. Lang fired, trying to hit his assailant. He saw no results.

Another man fell, then a Baerd. Both were closer to him then the security guard had been. Lang kept firing, trying to anticipate.

Then the hammer on his gun fell on an empty cartridge.

◆ ◆ ◆ ◆ ◆

Jim stood up and spoke as quietly as he could. "Pearl, were there just three of them?"

"I believe so." Pearl sounded miffed. "But there are two other groups. One is fighting on the bridge, the other is trying to free the prisoners."

"Damn. Lights on."

He looked around. There was a body partially visible with fireworks going on around it, and the third assassin he'd killed. He felt around with a foot until he nudged something where his eyes told him there was nothing.

One good kick convinced him the unseen dead body was just that, and he went to inspect the one whose stealth system had failed.

The alien was barely four feet tall, had dark grey fur, and a long narrow skull. The face was in a death grimace that revealed long, extremely dangerous looking teeth. Lots of them.

Jim was intrigued to see that the entire bady was encased in a suit that was mostly transparent. What he assumed were power lines ran from a wide belt around its' waist about an inch thick and three inches wide.

He couldn't see any seams, and there appeared to only be a few breaks in the material. One was a flap that fell over the mouth, but allowed air to pass.

Jim wondered what weapons besides the teeth there were. The creature seemed to be unarmed. Then he noticed tiny circular flaps on the knuckles. Cautiously, he stepped on one of the forearms.

Three long claws slid out.

Yow, Jim thought. Three very sharp looking claws, at that!

"Pearl, do you know what these are?"

"By piecing together a number of unconfirmed reports, myths, and legend, I surmise these are members of a race called the Reigna. There are no visual records, only rumors and stories."

"Hmm." Jim lifted his foot, and the claws slid back out of sight. "Dangerous looking little buggers."

"More than you realize. The claws are reputed to be extremely poisonous to most species."

"Wonderful," Jim muttered. "And you say we had two other groups attack? I assume they were beaten?"

"Not yet. One remains at large on the bridge, and although all three were killed at the brig, they managed to release some of the prisoners. I've summoned security to recapture them."

"Damn!" Jim swore, and took off at a fast trot. "Why didn't you tell me?"

"You would be safer if you remained here until I issue an all-clear," Pearl said in a defensive tone.

"You know me better than that, Pearl." Jim was furious. He'd had enough.

"Jim Morris, you are going to intersect the course of two Tryr. Help is close, and you are unarmed. It would be wiser to wait for back-up."

"Pearl, I'm never unarmed," Jim snarled, then turned a corner and saw the approaching Tryr. One was approximately twenty yards in front of the other, obviously a decoy to draw fire and allow the other to react.

They spied him, and the lead Tryr snarled triumphantly as he saw Jim had no weapon. He loped forward easily, looking confident. His cockiness turned to surprise as Jim snarled back and began striding purposefully forward.

"Look at this hairless little Hoag," he called back to his pardner. "Rushing to his death!"

Jim snarled again and kept his pace deliberate. The Tryr slowed to match him, and laughed when Jim raised his arms so his hands were at shoulder level.

They came within a yard of each other, and the Tryr straightened as he came to a halt.

"Time to die, Human," he said as he watched Jim's hands.

Jim's response was a front kick, as fast and as hard as he could make it. He hit his target perfectly, and the Tryr bent forward, screaming in pain as Jim's foot caught him squarely between the legs.

Without any hesitation, Jim did a crescent kick with his left foot, hitting the other along side his head. The Tryr spun around and down to his knees, both from the pain, and from shock.

In a flash, Jim kneed him where Humans would have kidneys. Obviously Tryr had something comparable, because his head reared back and he screamed again.

He grasped the large, black furry head and twisted as hard as he could. There was a loud crack, and the Tryr slumped to the deck.

The other Tryr had stopped and was staring at him in shock, then anger. He roared and Jim roared right back and stepped past the body on the deck.

Jim knew he wouldn't be able to catch this one by surprise, and the odds were now heavily against him, but he didn't care. A heavy film seemed to be growing over his eyes. It didn't block his vision, just his judgement.

Even so, he had the presence of mind to continue analyzing as they met. The Tryr was throwing himself forward, so Jim helped him, catching one hairy arm and falling backwards to send the catman flying over his head.

The Tryr landed heavily, obviously surprised, but was still back on his feet and charging far faster than any human would have been able to.

This time, he slowed as he neared Jim. Fast learners, Jim admitted through the haziness. He feinted with a kick, then punched as the Tryr reacted to the threat of his feet. It hurt his hand.

The Tryr looked surprised, then grinned, revealing his long fangs. It may have hurt him, but not nearly enough, Jim saw.

"Now you die." The Tryr took one step forward, then a look of absolute shock, then pain flew across his face. Jim watched in confusion as the Tryr started to turn around, then became immobile as the tip of a sword suddenly protruded from his chest.

Jim watched him look down at it stupidly, the light go out of his eyes and collapse. Behind the dead Tryr, Captain Koro Asaya hurriedly pulled his katana out to prevent its breaking.

Asaya wiped the blade on the furry arm of the dead Tryr to clean the blood off, then sheathed it with a flourish. In his eyes, Jim saw a reflection of the madness he felt.

Two armed security guards stood behind Asaya, assault rifles at the ready. One of them carried an extra one, and he offered it to Jim.

"Pearl told us you needed help," Commander Asaya had returned to his unflappable self, the fury of battle temporarily buried.

"What about the bridge and the brig?"

"What about them?" Asaya looked puzzled, and Jim saw the truth. To make sure he got assistance, she had neglected to inform Asaya of the other battles taking place.

"Damn!" Then to the confused Asaya and his men, "come on, we're not through, yet."

"Sure, don't anyone tell me what the hell's going on, no..." Asaya grumbled as he motioned for his men to follow Jim. "Why would I need to know anything?"

They left the two dead Tryr where they lay.

Randy Luca saw the governor firing from where he sat frozen in his seat. Bodies were dropping all around, blood was everywhere. He watched Danny yell in triumph as his shotgun got another assailant.

Two down. How many more?

His attention came back to the governor, who had stopped firing. He seemed to be searching his pockets frantically for something. Dimly Randy became aware that Lang was trying to find more ammunition for his revolver.

The governor was still laying on the deck as he finally pulled a small box out of his trousers. Randy wished he felt as calm as Lang looked as the older man began emptying the spent casings out, and replacing them with fresh shells.

Randy felt his eyes widen in horror as he saw a footprint appear as if by magic in a puddle of blood between him and Lang. But no one stood there! Another print appeared, bloody drippings on an otherwise clean spot of the floor. Then another, as the hidden enemy approached Lang from outside his line of vision.

"No!" Randy didn't know he was moving until he suddenly had something cradled in his arms. It squirmed and tried to break free, but Randy held on, yelling to the captain all the while.

"Behind you, sir. I've got it! I got..." He felt something give and thought his belt had broken. Then he realized it wasn't his belt.

A sensation he knew had to be pain was flashing from his center outwards, but he ignored it and crushed the invisible foe close to his chest, trying to hang on, even as he felt something start oozing down his legs.

Lang suddenly was at his side, and put his pistol up against whatever Randy held and fired. His burden reacted spasmodically, then slumped unmoving. Randy tried to shake his head as Lang told him he could let go now.

Didn't the captain understand? The dead body he clutched was all that held his insides in place as he slowly sunk to his knees. He tried to speak, but all that came through his lips was blood.

He didn't want to go, yet. There was too much to do, and he was needed. But now, he could recognize the sensation sweeping throughout his body as pain. Raw, overlapping waves of pain.

Leaving didn't seem to be so bad anymore.

Jim left Asaya and his men behind as he ran full tilt towards the sound of gunfire. Good, as long as there were shots being fired, they hadn't lost yet.

He rounded the last turn, and saw McGregor and a slew of armed men on both sides of the open hatch. No one stood right in front of it, though. McGregor was directing controlled fire from both sides, diagonally through the hatch, creating a crossfire of death the Ananab and Tryr couldn't break through.

There was a sudden flash and a loud thundering from inside the compartment. McGregor and the others fell back from the blinding light. A rumbling sustained for several moments, then the light and the sound ceased.

"Please do not enter the compartment." Pearl sounded cold and efficient. "You will want to don heavy footwear."

"What did you do?" Jim whispered. "What did you do?!"

"I increased the gravity in the chamber to four hundred times normal. There is no further threat. You may enter now."

Jim and McGregor stared at each other in horror. Asaya came running up, gasping for breath. He put a hand on McGregor for support. "What happened?" As his two men belatedly arrived, he looked at Jim. "You know, you can run a hell of a lot faster than I realized..." Asaya's voice trailed off as he saw the looks on their faces. "What is it?"

Jim pointed mutely. As one, the three of them took hesitant steps to the hatchway and looked inside.

Carnage greeted them.

Behind him, Jim heard Ellis retching as he jettisoned his lunch against a wall. One look at Sean showed it was all the slender young man could do to keep from joining his friend.

"Why, Pearl?" Jim asked simply.

"To reduce casualties." Pearl said in a matter of fact voice to his personal transceiver. "You would have attempted to overwhelm them without having to kill them all, and they would not have surrendered.

Your life would have been at extreme risk."

"It's my life!" Jim almost screamed it. "You do not dictate my life, and what chances I take!"

"I have no choice in the matter," Pearl countered. "My programming does not permit me to stand by and not take action, when there are other options."

"I order you to stop making these choices for me!" McGregor and Asaya both took a step back at the venom in his voice, looking around to see where it was directed.

"I can not." Pearl said simply.

Jim stood there, looking at the bloody sludge that was ankle-deep throughout the compartment. "What's the situation on the bridge."

"All fighting has ceased, and all Reigna are dead. But there were casualties."

"Casualties," Jim repeated, looking at Asaya. Without another word, they turned and hurried to the bridge.

What they saw stopped them cold.

Dead bodies were everywhere. Not just Human, either. Jim could see both Hoag and Baerd strewn across consoles, in aisles, halfway to the exit, evidence of failed attempts to flee.

Horrible as those sights were, Jim's eyes didn't linger as they passed on to rest on the figures huddled next to the command console.

Governor Lang, knelt holding Randy Luca's body in his arms as he would a child's. Jim caught his breath as he saw the extent of the damage to the ex-purser.

Randy had been disemboweled from sternum to crotch. Draped across his legs was a dead Reigna with most of it's head blown off.

Lang's shoulders shook as he silently sobbed. Tears ran down both cheeks, soaking his white beard. For the first time that Jim could remember, Lang actually looked his age.

Or older, Jim admitted to himself. Much older.

The survivors of the bridge crew stood around, staring at each other and at their leader. Jim caught the eye of the senior Hoag.

Jim raised a questioning eyebrow, and Spat slowly nodded. With great effort, he spoke to the sole other surviving Hoag in the room, and they huddled over their work station, calling other departments to send help for the wounded.

And for the dead.

Jim started towards Lang, not quite sure what to do.

"No." He stopped as Suyo Takashi stepped in front of him. She raised one hand imperiously. "I will help him."

"Are you sure you can..." Jim stopped as she smiled tiredly at him. She was so small and Lang was so big. But he didn't doubt she could cope, not for a moment.

"I will take care of him." Suyo looked at him intently. "You have a ship to prepare for departure."

"How can I..." Jim glanced around the room. The station was in total disarray. He couldn't leave them like this. But, he couldn't delay getting Afsaneh back to Earth, either.

"We will manage. No one will blame you for trying to save your only daughter." Suyo crouched next to Lang. "Now, go," she said over her shoulder as she placed a hand on the grieving man's shoulder.

"She's right, Jim. We can handle this, and the Captain, uh, Governor, will be back after he gets about twelve hours of sleep." Danny watched Suyo gently pry Lang away from Randy so the Hoag could remove the body.

Jim was amazed to see there were already dozens of Hoag helping people all over the bridge. Dr. Gonzalez was walking from body to body, shaking his head in resignation almost every time.

For a moment, all activity ceased, and Jim looked around, alarmed. But they were just watching Suyo lead Governor Lang off the bridge. He walked in short, uneven steps, leaning heavily on her.

They passed a Baerd kneeing next to the body of a fellow Baerd. He was trying to straighten the shredded remains of her tunic to preserve her modesty.

Lang stopped and fumbled through his pockets. He found a hankerchief and knelt next to the grieving male. He opened the hankerchief and laid it across her chest. The Baerd looked up at him, grief stricken.

"Please come, Sir." Suyo's voice was soft, but firm. Lang nodded and, as he stood up, patted the shoulder of the Baerd almost absentmindedly. He took one last look at Randy, then his eyes met Jim's.

"He saved my life," he said simply. Jim could only nod, his throat too thick for words. He watched Suyo lead the man away.

"Will he recover?" Spat kept his eyes averted to the ground as he spoke. Jim glanced at Danny who shrugged.

"I've never seen him like this. He's usually so reserved and in control." Danny stepped aside so a Hoag could pass with an antigrav sled. "But he cares so much..."

278

"Will he be...okay?" Spat persisted, timidly looking up at Jim.

He saw the old man leave again in his mind, and thought about the tiny handful of Humans, Baerd, and Hoag left on Osaka. He pictured ships landing on the White House lawn, on university campuses all over country, all over the world.

And he thought of Afsaneh lying so small, so still in her bed on 'Wolverine. And of his wife, far away back on Earth. His answer was more brusque than he intended.

"He will, because he has to."

CHAPTER NINETEEN

Ann Arbor, Michigan

"Finally," Iori sighed in relief. "They're checking into the Marriot."

Sasama frowned. "That's weird. Jim and Kimberly are married, and he's got a great house on the other side of town."

"Well, look." Iori pointed triumphantly. The two women had pulled up to the main entrance, and Kiri hurried inside. Sasama pulled into a parking spot and adjusted his rearview mirror so he could watch Kimberly waiting in her 'Beamer.

A few minutes later, Kiri came out with some papers in her hands. She got back in the car, and Sasama cautiously followed as they circled the tall building.

Kimberly suddenly whipped into a parking spot, and Sasama sped up so he passed before the women got out. He went down about twenty parking spots and found an empty one.

They watched as Kiri started to get a suitcase out of the back seat. Iori chuckled as Kimberly convinced her to leave it, and they went inside the hotel.

"That's right, Kiri. Let the bellboy get the luggage." He grinned at Sasama. "Let's go get a room and sleep for about two years."

"We can't stay in the same hotel," Sasama argued. "With our luck, we'll run into them in the elevator or something. We need to find another place."

"Like, perhaps, that world famous hotel chain situated so conveniently next door?" Iori asked, pointing. "If we get a room on this side, we can see their parking spot and sleep in shifts."

"Vicki, we're checking into the Hyatt. Any problem with that?" Sasama began to drive next door as he waited for the response. "Jade Viking? Captain Tachibana?" He and Iori exchanged worried looks.

Iori looked out the car window up into the sky. "Are they on the other side of the world, or the moon?"

"That didn't stop communications before," Sasama said, parking. "Come on, let's get into a room and we'll try again."

Five minutes later they were signing in at the desk. Sasama glanced at what Iori was writing and winced. Hirohito Yamato was a pretty unlikely Japanese name in this day and age, but the clerk didn't seem to notice.

"We'd like to pay in cash, please." Sasama smiled at the young man behind the counter as he pulled out his wallet. "We'll be staying two nights."

"Fine, but I'll need a credit card for security."

Sasama and Iori looked at each other, alarmed. "Um, I don't want this visit showing up on my credit card bill...uh, Bryan." Sasama improvised, looking at the clerk's name tag.

"It won't, as long as you settle up when you check out." Bryan gave him a reassuring smile. "It's just a normal precaution, in case you make long distance phone calls or something."

"Uh, well, I may have a little problem." Sasama's mind raced as he tried to think of a way out. "You see, I can't let my wife find out I stayed here. She's the jealous type."

Bryan looked at him, then at Iori. A slight smile came to his lips. Wait, he thinks...hmm, that might work, Sasama thought.

"I could lose my job." Sasama tried to look very worried. "We both could." Iori gave him a dirty look, that, fortunately, the clerk missed. "We're both from out of town, you see. We always try to meet in...liberal cities. And Ann Arbor...well, you know."

"Yes, I do." Bryan's mannerisms changed subtly. An air of conspiracy entered the conversation. "Don't worry. We don't actually charge anything to it, as long as you settle up when you check out. The paperwork just sits here until then, and you can have it all back when you leave."

"But the name's not the same." Sasama made one last attempt, but Bryan squashed it.

"Oh, that's okay," he assured Sasama. "We get people staying incognito all the time. But I'm afraid I do have to get a card imprint. If it was up to me..." The clerk let the sentence die away as he leaned forward onto his side of the counter.

"You're sweet." Sasama gave up and pulled out a credit card. He forced himself not to snatch his hand away when Bryan's fingers lingered as he took it. A few moments later, it was returned.

"See? No sweat." Bryan glanced to either side, then spoke in a quiet voice. "Do you know any of the local clubs? I could suggest a few. In fact, I was thinking of going out after work tonight..."

"Uh, not tonight. We both came a long way and are going to stay in tonight." Sasama tried not to overact. "You know what I mean? But, maybe tomorrow..."

"I work the late shift tomorrow," Bryan said regretfully. "It's probably just as well. My boyfriend is such a bitch, and so suspicious."

"Aren't they all?" Sasama said as he backed away from the counter. "Thank you again, and it was nice talking with you."

When they hit the sidewalk, Iori turned to him. "Did you have to give him the impression I'm your boy toy?"

"Yes," Sasama said, then giggled.

Iori snorted and shoved his hands into his pockets. "That room better have two beds."

❖ ❖ ❖ ❖ ❖

Bryan watched the two young Japanese men walk out. Oh, I just love oriental men, or would if I had a chance, he admitted. And to spend the night with two at once...

They were so athletic looking, and could probably go for hours and hours. He forced himself to stop picturing that particular scenario. His pulse raced just thinking about it.

"Another one that got away," he whispered to himself as he did a routine hold on a portion of the credit card's available funds.

❖ ❖ ❖ ❖ ❖

Groundhog watched the two Japanese men wearily carry suitcases into the hotel. He'd caught enough conversation between Kimberly and Kiri to piece together why they were at the Marriot. It's too bad he hadn't

283

bugged their car for sound as well as beacon signal. He'd only been able to use his snooper laser at the rest area, and the conversation had been limited.

He decided there was time to go to Jim Morris' house, bug it for sound, and return in time to pick up the trail in case of more diversions. Later tonight, he would bug the red sports car as well. It would be much easier to keep track of both cars without as much risk of detection.

◆ ◆ ◆ ◆ ◆

Sasama felt like it had only been minutes since he laid down when Iori shook him roughly. "Come on! They're getting into their car! Hurry!"

Five minutes later they were racing down the expressway, looking for Kimberly's BMW.

"This goes towards Jim's place," Sasama suggested, not taking his eyes off the traffic around them. "They must be headed there." He saw the gold 'Beamer ahead in the next lane. "There they are. Slow down. Don't let them see us."

He sat back and rubbed his eyes in frustrated exhaustion. He swore if the two women tried to drive past Jim's house, he'd shoot out their tires.

◆ ◆ ◆ ◆ ◆

"We have to watch ET Thursday!" Kiri announced. Kimberly nodded wearily.

"I know, I know." Kimberly glanced over at her. "You've only said that fifteen times since we got in the car."

"It's not been more than ten times," Kiri argued. At Kimberly's skeptical look, she conceded. "Maybe a dozen."

"Personally, I enjoyed seeing everybody again more than that boring interview." Kimberly waited for the storm to hit and she wasn't disappointed.

"Boring? Did you say boring?" Kiri was indignant. "I'll have you know, I was witty and charming. Ask anyone."

"Yeah, yeah." It had been an amusing few minutes on camera. Kimberly tried to stay far away from the ET people, immersing herself in the small crowd of Jade Viking veterans. Although it hadn't been that long since they'd seen each other, everyone had wanted details on what they'd been doing. It reminded her of a class reunion, but without the usual jerks.

Yvette and Janice were the same as always, but their banter couldn't conceal the fatigue or the worry in their eyes. Earlier, contact with Vicki abruptly cut off. It might be nothing.

Or, it might not.

Yvette told her she'd started paperwork on a corporation to be based out of the Bahamas.

Eric Miles had found an island off the coast of Columbia. As soon as the corporation was up and running, he would try and purchase the island outright. He assured her that enough money in the right places would get the Columbian government to cede it outright.

After all, it was tiny, only about eighteen square miles. It had no source of fresh water, and almost no vegetation. It didn't even appear on most maps. No one lived there.

Perfect.

Eric had been busy with other things, too. He'd actually arranged to buy several 'retired' oil tankers as scrap. The Hoag had assured him that any scrap metal could be salvaged and used efficiently by Jade Viking or Station Osaka.

Which was why, when he wasn't recruiting for the Remote Sites employment agency, Ron Hoffman was spending most of his time buying up automobile junkyards. This also meant Kimberly had a backpack full of papers to go through, the sooner the better.

She came back to the present with a start as Kiri directed her into a long driveway that wove through heavily wooded land. She rounded the last turn and let the car roll to a halt.

A large, mostly ranch-style house faced the driveway. It was a tasteful combination of stone and grey stained wood, with an A-frame face lined with windows. Kimberly's brow wrinkled in puzzlement. It was nice, but not as pretentious, or decadent as she had expected of Jim and Hakim. She shrugged and drove up to the driveway door at the right end of the house. Three-car garage, she noticed. No surprise there, she thought wryly.

Kiri eagerly got out and jingled the house keys at her as she walked to the front door.

That's my front door, Kimberly belatedly thought. This is...home? She sighed and climbed out of the Beamer.

Kiri had disappeared somewhere inside. Kimberly entered the foyer and admired the framed picture that greeted her on the left wall.

It was a nice print of Mount Fuji, she decided. A closer look showed it to be an original painting. And a very good one, at that. A large family room seemed to occupy the entire center of the house. The left corner was dominated by a huge black grand piano.

Glass doors to the left led to a formal dining room that looked like it never got used. To the right, a bar and a fireplace separated the family room from the kitchen beyond. The back wall was mostly sliding glass doors and windows, all heavily draped.

It smells musty in here, she decided. There was a hallway to the right of the dining room, and she heard the faint sound of a toilet flush. That sounds like a good idea, Kimberly thought, but first let's open this place up a little.

She drew the drapes to one of the two sets of glass doors, and gasped. What she thought had composed most of the house was really only about a third of it. It was a big "U", and she was standing in the very middle.

In the open space inside the "U" was a huge swimming pool and deck area. There was a large separate building that looked for all the world like an apartment complex clubhouse, complete with Tiki Bar at the far end of the pool.

"Whew, that wine runs right through me." Kimberly started as Kiri spoke, but it reminded her of her own need.

"Where did you find a bathroom?" Kimberly asked, tearing her eyes away from the pool with some effort. "This place is a lot bigger than I realized."

"Yeah, it's pretty cool," Kiri said, nodding. "Come on, I'll show you around."

"Let's start with a john," Kimberly reminded her.

"Right this way, Ma'am." Kiri spoke with an exaggerated drawl that was incongruous with her Asian features. It would have done Janice proud. "On the left here we have the formal dining room, as far as I know, never used. Next, we have..."

"I know what that is, and I'll be right out." Kimberly only took a moment, but by the time she got back out, Kiri had disappeared again. She walked down the hall, checking doors as she went. Guest bedroom, another guest bedroom, another guest bedroom. A door stood slightly ajar at the end of the corridor, and she pushed it open, then gasped with pleasure.

This had to be Jim's, she decided. It was a lounge and office, all in one. A small baby grand piano occupied one corner. A neat desk area with numerous shelves above it, took up another. Several very comfortable looking chairs and sofas were scattered about, seemingly at random.

Every wall was filled with bookshelves that were jammed with literally thousands of books and videos. Several photo albums were strewn across one coffee table and Kimberly idly flipped one open.

A very young Jim Morris stared back at her. It was obviously his high school graduation picture. He looks so...young! Kimberly smiled as she flipped through the pages.

He was so clean-cut when he was younger! At least now she had a little better picture of how he looked without a beard. And about fifteen years, she added silently.

She regretfully left the photo albums for future perusal, and went into the next room. She didn't need anyone to tell her this was Jim's bedroom.

It was about what she would have expected. A king-size bed barely made a dent in the floor space. The walls were covered with a strange conglomerate of Japanese, University of Michigan, and other assorted adornments from all over the world.

There were several stuffed chairs against one wall, with a large coffee table between them. Kimberly stared at the large framed picture that hung above the table. A very pale, black-haired woman with eyes of sapphire gazed at her with a calm expression. Behind her was either the sea, or one of the Great Lakes, but at first you didn't even notice.

Kimberly didn't need anyone to tell her it was a picture of Afsaneh's mother, Nasri. Jim had told her how beautiful Nasri had been, but Kimberly had assumed it was just his romanticized memory at work. She wasn't just beautiful, but...captivating.

"Gorgeous, isn't she?" Kimberly didn't turn at the sound of Kiri's voice. "I think Afsaneh inherited most of her better features."

"I see why Jim was in love with her," Kimberly admitted, a little wistfully. She tore her eyes away and saw that Kiri had brought some of their bags in from the car. "You should have waited for me," she protested.

"There's more where these came from," Kiri promised. "You might as well stay in here, don't you think?"

Kimberly looked around the room with some trepidation. She felt like she was intruding on Jim's privacy, and his past. She glanced back at the picture of Nasri. The Persian woman stared back at her imperiously.

"I don't know..." she said hesitantly. "I feel like I'm intruding."

"Kimberly." Kiri lay her hand on Kimberly's arm and gazed into her eyes. "This is your home, now. You are the lady of the house, Madame."

"Get outta here," Kimberly laughed and impulsively gave her a hug. "Thanks for being here, Kiri. This is all pretty strange to me."

"You'll probably want me to stay in here with you..." Kiri began, then, with a big grin, waited for Kimberly's reaction. Kimberly was gratified to see shock on her friend's face at the answer.

"That would be great. Otherwise, I'll have to cover that picture." She gestured at Nasri.

"Really?" Kiri asked, looking as though she thought Kimberly was pulling her leg.

"No, stay in here with me," Kimberly insisted. "This bed is humungous! But, you have to promise not to feel me up in the middle of the night."

"Ha! No way, round eyes." Kiri nudged her playfully. "I don't make promises I don't plan to keep."

Suddenly, nothing seemed as threatening or foreign to Kimberly. She grinned at her friend in gratitude.

"Come on, Valley Girl. Let's go get your other fourteen suitcases. A hot bath beckons."

As usual, Kiri got the last word in.

"Yum!"

Groundhog felt his jaw harden, but kept driving. He'd let the red Viper get far ahead, since he'd known where they were going. Sure enough, they were pulled off on the side of the road just within visual range of the turnoff into the driveway.

What he hadn't expected were the two other vehicles hidden in the trees across the road. He was absolutely certain they hadn't been there a few hours ago when he'd bugged the house.

Speaking of which, he turned on his monitor and kept trying channels until he found the two women. They were in...Jim Morris' room. One or both of them were lesbians, or bisexual.

That was something the files hadn't given a clue of.

He pulled off the road onto a dirt trail. Fifty yards later, he pulled as far off the trail as he dared and parked. He looked at the darkening sky, and sighed. At least he would have the night on his side.

Fifteen minutes later, dressed in black, he began the tedious chore of working his way through thick foliage, aided by night goggles that lit the terrain an eery green.

It took almost half an hour, but he didn't rush. Finally he made out a rough outline of an automobile ahead. It looked like a typical rental. What was less typical were the four men leaning against it, looking across the road towards the house.

He turned to check. Sure enough, his goggles allowed his to catch the faint glow from the windows. He tried looking through his night scope, but there was too much underbrush. A thought occurred to him. He began a careful scan and wasn't surprised to see they had goggles and scopes, as well.

There were two vehicles hidden in the woods. He began a careful search and, after several minutes froze.

They had set out pickets.

Two men were elbow to elbow, at the base of a tree, and they had what looked like sniper rifles with night scopes mounted and raised to their eyes. They didn't move, they just kept watching.

He had stopped bare yards before their line of vision! He was lucky they hadn't spotted his motion when he arrived. He slowly shifted his line of vision to the second car. It was a van, and there were four more men huddled behind it, doing something he couldn't make out.
He checked the two sentinels again. No change.

It took five minutes to work his way behind a thick oak. He clicked on his receiver and found the two women talking about getting some sleep. Good, they were settled for the night.

The sound of an engine starting made him flinch. It was the two Japs in the sports car. They made a U-turn and drove off.

He turned his attention back to the men hidden nearby, pulling out a directional microphone and holding it around the trunk of the tree.

He couldn't understand what was being said and put a finger to his headphone, trying to pick up the words.

They were speaking Japanese, but the words were too faint. The sound of an engine starting blasted in his ear. Suppressing a grunt, he jerked his headphones off.

A quick peek showed the van working it's way out of the woods onto the road. Moments later, it disappeared after the red car. Groundhog ascertained both guards were still in place, but there were only three men by the rental car now.

He was reasonably certain the Martin woman and the actress were staying put, and a quick listen to his bug confirmed it. And, he was recording all over the house. If anything happened, he would know about it.

Groundhog began creeping away from the concealed men. He suppressed the urge to hurry. Hurrying got people killed, as he knew very well.

"Set the alarm for five A.M.," Sasama said, shuddering. Gods, he needed some sleep. Please, Kiri. Sleep in, seduce Kimberly, whatever. Just don't leave the house before we get back there in the morning!

Iori groaned, but did as he was told. *If that kid lives long enough, he's going to amount to something*, Sasama thought as he turned the light out and settled back into his side of the bed.

Next to him, Iori muttered under his breath.

"What?" Sasama asked. "I couldn't hear you."

"Just as well," came the answer back. "You just had to use the one excuse that would make it awkward for us to insist on two beds, didn't you?"

Sasama smiled in the dark, and turned on his side.

He was almost asleep, but his mind kept coming back to a vision of Kiri and Kimberly in Jim's hot tub, splashing and laughing. In the nude, of course. He didn't know if that was what they were doing, but it was an easy picture to visualize.

In his mind, Kimberly started to stand up, twin pale globes emerging from the bubbling water, when the door clicked open. He heard motion in the dark and gave Iori a hard shove, then rolled in the opposite direction.

He landed on his knees and scrambled across the floor. Something made a slithery sound, and he realized it was a blade, cutting the sheets he'd just been underneath.

Iori shrieked, and Sasama choked back a shout of rage as he tried to find the shotgun he'd left behind the little table by the window. As his hands closed around it, Iori's voice abruptly cut off in mid-scream.

He stood and brought the weapon up to waist height. A dark figure hurtled across the bed at him, and he pumped and fired. The sound was deafening in the closed space of the hotel room, but Sasama didn't even notice.

The attacker on the bed was gone, but in the corner of his eye he saw another figure raise an arm. Sasama whirled and fired as the arm came forward. The other man flew backwards and crashed against the wall.

At the same time, Sasama felt something hit his right shoulder, turning him as he pumped another shell into the chamber. Something slashed his right side and he screamed in pain. The shotgun fired out the window, shattering glass everywhere.

Sasama couldn't take his eyes off the glittering shards as they flew outward and down in slow motion. He staggered away from the pain and tried to chamber another shell, but his hands didn't seem to want to work right.

As he turned away from the window, he saw a large man in the dim light from the outside. The man was dressed entirely in black, even to the strip of cloth across his face, leaving only his eyes visible. He held a sword loosely as he watched Sasama stagger backwards.

Ninja! Sasama registered the thought from a distance as he stared at the sword's blade. Why didn't it gleam in the moonlight? He vaguely realized it was a dumb thing to focus on, but he couldn't tear his eyes from the blade.

As the backs of his legs touched the low window sill, he figured it out. The blade didn't shine because it was covered with a dark fluid. It slowly worked its way into his brain that the fluid was his blood as he tipped backwards out the fourth story window.

He seemed to take forever to fall out the window. If he could only reach out, surely he could catch himself in time, couldn't he? But all he could do was clutch the shotgun as the pressure behind his knees suddenly disappeared and he watched the window grow smaller and smaller.

He was flying!

An eternity, or an infinitesimal split second later, his feeling of freedom came to a smashing halt, and a tremendous roar sounded in his ears.

Then he heard nothing.

Takeda Nagashino swore as he jerked his head back and pellets from the shotgun struck all around the window framing.

The bastard had nearly gotten him with his dying breath! Wouldn't that have been ironic? He snorted in self-derision.

As it was, two of his men were either dead or dying because that stupid actor had been able to reach his gun. An actor!

"Is this one still alive?" Takeda walked around the corner of the bed and looked down at the crumpled boy.

"He's with his ancesters by now," one of the two remaining men wheezed, trying to catch his breath. "He fought like a tiger!"

"He fought like the child he was," Takeda snarled. "Trying to escape the bite of the blade is not fighting, it's survival instinct." He cautiously peered out the window at the still figure lying in the dumpster below. "Now this one, he was a fighter. With his last bit of blood pumping out of him, he tried to take an enemy with him."

Takeda focused on the matters at hand. Someone had to have heard that damn shotgun firing. He came to a decision.

"Throw the boy after his friend. Gather their belongings together. And bring these two idiots." He pointed at his dead. "Come! The police will be here any moment."

Takeda walked in the lead as they left, sword at the ready. His remaining two men were heavily laden, each with a body over their shoulder and suitcases in hand. It would be up to him to deal with any witnesses, security men, or even the police. But they saw no one as they made their way down the emergency stairs.

Five minutes later, they were driving at the speed limit back to the house in the woods.

Sasama distantly felt something strike him. An eternity later, he managed to open his eyes and see what was draped across him.

It was Iori. His eyes stared unseeing, and his head was at an unnatural angle to the rest of his body. There was blood everywhere.

Sasama tried to speak, raise his hand, anything. But even though he could feel tears welling up in his eyes, he couldn't weep. He could only lay there, unmoving, barely aware of his surroundings.

Eventually, even that left him.

◆ ◆ ◆ ◆ ◆

Groundhog parked and glanced up at the window he knew belonged to the two Japanese. Something didn't look right, and he pulled out a tiny snooper scope.

The window was shattered. The metal framework had bright streaks that reminded him of something. There were also gouges in the brickwork above and below the open space.

He allowed the scope to sink downward until he reached ground level. There was a dumpster with an open lid beneath.

He lowered the scope and stared at the big metal box. He felt like an idiot, but after checking for faces in windows and approaching cars, he reached in his car and pulled out an empty cola can and walked across the parking lot with a nonchalant air.

Groundhog didn't need to stretch to be able to see inside, and his suspicion was confirmed. The bodies of the two young Japanese lay inside, one draped over the other.

As he tossed the beverage can inside, he looked around, seeing no one. Considering it wasn't even midnight yet, it was almost too quiet.

He quickly walked back to his car and drove to the dumpster. Muttering to himself, he got the first body out of the trash and into the trunk of his car. But when he went to drag the second one out, the man groaned.

Groundhog stopped and thought. With one last look around, he pulled the body out and also put it into the trunk, but more carefully.

Without a pause, he closed the trunk, got behind the steering wheel, and drove off, making sure he didn't speed.

◆ ◆ ◆ ◆ ◆

Kimberly lay on her side, facing away from Kiri. The young woman had shifted gradually until her backside was up against Kimberly's. If she hadn't been lying there, unable to sleep, she would have thought it deliberate.

But Kiri's breathing had grown regular long ago. She was either asleep or far more patient and a better actress than Kimberly gave her credit for.

Now that was catty. Why can't I fall asleep? Sure, that marvelous shower rejuvenated me, but even so, I'm exhausted. But she knew the answer. It was that damn picture.

Nasri Riahi stared at her, even in the dark. She didn't have to see it to know she was there, watching, never blinking or shifting her gaze elsewhere.

Kimberly knew being jealous of a woman dead for fourteen years was stupid. It was more than that, it was petty and mean. *Come on, Martin, you're bigger than that.*

She did the only thing she could. Being careful not to disturb Kiri, she slid out of bed and made her way over to the picture.

Kimberly knew she was close when she whacked her shins on the coffee table. Suppressing the curse that tried to pry its way through her lips, she maneuvered around the table and felt the wall until her fingers touched framing.

Kimberly lifted the picture off it's mounting and lowered it until it touched the floor. She paused for a moment, then lifted it back up, turned it around, and replaced it on the floor, facing the wall.

I'm pathetic. But her heart felt lighter as she climbed back into bed. On an impulse, she snuggled up behind Kiri and put her arm around her friend's waist.

In no time, she was asleep.

A bright light woke Kimberly. At first she thought it was the morning sun, but a voice quickly cured her of that notion.

"Well, this is a pretty picture. It makes me wish I were one of you two." The man behind the voice laughed. "Almost."

Kimberly found they were curled up in spoons, her hand cupping one of Kiri's breasts. She snatched her hand away and felt her face start to redden as she tried to focus on the group of men standing at the foot of the bed.

Kiri rolled over and sat up, her pajamas rumpled and bunched up. She glared at the men.

"What the hell is going on here? Who are you. and what are you doing in this house."

"You're trespassing." Kimberly fought to regain her usual calm self-control. Besides the Japanese man who had spoke, there were four others, all dressed in black, all apparently Japanese. "If you don't leave right..."

"Enough." The man sneered at her and motioned to his men. "You will do as you're told, and you might not get hurt. Get up and get dressed."

Two men came around either side of the bed, and Kimberly raised her hands meekly. "Please, we'll cooperate. Just don't hurt us." As she spoke, she sat up and swung her legs over the side of the bed. She could sense Kiri doing the same in the other direction.

Kimberly stood up. She had one of the men slightly behind her by the headboard and faced the other. She didn't dare think about what she was doing or she would start shaking.

Without warning, she snapped a backhand at the head of the man behind her, trying to land the blow both Jim and Kiri and assured her would instantly kill anyone.

The man was fast enough to save his life, but not quite quick enough to escape injury, and her hand smashed into his nose at an angle instead of straight on.

Kimberly felt cartilage give way beneath her blow, and the man screamed in pain and fell back against the wall. She tried to kick the second assailant, but he was ready for her and caught her foot with his hands.

The next thing she knew, her face was being pushed into the bedcovers, and her hands were being held from behind. She kicked backwards, but met only air. From the sounds of it, Kiri was faring better.

The leader yelled in Japanese. He sounds angry, Kimberly thought. Good. She was able to raise her head enough to see Kiri throwing one of the men against a wall. The other seized her from behind, then somehow or other, was flying through the air to land on top of his cohort.

With a quick stride, the leader was next to Kiri and chopped her on the back of the neck with a stiffened open hand. She collapsed with a groan.

"Kiri!" Kimberly tried to shout, but the bedcovers pressed against her mouth muffled the sound.

The leader leaned over the bed until his face was only inches from hers. He had cruel eyes that glittered darkly with anger.

"I give you only two choices." His voice was cold, with clipped tones. "One, you stop resisting and get dressed. We let you get some more appropriate clothing on your lover." She started to protest but stopped cold when he raised one hand threateningly. "Two, we knock you out as well. Then we strip both of you naked and tie you up. You get no clothing whatsoever for the duration of this..." he paused and smiled thinly. "...encounter. I also let my men relieve their tension and...distress with your resistance. Whenever, however often, and in whatever fashion they desire."

At that moment, Kimberly couldn't have spoken if she'd tried. Her mouth went cotton dry, and it was hard to breath.

He correctly interpreted her thoughts and smiled. Kimberly had to fight to stop the urge to shiver.

"Would you like to get dressed?"

For a moment, she couldn't move, and was afraid he would think she wasn't agreeing to cooperate. But he waited patiently until she was finally able to give a tiny nod.

"Good." He straightened and nodded to the man holding Kimberly down. "You can let her up, now. Ms. Martin won't be giving us any more trouble." His eyes shifted over to the other man that Kimberly had struck and a look of displeasure appeared.

"Is your nose broken, again?" He shook his head in apparent disgust. "Didn't you learn anything the first time?"

The grip on Kimberly loosened cautiously, and she pushed herself to her feet, giving the injured man a quick glance.

Was that the guy from Sukuru that Afsaneh had flattened? What was his name? Takuan something or other. She was pretty sure it was him and felt a chill in her spine. That answered the question of who these people were.

"I would appreciate it if you would move a little faster, Ms Martin. The leader gave her a look that just missed being a leer. "I'm afraid you'll have to get your clothes on with us in the room." His apologetic look didn't look remotely sincere to her. "I'm sure you understand."

His thin veneer of good humor abruptly disappeared.

"Get moving. Now. Or both of you go as you are."

Kimberly hurriedly began searching for her clothes.

Groundhog slowed his car in front of the drive. The two vehicles hidden across the road were gone. On an impulse, he turned into the driveway and stopped in front of the garage door.

The lock on the front door took less than a minute, and it took even less time to get to the bedroom he knew they'd been in.

He took in the obvious signs of struggle. When he saw the bloodstains to the left of the bed, his eyes narrowed. He started to turn to leave, and saw bedclothes lying on the floor.

Groundhog knelt next to them. There were two sets. More importantly, the only traces of blood were on one sleeve. He stood up in satisfaction.

It looked like the women exacted a price for their capture, he decided with a grin that didn't reach his eyes. The recordings would hopefully give him a clue as to where they were being taken, and by whom.

He turned to leave, but stopped again. There was something different. Something out of place besides the obvious signs of struggle.

Then he saw what his subconscious had noticed. There was a large bare spot where there had once been a painting. He saw the top of the frame behind the low table and gave it a closer examination.

It seemed unlikely a fight would have knocked just that one picture off the wall, and he quickly saw that it was facing the wrong way to have fallen.

It looked like Mrs. Morris wasn't too happy with Mr. Morris' interior decorating when it came to old flames. He filed the observation away for further contemplation. That might be something he could use at some point in the future.

After all, he thought, information was the primary product he dealt in. And it was one thing you could never have too much of.

CHAPTER TWENTY

Jade Viking

The shuttle hanger was almost completely dark. Emergency lights had been burning for twenty-four hours and were noticeably dimmer. A few people had handheld lights but an effort to conserve the batteries meant there were never more than a couple lit at a time. Scattered around were small clumps of people, huddled together for warmth. An effort had been made to find any extra heavy clothing and blankets, but there wasn't near enough for everyone to be properly protected from the bitter cold.

Hiroaki Tachibana grimaced as he noticed that even now, in what might be their last few hours alive, the crew was segregated. Humans snuggled close to other humans, Hoag and Baerd did the same.

The Baerd didn't seem to be holding up too well to the cold, he noticed with concern. Although it would be high levels of carbon dioxide and oxygen deprivation that would kill them all, the extreme temperature drop was affecting them more than humans of the furry Hoag.

His first officer, Commander Randall, rubbed his hands together briskly to warm them up. Hiroaki cleared his throat, just loud enough for the young man to hear. Randall crossed his arms, tucking both hands under his armpits, and looked at him in embarrassment.

"Sorry, Sir," he muttered. "It's hard to remember we need to keep still, to save oxygen."

Before Hiroaki could respond, the lights in the two shuttles came on, and a whoosh of fresh air came out the open hatches. He quickly entered one and strode to the controls at a fast pace.

The screen still said the same thing it had for the last twenty-four hours.

Wait.

"Commander, send a runner to the other hanger and find out the status of those shuttles." He heard the young man leave, but didn't take his eyes off the screen. What was Vicki doing?

Hiroaki tried not to think about one possibility. Vicki, as he and the crew knew the ship's computer, might be brain dead.

Inam appeared at his side. He glanced over at her and started. Her normally deathly white skin was closer to a pastel blue, now. Her teeth were chattering as she tried to speak.

"S-s-so, b-back to th-th-the s-s-s..." She gave up trying to finish the word, and gave him a wan, thankful smile as he helped her.

"Yes, same situation we were in twenty hours ago." Hiroaki pulled off his jacket, ignoring the chill that immediately set in. He draped it around her shoulders, despite her feeble attempts to refuse. "Do not argue with your Captain."

She gave in without any further argument. The Baerd wore thin tunics that reached below their knees. But it was about all they had. Space didn't have climate changes. Inam wore three layers of tunics, and it still wasn't as thick as a good sweater would be.

Hiroaki began striding back and forth on the tiny bridge to conceal his own coldness. At least for the moment, fresh air was not a problem.

"Before we get too excited about this, we should remember that early on, this same event occurred." He glared at the unhelpful screen for a moment. "Two shuttles worked at full life support capacity while the other two used all their power to provide a stealth screen to hide any sign of power outage from the Egelv. If they observed us in that time, hopefully all they saw was a dead ship."

Hiroaki rubbed his arms left unprotected by his short-sleeved shirt. He changed the motion into a stretching one when he saw Inam give him a guilty look. He was gratified to see her color returning to it's normal pallid state.

"She intentionally severed all lines connecting the four shuttles to the ship," Inam said, her voice already stronger. "She did leave a system of circuits jury-rigged between them."

"So, just when we're about to suffocate, life support kicks in for awhile, then all power goes out again." Hiroaki glared at the screen, his arms folded, feet squared. "Any idea why?"

"The shuttles were operating on batteries," Inam pointed out. "She probably estimated how long it would take two shuttles to refurbish the air supply. She also must have figured how long we could survive without life support systems being on."

"Well, she did an excellent job of guessing," Hiroaki admitted. "I don't know that we would have lasted much longer."

A teenage girl trotted into the bridge, panting heavily. She leaned against a control panel to regain her breath, then straightened at Tachibana's measured gaze.

"Uh, sorry sir!" She tried to stand at attention and Hiroaki hurried to set her at ease. There would be time for instilling discipline later. At least, he hoped there would be.

"What's your name, young lady?" he asked, not unkindly.

"Uh, Amy, Sir." When he continued waiting, she stammered out the rest. "Th-that's Amy Sterling, Sir."

"Was there something you wanted to tell me, Miss Sterling?" Hiroaki fought down his own impatience. "You did run here for some purpose?"

"Oh. Of course, Sir!" Amy gave him a dimpled smile. She can't be over sixteen, he decided. "Commander Randall says the other two shuttles are providing the same image they were before."

"So what happens now?" Hiroaki turned to Inam, who shrugged.

"All controls with shuttle computers are turned off. The only way we can circumvent that is physically tie in a new set of controls."

"Can we at least tell if these computers are doing anything?" Hiroaki hated inaction, especially in a crisis.

"There is definite activity between all four shuttle computers, and at least one of the new connections is showing use." Inam looked around the room. She looked at least as frustrated as Hiroaki felt. That made him feel a little better, he realized with a pang of guilt. "My first guess would be she backed up as much as possible on the shuttle computers, with a deliberate schedule of rebooting designed to drain the batteries as slowly as possible."

"All computer activities shut off," Hiroaki pointed out. "That doesn't necessarily mean 'Viking's power systems did the same."

Inam shuddered, and it wasn't from the cold. "You should be very thankful a failsafe insures a shutdown in case of computer systems failure. Otherwise..." She didn't finish the sentence.

"Boom?" the Sterling girl asked tentatively.

"Boom," Inam agreed with a quiet smile.

"Thank god Vicki considered the translator to be a crucial part of life support," Hiroaki muttered. "So, is there something we can do?" Hiroaki asked her, hoping she would give her real opinion. Both the Baerd and the Hoag had come a long way from the days of working under the Ananab, but they were far from comfortable with making suggestions to their new leaders yet. "Or do we trust Vicki and wait."

Inam gave him an impassive look, her face telling him nothing. Or was there the slightest hint of an expression around her eyes? He sighed and sat in the seat next to her and, after a moment's consideration, propped his feet up on the control panel.

Well, why not? They weren't active, anyway.

"We wait?" he asked her, not really asking.

"We wait," she agreed, and in a rare moment of Baerd bravado, propped her own sandaled feet next to his. He could feel her watching him out of the corner of her eyes, waiting for his reaction.

He smiled at her and nodded approvingly. Amy Sterling sniffed and headed for the exit. Her parting words drifted back to them.

"Oh, like anyone would think it was okay if I propped my feet up on the furniture..." Her voice faded in the distance.

Glowing Mist

Matt stared at the screen in front of him, unseeing. The excitement of coming out of orbit into the atmosphere and into a landing had lost it's thrill.

In fact, he admitted to himself, he'd completely lost his awe and sense of humor. *Du Brimar isn't clever or funny any more. He is a sick fu...*

"Don't hate us," Jo Coran startled him by saying. She very rarely even condescended to speak to him when he asked her something. Her initiating speech was a first. "We only are doing what we know has to be done. Your people are too talented to be allowed free access to our universe. Anyway, you didn't know any of them personally, did you?"

"That wouldn't make any difference." Matt bit back a snarl. It was time to use the brains he always bragged he had. "We cherish human life, not just the lives of our friends."

"And yet, your history is nothing but a connection of wars, one starting even before the last has ended." Du Brimar had none of his usual cockiness when he spoke. He isn't deliberately malicious, Matt reminded himself. He's just inconsiderate and arrogant. "Even today, there is fighting somewhere on your planet between different factions of the same people, neighboring countries, even families split on two different sides."

Matt didn't answer immediately. He wasn't sure that his professing a difference was anything more than rationalization. "Couldn't we have saved some of them?"

Du Brimar snorted and said nothing. Jo Coran shook her head. "Matt, do you remember what that teacher said about how they first obtained that ship. The last thing we want to do is board a dead ship with an unknown number of angry, armed Humans."

"Much less let them on our ship," Du Brimar said dryly. "We're coming into the lower atmosphere and I need to pick a specific destination. I've been monitoring the bug we had on that FBI agent. He seems to think this Kimberly Martin will be at one of Jim Morris' residences. Probably..."

"Hey." Matt sat up straight. "That's right, Jim Morris lives in Ann Arbor. That's not too far from where I live!"

"...in Tahoe, or San Francisco," Du Brimar finished. He looked at Matt with the briefest moment of suspicion. "He didn't mention Ann Arbor."

Matt shrugged. "I know he has a place there. I've read about it. He's a Michigan alumni."

"Well." Du Brimar nodded to Matt. "Since this Mr. Costa has sent agents to the other two places, we'll start in...Ann Arbor."

"Wow, nice place," Matt said, watching as the ship approached the grounds. They were landing behind the house, beyond the clubhouse at the end of the huge pool. Next to what Matt suspected was a five wall racquetball facility, which was next to the tennis/basketball court, which bordered the clay infield of what looked like a regulation-sized softball field.

"Ah, a welcome mat," Du Brimar said, his usual grin back in full force as they exited the ship. Matt dutifully stepped on the second base 'welcome mat' at the foot of the stairs.

He couldn't help staring as they passed the pool area to come to a

303

halt before one of the glass patio doors. Jo Coran had disappeared some-where in the process but she quickly showed up inside the house. She unlocked the doors and as they entered, Matt looked at her curiously.

"My little secret," she said, her face deadpan, but there was actually a little humor showing in her eyes.

"I think you're a bad influence on Jo Coran," Du Brimar observed.

Matt ignored him and began exploring. A left turn took him down a hallway past several bedrooms to the final two doors. One was non-descript and one quick inside glance told Matt it was of little interest to him.

The other door had a full-size poster of Jim Morris tacked to it. The picture was from one of his movies, and Matt had seen it before. He put his hand on the doorknob and, with a deep breath, opened the door.

He knew that Jim Morris lived with a friend and his daughter. If Mr. Prause was to be believed, the girl was actually Jim's daughter. This was definitely her room, he thought in disgust. And they think guys are sloppy. One quick look confirmed something he'd already suspected. Most girls were pigs in the privacy of their own room.

Clothes, both clean and dirty, littered the floor. Including undies, he thought, crouching to look at a pink bra lying at the foot of her bed, which was unmade.

"Ooh," Matt breathed in. There was an entire shelf of DVDs, all of which seemed to Jim Morris movies. He picked one up. It was the one the poster on the door was from. This was a great action flick.

He noticed a picture of Morris on the night stand next to her bed. She really had a thing for the guy. Kind of unhealthy, if you ask me, Matt thought. There was a photo album next to the picture and he idly picked it up and flipped it open.

He had no idea how long he stared, but eventually he shook himself and went back to the beginning of the album and began looking at each page.

He could tell that the toddler on the first few pages was the same girl as the preschooler sitting on her bike with training wheels between a younger Jim Morris and an incredibly ugly, dark complected man.

Which was the same as the preteen girl in the swim suit standing on the diving board. Which was the same teenage girl standing in a quite different swimsuit on the same diving board.

"Well, what have we here?" came the all-too-familiar sarcastic voice from behind. Du Brimar pulled the movie from his unresisting hand and glanced at it. "So this is the guy we've heard so much about. You know, none of his films seem to show up on broadcasts we can intercept. Any more?"

"Most of his early movies went straight to video," Matt said, hardly paying any attention. He tore his eyes off the girl's picture in time to see Du Brimar scooping up an entire armload of the disks.

"Hey, those aren't yours," he protested. "You can't just take them."

"Why not," Du Brimar asked, his tone bored.

"It's stealing," Matt said, for some unfathomable reason worried about what the girl would think.

"I prefer to think of it as an archeological find," Du Brimar said. He held them out to Matt and literally piled them in his arms, on top of the photo album. "Come on, let's go. No one's here."

"They might be out shopping or something," Matt said quickly. "Maybe we should wait a while."

"No, they've already been here. And so has someone else." Du Brimar led the way through the house and back outside.

"How can you tell" Matt asked, confused.

"Their luggage is here. And there's recent blood on the floor in the room they were sleeping in."

"Maybe it's theirs," Matt pointed out. Du Brimar shook his head.

"Did a quick scan." Du Brimar looked smug. "It's definitely not either of the two women's. In fact, it's from a male. Undoubtably one of their kidnappers."

"Kidnappers," Matt gasped, then blushed as Du Brimar looked at him in obvious amusement.

"Yes, kidnappers," he said. "It does happen, you know."

"Only too well," Matt mumbled under his breath.

"I heard that," came the swift response. "Now, let's go. Jo Coran is in a hurry for some reason."

"So what do we do now?" Matt asked, giving the house one last longing look before he entered the ship.

Du Brimar laughed. "That's up to Cromar Try. Me? I'm going to watch some movies."

❖ ❖ ❖ ❖ ❖

Jade Wolverine

305

Far away, Jim Morris sat in total ignorance of the invasion of his home, holding his daughter's hand as she lay unmoving in her bunk. His eyes, when they bothered focusing on anything, flicked back and forth between the two sides of the split screen on the wall.

One showed Station Osaka. He felt guilty for leaving the station with everything so unsettled. People were depending on him.

But so does Afsaneh, he thought, looking down at her bandaged head. Right now, her need surpasses any other.

That thought made him look back up at the other side of the screen, where an unmoving still shot of the Earth hung in space. It was from the records of the previous voyage. Irene had found it for him. He'd been here almost non-stop since their departure from the station and could see no good reason for being anywhere else.

"Jim Morris." He jumped and glanced down at Afsaneh in surprise. But it wasn't she that had spoken, but Irene. "An object has been spotted moving this way on a direct heading from Earth."

"A ship?" His voice was hoarse from lack of use.

"No, it's an unmanned probe from Jade Viking. It was probably launched about thirty-six hours ago. We will be close enough to receive any message it carries in about ninety minutes."

"Call me in an hour," he said, and looked back down at his daughter.

Station Osaka

Suyo Takashi asked for one final verification, then sat back in her seat with her shoulders slumped. She didn't want to disturb the governor with this, but knew she had to.

"Connect me to Governor Lang," she finally said. His voice eventually answered, but the screen pickup was turned off in his quarters.

"What is it?"

"Governor, this is Suyo. Pearl has spotted a Tryr ship approaching the station. It will be within firing range in about four hours, on its present course."

"Has the station been alerted?" the tired sounding voice asked in resignation.

"Yes." Suyo hesitated, then told him the remainder of the news.

"There are what looks like five more Tryr ships in sheathed status holding position just within our detection range. They probably think we can't see them."

There was no sound, and Suyo bit her lip.

"I'll be down in twenty minutes," he surprised her.

She cut the connection, then bowed her head forward and uttered one word in heartfelt relief.

"Yes!"

◆ ◆ ◆ ◆ ◆

CHAPTER TWENTY-ONE

San Francisco, California

Agent Costa was sick of this case. There were too many strange events, coincidences, unexplained details, blatant impossibilities. Even being back in San Francisco didn't improve his mood.

"I think I preferred when they were all missing," he said to no one in particular.

"Excuse me, sir?" Patrick Beatty looked at him doubtfully. When Costa made no attempt to answer, he gave a bright, beaming smile and checked the clipboard he held. "There's no sign anyone has been here since Martin and Oshiba left."

Costa ignored the young agent and stared out the window. It was a bad sign when the most logical explanation was also the most outrageous.

"I'm going home," he announced. Beatty looked at him in surprise. "You better get started on the paperwork. I want a complete report of the last week on my desk tomorrow morning, nine a.m."

Beatty looked at his watch with resignation. "Yes, sir. Nine A.M. Anything else?"

"Yes." Costa sighed. "Put out a bolo on Kimberly Martin and Kiri Oshiba. I want to know where they are. Their stories conflict with other passengers, and they've been constantly on the move." His voice hardened. "And the only theory that makes sense will land me either in a mental facility, or the ranks of the unemployed."

"What theory is that, sir?" Beatty looked puzzled, and Costa couldn't blame him.

"That the Jade Viking was hijacked by aliens, but somehow, some of the missing people are back, and with an agenda I can't begin to fathom.

Costa exhaled heavily as he walked out of the room, ignoring Beatty's incredulous stare.

◆ ◆ ◆ ◆ ◆

New York City, New York

Will Spencer saw the message light come on, and picked up the phone.

"Yes?"

"Mr. Toshida is here to see you, Mr. Spencer." His secretary had a beautiful contralto voice, almost as beautiful as her face and figure. He started to answer, then noticed she had only said Toshida, not his goons.

"He's alone?"

"Yes, sir."

Curious, and more curious, said Alice, he thought. Or was it the rabbit? "Send him in."

Toshida was seated across the desk from him, and refused refreshments while Spencer sat back in his chair and waited.

Toshida gave him a thin smile. This man is dangerous, and not just in a business sense, Will thought.

"I trust your 'associates' are enjoying a little sightseeing in the big apple?" he asked as he channel-surfed through the security camera system. He found Toshida's men down on the main floor in the lobby.

But only two.

"Where are the rest?" he asked.

Toshida nodded, as if to show his appreciation for Spencer's efficiency. "They're keeping busy," he answered vaguely.

"I'm sure they are." Spencer felt his lips tighten over his front teeth. They must be out looking for Kimberly Martin. He didn't know who he felt sorrier for, Kimberly or Toshida's goons. "You know, you're going to find that Ms. Martin is a formidable woman. She's already been interrogated by the FBI. I tried to question her as well, but she stuck to that nonsense about having a memory lapse. What makes you think you'll have any more luck than we did?"

Toshida smiled thinly, and Spencer fought the urge to flinch. Again, he recognized that this was a very dangerous man, and not just to Kimberly. It was time to walk very carefully; and to increase security measures, both for the company and himself.

"Oh, I sure we'll handle her just fine."

Somewhere in the mid-west...

Kimberly brushed the hair out of Kiri's sleeping face. She was worried. Kiri had been unconscious for what seemed like hours now. What if she had a concussion or worse?

As if in answer to her unspoken question, Kiri gave a little moan.

They were on the floorboards of a moving van, Kimberly propped against one sidewall, Kiri's head in her lap. Sitting across from them were two Japanese men. They had taken their masks off, which didn't bode well. Kimberly had heard that once a kidnapper showed his face, he didn't plan on live witnesses.

Kiri moaned again and lifted a hand to the back of her neck. "Ow, ow, ow," she half whispered and her eyes opened to stare into Kimberly's face. "Hey, what happened? You pop me one, round eyes?"

"Do you remember waking up?" Kimberly asked, worried by the look of disorientation in her friend's face.

"Waking up?" Kiri asked dumbly. Kimberly stiffened as she felt Kiri tensing and gathering herself to spring. And she was deliberately not looking towards the two men sitting only a few feet away. Kimberly was sure of it. "The last thing I remember is trying to get to sleep. I fall outta bed?"

"No, Kiri, don't." She put a hand on Kiri's arm, holding her down. "Not a good idea."

Kiri glared at her in anger, then at the two men. "Dammit, Kimberly, why'd you stop me from trying?"

One of the men smiled and pointed a pistol with a silencer at her kneecap.

"No!" Kimberly shouted, then quickly lowered her voice. "I'm sorry, I didn't mean to shout. But please don't shoot her. Kiri, don't make it worse."

"What's the matter with you?" Kiri demanded.

311

"She has seen the eye of the dragon," came a voice from the front of the van. Both women looked at the source, and Kimberly couldn't help herself. She shivered violently.

The man who spoke was in the passenger side of the front seat, and sat sideways in his seat so he could see them. He was the most muscular oriental man she'd ever seen. He was the leader from their kidnapping, and Kimberly was terrified of him.

She'd seen him take his black costume off, revealing street clothes. Both arms and legs were heavily muscled and his chest seemed to strain the buttons on his shirt. His shoulders were layered with thick slabs of muscle that continued right up his neck to the base of his skull.

"Where's your neck," Kiri spoke up, her voice showing no fear. Kimberly groaned inside and shook her shoulder.

"Kiri, I had to promise we wouldn't give them any trouble. I had to." Her voice rose and she felt her face redden with shame. She wasn't a coward, but in the presence of this man, she could barely hold control her panic. "It was that or gang rape and no clothes for either of us."

"You believed that?" Kiri demanded, sitting upright. She glared at the leader and something in her expression changed as she got a good look at his eyes for the first time. She shuddered. "Well, okay, I guess I can see that." She didn't fool anyone with her attempt to maintain her bravado. Kimberly gave her a gentle pull, and they settled back into sitting positions next to each other.

The man with the pistol leered at them. Both women ignored him, but Kimberly noticed Kiri staring at the other guard. It was the one Kimberly had punched when they were captured, and his eyes were bloodshot and rapidly blackening. His nose was bright red and swollen.

"Shinzo Takuan?" The man wouldn't raise his eyes to meet theirs, and Kiri snorted, and glanced at Kimberly. "What happened to him this time?"

"I tried to punch him the way you and Jim taught me, but I missed." Kimberly tried to keep her voice low.

"Not completely, you didn't," she said, looking at Takuan again. "What is it with your nose and women, anyway?" she demanded. "First Afsaneh breaks it, then Kimberly. Do I get a chance for the trifecta?"

Kimberly groaned, then brightened as the rest of the men started laughing. Thank God, Kiri's big mouth still hasn't gotten us raped or killed. Takuan's face reddened to match his nose, and he started to get up, but one word in Japanese from the leader, and he sat back, looking angry and frustrated.

"I'll get my chance," he muttered, just loud enough for those in the back to hear.

"Yeah, right." Kiri turned back to Kimberly and proceeded to ignore him. The other guard snickered and whispered something in Japanese. Takuan just stared at the two women, pretending not to hear.

Kimberly looked at Kiri questioningly. "I guess he neglected to tell them exactly who broke his nose the first time, on Jade Samurai." Kiri said, and a curious expression appeared on her face. She peeked inside her sweatshirt, then sideways at Kimberly. "Where's my bra?"

"You're lucky I was able to get you panties and sneakers," Kimberly retorted, glad to change the subject before Takuan lost his head and did something they would regret. "They were in a hurry, and I got what I could find quickly."

"Thanks." Kiri patted her leg and gave her a sympathetic look. "I mean that. I guess I slept through the tough part."

"The tough part is still to come," came the voice of the leader. "Now be quiet. Any more talking, and we play that fine American game, strip poker. Every time you speak, you lose something."

Kimberly and Kiri looked at each other in frustration, then settled back to wait.

But wait for what?

Ann Arbor, Michigan

Sasama's first awareness was of pain. Then it was of lots of pain. Each breath seemed to rattle in his throat and he couldn't see! Then he realized that caked blood had his eyelids glued shut. He tried to lift his arm to his face and screamed.

"Stop that," a voice said in English. It was a man's voice, soft and high-pitched. "You've got a broken back and need to lie still. Hopefully, I can get you to a hospital soon, but for the moment, don't try to move."

Sasama needed to know something. It took everything he had, but he finally forced the words through his lips.

"I-Iori? Is he..." It was all he could manage to get out.

"Your friend?" Sasama tried to nod without thinking and he gave a strangled gasp. "Don't move or try to speak anymore. I'm sorry about your friend, but he didn't make it."

The voice sounded like it carried genuine regret, but Sasama hardly noticed. Tears tried to force their way out through the dried blood, and Sasama fought to retain consciousness.

But he lost that battle and darkness reclaimed him.

Groundhog watched the injured man pass out again. The pain had to be intense. He lost interest in that as his laptop signaled from the front seat that the transmission was complete.

He listened to the capture of Kimberly and Kiri, and the threats that followed. Then he listened to all the recordings that had any speaking. Away from the women, the kidnappers had been lax in their security. They were definitely from Sukuru, and were taking the women back to San Francisco by van. Even driving through, trading off to rest, it would take several days for them to get there.

Groundhog needed to make a decision.

He had a good description of the van, and could fabricate an all points bulletin that would probably get them pulled over. They would almost certainly blow the cops away, and it was uncertain how that scenario might end.

Two, he could try and intercept them. Much more difficult, but if he could find them, a much better chance of getting the women free alive.

But, they had several hours head start, and he was alone, with no relief driver. And, he hadn't slept in over twenty-four hours already.

He knew they were taking Kimberly and Kiri to the Sukuru dock facilities recently acquired from Spencer Corp. in San Francisco. Metro airport in Detroit was a forty-five minute drive. He could be in San Francisco, well rested, waiting for them.

He saw he had numerous messages from Spencer and Costa, among others. He was at various stages in several other projects, but this was far more interesting, and they could wait.

Groundhog was tempted to call both men now, in the middle of the night. Keeping them off balance had some entertainment value, but he decided to wait until morning.

And until he decided exactly how much to tell them.

He had one other detail to attend to. Two bodies, one dead, one near-

314

ly so. He could drop them off at one of the entrances to the hospital at the campus. The University of Michigan had one of the finest medical facilities in the country.

But they would be identified, and he wasn't willing to give up that little secret yet. These two men were listed as missing passengers aboard the Jade Viking. Showing up under these circumstances would generate a serious reaction from Costa, Sukuru, the media, for that matter.

His laptop gave a warning sound. Someone had returned to the Morris house.

He found which rooms were picking up sound and began flipping between them. There was little being said at first, then he heard an exclamation from someone. He checked his list. The girl's bedroom. It sounded like a male voice.

After a few minutes, another male spoke. But it was in a tongue he couldn't place. It was kind of like...Celtic-Korean, or some other strange combination. Maybe the computer could place it. He heard more English, presumably from the first male.

"Most of his movies went straight to video." Then the other spoke in the strange language. He listened as the two voices spoke to each other in two separate languages, both sounding as if they could understand each other.

A high-pitched screech made him tear the headphones off. He rubbed his ears, trying to relieve the agony, caught his breath and cautiously lifted the phones back to his head.

Nothing. He frowned at the headphones. Had the high volume fried the tiny speakers? A quick test showed they were still working fine, but he couldn't pick anything up from any of the hidden microphones in the house.

He tried a diagnostic, but couldn't get anything at all from the house. It's as if something nailed every one of my plants, he thought, puzzled. All at once.

He tossed the phones on the seat next to him, then opened his car door and stood up. He'd parked back in his original hiding spot in case the women had gotten a call off to the police. He debated working his way through the woods to the house, then heard a distant whooshing sound. A moment later, there was a cracking sonic boom.

It sounded like it might have been a Harrier jet, but he suspected it wasn't. He got back in the car and checked the recordings for the rest of the rooms before his pickups were destroyed. At the same time the two men had been talking, someone else had been going through several other rooms.

A higher, possibly feminine voice said something he presumed was in the same strange language. Then the voice spoke in clear, slightly accented English.

"I could find who, and where, you are. Maybe next time."

This time he was ready and pulled his ears away before the screeching began. He stared at the headset. That was unexpected.

He sat in his car, considering. For the moment, the danger was gone. The injured Japanese in the back seat gave a groan, reminding him of a loose end.

Groundhog got out of the car and opened the trunk. He placed one big hand over the dying man's face, covering his mouth with the palm, and pinching the nose shut between his thumb and forefinger.

After a moment, the Japanese tried to lift his arms to free himself, and screamed through his hand. Groundhog maintained his grip and Sasama's struggling grew weaker, then stopped entirely.

Groundhog closed the trunk, got in the car and headed back to the campus area to find a dumpster, his mind already focused on San Francisco.

Glowing Mist

Matt Stickel sat next to Teresa, trying to watch the screens over both Du Brimar's and Jo Coran's shoulders. At Siph Carni's insistence, chairs had been brought to the bridge so they wouldn't be 'lurking' as she put it.

"This is great!" Du Brimar announced, slapping an arm of his seat, with glee. "Did you see that?"

Cromar Try shook his head. He watched as Du Brimar backed up the disk and replayed the sequence. The Egelv had brought one of the DVD players back from Jim Morris' house, and it had only taken him minutes to tie it into his computer.

On the screen, Jim Morris was fighting a man with a Japanese sword. The villain swung, trying to cut off his head, but he ducked. He then went into a back flip just in time as the man came back with a low slice that would have surgically removed his legs at the knees.

Morris then leaped high in the air, turning sideways to kick the man in the face as he swung yet a third time, this at waist height. Morris rolled right back to his feet and kicked the man's arm dislodging the sword.

Moments later, the villain lay unconscious on the ground.

"I ask you, if that isn't just hilarious, what is?" Du Brimar was chortling at what was to him, an obviously impossible series of feats. "I love this stuff. You know, there is a market for this. They are funny!"

"Those stunts aren't physically possible, are they?" Siph Carni was watching Matt's reaction very closely. He shrugged.

"In real life, a fight sequence like that probably couldn't happen," Matt admitted. His mind raced as he tried to decide if he could somehow use this to their advantage. He reluctantly decided on honesty. "Although every one of those moves is physically possible, and someone probably could do the whole series of actions." He remembered something he'd read once. "Although I don't know if Jim Morris can do it."

"Isn't that him?" Cromar Try was looking interested despite himself. "Are you saying all those moves are faked?"

"I don't know," Matt said, watching as Morris proceeded to pound on three bad guys at once. "Using filming techniques and stunt men, this could be faked without him having actually done any of it." He saw Siph Carni give her mate a confused look and tried to explain.

"Look, they could have filmed each move separately, using a stunt man, then shot the close-ups of Morris' face, and him standing ready, then spliced it all together." He grinned. "Or, maybe he actually did all of them, one after another, just like we saw a moment ago."

"It doesn't seem likely, considering the techniques of filming you just mentioned are obviously commonly used," Jo Coran spoke up. "It seems impossible that an unarmed man could defeat a man with a long sharp blade. Especially since the man was evidently experienced with the weapon."

"It can happen," Matt said, then shut up. There was no reason to try and impress them with how capable his race was. That was part of the problem now.

"I found it interesting that someone installed listening devices in that house," Jo Coran said casually. Du Brimar looked at her in confusion.

"What are you talking about?" he asked, frowning. "You didn't say anything about listening devices."

"I didn't want your incessant curiosity and tendency to torture small animals to interfere with our mission," she retorted. "And as it happens, Cromar Try agreed."

"So we let some Human get a recording of our language? Did they have visual capacity?"

"No video," she said, grinning. "But did I say I let him get away with it?"

"What did you do?" Matt asked, dreading the answer.

"I believe your language has an excellent term for it." Jo Coran looked first at him, then at the fuming Du Brimar. "As you put it, I...'fried' his system. His ears will ache for a while, but that should be the extent of his physical damage."

"His?" Du Brimar looked at her suspiciously. "How do you know it was a 'he'?"

"As we lifted off, I scanned the surrounding terrain and..." she turned to her controls for a moment, and an aerial view of the area surrounding the Morris House appeared. It zoomed off to a spot across the road and even Matt could see the heat signature. "One vehicle, crammed with electronic gear, and two males, Human. Therefore..., he."

Du Brimar stood up, his hands on his hips. He was definitely irritated now. "We could have snatched them with no problem at all!" He looked at Cromar Try imploringly. "She was out of line, withholding this data from me."

"I don't think so." Cromar Try looked as if he was used to this kind of argument between his crew. "We don't really need any more samples. In fact, I don't know that we need to remain much longer in this area. We'll monitor newscasts for a few more days to be sure none of the shuttles were away from the P'Tassum, then we're off to Station Chaq."

"There's still so much to find out," Du Brimar protested. "What about...?"

"What about our primary mission, which was to find Ty Musa, or any sign he'd been here?" Cromar Try reminded him. "We've gotten sidetracked by all this. So, we wrap up here, go to Chaq, deal with the Humans there, then head straight to the nearest Egelv world, which would be...Argov."

"Argov?" Du Brimar wrinkled his nose in evident distaste, and Matt watched the other Egelv give a similar reaction. "It's on the edge of... nowhere! It's barely civilized!"

"It's the closest," Cromar Try said in a tone that announced the end of the discussion. He turned to his mate. "Have you checked the P'Tassum at all?"

"I've viewed them several times," Siph Carni answered. She started to glance at Matt and Teresa and visibly restrained herself. In another situation, Matt would have liked her. "There's no change. It is a dead ship. They didn't even get any shuttles away. By now, either the cold or oxygen deprivation has killed them."

"Just the same, I think we'll give them one last close-up scan on our way out of the system," Cromar Try said thoughtfully. "I can see why our ancestors wanted to be sure about the Hashir. These Humans have all kinds of hidden talents."

"I think they're fun," Du Brimar said. He sounded regretful to Matt. But it wasn't anything remotely related to sympathy, he knew. No, if anything, he just regretted the loss of a source of entertainment.

Matt glanced at Teresa and she motioned to the door, using only her eyes. He stood up, making sure his moves were casual.

"I'm tired. I'm going to my cabin to rest."

"I am, too," Teresa announced with a yawn. "I'll join you."

They got to their cabin. The sleeping area was split by a screen, giving them both some sense of privacy. He wasn't really surprised when she followed him into his half.

He stood by his bed, hesitating. She came straight into his arms and held him close. He returned the embrace cautiously, not entirely sure what she wanted of him.

When she spoke, her voice was almost completely muffled by his shoulder. "They're not going to let us go, you know."

Matt closed his eyes for a moment. Then he slid his mouth over next to her ear and spoke as quietly as he could.

"I know."

They stood there, holding each other. Matt felt her lithe body against his and felt lightheaded. This was what he'd wanted since they first met, but now? Under these circumstances? He gently kissed her ear, no longer angry, but sad.

She stiffened and he froze, knowing she'd misunderstood the kiss.

"No," was all she said. Several minutes passed, and Matt stood there holding her, without a clue as to what he was supposed to do now. Then she went on, as if the 'no' had been just a moment before.

"I'm not going to give them a show. They're probably watching, this very moment." Her voice softened. "If this was my last few moments, I would be happy to share them in bed with you, Matt Stickel."

"That kiss wasn't a preamble to love-making, Teresa." Matt spoke slowly, wanting to get it right. "It was intended to give comfort, and to show you I care about your well-being. Being a guy, I thought about this issue long ago." He controlled his anger to keep his voice quiet. "I wouldn't entertain them, even if it was to do something I wanted to so badly."

He felt Teresa's lips against his neck, turning upward in what he suspected was a smile. "I like you a lot. You're fun to be with, even though you're so young." Matt winced at that. "But I'm not conceding anything yet. This is not my last few moments, and there is still hope. Still hope of regaining our freedom..." She put her lips to his ear as if nuzzling it. "...or the chance for revenge!" Her whisper was fierce, and he resisted the urge to look around, as if that would tell him if they were overheard.

"Freedom or revenge." he whispered the words as if they were a litany. She pulled away a little and looked up at his face. Her words reminded him, if he needed any reminder, that she was a lawyer and a woman. Her expression made him thankful it wasn't directed at him.

"Or both."

Jade Wolverine

Jim Morris stared at the screen, as if he would be able to see any threat.

"We're getting into range to scan the entire system," Lasty said from his own seat.

"Can we be seen?" All Jim knew was that the Egelv were far more advanced than the Ananab, and if he could see them, it only stood to reason that they would be able to see his own ship.

"With the entire ship under power discipline, stealth shields at maximum, and the engines turned off, it is unlikely." Irene sounded a lot more confident than he felt, or than Lasty looked, for that matter. "We are using passive scans, not as efficient, but necessary. I have sighted Jade Viking."

"Where is she?" Jim looked at his screen, and waited for Irene to show him what she saw.

"Jade Viking is approximately a third of the way between Earth's and Mar's orbits."

"She's not under power!" Dutter looked up from her console, fear in her face. "It's a dead ship!"

"Dead?" Jim stood up and looked over her shoulder at her display. It told him exactly nothing. "Are you sure? Maybe they're just not under way."

"It's not just that," she said, pointing to one display. "They aren't even under stealth shielding! They can be seen, even with the naked eye. And their power grid is cold. That means no engines, no stealth, no computer." Her words trailed away as she realized something a moment before he did. "And no life support."

"You are almost accurate in your assessment, Assistant Commander Dutter." Irene spoke the words calmly, but they had an electrifying effect on the bridge. She continued. "What we are seeing is at least partially a ruse."

"Can you clarify, please, Irene?" Jim asked, glad to see from Lasty and Dutter's expressions that he wasn't the only one in the dark.

"Jade Viking is a dead ship, at the moment. It appears that all systems are off, for some reason. But, two shuttles are producing a stealth screen that is actually a projection of Jade Viking as a dead ship. A logical assumption would be the screen is to hide the activities of the shuttles themselves. The other two are powered up and performing some function, probably life support."

"So there may be survivors?" Jim exchanged relieved looks with the rest of the bridge crew.

"We are still too far to be able to tell for certain, without revealing our own presence."

"How long?" Jim's voice was terse.

"We will be able to scan the ship for life in about four hours, at our present speed. But we should be able to converse with them reasonably securely in less than half that time. If we continue at our present speed."

"What do you mean?" Jim asked.

"At this speed it would be impossible to conceal ourselves if we wanted to stop and give them aid. To remain undetected, we need to start slowing immediately."

"Well then, do so." Jim didn't understand at first why Irene was making this a tough decision. Of course they would stop and help. Hell, that was why they were here...

"Oh."

"Precisely," Irene said, with what sounded to Jim like sincere regret in her voice. She shifted to speaking through his personal transceiver. "A primary objective in my programming is to protect Afsaneh Riahi. To do so, I must continue on to Earth, first."

"Not necessarily," Jim said, thinking fast. "There's another option."

"I can not permit what I assume to be your other option." Irene was firm. "With a potentially hostile force concealed somewhere within the Solar System, I can not permit you to take her in a shuttle. There are not adequate defenses."

"You seem to be under the mistaken assumption that you are in command." Jim spoke softly, but with an edge of steel in his voice. "I am in charge here, and you will do as I say. Do you understand?"

"I understand you, but that does not change the fact that I can not permit you to go to Earth with Afsaneh in a shuttle."

Somewhere on the bridge someone growled. Jim distantly realized it was Angela Dawson. "Is there a reason Irene isn't letting us hear her?" He ignored her as he stood and faced the main screen. Even though technically she was the entire ship, he still pictured that as her main presence. A central point to focus on.

"Irene. As you pointed out, there may be a hostile ship in this system. You may or may not be able to defeat an Egelv ship by yourself. If we can get Vicki back in commission, it has to improve our chances."

"Your safety is paramount, Jim Morris. I can not change that programming."

Jim glared. "Can you give Fang or Claw adequate instructions to approach Earth under maximum caution, and bring her to Ann Arbor?"

"Yes, but that is not..."

"Yes will be sufficient." Jim was mildly surprised she let him interrupt her. "Something turned Vicki off like a light switch. We have to know what happened and fix her. You can do that. If something happens while I'm approaching Earth, you can be with me in minutes."

"Look, I don't want to take any chances on either Afsaneh's or my safety. If anything happens, come running. But we need Jade Viking. We need Vicki. We have to help her if we can. She's our friend. And so are all the people in her crew."

He waited for her response. He couldn't believe he was having an argument with a computer, but then again, Vicki, Irene, Pearl, Sam, and the new ship, Connie, for that matter, were far more than just computers.

"Your suggestion does appear to have the most positive aspects," she finally said, now speaking through the common wall speakers. "We will need to begin preparations immediately. You will need to launch within the next twelve minutes."

"Twelve..." He gaped. Jesus, when she made up her mind, she got right down to it. "Well then let's get moving!"

He grinned at Lasty. "You've got the con, Mister."

Lasty watched the Jim Morris hurry off the bridge, still staring. It took several moments for the words to sink in. He looked at the fearsome Security Chief Angela Dawson.

"Con?" he asked.

"Controls," she said, her white teeth brilliant against her dark skin as she grinned at him. It reminded him of the Tryr a little, but he didn't even shiver at the image. "Is it just me, or does it seem that Vicki is more like a wife or mother with control issues than a computer?"

Lasty only half listened to her as he considered what needed to be done. He would need to begin making adjustments to the new course in a minute or two, but for at least one moment, there was only one thought in his head, and he couldn't resist saying it out loud.

"I have the con."

❖ ❖ ❖ ❖ ❖

CHAPTER TWENTY-TWO

Aboard the Tryr Warship Trhktah, approaching Station Osaka

Commodore Tka leaned forward in anticipation. Beside him, his brother Captain Tzi did the same, as did most of the rest of the personnel on the bridge of his flagship, Trhktah. On his other side, their nephew, Commander Tne gave a toothy grin as he spoke.

"Bokh take it, that ship is Tryr. I've seen it before, the Trawk. Clan Tcha never was worth Hoag dung, can't even hold their own ships."

Tka looked at his nephew affectionately. Ah, to be so young again. Tne was tall, even taller than his father Tki, and his fur was, of course, still blacker than the deepest space and glistened with health. He'd already noticed the effect Tne was having on the females in the crew.

"If they were worth the fur that enfolds them, they never would have indentured themselves to the Ananab," Tzi snorted. He still stood ram-rod straight but, like Tka himself, was beginning to show a little grey and white around the ears and whiskers.

And around the scars. His brother knew all about scars, Tka thought, glancing at the long white ribbon that wound from the captain's left shoulder all the way down to his right hip. Tzi had been lucky he hadn't been disemboweled by the slashing blow that had caused the scar.

But enough of that. Tka was also eager to see these Humans that had caused such an uproar. He had instructed the technician to allow full visual, but Station Chaq had not reciprocated.

"Tryr ship, you are cleared to dock at Berth One, 'E' Concourse. Please follow the buoy signals. Any attempt to dock at any other location will result in your destruction." Tka bared his teeth at that.

But he had his orders. Reconnoiter first, find out what he could about these Humans. At that point, if he felt comfortable with the odds, attack in full force. But learning about what the bumbling Ananab had unleashed was more important. The station could be reclaimed or even destroyed at a future date.

"Do as they say," he said through clenched teeth. He could hear rumbling in the throats of a number of the bridge staff, including his brother. "Keep your opinions to yourselves," he said. "There'll be time enough for putting them in their place later."

His nephew tapped his monitor with an extended claw from a single finger. "Look at the damage along the northern regions of the station. I'll bet none of the defenses in that section of the station are functional."

"And isn't that one of the Ananab ships from the last task force sent out here?" Tzi increased the the magnification so they could all see the damage to the hull and one of the engine nacelles. "I doubt that ship can even navigate, much less go to battle." He turned in his seat to confront Tka. "We could probably end their defiance with just our ship!"

"Perhaps," Tka admitted. "But, perhaps not. There has to be more to these Humans than what we can scrape from beneath our claws. I want a pledge of restraint from each and every one of you that accompanies me."

"Look where they've placed us," growled Tzi, pointing at the lights signaling from the end of one of the arms that stretched out away from the main body of the station. "We will die of old age in the time it takes us to walk to their bridge."

"Placing us in such an inferior docking is an insult." Tka's young nephew rose halfway from his seat. "We should insist on a closer berth."

"We will dock where they say." Tka let some talon show in his voice. There were more rumblings, but more cautious this time, almost subliminal to avoid his wrath. No one on the bridge spoke until the ship came to a halt within grappling range of the station and was reeled into its berth.

Tka rose and turned to his brother, who was also obviously planning on boarding the station.

"Captain Tzi, you will remain on board and monitor our progress. Should anything go wrong, you are to take any measures necessary to avenge us and recover the station." His brother opened his mouth to argue and Tka cut him off, stepping in close so they could speak with an illusion of privacy. "Brother, I need you here. Should we find ourselves in battle, I'll be counting on you to pull our fur from the flame."

He tried to put a little amusement into his voice to give his brother face in front of his own crew. "Anyway, you know you are the only Tryr in this sector besides myself that Tne's sire will take orders from." He was relieved to see Tzi grin at that. They both knew how difficult their brother Tki could be. He was captain of one of the five ships in sheath mode hanging back, eagerly awaiting the command to attack. Of course they both also knew that at least part of the reason Tzi was staying on board was that his old wounds slowed him up, making him a liability in close combat.

But things like that were almost never said out loud. And when they were, someone usually died.

A short time later, Commodore Tka stood waiting for the hatch to open. Although the ship was moored, direct computer and power lines between the ship and station had not been established. This meant he couldn't view the reception waiting with the station's own sensors.

With an uneasy feeling, he gave the command to unseal the ship. His nephew stood slightly behind him, as did another officer, Commander Tql, a distant cousin. Behind them were the three guards assigned to accompany them. All six of them were armed with disruptors.

The hatch opened, revealing an empty passageway.

For a moment, Tka just stood there, fighting down irritation. Normally, this act of rudeness would cost someone their throat. Since this was an official visit, there should be a greeting party.

Fighting down an inward growl, he marched down the empty corridor. It was only a few clarns long, and when he reached the junction at the end, he got his first glimpse of a Human.

There were two slightly to the left of the passage. Both had unfamiliar weapons pointed at him and his party. Two more stood just to the right, doing the same. Good idea, he nodded to himself. They could bracket the corridor without coming under direct fire from anyone standing back in the hatch of his ship.

Farther down the main corridor to the right, four more Humans waited. Two were guards, with weapons raised.

The other two were obviously officers, or leaders of some sort. They were both armed with handguns sheathed at their hips. One had something strapped to his back that looked like it might be a weapon, the other held one of the same weapons as the guards loosely in one hand at his side.

But these Humans were...small.

The biggest of them barely came up to Tryr shoulder heighth. And they seemed to come in quite a variety of colors and sizes. Two of the guards were dark skinned, almost black. Several were pale, not unlike the Baerd. Others ranged in shades in between. The officer packing the second weapon actually had a yellowish tinge.

And they had an even wider variety of fur, both in color and in style. All in all, an interesting spectacle.

But they just don't look very dangerous. He wondered why even the Ananab, incompetent though they were, would have so much trouble subduing these creatures.

Tne muttered in a low tone designed to avoid the listening sensors. "There's an energy suppressing field. Disruptors won't work here."

Captain Tka caught his full-toothed grin before it got loose. These Humans didn't look like they had any claws to mention, and they certainly weren't big enough to match strength with even an immature Tryr, much less an adult warrior.

Not very good tactics. Or was it?

He looked at the weapon one of the guards held pointed at him. That didn't look like any energy weapon he'd ever seen. It had an opening at the end. Did it project something out at its target? He vaguely recalled reading about some such thing. Was it the Venn that used them? No, it was someone else. Tka mentally shrugged. It didn't matter. He would match his speed against another's aim any day.

He came to a halt in front of the two officers. The smaller yellowish one with the straight, black hair spoke.

"Welcome to Station Osaka." The translation into Tryr came through wall speakers. "I am Captain Koro Asaya. This is Security Chief James McGregor." Both Humans gave slight nods of their heads, then waited for him to respond. His cousin gave a growl at the lack of subservience, but Tka lifted a hand to silence him.

He waited to see if they would give a more proper greeting, but there was none offered. These Humans are either very brave or incredibly stupid, he thought. Or both. He decided he'd waited long enough.

"I am Captain Tka, of the Clan Tryhk. I have been sent by the Hshtahni to appraise the situation." He let his teeth show slightly, a muted threat that the Humans didn't seem to recognize. "Are you the leader?"

"I will take you to him." The Human commander gestured for him to precede him down the corridor. His men would have surged forward had he not immediately raised his hand again.

The Human seemed to understand, and gave what appeared to be a friendly grin, not quite showing any teeth as he spoke.

"Please excuse any ignorance we may show regarding Tryr customs. With humans, allowing someone to walk first is a gesture of politeness. May we walk together, Commodore?"

"Certainly." Tka took several steps before the words sank in. "My rank is Captain."

"Actually, you wear the emblem of a commodore, and our most recent information has your brother Captain Tzi commanding the Trhktah."

Tka was shocked, then remembered the captured Ananab ship. Still, that showed an efficiency and thoroughness that Tka found unsettling.

The corridor opened out to the left into a large receiving room. More guards were spaced around the walls, all armed and looking alert. A huge table stood in the middle of the room, and behind it was one of the taller Humans he'd seen yet. His eyes actually came up to his own jaw.

The Human had shockingly white fur on his head. He looked older than most of the others. Next to him was a much shorter Human that Tka belatedly realized was a female. He'd deliberately selected all males for this initial encounter, not sure of Human habits. Some races would have taken it as a sign of weakness to have females at a possibly confrontational meeting.

He wasn't sure if all females were that much smaller than males, or if it was just this one. Other than size, the only obvious difference between them were the teats. And even they weren't much bigger. Of course, since Humans seemed to wear more clothing than any race he could think of, it was hard to be sure.

"Commodore Tka, of the Clan Tryhk, may I present Governor Jason Lang." Tka gave the slight nod he had received earlier and the Governor returned it.

"May I offer you a seat, Sir?" Governor Lang gestured to the seats placed before the table. There were three, and they were designed for Tryr comfort. Tka felt the sense of uneasiness return. These Humans knew a lot more about him than he did about them.

He sat down gingerly in the seat in the middle. He tried to look nonchalant while still remaining in position to leap into action if necessary. His nephew and the others remained standing fanned out behind him. He watched as the Governor noted that and then sat down on his own side. The two officers split to stand, one at each end of the table.

The white-haired Human spoke first. "Thank you for agreeing to speak with us. This is the first contact we've had with your people that didn't involve fighting."

"I have been sent by the Hshtahni to evaluate the situation."

"You mean to evaluate us." Lang spoke softly, with a glint of what looked like humor in his eyes. Tka was a little unnerved by his candor.

And his apparent lack of fear.

"This station belongs to the Ananab." Tka decided to be equally blunt and candid. "The Ananab are vassals of the Hshtahni. As such, they are under their protection. You are to surrender this station and all weapons at once."

Several Humans stirred at his words, and he could feel his own guards tensing. So, evidently, could Lang.

"As you were, gentlemen," he said, and Tka wondered if the station's translators were working properly. But the words of respect did seem to match his mannerisms. Lang turned back to him and leaned forward to prop his elbows on the table, placing his hands together, palms open.

For a moment, Tka thought it was a sign of submission, then realized it was just a favorite position of comfort. He turned his attention to Lang's words. The Human spoke softly, but with firmness.

"We didn't ask to be brought here. The Ananab came to our world and stole us and our ocean vessel. We were left with no choice but to take matters into our own hands."

"Your choice is clear," Tka countered. "You can submit to my authority now. The Hshtahni are interested in your race and would probably not allow the Ananab to exterminate you as they wish to."

"No one will be 'exterminating' us." Tka couldn't get over the fact that the Humans showed no fear, either in body language or scent. If anything, it was anger that showed in Lang's words. "And we won't be surrendering to anyone. We took the Ananab ship that brought us here, and we've taken this station and the ships that survived battle with us. These are rightful compensation for the pain and suffering we've been caused."

"You don't know the meaning of pain and suffering. But you will if you don't surrender." Tka shook his head. "Don't you understand? All you've fought so far were thick-skulled Srotag, incompetent Ananab, and what has to be the sorriest excuse for a Tryr clan there is."

He gestured behind him.

"These Tryr are as superior to what you've faced so far as the Hshtahni are to the Ananab. You can no more stand before our forces than one of your men could defeat a Tryr without the use of weapons."

The smaller officer, Commander Asaya, spoke. "Humans have beaten Tryr in one to one combat."

Tka couldn't resist a grin, and he could hear his men laughing behind him. What a thought, that a Human could even survive a moment's time, much less actually defeat a Tryr.

The bigger of the Human officers, although still small by Tryr standards spoke for the first time. McGregor's voice, unlike the other Humans, was very nearly as deep as his own.

"It's true. In fact, Jim Morris beat more than one, several times."

"Who?" The translation had made the name sound just like a Tryr word that meant, of all things, danger.

"Jim Morris." Commander Asaya enunciated the name carefully, but it still sounded unnatural. "He killed many Ananab, Srotag,..." The Human grinned, his teeth shown to be even and devoid of fangs. "...and Tryr."

Tka was getting weary of this. The Humans, intriguing at first, were becoming boring and foolish. As if he couldn't tell a deception when he saw it. "Anyone can kill from a distance, with a weapon. But when the energy fields are in place, as they are here, one has to rely on personal skills, strengths and natural abilities."

He looked around the room and gestured at the guards.

"We are not here to fight, at this moment. But if we were, the six of us could probably kill most or all of you with our bare claws, even with your primitive weapons. And you..."

He stopped. It took every ounce of courage and resolve to not react as Asaya suddenly leaped forward, his hands grasping the weapon on his back, drawing it.

Governor Lang spoke one word.

"Hold!"

Tka looked at the edge of a claw. Unlike his own claws, this one was of metal. And it was as long as one of his arms, and looked as sharp as a laser-blade along its edge.

Of course, at the moment, the most important aspect of this claw was that it was less than a finger's breadth from his eyes. The Human had moved with a speed that rivaled that of a Tryr. And his stopping at the command of his leader showed a control that Tka had never seen in a Tryr.

"Wait," he said to his men that had been as shocked as he, but were on the verge of attacking. The word was barely legible as he realized he'd stopped breathing and had no air in his lungs. Someone behind him snarled, and his voice grew thick with rage as he repeated, "I said wait."

"Commander Asaya, return to your post." Lang's voice allowed for no other choice, and Tka watched Asaya's face in fascination as emotions struggled for control. Finally, reason won out.

"Yes, sir." The Human took a step backwards, then another. His blade shifted slightly as someone behind Tka started to move.

"I will not repeat myself without drawing someone's blood," Tka warned, his eyes never leaving Asaya's face. The blade disappeared as fast as it had appeared back into the sheath on his back. The Human looked back at him for a moment, then bowed his head, much lower than he had earlier.

"Please forgive my impetuousness, Commodore Tka. I am young, and drawn too quick to anger. I lost friends in those battles we were speaking of."

"It is forgotten," Tka said, moving in his seat stiffly. He felt like he'd strained muscles, even though he hadn't budged a bit. He heard the expected rumbling behind him. "It is forgotten," he repeated firmly, and the rumbling stopped.

"Which one of these men is the Jimmorss you speak of?" He looked around at the guards. Lang looked...apologetic?

"I'm afraid he's not available at the moment," he said, giving Tka an innocent smile. "As you probably know, we have more ships than what are docked at Osaka. He is presently on one, in stealth mode, not unlike the five ships you have posted out near the perimeter of scanning range."

Tka hoped he didn't show the surprise he felt. He'd been sure that no Ananab sensors could detect his ships when sheathed. He'd heard the Humans had no advanced technology of their own. How could they have improved the Ananab equipment so quickly, and so effectively?

If their detection gear was so much better than expected, maybe they could have more ships hidden nearby. He spoke in a low tone in his Clan dialect, for the benefit of his brother.

"Scan everywhere and see if this is so."

Lang gave him an amused look. "It won't help. They won't be able to spot our ships." *Did they have access to his clan's secret language?*

332

No, no, it was just a lucky guess, or a logical assumption. It had to be.

Commodore Tka sat back in his seat, shifting to allow his tail to drape comfortably off to the side. He didn't understand any of this. Why weren't these Humans quaking with fear? He could see wariness, and even smell the rancid scent of cold sweat on several of the guards.

But, by and large, most of the Humans were simply determined, confident. The leaders showed respect, but any fear they felt was firmly held under control.

Tka was honest enough to know the odds of only six Tryr defeating this many armed enemy was slight. But he also knew what an intimidating sight they were. A Baerd or Hoag would have soiled themselves by now. Even Srotag and Ananab showed caution that was equal parts respect and fear.

Of course, they had been dealing with the Tryr Clan Tcha who were the laughing stock of the entire Race. Modest success against such incompetent Tryr might give them a false sense of confidence.

His brother reported through his ear implant that there was no sign of any other ships in the vicinity, and that the Trawk had docked nearby, on the same concourse, at the same time they had..

"I would be candid with you." Tka started to lift a foot up to rest on the table, but thought better of it. He flexed one hand, allowing the claws to extend fully. Every Human eye at the table followed the motion. "So far, the Hshtahni haven't gotten involved in this matter. They considered it an Ananab problem, and one of their own causing. They had no business taking the initiative they did with your race."

"About time we heard something like that." Governor Lang sat upright. "I was beginning to think there weren't any civilized races in space. Nor respect for other races, or their property. And the way they treated the Baerd and Hoag on this ship, little better than slaves!"

"You misunderstand me," Tka said, keeping the astonishment out of his voice. Did they really think they had inherent rights? "The fault of the Ananab lay not with their attitude to lesser races, but with their presumptuousness in taking any action regarding your planet without first contacting their superiors. Namely, the Hshtahni."

"Oh?" Lang's face was implacable, but for the first time, Tka saw a glimpse of a struggle for control. His face had acquired a Baerd-like tinge of red, but unlike the Baerd, a sign of anger.

"They made a complete mess of things, and it will be just that much harder for your people to reconcile themselves to their position in life."

"Position in life?" The Human's face had darkened even more, but his voice was very quiet now, and Tka saw that battle was probably inevitable within the next few moments. He hoped his men were ready.

"Yes." Tka felt sympathy for this Human. Under the proper supervision, he would have made an interesting vassal. They were all spoiled now, though. They'd had a taste of success, and the only thing that would put it into proper perspective would also cost them their lives. "Until now, the Hshtahni were content to allow the Ananab to retake their own property. Since they seem unable to do so, we've been instructed to investigate. The Hshtahni can no more allow this area of space to fall out of their sphere on influence than they can allow rebellion or insolence."

"You and your friends the Hshtahni may find us insolent." Governor Lang spoke slowly, and his voice was thick with intense emotion. "But to be rebellious implies we were once under your control. And slavery in any form is repugnant to us and we will not comply."

Without noticing, both Tryr and Human had risen to their feet, glaring at each other across the table. As Lang continued speaking, Tka was only half-listening as he began to plan his first attack.

"We were knocked out and kidnapped, tortured by Tryr, Srotag, Ananab...but we fought back and took the P"Tassum and made it our own, as we did the Trawk when we arrived at Station Chaq. We took that as well. And two assaults later, we still have the station, and even more ships. Even your damn 'ghosts' were defeated. If you think we're..."

Tka stared at him. He took a step forward and Humans all around the room snapped their weapons up into a prepared position. It also stopped the old Human's tirade for a moment.

"Did you say 'ghosts'?" Tka ran his tongue across his chops nervously. *He couldn't mean...could he?* "What do you mean?"

"As if you didn't know." Tka marveled as the expressiveness of the Human's face. This was true hatred. He could admire that. "Gray, furry little bastards about this tall. Each with his own personal stealth field. Retractable claws, poisonous if they don't just gut you from stem to stern."

Tka took an instinctive step backwards and turned his head to look at Commander Tql. His cousin's eyes were wide with shock. And fear, probably reflecting his own, he admitted to himself. He called out to his brother.

"Tzi, did you hear?"

His brother's voice was grim in his ear. "Yes. Could it be the Reigna?"

"The Reigna," Tka breathed. "I never really believed..."

"Those are the bastards," Lang agreed vehemently. "The Reigna."

Tka stared at him, hardly seeing. "You've seen Reigna? You fought them?"

"Haven't you?" He could tell the Human suspected him of deception, but was too stunned to be insulted. Lang snorted and leaned forward across the table. "Would you like to see how they look...dead?"

"Wait!" Tka felt like he was fast losing control of the situation. This was very dangerous, and not just for him and the boarding party. He turned away from the Humans and his men closed around him to give him the illusion of privacy.

"Tzi, I need your advice. Second brother of my litter, need I tell you of the inherent dangers?"

Tzi snorted through the connection. "Not likely. Need I remind you that the more we speak in our Clan tongue, the more likely their computer will acquire a translation?"

Tka winced. The elders wouldn't thank him for giving an alien race of unknown potential keys to one of their most highly prized security measures. He slowly wheeled around to face the table of Humans again. His men faded back behind him. He felt like his arthritic sire as he fumbled his way back into his seat. He stared at Lang, who stared back with open curiosity.

"Do Humans understand the concept of 'Honor'?" he finally asked. Lang glared at him and his answer was swift as it was abrupt.

"At least as well as any Tryr!"

Tka felt his nostrils flare in outrage, but fought down the automatic desire to throw himself at the Human. His raised paw stopped any of his party from the same. "So you understand the binding nature of a pledge? An exchange of pledges?"

Lang looked like he would have liked to have asked for more details, but took no time to answer. "Of course."

"Brother, is this wise? You risk..." Tzi's voice was urgent. Tka impatiently interrupted him.

"I know what I do," he said in basic Tryr. He could tell Lang was deducing who he was actually speaking to. Tka took a deep breath, then stood. Lang looked wary, but there was little or no fear.

Tka cleared his throat. His men stirred uneasily behind him, but one twitch of an ear and they were silent again.

"I, Commodore Tka, of the Tryr Clan Tryhk, note the time and date.

I vow on the honor of my clan that no Tryr nor Human shall do battle or die this day." He watched as Lang digested what he'd said. The urge to turn and look at his companions must have been strong, because his head started to twist sideways two or three times before he finally stood, bringing him nearly to eye level with Tka.

"I, Jason Lang, Governor of Station Osaka, ex-Captain of the Jade Viking do..." Tka suppressed the temptation to laugh as he watched the Human try and remember exactly how he'd phrased his pledge. "...note the time and date, and vow upon my honor that no Human nor Tryr shall do battle or die this day."

Lang grinned at him, obviously trying to keep his teeth from baring. "If you want, I could swear on a stack of bibles?"

Tka didn't understand the connotation, but appreciated the lightening of the mood. "Not necessary. But at least now we can relax and not have to do battle at the flick of fur."

"May I offer refreshments?" Lang sat back down, and Tka thankfully joined him. His cousin and nephew sat at his sides. "We have several different selections of Tryr food and drink that we've...acquired. Although I'm afraid I don't know your brands well enough to know which are good or bad."

"If Tcha trash bought it, it's all bad," Tne spoke up. "They have the discriminating tastes of Hoa..." The young Tryr froze in mid-sentence at Tka's glare. As Tne sensed someone was standing next to him, he looked over to see a Hoag displaying a list.

Tka almost felt sorry for him. Very few Tryr had a knack for tact. He liked to think he did, but being courteous and sensitive to the feelings of a Hoag was far beyond Tne's reach at his age. He was old enough to recognize he should shut up, though.

"Perhaps you would like to check the list for your Commodore," Lang said in the dry voice Tka was beginning to recognize as understated sarcasm. He rather liked it. "I'm sure there's something that will do."

Tne barely glanced at the list before pointing at an item, then another. Then he made a pretense of examining the fur on the back of his wrist. The Hoag left.

Tka watched the small creature leave through a small hatch he hadn't even noticed before. It was interesting that the Hoag hadn't been paralyzed with fear. These Humans must be contagious, he thought with a wry smile. He looked up to see Lang watching him.

336

"Sir, did you wish to see the body of one of these Reigna?"

Tka noted the pain and anger in Lang's voice when he said their name. That must have been a very costly battle for him. He shook his head. "Not quite yet. I'm still trying to decide if it's wise or not."

"Oh?" Lang encouraged him to continue.

Tka felt restless. "Is there somewhere we can walk? I think and talk better when I'm moving."

Lang laughed out loud. "I know what you mean. I'm much the same. Come this way, please."

Tka held up his hand to his men as they made to accompany him. "That won't be necessary. I want you to mingle and learn more about these people."

Tql shook his head firmly, and Tka could see it would be difficult, if not impossible to disuade him. He could see Lang having the same problem with the...what was he called? Ah, the McGregor.

"We seem to be overruled, Governor," he said politely.

Lang nodded his agreement. "Well, they can tag along as long as they stay out of our way."

"I concur," Tka said, and they strode down the concourse towards the hub of the station.

"Commodore, may I assume the Reigna are not a commonplace resident in your neighborhood?" Lang's voice still showed pain at mentioning them.

Tka raised an eyebrow at the way he phrased it. "Common? No. In fact, I've never really been convinced they existed, until now."

"There were nine of them on the Ananab ship you passed when you came into port." Lang's voice grew grim. "We captured most of the crew alive and incarcerated them. But we didn't know there were invisible enemy hiding on board. We lost about fifteen people, from all three races, before we got them all."

"Three races?" Tka looked over at him, noticing Tql and the McGregor walking uneasily next to each other behind them.

"Well, yes. Human, Baerd, and Hoag." Lang gave him a shrewd look. "I don't suppose Tryr spend a lot time worrying about the welfare of the 'lower races'."

"No, we don't," Tka said bluntly. "There are more important things for us to 'worry' about." He wasn't about to start apologizing for perfectly natural behavior. After all, he was a Tryr. He decided to change the subject.

"What about your race? How advanced are your people?" He tried to think of a polite way to put it. "Have you begun to develop any of your own...technology?"

"Yes." Tka waited for him to elaborate, and realized he wasn't going to. Ah, he understood.

"Don't worry," he said. "You're not going to give up any secret that really matters. It's not as though it'll change anything in the long run. Whether you've discovered electricity, or the dynamics of flight, or any number of other things, it's far too late for anything you learn on this station to protect your planet once the Hshtahni find it. And they will find it."

"Because we've seen these Reigna?" Lang had a curious mixture of emotions on his face. Tka couldn't quite place them, although he did seem...amused?

"No, that's more likely to get the Reigna going for your jugular," Tka said, grinning mirthlessly. "No, the Hshtahni rule a large portion of this part of the galaxy, and this station is firmly inside their sphere of influence."

"Our planet isn't," Lang countered.

"No?" Tka felt sympathy for this Human. In fact, he was surprised to find that he actually liked Lang. "Well, that will change. We're just close enough to Egelv space that they won't take any chances."

"Hmm," was all Lang said.

Tka looked at him suspiciously, then shook his head at his own paranoia. It wasn't as though these Humans had a chance to go seeking aid from the Egelv, even if they were inclined to give it. Unfortunately for them, they were in way over their head.

"So, how were you able to smuggle your own weapons on board." Tka decided yet another topic was in order while he tried to digest what he'd learned so far. "I would have thought even the Ananab would have taken better precautions. They're a paranoid race."

Lang stopped and looked ahead to where the concourse joined the hub. He turned and smiled at Tka. "We should head back."

Tka nodded understandingly. Lang wouldn't want to show him his defenses. He probably had the concourse junction rigged to be destroyed if they lost control.

They began walking slowly back, both seeming to want to extend the pleasant interlude. Tka noticed Tql and the McGregor were exchanging grudgingly polite comments. Tka suspected that was one Human that

338

would be good in a fight. He walked like a Tryr.

"How did we take the ship, then the rest?" Lang continued where they'd left off. He looked at Tka and his eyes twinkled.

"Want to see?"

"So these are actual computer recordings made, with no doctoring?" Tka gave his brother a pained look. Couldn't he at least try to be tactful? After Tzi had cut into the conversation via Tka's implant for the fourth time, he'd given permission for his brother and some of the crew to leave the ship. They were all gathered in the large reception room. More seating for Tryr bottoms had been brought in, and if one ignored the half a dozen armed Humans still posted around the perimeter, it was a comfortable and friendly gathering.

The small Human female, Suyo, ignored the insult and smiled at Tzi. "We've made no changes. This first scene is how we were greeted by the Captain of the Ananab.

There were numerous large screens scattered around the room and they all suddenly displayed what Tka recognized as the typical bridge to an Ananab merchant ship. His lip curled up in distaste as he recognized the Tryr commander.

"Remember that bog slime Tak, brother?" Tka nodded to Tzi, only half listening. He was more interested in the Humans in the picture. One was obviously the leader. From his relative size to Tak, he knew the Human was about half a head shorter than McGregor(his name, not designation).

So this was the Jimmorss they spoke of. He had longish, light-brown fur on top of his head and a short stubble of darker brown on his face. Tka always felt he could tell a lot about someone from the way he or she walked.

Jimmorss walked very well. He showed a confidence Tka wouldn't have felt under the same circumstances. Tka looked around and saw that all of his Tryr were watching with barely contained boredom, talking among themselves, whereas the Humans leaned forward in their seats, as if they could leap to the aid of those showed on-screen.

The room grew quiet as they watched the Ananab Captain rant at the Humans. A Srotag stepped behind Jimmorss. A few of Tka's men shouted good-natured warnings that the figures on the screen of course couldn't hear. A few Humans gave his men dirty looks.

When the Srotag grabbed Jimmorss from behind, Tka shook his

head in confusion. He had the impression the Human lived through this battle, even won it. Then he gawked as the Human literally ran up the Tryr's chest in front of him to end up on the back of the Srotag that had, only moments before had him in a deadly grasp.

The Tryr grew silent when Jimmorss broke the Srotag's neck.

Tka watched as his men surreptitiously tried to get a good look at the biceps of the Humans closest to them. He found himself eyeing Governor Lang, doing the same. How in...?

Several Tryr chortled as they watched Jimmorss dispatch two of the Ananab with his bare hands. I could do that, Tka thought. Then his inherent self-honesty kicked in. I could do that, when I was Tne's age.

They watched as the camera angles kept changing, showing Humans produce weapons from seemingly innocent devices. The carnage was impressive. A low growl started around the room when Jimmorss killed a female Tryr guard.

Tka and Lang looked at each other in alarm, but his brother Tzi, brought things back into perspective.

"She's a Tcha Clan bitch," he said, nudging his Tryr neighbor roughly. The young Tryr gaped at him for a moment, then nodded his head in bemused agreement.

"That's true. What's one more bit of trash, male or female?"

The scene ended and Tka found himself eyeing the blood dripping from Jimmorss' shoulder.

"Is there more?" A Tryr voice asked huskily.

"Yes," Lang admitted. He looked at Tka with concern showing on his face. "Commodore, will your men get too caught up in this?"

Tka felt the heat of shame rise to his face. He had been the first to make the pledge. If anything happened, it would his dishonor entirely. He shook his head.

"No. Please forgive my men, and myself. It is an unusual experience watching Tryr die at another race's hands while in their presence." Tka took a deep breath. "Governor, please allow me to assure you, we will not lose control."

"Good," Lang said, giving him an encouraging nod. "And please, call me Jason."

He heard his nephew gasp and start to rise in horror. His hand shot out and deposited Tne right back in his seat. He pivoted and stared directly into the young warrior's eyes. Nothing was said, they just stared at each other until his nephew dropped his gaze. Hiding his sigh of relief, he turned back to the govern...to Jason, who watched with growing concern on his face.

Tka smiled, careful to keep his teeth covered. "The right to use a familiar name is not one given lightly in Tryr society, ...Jason. Please, call me...Tka."

He ignored the shocked gasps of his men. He and Lang locked eyes for an eternity, then to his shock, Lang bowed to him.

"You are a gentleman, and a noble being, Tka." 'Jason' smiled and held out his hand. Tka looked at it in confusion.

"This is how my people greet each other with respect." Lang left his hand extended, waiting. After a moment, Tka held out his own. Although he suspected what would happen, he was still shocked when the Human took his hand in his own.

Then he shook it, up and down several times, squeezing as if to show there was strength, but no threat intended. Tka automatically returned the pressure. His fist was much larger than the Human's but there was a sense of balance in their grasped hands. Then, as if by mutual agreement, they both released grips.

Tka stared at Jason, deeply disturbed by a feeling he had never, ever, had with an alien.

A sense of kinsmanship.

He didn't have the slightest idea what to do next, but his new friend, Jason, saved him.

"Shall we watch more?"

Tka nodded, not trusting his voice. Jason nodded to Suyo, and she continued her instructional monologue.

"That was the battle for the P'Tassum, which we now call Jade Viking. The first thing we did when we docked at Station Chaq was secure the Trawk."

"I'm afraid that since all the fighting took place on the Trawk, we didn't get any decent footage of those events. Basically, we caught them by surprise." Her smile seemed to lighten the weight of those words. "Once again, Jim Morris led the attack, although many were involved in the fighting. This was the final battle for control of Station Chaq, or Osaka, as we now call it."

The picture changed to one of a large squad of Tryr surprising and overwhelming several Human guards, not letting them get more than a couple of shots off. Several of Tzi's crewmen cheered, then covered their mouths guiltily.

Suyo spoke in a strained sounding voice. "That was Hakim Riahi there with the black hair and dark complexion. He was Jim Morris' best friend."

Tka watched her out of the corner of his eye. To his amazement, she wiped a tear away from one eye. Her voice was thick and she had to clear it before continuing. His third cousin's daughter Tht, a security guard aboard the Trhktah, put one hand under her elbow, as if she would need support.

The Human woman gave the Tryr a startled look, then, with her other hand, patted Tht's hand in gratitude and continued.

"What they didn't know was that Jim was nearby, and heard them."

What Tka saw then he would take to his grave. If someone had described it, he would have scoffed in disbelief. He counted at least a dozen Tcha Tryr warriors clustered around the two fallen Humans.

Then the whirlwind descended upon them, in the form of a wild-eyed Human. He had some sort of hand weapon that he fired at Tryr from point blank range.

It is a projectile weapon, Tka marveled. In a spaceship, they're firing projectile weapons! Give them enough time, they'll kill themselves off, he thought, shaking his head in astonishment.

The man known as Jim Morris, Tka said it silently as two words, as the Humans did, made every shot count. When he reached the two dead Humans, only five Tryr remained standing.

Then Tka saw that the one called Hakim Riahi wasn't dead after all. The sound was off so Tka couldn't hear what was said, but he understood when the wounded Human fell back and died.

And as he watched in growing awe, five Tryr quickly joined him. A roar of approval rumbled out all around him when the Human walked right up to the nearest Tryr, holding his weapon extended. When the weapon proved to be fully discharged, they howled!

The stick he held proved to have hidden claws, and he dispatched most of the Tcha Tryr with that. When Jim Morris fought the Tryr with his bare hands, Tka actually heard his own men yelling support and encouragement to the Human.

When Jim Morris knocked his last opponents arms to the side and stabbed forward with one extended hand, his hand actually penetrated the Tryr's chest!

The hand of Jim Morris penetrated the body cavity past the wrist! Then, as the room watched in shocked silence, he lifted the dying Tryr, sliding his body up the wall.

When Jim Morris retracted his hand, holding the still-beating heart in his grasp, the silence could have suffocated. In the left corner of the screen, the watchers could see more Tryr, Srotag, even Ananab, approaching at an accelerated pace.

Tka heard his nephew cry out a warning to the Human, and breathed a sigh of relief. In another moment, he would have been the one calling the warning.

He stared as the Human pivoted and raised his gory hand, screaming his defiance. Then, a look of confusion appeared on his face. That's battle shock, Tka thought. I know that expression only too well.

Jim Morris stumbled backwards and a groan went up around the room from the Tryr. It turned to cheers as a transparent wall crashed down, barely missing Jim Morris. Then the picture went blank. Tka glanced sideways at his brother, who was looking back at him with the exact same expression.

There would be no battle today. At least not between Tryr and Human. Although his pledge had guaranteed that, he had fully expected to spend the next day securing the station for his Hshtahni overlords.

But now?

Tka felt someone's gaze and looked over to see Jason Lang staring at him, knowing full well exactly what he was thinking.

They stared at each other as the room around them erupted into sounds of amazement, and honest exchange between warriors and veterans of battles that weren't asked for, but accepted as necessary.

Dialogue between Tryr and Humans.

Tka grinned a full-toothed grin that would have made even a Hshtahni pause, and the white-haired Human grinned right back, not the least bit intimidated.

"Jason Lang, my Human friend?" Tka said, standing to meet him nearly eye to eye.

"Yes, Tka, my Tryr friend?" Jason Lang held out his hand.

Tka nodded, accepting the inevitable, and engulfed the Human's hand in his own, careful to not let his claws extend.

"You will be the death of me yet."

CHAPTER TWENTY-THREE

In a van, somewhere in the mountain states...

Kimberly watched Kiri do simple isometrics. She knew she should be doing them too, but couldn't dredge up the energy. She wished she could channel her concern and fear the way Kiri did.

Normally, Kiri was the bubbly, enthusiastic, optimist. Her mouth rarely stopped running under any circumstances. Now she sat in silence, staring stonily at the men in the van. Her only movement or sign of awareness was the nearly constant pitting of muscle against muscle as she did the only form of exercise available to either of them at the moment.

Kimberly had spent most of her waking hours watching her captors, trying to see out the front windows to figure out their location, racking her mind for ideas and plans. It hadn't been very fulfilling. The few details she had picked up were mostly negative.

The leaders's name was Takeda Nagashino, and she suspected he was high up in the Sukuru hierarchy, probably in the security division. They were being taken to San Francisco, to be put on a freighter bound for Japan.

Never to be heard from again, she was sure.

Come on, Martin. Let's use this highly trained brain of yours for something positive. Of course, it was difficult devising any sort of plan when you couldn't talk.

Both women were barefoot, and lucky not to be topless or clad in mere bikini panties below the waist. Kiri hadn't lasted half an hour before she'd tried to speak, and been told to take off some piece of clothing. Both women protested, and their captors had risen to their feet threateningly.

Kimberly removed one shoe and Nagashino had laughed and told her she'd spoken twice. He almost got her with that, and her mouth opened to protest the unfairness, but stopped upon seeing the anticipatory grin on his face.

So, their shoes were piled behind the driver's seat, and every now and then, one of the men would try and goad them into speech.

Kimberly hated the feeling of being helpless. The idea of having to rely on rescue by anyone was against everything she believed in. On the other hand, she was looking forward to seeing Jim's reaction to being told how she'd been treated.

Jim's going to wipe the docks up with these bastards, she thought, allowing a slight smile to come to her face. It didn't go unnoticed.

"Ah, Ms. Martin, thinking of rescue, perhaps?" This one's name was Yoji Iwasaka. In his mid-twenties, he was actually kind of handsome, if you didn't notice the cruel twist of his lip when he spoke. *And, if you ignored the gloating sneer in his voice.*

Kimberly shrugged her shoulders, not deigning to look at him. He laughed and nudged Takuan, who just shifted away from the contact and resumed his primary purpose, which was glaring alternately first at Kimberly, then Kiri.

Iwasaki wasn't discouraged though. "They probably think those two kid actors are going to come busting in, and save their pretty little bottoms."

Kimberly saw Nagashino, who was driving at that point, glance at them in his rear view mirror. His eyes were expressionless, and he didn't speak. She was so busy watching him, she almost didn't get the meaning of Iwasaki's words.

Kiri did though, and gave the man a puzzled look. Kimberly watched as he sneered at her friend.

"Was one of them an old boyfriend of yours?" He saw their confused looks and laughed contemptuously. "Oh, go ahead, play dumb. That's right, you didn't know you had a tail. Those two actors just happened to follow you and stake out your house."

Kimberly and Kiri looked at each other in surprise. This was the first she'd heard about a tail, and it didn't look like Kiri knew any more about it than she did. They both looked back at the big-mouthed guard.

"You really didn't know?" Iwasaki got a triumphant expression on his face as he realized he'd caught them unawares. "Sasama Sakakibara and uh, Iori Kojiro? They were driving a car registered to Jim Morris? Your husband, isn't he, Ms. Morris? A red Viper, Nevada plates?"

Kimberly looked at Kiri in bewilderment, and the young actress had a worried look. Kimberly lifted her eyebrows as if to say, does my husband have a red Viper? Kiri nodded, biting her lower lip nervously.

Both women looked back at the man mocking them. Iwasaka grinned as he saw he had their undivided attention. He leaned forward to speak in a conspiratorial whisper.

"They're both dead. We killed them, at a hotel in Ann Arbor. Then we threw their bodies in a dumpster for the rats to enjoy." He sat back, as if to savor their shock.

Kimberly believed him, and a soft sniff from Kiri confirmed she did too. She put her arms around her friend and hugged her close. Kiri began sobbing quietly and Iwasaki clapped his hands in glee. She ignored him and looked forward to meet Nagashino's eyes still watching them through the inside driver's mirror. She ground her teeth together and met his eyes, glaring.

Nagashino's eyes gave no hint of any sympathy, or any other feeling, for that matter. Kimberly patted Kiri softly on the head and murmured little wordless sounds of comfort. Her eyes never left his.

In law school, she had practiced her steely-hard glare in the mirror for hours. She had no illusions that women got an even deal, even in law practice. Or perhaps, especially in the legal world. The ability to stare down anyone, to intimidate with a glance, was a skill worth developing.

The look she was giving Nagashino had no relationship to those hours of rehearsal. At that moment, if she'd had a gun, she would have shot all of them down without a moment's hesitation. If Jim had showed up, she would have told him to stay out of her way while she dealt with these bastards.

At that moment, she didn't want to be rescued. She wanted the power to deal with this scum herself. And somehow, she would.

Perhaps Nagashino saw some of that, perhaps not. Maybe he just saw a refusal to be intimidated any further. In any case, when Iwasaki demanded they remove more clothes, he spoke in his expressionless voice in Japanese. Iwasaki protested, and he uttered a single fierce sounding statement.

Kimberly and Kiri's tormentor sank back into a sitting position in disappointment. He quickly transferred his irritated look back to them, grabbing himself in the crotch suggestively.

Kimberly didn't talk or look away. She just stared at the man, wondering when and if she would get a chance for retribution.

Jade Viking should be able to trace them. They still had their flesh colored patches behind their ears. Evidently Takuan hadn't noticed them.

But why had there been no word? What had happened to the Jade Viking?

Jade Viking

"Captain Tachibana?"

He gasped in relief as he heard the nearly familiar voice in his transceiver.

"Vicki?"

"No," came the swift reply. "This is her...niece, Irene. We are approaching your ship and will establish a tractor beam tow in two minutes.

Hiroaki started as people around him began cheering. Then he realized they were all picking up the same broadcast. A rescue ship from Osaka? It was too soon. The probe should just be reaching the station right about now.

But he wasn't about to slap a gift horse in the mouth. And neither were the people around him, hugging and shouting in excited relief. He raised his hands.

"Let's hold it down, people. Calm down. Do you want them to hear us all the way back on Earth?"

"Captain Tachibana, I am separating your channel from the group, and will continue to do so with the others as I connect the frequencies to specific members of your crew. In the meanwhile, could you please give me a brief overview of what happened?"

Tachibana quickly recounted the last seventy-two hours, finishing with the opinion that Vicki had used the few seconds before allowing contact with the Egelv ship to devise and prepare some sort of scheme to keep them alive until she repaired herself or rescue arrived.

"That would appear to be essentially what she did," Irene agreed. "I have set up a subroutine to begin rebooting her main systems. If the self-destruct command is still present, it will be isolated, with no harm done to my primary systems. We have secured Jade Viking with tractor beams and extended our stealth shields to conceal both ships."

"What if the Egelv notice our ship is gone?" Hiroaki wasn't eager to have the aliens rush back out here to find where the supposedly dead ship had gotten to.

"We are leaving a probe with stealth shields projecting an identical image of your ship as when we approached. As long as they don't happen to be watching the very moment we exchange the probe for Jade Viking, it should be impossible to discern the difference at that distance."

"Excellent," Hiroaki nodded enthusiastically, forgetting Irene couldn't see him. "What ship are you, anyway?"

"I am Irene, the computer of the Jade Wolverine, the first ship made specifically for Human use, under the command of Jim Morris."

"Ah, Mr. Morris!" Hiroaki smiled broadly. "I mean, Captain Morris! May I speak to him, please?"

"I'm afraid Jim Morris is beyond safe transmitting distance at the moment." Hiroaki's brow furled in confusion that became troubled as Irene continued. "He took the armed shuttle Claw to Earth with Afsaneh Riahi. He separated when we began to brake to rendezvous with you. We will catch up with them on Earth."

"Why did he go ahead?" Captain Tachibana couldn't believe the actor hadn't waited until his ship was rescued. Surely he didn't miss his wife that much. His irritation turned to embarrassment and worry when he was told of Afsaneh's condition, and how it happened. "I see. Of course, I would have done the same."

Actually he wasn't so sure, but he tried to give Jim the benefit of a doubt. After all, he'd been a Captain for years. Jim had no experience with the job, and the exchange of trust and commitment were something he would have to learn over time.

Assuming there was time. There was still an Egelv ship out there. Would he even manage to sneak by it?

❖ ❖ ❖ ❖ ❖

Aboard Claw, Jade Wolverine's shuttle

Jim gave a sigh of relief as he felt the slight turbulence caused by the atmosphere on his ship. They should be over Michigan within a few minutes. He didn't like Afsaneh's color a bit. It seemed to him she'd worsened in the past few hours.

He gingerly placed his hands on the joy stick and mouse. The shuttle should be able to handle a landing on automatic pilot, and he wasn't any too confident of his abilities to take control if necessary.

This was a little trickier than a Cessna, he conceded.

"How's it going, uh, Claw?" He knew this computer was much more limited in it's capabilities and he didn't have a clue how far to trust it.

"We are within .02 percent variation of our flight plan, Jim Morris." The shuttle's voice was female, like the rest of the ships, but much more impersonal. In fact, it reminded him of Vicki when she was first...born? Now there was a thought to provide him with much deliberation some evening.

"Any sign of the Egelv?"

"None. However, we are not scanning for them, other than passive data observance."

"Right." Jim felt very much out of his element. Then he leaned forward in excitement as the Great Lakes grew in size until they lost their shape in the early morning light. "You know where we're going?"

"Yes, Jim Morris." If that had been Vicki or Irene, there would have been a suggestion of irritation in their voice. Claw's tone never modulated. "I am operating on the assumption we are proceeding directly to the University of Michigan Medical Center, the emergency room entrance."

"Good." Jim nodded in approval, then rolled his eyes at his subconscious gesture. "When we get close, let me point out a place to park. We'll need to approach at a very moderate speed so that we don't create a lot of wind."

"Of course." Jim got the hint and shut up.

Ten minutes later, he was pulling an antigrav sled carrying an unconscious Afsaneh down the ramp of the shuttle. "Seal the hatch and wait for my return," he ordered. "And when I say now, cut power to the sled."

"Yes, Jim Morris."

He watched as he approached the emergency doors until no one inside seemed to be paying close attention to the entrance, then scurried inside, pulling the sled over a conveniently placed empty gurney.

"Now," he said, and the sled settled on top.

Then he began to shout. "Emergency, emergency transfer for head injuries. I need a doctor here, right now!"

Startled ER attendants looked up from what they were doing, then an intern was bending over Afsaneh, checking her vital signs.

"This girl has already received medical attention. What is she doing here? Who was the attending doctor?"

"She's had a serious blow to the head, and fluid is building around her brain. That pressure needs to be relieved immediately. And she has a broken arm and leg. Who's the Doctor in attendance tonight?" Jim tried to sound officious.

"What?" A nurse looked at his non-regulation scrubs, then at his face, as if to recognize him. She flinched involuntarily as she saw the long scar on the left side of his face. "Who are you? I don't know you."

"Of course you don't," Jim said, stalling for time. He was saved by the intern.

"She's in stable condition, but I don't like...call Dr. Tinsley down here at once. And find out what O.R.'s available."

Jim backed away as attention centered on Afsaneh. He thought he'd pulled it off when a hand took hold of his elbow. It was one of the attendants, with a clipboard in hand.

"Sir, we need some information..." she started but stopped as Jim raised a hand.

"Her name is Afsaneh Riahi. She was injured on a camping trip. You have her records on file. She was born here and has received most of her medical care at this facility." He made a pretense of checking his pockets. "I don't have my wallet on me. I must have left it at my friend's house. It has my insurance card..."

"We'll need her insurance company," the young black woman taking the information down pointed out.

"We have the same company, same agent, same coverage..." Jim really didn't want to give his name. It was bad enough they had to know hers.

"Are you related to the patient?" She was giving him a shrewd look that changed into one of near-recognition. She obviously knew she'd seen him before, but couldn't place the circumstances.

"Kind of," Jim answered vaguely. "Let me call my friends. They can swing by the house and pick up her card, too. I'll be right back..."

"But..."

He quickly left her and looked for a pay phone. He saw they were getting ready to take Afsaneh somewhere and hurried. He picked up the receiver, then stared at the phone in dismay.

Deposit fifty cents!

He didn't have a red cent on him. Of all the things to forget! He started to slam the receiver down and restrained himself just in time and gently put it in place. Turning, he was unnerved to realize the black attendant had followed him.

She smiled and held out two quarters.

"Since you were nice enough to not break it," she said sweetly. "... Mr. Morris."

"Thank you," Jim said, sighing in relief. He started to turn back to the phone, then her last words sank in. "Ah, I'm sorry. I think you've got me mistaken..."

"I've seen enough of your movies, and wouldn't be mistaken." She gave him a smile. "Even with that great scar disguise. I heard you were missing or dead, or something like that."

"Ah, well, you know how the tabloids are..." Jim was chagrined. He was an actor, damn it. And he was drawing an absolute blank on what to say.

"I'll be waiting to complete this form. Please don't go anywhere until we do." She gave him a calculating look, then turned and strode back to the nurse station. He stared after her for a moment, then made his call.

"Janice? This is..." She recognized his voice and began chattering. He cut her off. "Janice, not now. Please listen. I'm at the med center with Afsaneh. She's been hurt pretty bad." He went on to tell her what was going on.

"You two come on down here, okay? I'll wait as long as I can, but I've got to get out of sight." She started in again. "Yes, I know what's going on with Vicki. You should be back in contact again shortly. But in the..."

She was at it again, and he stood listening for a few moments, then cut her off. "Janice, will you please be quiet and get moving? Thank you."

He finally got her off the phone, but didn't hang up. Instead, he pivoted with the phone still at his ear, to see the attendant watching him. She gave him another sweet smile, then turned to answer a question.

He quickly hung up and went through the doors they'd taken Afsaneh through.

Several frantic minutes later, he found they already had her in an operating room, and were prepping her. He saw the empty gurney and casually went to it and compressed the antigrav sled down to it's smallest size, about two feet square and maybe an inch thick.

He turned to leave, and saw that a nurse was shaving part of Afsaneh's head. Her long dark tresses fell to the floor, and Jim felt tears well up in his eyes. The once vibrant, perpetually excited, beautiful young girl looked so tiny now. And she loved that hair so much.

But hair could grow back, and broken bones could mend. As long as she got the chance!

"Mr. Morris?" He about jumped through the ceiling again as the black attendant startled him yet again. "Mr. Morris?"

"Yes?" Jim conceded he couldn't fool her. He was astounded that she found him so quickly until he realized that she probably just checked on where Afsaneh had been taken, figuring she would find him nearby. He looked at her name tag. "Yes, Dawn?"

"You're not supposed to be here," she pointed out, then relented. "Just try to stay inconspicuous, okay? I checked for her records, and you were right. I've got most of what I need, but I thought you should know something."

Jim gave her a guarded look. "Oh?"

Janet nodded. "There was a flag on her file. Probably on yours, too."

Jim got alarmed. "You mean you can't treat her here?"

"No, no. Nothing like that. Her insurance is fine, and you and her father have given enough donations over the years, you could probably get anything you want around here."

"Then what?" Jim knew the answer the moment he asked, and she saw that and nodded.

"It sent a signal out, probably to the FBI, since you're both missing persons. There'll be someone here in no time. They'd be here now if it wasn't so early in the morning."

Jim made up his mind. "Okay, two women will be here within the hour. Yvette Stephanian and Janice Wooley. They'll act as her guardians for the moment. Yvette's her godmother."

"That's good," Dawn nodded. "Where will you be?"

"Better you don't know." Jim gave her a crooked grin. "Then you don't have to lie." He looked at her appraisingly. "Why are you helping me?"

Dawn just grinned. "Maybe I like your movies. Or maybe I'm just bored, and hope I get some free movie passes out of this. Or an autographed picture, or something."

"Or all the above," Jim said, relieved. He saw Yvette look through the small window of the door. She saw him and pushed through, Janice close behind.

Then Jim saw three or four men in dark suits behind them, half looking around, half following the two women. They hadn't seen him yet.

"Uh, oh," said Dawn, looking the same place he was.

"Is there a way to the roof?" Jim looked around. He saw an elevator and went and pushed the up button.

"If you go up there, it will set off alarms,' Dawn warned. "Unless you use the small access door in the northwest corner of this tower." She grinned. "That's where the smokers go for their drug fix."

"Thank you, and good bye." Jim gave her a warm smile. "Help my friends." He gave one last glance towards the O.R. they had taken Afsaneh to. "And my daughter."

"Your..." Dawn looked startled, then her eyes went over his shoulder. "You better go, now!"

The elevator chimed, and Jim quickly stepped inside and pushed the top floor, resisting the urge to look behind him. He heard Dawn call to Yvette, cutting her off from him for a moment.

Good girl, keep them out of it, if possible.

The doors began to close, and he heard an unfamiliar male voice. "Isn't that Morris? Hey, hey!"

Then the door shut and the elevator began to climb. Jim leaned against the wall and closed his eyes. It didn't change the vision of the tiny little figure under the sheets downstairs, lying so still, so pitiful with her long, luxurious ebony locks shorn.

But not alone. Never that, he vowed. Then he set about calling Claw to the roof.

He made his way to the northwest corner, and sure enough there was a metal door that said no admittance, and beyond that, a narrow stairs to the roof. He hurried up the steps.

When the FBI agents made it to the roof, less than two minutes later, they were met with a swirling wind, as if a large volume of air had just been displaced.

But they found no trace of the man they'd chased up there.

They would report later that it was as if he'd just flown away.

Glowing Mist

Siph Carni swore to herself. She checked things twice, to be sure. Then she turned to her mate.

"I've got a recent entry into the atmosphere. I make it out to be a shuttle."

"From the...?" She didn't give him a chance to finish.

"No, I already checked. No change with P'Tassum. It must have been somewhere else when we killed the ship."

"Where's it going?"

"Beyond somewhere in North America, I can't say, as yet. Whoever the pilot was, they went down close to ground very quickly. I'm pretty sure it's gone to roost, at the moment."

"Any chance it might be from another ship?" Jo Coran sounded worried. "What about a response to the probe they sent out."

Siph Carni shook her head. "Not enough time for them to get here, yet. And anyone else wouldn't be expecting us, so we should be able to pick them up when they enter the system."

"This is a long shot, but as our illustrious captain pointed out, we are here searching for Ty Musa," Du Brimar drawled. He was still sulking about Cromar Try's decision to leave soon. "Is it an Egelv shuttle?"

Siph Carni felt all eyes gravitate to her, and reviewed the data once more, just to be sure.

"No," she finally said. "I'm fairly sure it's not Egelv. But I can't seem to pin it down as either Ananab or Tryr. It has elements of both signatures." She shrugged and looked at Cromar Try in resignation. "Until I see it, or catch it in flight, I can't say, definitively."

"Keep a watch for it, then." Cromar Try said. "If it's from the P'Tassum, it's a loose end we need to snip. And keep an eye on that ship. I don't trust these Humans."

Du Brimar summed up her thoughts as he gave Cromar Try a sardonic look.

"What could they do?"

San Francisco, California

"You've been trying to reach me." Groundhog waited for the voice at the other end of the call to wind down.

"Now, Mr. Costa, let's get down to business. I think you should check into the Ann Arbor area closer. My resources tell me there have been recent Jim Morris sightings...oh, you knew that, didn't you?"

He'd found out about the hospital the same time the FBI did, and he knew Costa's reaction had been swift, though not swift enough. But he wanted to make sure the senior agent knew he was as aware of events as the FBI were.

"No, I don't know where he is, at the moment. But I do have inside sources to the survivors of the Jade Viking."

Costa's tone grew menacing, but Groundhog wasn't having any of it. "Don't threaten me. You can't carry it out, so save your breath. No, I won't tell whom I have close to who. What I will tell you is that Sukuru is up to something. They've had men swarming all over the east coast and Michigan."

Wind blew into his face, and he turned away to shelter the phone. Costa must have heard the sound, though, because he asked where Groundhog was.

His mind raced. He didn't want Costa to know the action appeared to be headed towards the bay area. Keeping all attention out east was the best idea.

"They don't call it the windy city for nothing," he said lightly, hoping he was convincing. "Oh, by the way. I understand the Riahi girl is going to be okay. Have you found out what happened to her."

Costa cursed, and Groundhog let him go on for a moment. He fully commiserated with the agent.

"I don't know, Costa," Groundhog said, his voice deadpan. "Maybe you should be checking into alien abductions."

The long pause at the other end of the line meant confirmation to him. Costa was actually considering the possibility. Groundhog hoped the man didn't try and convince his superiors of that theory. He rather enjoyed working with and baiting the man.

Karl Costa glared at his phone long after he'd hung up. If there was anything he would bet his life on, at this moment, it was that the one place in the entire universe Groundhog wasn't, was Chicago.

In fact, knowing how devious the man was, he was probably right here in San Francisco. Or was that what he was supposed to assume?

My head hurts, he decided. And after my four o'clock, it's going to hurt more. Everything seemed to be happening at once.

Item one, another member of the missing passenger list had turned up. In Ann Arbor, of all places! Broken arm, broken leg, serious head injuries requiring immediate care.

I wonder if she'd be there now if it was just two broken limbs, he theorized cynically.

Item two, it appears Jim Morris, another missing person, is the man that brings her to the emergency room. Then he disappears, off the roof of the hospital itself.

Item three, within hours of her arrival, legally licensed armed men show up and post themselves around the young girl's hospital room, refusing to be moved. They have a court order filed by that Stephanian woman. The men are employed by a firm that traces back to Ron Hoffman, a Texas businessman. And who was also, of course, a passenger on that ill-fated cruise.

Item four, that irritating teacher, Howard Prause has disappeared again, sans cruise ship. Hasn't been seen for days.

Item five, no matter how hard my men search, they can't find a single trace of Kimberly Martin or Kiri Oshiba. They left New York in her BMW, which was found at Jim Morris' house in Ann Arbor a few days later, along with most of their luggage. No trace of the two women, but perhaps of some sort of struggle or robbery. A few pieces of furniture overturned, several appliances missing, but all the vehicles accounted for.

Item, six, was it? A red Viper registered to Jim Morris is found in a Hotel parking lot in Ann Arbor. But it's got Nevada plates, and was evidently being driven by two Japanese men, tentatively identified as Sasama Sakakibara and Iori Kojiro. They used a credit card registered to Sakakibara to pay for the room in the hotel, which in turn, gets trashed. Even the windows are broken. Firm evidence of gunfire, a shotgun. And lots of blood, and not just the same types as the two missing men.

Had Jim Morris and Afsaneh Riahi been with them secretly? Is that how the young girl got hurt?

Item seven, someone assaults and almost kills Eric Miles. Through a fluke bit of luck, a bystander interrupts the attack and saves Miles. He now travels with a bodyguard everywhere he goes. This took place in Miami, Florida.

Miami, San Diego, New York, Ann Arbor, San Francisco, Texas.

They're freakin' everywhere, he thought glumly.

A light appeared on his desk, and he groaned.

Item eight. His immediate supervisor, and _his_ immediate supervisor, the Director himself, were here to discuss his case.

Item number nine. Maybe he should start checking the classifieds for job listings.

◆ ◆ ◆ ◆ ◆

CHAPTER TWENTY-FOUR

Station Osaka

Commodore Tka started as his brother nudged him. Tzi tapped his holstered disruptor pointedly. Tka looked down at his own holster and was shocked to see he'd been on Station Osaka for over half a short cycle. His chronometer showed it to be past night midpoint!

No wonder he was so tired. He tried unsuccessfully to cover a yawn. Nearby, a Hoag automatically flinched. He was more successful at hiding his grin. At least some things endured.

That Humans would mean change, he had absolutely no doubt about it. How it would affect he and his own still remained to be seen.

They even had him thinking of this station as Osaka now, instead of the Ananab name, Chaq. Well, why not? By his own standards and those of the other races that made up the collective galactic community, they'd already demonstrated their domination over the Ananab.

Personally, he had no problem with that. And he doubted any other Tryr, with the obvious exception of Clan Tcha, would feel any different if they got a chance to meet these Humans.

But therein lies the problem, he thought dourly. If the Humans swore fealty to the Hshtahni, something would be worked out. The Ananab would be tossed some partially gnawed bone, and told to behave. Clan Tcha would be jumped on by the rest of the clans and held under control. The Srotag, even with their sworn race vendetta, would be dissuaded from any action.

The Reigna... How would the Hshtahni control a race they wouldn't even admit existed, except in myth.

Until this last day, Tka himself hadn't really believed the stories.

Oh sure, everyone had seen some unlikely assassinations in their day, unclaimed murders, punitive strikes. But he knew of no one who had actually seen a Reigna, much less killed one.

Or nine, he thought, fighting the shiver that made his fur stand out.

And the Humans had done just that. He knew it to be true because, after much deliberation between himself and his two brothers, he'd gone to personally view the bodies.

He'd expected to be disappointed. After all, what enemy, no matter how worthy an opponent, ever looked as menacing in death as his actions had warranted.

But these Reigna did. Even in death, their features were distorted by a loathsome hatred-filled snarl. Without exception, every face had its lips drawn back into a teeth-filled grimace.

Tka noticed six of the nine had wounds obviously induced by the projectile weapons the Humans carried. The other three had no marks whatsoever, except for the burns caused by their sheathing system shorting out. All nine had some variation of those.

Tzi and Tql, the only other Tryr he would allow to verify the Reigna, had stood and stared at those three, trying to decide what had killed them. One's neck was broken, and another seemed to have a caved in chest, but there was no obvious sign of what caused the trauma.

"The Jim Morris," Tzi said suddenly. "Did these three fight the Jim Morris?" Tka stared at his brother in admiration. Of course, that had to be it! But three? Surely not all at once. But that thought was contradicted by Lang's next words.

"Yes, these three went after Jim."

"All at once?" Tka fought down the excitement. "How? When he fought them, were they were still in sheathed mode? How could he have..."

"Jim Morris has skills beyond the human norm." This was the small woman, Suyo, that spoke now. "There is also a belief that if one is willing to be receptive, in time, with discipline, one can acquire an awareness that can not be explained simply with the senses we now agree exist."

Tka and Tzi looked at each other, nonplussed. It sounded like magic! But one glance at the other Humans present confirmed her statement to be an opinion commonly held by many.

"And this Jim Morris?" Tka spoke slowly, crouching to look at one of the dead Reigna more closely. "He has these heightened senses?"

"He is the most attuned Westerner I've ever seen," Suyo said. "For someone so young, he has training, discipline, and abilities I've never seen matched before."

"Jim Morris, disciplined?" Governor Lang, no, Jason, looked at her in astonishment. "You ever watch him at a party?"

"That is something different altogether," Suyo argued. "Personally, I believe his social skills to be some of his most effective acting. When he drinks, he plays a role."

"Acting?" Tka asked, a little confused. "Drinks?"

That opened a line of conversation that had gone on for hours after they returned to the reception room. That one of their most prized warriors was an...entertainer by trade. Not even in the military!

And this alcohol...well, it seemed insane to both Tka and Tzi. Although he had heard stories about some of the more decadent races closer to the galactic core...

Tka decided he had as much data about Humans as he could assimilate for the present. He glanced over at Jason, who looked as tired as he felt. Their eyes met.

"I think it is time we left," Tka said, not surprised that he felt regret. Going back to report to Lord Qatahkh was almost guaranteed to be an unpleasant experience. The Hshtahni would not let this matter go, and the Humans weren't going to submit.

Perhaps by the time he got back to base, he would have decided what to say about the Reigna, if anything. That he, and by extension, his officers and crew were now in very real danger was beyond doubt.

It was unlikely that the Reigna would allow proof of their existence to be presented for all to see.

Sighing, he climbed to his feet, feeling aching muscles protest. Jason joined him, giving a slight groan of his own as he held his back. They both smiled at each other.

I could call this Human friend, Tka thought. But I may have to kill him instead. The thought depressed him.

"You have a difficult road ahead of you," Jason said, sympathy in his voice.

"You have no idea," Tka retorted.

"Oh, I don't know about that," the Human said. "I doubt you're going to get much approval for being a reasonable person."

Tka snorted. These Humans had such amusing ways of saying things. They could make such clever understatements. He signaled to his nephew, and Tne began gathering the crew. He noticed his nephew had spent a lot of time talking with the small yellow Human that carried the claw on his back.

Sword, he thought. They call it a sword. He'd heard of such things, but never seen such an effective-looking one.

And his cousin Tql seemed to get on well with McGregor. He'd watched them exchange pictures of their respective get, and had gotten a look at them himself. Human babies looked completely helpless.

Tql had expressed sympathy over the smallness of the litter, and nearby Tryr had cringed at his lack of tack. But McGregor had just nodded, and said two wasn't the standard size of Human litters, but that his wife had seemed satisfied it was enough.

Tka shook his head at the thought. His sister, Tma, had a smallish litter of two and had to be restrained from hurting herself in grief and shame.

He looked up in surprise. He was at the hatch to the Trhktah already. He turned to Jason.

"I wish we had more time," he said truthfully. "I've enjoyed your company."

"As have I, Sir." Jason held out his hand, and Tka took it gingerly. They shook, but didn't release their grips immediately. "Did you get everything you needed on tape?"

Tka winced. Of course his cousin and one of the other guards had been wired for visual recording to supplement the usual audio record kept via tranceivers. But he hadn't realized the Humans had figured that out.

"Ah, yes, I think we have all we need," he said truthfully. "In fact, probably more than we need, or should have." He thought of the line of nine grey bodies stretched out on the deck deep within the station.

"If you'd like, we could provide you with a copy of the video presentation we gave you when we first met." Tka looked at Jason in mild astonishment, although nothing these Humans did should surprise him anymore.

He shook his head. "No, I think my cousin got a pretty good copy." He grinned at Jason, or Governor Lang, as he tried to think of him as. "You Humans have the most annoying habit of being helpful and unyielding, all at the same time."

Lang laughed and nodded his agreement.

"Good luck with your superiors," he said, looking like he meant it.

362

"May we not meet at claw point," Tka grew more formal. "May your get be strong and fruitful."

Lang's face seemed a little longer, but he forced one last smile as they parted hands.

"Good winds and safe harbors."

A short time later, the Trhktah backed out of the berth and gained speed towards the remainder of the fleet. His brother, Tki, came on screen.

"Brother, you endanger yourself and your clan." Tki looked over at Tzi, as if for support. Tzi just shrugged, letting Tka deal with it. "The Hshtahni aren't going to like your failure."

"Did I fail?" Tka leaned back pensively. "I'm not so certain. These decisions need more voices in the making than we have here, and I did pick up a wealth of information. It could prove very useful."

"It could also get us killed some lonely night," Tzi muttered, and Tki looked at them both suspiciously.

Tka sighed. He knew how his brothers felt, both of them. But the topic of the Reigna would have to wait until the privacy of his chambers when they rendezvoused.

But would it be private?

Did his ship have an infestation of small grey shadows, even now?

He looked around the bridge, and saw that Tzi understood exactly what he was thinking. Damn these Humans, anyway. Because of them, he would take fear to his grave. The fear of eyes looking over his shoulder, viewing him in his sleep. The fear of never really knowing if he was alone in an empty room.

"I thought they'd never leave," Suyo said. Lang smiled to show he appreciated the humor, but his eyes never left the screen in the reception room that showed the departing ship, discreetly followed at a distance by the Jade Samurai, Captain Asaya back in the command chair.

Had he made a difference? Made a friend or an ally?

Only time would tell.

Seattle, Washington

Karl Costa put his hand on the doorknob and paused. This meeting could very well be the end of his career. At least the significant, worth-while portion of it. He might be desk bound and counting pencils until the day he retired.

He sighed and pushed the door open. The conference room had a long oval table with six chairs. Five of those chairs were clustered around the far end, with one at the head, and two on either side. All five were occupied. The sixth chair was at the foot of the table, isolated and of course, empty. He ran his eyes over the crowd at the far end of the table as he sat down.

Closest to him on his left was his regional director, Daniel Blake. He was in his mid-fifties, ruthless and very ambitious. He made no secret of who he thought the next Director should be. But it would never happen. Blake was short, very over-weight with a florid face that spelled impending health problems.

And he drank like a fish.

Next to him was the Director's aide. Quite frankly, Shelly Trent scared the hell out of him. She was relatively young, in her early thirties, and had latched onto the Director as a gofer before his star had taken off.

She was irritating, cheerless, talked way too aggressively, but rarely said anything of consequence that could be used against her. Tall, dark long hair without a hint of age, a little fleshy, she was attractive enough to be pleasant on the eyes, but not enough to make anybody do something stupid.

Shelly had the best memory Costa had ever come across. As the Director's personal aide, she could filter his data, or focus his attention. She wields a lot power, he thought, giving her a cautious smile, which she ignored.

Uh oh.

The Director was, of course, the Director. Nothing worth adding to that. His power and influence was enormous, and he had no scruples about using either.

Sitting next to the Director was a member of the National Security Agency. He didn't have a title Costa knew about, but he always seemed to be around whenever foreign powers were mucking about in the States.

The fifth person was an Air Force Colonel, and Costa had no idea who he was.

He became uncomfortably aware that the silence he'd been greeted with was growing, making him wish he'd brought some papers or something for his hands to play with.

He'd heard the Director once make a sarcastic remark about people who relied on stacks of notes, instead of their memory. Ever since, Costa had tried to never take any files to any meeting the man might be at.

He decided to take the bull by the horns and met the Director's eyes.

"You sent for me, sir?"

"Hell no," the man snapped. "I'm the one who had to fly clear across the country. That makes you the one who sent for me. Now report."

Costa didn't try to be coy. "Yes sir. My report, which you seem to have anticipated by hours, is on its way to Mr. Blake's office now, via courier."

"Why didn't you just fax, or send it through the computer?" Blake growled, giving him a dirty look. He probably thought Costa was trying to circumvent him.

"I didn't want it to be handled or read by the wrong people, due to its delicate nature." Costa took a deep breath, knowing it was coming, and Shelly didn't disappoint him.

"What delicate nature?" She leaned forward as if to offer encouragement. "Is there some sort of damaging material in it?"

"Only to my career," he muttered, and got a sharp look from the Director. "Sorry sir. It's just that the facts don't seem to add up at first. Then, when they lean towards an explanation, it's so absurd it shouldn't even be considered." He paused, then leaned forward in resignation.

"At this point, after having reviewed the statements of the survivors, I find that most fall into two categories. First, total loss of memory for the entire period of time. Nothing seems to break their consistency."

He glanced around the table and saw five stony, blank expressions. They weren't giving away a thing. Okay, he thought, here's the first nail in the coffin of my career.

"The second group all have a wild story about the entire ship being lifted off the planet's surface by aliens from outer space. There are five distinctly different types of aliens described. The problem is, there aren't some people saying there were big crawfish, others saying giant cats and a third talking about four-armed albinos."

"Why is that a problem?" It was the first time the NSA guy had spoken and it startled Costa. "Are their stories consistent?"

"They're consistent enough that every single person that says they were abducted is describing all five races, and giving them nearly identical traits and duties."

"Do they have any commonalities in their lives previous to the incident?" That was his immediate superior, trying to sound thorough. It didn't fool anyone.

"It's a cruise ship. There are people from all walks of life, and from all over the world." Costa gave them a crooked grin. "But, they all agree on some things. Similar aliens, basically the same sequence of events, that actor Jim Morris and Kimberly Martin got married a few weeks before the ship returned to Earth, which people died, none of which have shown up, by the way." He paused.

"One of the first things Kimberly Martin did when she got back was go to Morris' apartment here in San Francisco. She had keys, is traveling with an actress from Morris' cast, Kiri Oshiba who is a longtime friend of Morris and his housemate, Hakim Riahi. Riahi, by the way, is one of the men reported dead by literally every single person claiming abduction."

"Let me make sure I understand you, Karl." His boss stared at him. "You're saying you believe the second story, the alien abduction one."

"I'm saying that these stories are consistent, and that circumstances seem to support the concept." Costa closed his eyes and rubbed them. Opening them, he ignored everyone except the Director. "Until something new breaks, based on the facts, the most logical assumption is that the Jade Viking really was hijacked by aliens. If so, we have to wonder what the Martin woman and some of the others are up to."

"What do you mean?" It was the NSA man again.

"I mean that almost everyone who stuck to the memory loss story seems to be establishing connections in their businesses, personal lives, everything." No one was laughing, he saw with amazement. Could it be they actually believed him? "We found two separate groups of survivors. The first, without exception, remember nothing. The second group consists, almost without exception, of those that remember aliens, and the rest. A small portion of the second group claim amnesia, but I think it's just for privacy's sake, a desire to sink into the woodwork.. The first group appears to be working in collusion, with a few obvious leaders controlling the actions."

"A conspiracy?" Shelly Trent raised an eyebrow.

Costa shrugged. "Or the ultimate in networking."

She looked irritated, but let it pass. "With what agenda?"

"I haven't a clue," Costa admitted. "But I've tried to bring Martin and Oshiba in for more questioning, and they seem to have..." He smiled apologetically. "...dropped off the face of the Earth." Blake snickered, and even the Director allowed himself a slight twisting of the lip as the others either smiled or nodded their heads in appreciation.

Except for Trent. "Have you considered bringing everyone back in?" She examined her fingertips carefully. "Maybe a littler harder line of questioning than the first time..."

"We'll be dealing with their lawyers," Costa warned. "I can hear the news now. 'FBI harasses ocean liner victims. Claims UFOs kidnapped all. Class action suit at eleven.'"

This time no one laughed or grinned. It was a scene all too easy to imagine. Costa suddenly sat back and stared around the table.

"You all expected this from me. You think there's a chance it's true, as well." His attention narrowed to the Air Force Colonel who so far, had contributed nothing to the meeting. "You have something I don't know about."

"What's the matter, Karl." Blake laughed, not seeing the measuring gaze he was receiving from the Director. "You come in here expecting to get canned?"

"Either that or committed," Costa admitted, not taking his eyes off the colonel. "What have you got?"

The colonel and the NSA man exchanged glances, then looked at the Director. He nodded once, and the colonel set his briefcase on the table in front of him. Opening it, he pulled a thin folder out and handed it to Costa.

Opening it, Costa found a stack of eight by ten photos. They were all shots of outer space, undoubtably taken by one of the orbiting telescopes. In the first, one star shone slightly brighter than the rest. It increased, first in brightness, then in size in each progressing print until the final picture, which it filled almost completely. Costa held it up and stared.

A ship?

It didn't resemble anything Nasa or anyone else had. Or anything like in the movies either, for that matter. But it had to be a ship, although what it looked like was a shoe box with four tubes of tennis balls attached to it, two on each side.

Or was that the top and bottom. In space, it didn't really matter, Costa decided.

"Are those engine nacelles?" he asked, trying to hold his excitement under control. It was making him feel lightheaded.

"We think so," said the Air Force Colonel. If he was trying to contain his enthusiasm, it wasn't apparent. "We don't think it's designed to enter the atmosphere."

"It looks dead," Costa said, frowning as he flipped back through the earlier prints. "It appears to be in the same position in each one of these shots. What was the time duration?"

"A few minutes, but it hasn't shown any sign of life since we sighted it. One second there was nothing, the next second it was just hanging there." The colonel glanced around the table. "We've restricted use of the satellite telescopes for the moment. But there's nothing to keep someone with a good eye on the ground from spotting it if they happen to focus on that part of space."

"Good eye?" Blake asked, looking blank. The others around the table exchanged amused looks and Costa couldn't resist being the one to say it.

"He means telescope. Anyone with a reasonably good telescope can see it." Blake shot him an angry look, and he kept his face impassive.

"For all we know, that ship might look just the way it's supposed to," Costa pointed out. "What about these people? My men tell me that the man that brought the Riahi girl to the hospital supposedly looked like Jim Morris. We have no idea what's..."

A knock on the door interrupted him. His secretary looked in apologetically and held up a cellular phone. He stared at her, exasperated. "It's Michigan," she said, glancing around the room at the disapproving faces. "It sounds important. Orinsky says they've got another Morris sighting, and two dead bodies."

Costa took the phone. He turned to look at his boss who, in turn, looked at the Director. The man stared at the phone, as if angry at the physical bearer of the news. His lips tightened as his look transferred to Costa.

"The leaders. Just the leaders. For the moment, leave everyone else alone."

"Got it." Costa put the phone to his ears. He wasn't convinced this was the best decision, but least it gave him something to do.

But as he talked to his man in Ann Arbor, he couldn't keep his eyes from straying back to the pile of photos on the table.

What if they didn't want to be brought in again?

Ann Arbor, Michigan

Jim felt pressure slough off him as he watched the city scroll beneath him. He was still worried about Afsaneh, but at least she was in the best possible hands now. As the tension faded away, exhaustion took its place.

"Home, James," he muttered. He was relieved when the ship didn't question him. He didn't feel up to trying to explain cute colloquialisms. He rubbed his scar and winced. Parts of it were still a little tender.

He recognized his neighborhood and watched as his house came into view. He couldn't help but grin as he saw it from the air for the first time.

Talk about decadent. The sprawling house and grounds didn't seem so opulent when you were down there, but from up here you could see how big the house and pool really were. As well as the clubhouse, the racquet and tennis courts, the softball field, and the open field that had served for everything from soccer to tackle football to target shooting at one point or another.

Jim frowned as he saw deep indentions in the grass of the softball field. Why the heck hadn't they used the practice field instead? He would have to say something to Kabu about that. It was probably the young actor's way of showing the relative importance between soccer and softball. "Claw, bring us down behind the tennis court, please."

"Yes, Jim Morris."

Jim looked for signs of life in the house below, but couldn't see any. Not that there would be much to see, he admitted to himself wryly. I can't see either Kimberly or Kiri swimming in the pool this time of year. We'll probably have our first snow within the next few weeks.

"Anybody home?" He didn't realize he'd spoken out loud until the computer answered him.

"There are no occupants within the house or grounds at the moment." The shuttle lightly set down and Jim stood and stretched wearily. He told the shuttle to stay in stealth mode. It would only be a matter of time before the FBI, if that's who he'd crossed paths with at the hospital, showed up looking for him.

Whistling, he hurried down the ramp and walked around to the back of the clubhouse. He reached behind a drain and pulled a little metal pillbox loose. It had a magnet on the back to hold it in place, and inside was a key to the house.

Having a teenager made a drop key absolutely mandatory, he thought, smiling as he remembered Hakim and himself lecturing Afsaneh about losing her keys, or leaving them in her room.

Jim let himself in the front door, disappointed. He'd been imagining this scene for days. But his version had Kimberly greeting him at the door, dressed in little more than a smile.

Heck, with the awkward parting we had, I'd settle for her sitting over by the fireplace, waiting for my apology. Jim started to sigh again and deliberately stopped himself.

You're getting far too self-indulgent and self-pitying, Jim Morris. Time for you to get your...

He stopped that line of thought as he caught a slight whiff of something burning. Or something burnt, he thought as he stepped to the center of the room and closed his eyes. Several deep breaths later he was inspecting the wall behind the entertainment center.

Directly behind one speaker he saw a little box with signs of scorching on the wall around it. He pulled it loose, then mentally slapped his head. Sure glad it wasn't booby-trapped, you idiot, he thought grimly as he peered at what appeared to be a highly sophisticated microphone transmitter.

He ground his teeth together at the idea of the FBI bugging his house. As he made his way through the wing to his quarters, he found two more, both burnt like the first.

I wonder what fried 'em, he thought as he tossed them on his desk and entered his bedroom. Three steps inside he stopped in consternation. He stood perfectly still as he decided what had made his mental alarms go off.

First, the covers to his bed were pulled to the floor, and there was women's clothing scattered all around. In itself, and knowing Kiri, not that alarming.

Second, the stain on the floor next to the bed looked suspiciously like blood.

There's been a fight in here, he concluded. There were just enough things knocked over that he knew it wasn't just sloppy housekeeping.

He saw the blank spot on the wall and stared in confusion. How could that picture get knocked over? He picked it up and noticed it wasn't damaged. He turned it around and looked at Nasria's face.

Turned it around? How the hell could it get knocked down and flip completely around? He looked at the picture, then looked over at the bed in sudden understanding.

He'd always felt a strength in her piercing gaze. Those huge eyes would follow him around the room and provide comfort few visitors to his bed could ever match.

Until Kimberly. He pictured her laying in bed with the lights out, knowing Nasri watched in the dark. He gently set the picture down against the wall, facing out. Her strength would always inspire him, but it would have to be from another spot in the house, he decided as he crouched there in front of it.

Jim stared at Nasri, and laughed out loud as he imagined her mouth twitching slightly, as if hiding her amusement. It didn't seem the least bit strange to be talking to her through the picture, even after all these years.

"I love her, Nasri. She's made me care about things that haven't mattered in years. You'd like her..." He grinned. "Okay, you wouldn't like her at all. But she's good for me, and I think she'll be good for Afsy, too." His eyes misted as he remembered the small form on the operating table across town.

"Our little girl's been hurt. But she'll be okay." He smiled. "You can laugh, but I always knew I was her father..." Jim felt a stab of guilt as he remembered Hakim. "He died trying to save others, Nasri. You know him, never recognizing his limits."

Jim wiped a hand across his eyes, but they were dry. Were her brows furled ever so slightly? "You know as well as I do, he was always a better lover than warrior." His voice grew cold and distant, his forehead stiff from tension. "Unlike me. I don't know where this path is taking me, but I can't see another way. If I have to be mankind's god of war, then so be it."

He straightened and looked around the room. "My soul's been lost for years anyway. Kimberly and Afsaneh have what little is left of it. If she's been hurt in any way..." His voice broke off and he contemplated what to do next.

First things first, he decided. He picked up the phonebook to see what area code Texas was. Several calls, and twenty minutes later, he had Ron Hoffman on the phone.

"Jim? Is that you?" The voice sounded relieved. "I've been on the horn with Janice, and they wondered if you got away clear. What's up with Vicki, anyway? We've been cut off for a couple of days now."

"That'll have to wait, Ron." Jim quickly told him about the blood on the carpet and the house being bugged. "How far along is your security project?"

Jim didn't want to be too specific on the phone. It was probably bugged, too. One of Hoffman's plans had been to start a bodyguard/security company. He was relieved to hear that it was already operational on a limited basis.

"I just told Janice we'd be in the air within the hour. I'll add my electronic wizard to the crew. We should be setting down in Michigan in a couple hours."

"That's fine." Jim sagged in relief. At least Afsaneh would have good people watching over her. "I don't know if I'll be here or not. I think I can expect a visit from our friends in the bureau soon."

"Keep in touch," Ron spoke lightly, but Jim could hear the tension in his voice.

"Count on it," Jim said, and hung up. He scrapped some of the dried blood off the carpet, and pulled one stained pillowcase off the pillow and walked out to Claw.

"Can you do blood tests to see if this is either Kimberly or Kiri's blood?"

"I have records of their blood type and DNA. It may take several minutes, as I am not as well equipped for this as Jade Wolverine."

"See what you can find out," Jim said, and returned to the house. A quick walk-through found nothing else out of place except in Afsaneh's room. A blank spot on several shelves gave him pause for a few moments. Then he decided she was missing her DVD player and some movies. He didn't know which ones, but it didn't really matter. It could be that Kabu or somebody else had borrowed them.

It wasn't important.

He also discovered that the rest of the house was bugged, and that all the devices were trashed like the ones he'd already found.

What to do first, he wondered. The phone rang, causing him to raise an eyebrow. What had Hoffman forgot to find out?

"Hello?" he answered in a neutral voice.

"You don't know me," said a male voice softly. "In case you haven't already figured it out, you need to be careful on this line. It's bugged."

"By you?" Jim asked bluntly. Who was this guy?

"That doesn't matter." The voice remained smooth. "What does matter is that your wife and friend have been abducted."

"By who?" Jim felt his face tighten.

"They're being taken across country to San Francisco, where they will be put on a ship to Japan." The voice ignored his questions as if following a set script. "They will probably arrive at the docks this evening. A ship leaves at midnight. I believe they will be on it."

"Who are you?" Jim realized how stupid the question was even as he asked. "Why are you helping me?"

"Am I helping you, or them?" Jim blushed as he saw how self-centered he sounded. The voice stayed irritatingly even. "Remember, the enemy of my enemy..."

"...is my friend," Jim finished the quote. "Do you know why they've been kidnapped?"

"For the secrets of the universe, I would imagine," the voice answered dryly. "You can also expect the FBI to try and take most of your people into custody within the next few days."

"How do you know this?"

The line went dead.

Jim went to the gun cabinet and unlocked it with the hidden key hanging on the back. He surveyed the variety of rifles and shotguns that hung inside. Seeing what he was looking for, he pulled out a pump shotgun.

It had been his father's, and it was a beauty. Actually, every single gun in the house had belonged to either his father or McCoy. Sergeant Henry McCoy had been his childhood tutor in everything from math to shooting to martial arts. Especially martial arts. His Special Forces background had lent a different flavor to his teaching, both in subjects and in methods.

Jim held the shotgun and remembered hunting with the two men, from the time he was big enough to hold a rifle or shoot a bow.

He quit hunting for sport when he was eleven. He'd hit a four point buck with a rifle at four hundred yards, up in Canada. When they got to it, it lay on the ground, breathing heavily. It was dying, but far from dead.

McCoy hadn't hesitated. He'd pulled out his service revolver he always carried and handed it to Jim. His father had begun to speak, but stopped himself.

Jim had stared at the deer, horrified. It looked back at him with huge black eyes that were wide with fear. He tried to hand the pistol back to McCoy, but the man backed away, raising one hand.

"Finish what you started, Jimmy. Don't make him suffer."

Jimmy had reluctantly turned back to the injured animal and taken a step towards it. It quit struggling and lay there, as if waiting for him. He would carry the memory of those soft, dark eyes to his grave.

One shot and it was over. He handed the revolver back to McCoy, then ejected the remaining shells in his Remington. He put them in his pocket, and answered the questioning looks from the two men.

"I'll never hunt something that can't fight back again. And I'll never hunt simply for sport."

And he never had. He had no problem with the concept of hunting, and he loved meat, but he refused to participate in that form of 'entertainment' again.

He automatically checked to see the shotgun was unloaded, then pulled out the heavy metal case from the bottom of the cabinet. He emptied all the ammunition for the gun into another carrying case.

Jim held the shotgun up and admired it. He shook his head at what he was about to do. "Father would kill me for this," he muttered. Then he went out to the garage where he and Hakim kept all their tools.

An hour later he was finished, and gratefully went back into the house. He'd sawed the barrel off as close to the pump action as he could. Then he'd removed a good part of the stock. The result was a very deadly weapon, just under three feet long.

He attached a sling to the shotgun, and found a quiver intended for arrows that would fit it and rigged it to go over one shoulder.

Jim went back down the hall towards his bedroom. When he got to his reading room, he unlocked a drawer in his desk and pulled out a flat wooden box. He opened it gingerly and pulled out the holstered pistol.

It was the same one he'd killed the deer with. The only times he'd ever touched it since that day were to clean it, and to teach Afsaneh how to use it. Hakim had muttered under his breath until they got out in the yard and he watched Afsaneh use it for the first time.

She was a very good shot, and Hakim couldn't resist trying himself. He proved to be a quick learner and eventually became proficient with both the pistol and the rifles in the cabinet.

Jim set the pistol down and began rummaging through his drawers. When he finished, he had found four throwing knives, and several shuriken. Then he stood up and began taking things off the top shelf of one of the high bookcases.

Behind the clutter was a glass case with two swords. They had been a present from his father when he turned sixteen. Of course, by then, he was already very proficient with the Japanese style of sword fighting, but he'd never owned his own blades.

To this day, Jim didn't know where his father found the swords, or what he paid for them. He did know that they were over two hundred years old, and were considered masterpieces of workmanship.

He'd always thought they were a 'guilt' present, and out of character for his father. Both his parents had been good natured about his early interests in the martial arts, but neither had thought of it as anything more than a hobby.

His parents had been on the final leg of a two year tour in Japan, their fourth over the last fifteen years. The next station would be Germany, and Jim and Mr. Morris had flown there to look into schools and a place to live.

Jim had checked into what dojos there were in Stuttgart. He hadn't been particularly impressed by what he'd found, but was too polite to show his thoughts.

His father accompanied him to the school he finally picked out. Jim was told that the school catered to the finest students in Europe, and that he didn't appear to have enough formal training to be accepted.

It was the closest Jim ever came to losing his temper in a dojo. Mr. Morris had put his hand on his shoulder, and suggested they try elsewhere.

"Why?" Jim demanded, feeling his face go red. "This is the finest school in the country, and it's where I belong." He stood and bowed to the Master. "I would be willing to submit to an audition."

"I don't think that will be necessary. I'm sorry," he was told. His father exploded at that and started in angrily. Jim had stopped him immediately.

"No, Father. I understand. After all, it is they who have everything to lose." Jim had held his head high and stared at the Master. "I can understand their...fear of embarrassment."

The master stared back at him with no anger in his face. He finally sighed and nodded. "I understand your frustration. I would spare you the humiliation, but you will have your chance."

Jim then proceeded to defeat eight opponents in a row. The ninth was the most advanced student in the school, and he was the toughest challenge Jim had ever had. His adrenalin was pumping high, and the student was angry after watching so many of his schoolmates go down.

Both boys were going at full speed, oblivious to the potential danger to either of them. Fortunately, both the Master and Jim's father saw where the fight could lead, and stepped in and stopped it.

The Japanese boy had been so frustrated he'd grabbed two bokken, wooden practice swords, and tossed one to Jim.

"Now let's see," he'd snarled.

Jim caught the bokken and went into the proper stance. He wasn't angry. Actually, he was taking pride in the fact he'd kept his cool and not been arrogant through the entire process. But before anything could happen, the two men were between them.

John Morris had stared at his son as if he hardly knew him. Then he turned to the Master and waited. To the man's credit, he could admit when he was wrong.

"I believe you have proven yourself capable of attending this school," he began formally. Jim bowed deeply, then did several steps of Kata, coming to a halt before the man. He bowed again, laying the bokken on the floor before the master.

"I thank you for the compliment, but I don't believe this is the school for me. Thank you again for your time." He bowed once more, then turned to his father. "Let's go, Father."

Three weeks later, on his birthday, his father had given him the swords.

Jim found he was standing in the middle of the room holding the long sword. He stared at it, wondering when he'd picked it up. Then he shook himself and gathered the weapons together.

"Claw, have you analyzed the blood, yet?"

"Yes, Jim Morris." Jim held his breath. "It is the blood of Shinzo Takuan. We have his profile on record from when Afsaneh broke his nose."

"Really," Jim said, feeling his lips tighten. "Well, it looks like Kiri got a few licks in before they were taken prisoner."

He thought about checking the refrigerator. It had been hours since he'd eaten.

"There are motor vehicles slowing on the road. They appear to be headed to this address," Claw warned him.

"Damn!" Jim said as he heard cars pull into the drive. He hurried to the front door and relocked it. He then gathered the items he'd collected and left the house through the utility room behind the garage.

Jim tried to hurry without making too much noise, but he must not have completely succeeded because he heard a shout from behind him. By this time, he had rounded the racquetball court and could see to where Claw waited.

"Give me a two second visual on your open hatchway on my mark," he gasped as he broke into a run. "Now!"

He saw the ramp and the inside of the airlock appear briefly, and tried to note it's exact position. Then it blinked out again. He could hear three or four men behind him, and increased his speed.

"Stop! Stop, or we shoot!"

Then he was running up the ramp. "Close hatch," he said, trying not to shout. He heard it slam behind him as the inside of the airlock became visible. "Elevate ship one hundred feet straight up."

Moments later, he was on the bridge in his seat, watching what he assumed were FBI agents searching beneath his ship, baffled. Jim had the ship give him external ears.

"He can't have just disappeared!"

"I tell you, one minute he's running, then he's gone! Right out of midair!"

"Maybe there's a hidden bunker under this field?"

"Get equipment. Cordon the area off! Call..."

Jim frowned. If they dug holes all over his softball field, there was nowhere they could hide.

"Claw, please set a course for San Francisco Bay, avoiding all major cities, and at a speed and altitude the Egelv will be unlikely to detect. Can you do that?"

"Yes."

"Can you arrange it so we arrive just after dark, California time?"

"Yes."

That was what Jim loved about these computers. They were never wishy-washy or indecisive. A simple yes or no was their usual response.

"Have we gotten any contact with Irene, yet?"

"No."

"Any idea when we will?"

"No."

That was what he hated about these damn computers. They never volunteered any extra data. If you didn't ask the right questions, you didn't find anything out.

He stood and stretched as he walked to the bunk. On the other hand, this automatic pilot stuff sure beat the hell out of cruise control.

Jim lay on his back, staring at the bulkhead above him. As he thought about Kimberly, his face grew taut. Sukuru had kidnapped his wife. It had to be them.

It was time Sukuru learned that there were always consequences to every action. And kidnapping Kimberly and Kiri carried serious penalties.

God himself wouldn't be able to help them if anything happened to Kimberly.

Jim's mind wandered to the image of his daughter lying under the scalpel miles behind. He felt so helpless. With difficulty, he turned his thoughts away from Afsaneh, to Kimberly and her captors.

There was a situation he could do something about. He kept his mind focused on Kimberly and Kiri, tied up and helpless. And the hulking figures that loomed over them, faceless for now.

Not for long, he vowed.

CHAPTER TWENTY-FIVE

Station Osaka

Jason Lang opened his eyes and stared at the ceiling. He'd slept as much as he was going to this night. He swung his legs over the side of the bed salvaged from the original Jade Viking.

People might not realize it, but it was hard to find a comfortable bed when you were six and a half feet tall. When he had taken command of the ship eight years ago, he'd had his stateroom completely remodeled to accommodate this bed, and it had been worth it.

Lang got cleaned up and dressed. As he looked in the mirror, he pursed his lips in disapproval. It wasn't that long ago, he would have refused to leave his cabin without dress slacks, jacket, tie, and even his cap.

Now he considered slacks and any shirt with a collar acceptable. He hadn't quite made the transition in footgear yet, but it wouldn't be long. Dress shoes weren't the best either in comfort or practicality on a space station.

And he badly needed a haircut.

With one last glare into the mirror, he left and walked briskly to the bridge. There was almost no trace of the battle that had taken place just a few days ago. The Hoag had cleaned every blood stain from the deck, the seats, the walls... The only signs that remained were some scars on the bulkheads caused by gunfire.

And the strained, sad expressions on crewmen faces.

Lang nodded as he sank into his command chair. Now, what needed his attention? He probably should take a look at the time and material estimates on repairing the damage to the station, and the status of the nearly finished warship they were now able to complete with parts salvaged from the captured Ananab ship.

He started to look for Randy, and sank back in his seat, feeling the blood drain from his face. For a short, wonderful period of time, he'd forgotten the price they'd paid in that battle, and its aftermath.

"Sir, I have the construction schedule for completing the new warship, and the Hoag anticipate repairing the damaged sections of the station in the next three days." The voice startled him, and he turned to face Suyo Takashi. Even with him slouched in his seat and her standing, they were almost at the same eye level.

Lang suspected she'd made a shrewd guess as to what he was thinking. Either that or she's a telepath, he thought, allowing the tiniest of smiles to show.

"Aren't you supposed to be off duty?" he asked, taking the clipboard and wincing as he saw what Pearl was requesting.

"Aren't you?" With another woman, that would have sounded challenging, or flippant. She sounded...calm was the only way he could describe it. "I couldn't sleep."

"I couldn't either," Lang admitted.

He caught her eye as she turned to leave, and motioned to the seat next to him. She looked startled, then pleased. He watched her sink into the seat, looking around the bridge to see if there was any reaction.

Of course, there was none. The work around them went on with quiet efficiency. Due in no small part, to this woman's hard labors, Lang admitted. She'd been working with Randy since they took control of the station. "Who better?" He blushed as he realized he'd spoken out loud.

"I beg your pardon?" she asked, although he was certain she'd heard him.

"I was thinking about Randy," Lang said slowly, not quite sure of how to put this. "Someone needs to take over his duties, take his... place." Lang had trouble getting that last word out, but she seemed to understand. "Who better than you?"

"I would be honored," she said simply.

Lang settled back in his chair again, clipboard on his lap. They sat in a comfortable silence for a while as he took another look at it. Finally he looked up at the Baerd sitting nearby, coordinating the repair crews, checking on routine maintenance, in fact, doing most or all the actual work being done on the bridge at the moment.

"Do you play chess?" Lang asked suddenly.

"Certainly," Suyo answered.

"Care for a game?" He hesitated, and admitted. "I feel like a fifth wheel up here, right now."

"I know exactly what you mean," she smiled, and they stood up together. "I would love to."

"Shall we?" Lang stood and motioned to the door. She smiled, and led the way. Almost as an afterthought, Lang called over his shoulder to the Baerd manning the communication station. "Oh, please tell Danny... er, Captain DelaRosa that he can uncloak and bring Jade Conquistador back to the station, now that the Tryr are gone."

Jade Wolverine

"You have no idea how good it is to see you."

Lasty blushed in pleasure at the compliment from Captain Tachibana. "I'm glad we're able to help." He somehow kept the stammer out of his voice. "Irene tells me Vicki's recovery should be one hundred percent, but it's going to take some time."

"Can we reestablish contact with our people earthside?" Captain Tachibana looked worried, even through his exhaustion. "I'm concerned about the fact that we've been cut off for so long."

"Irene thinks we should wait until we're closer to Earth. She's concerned about the Egelv intercepting our transmissions." Lasty gave him an apologetic look. "We don't need to wait until all systems are up again, which will take another eighteen hours. But she wants to be in orbit so we can send tight beams."

"I understand." Captain Tachibana sighed. "I just wish we'd been able to notify Ms. Martin and some of the others before contact was cut off."

"Ms. Martin seems very self-reliant," Lasty pointed out, and saw Dutter nod her agreement out of the corner of his eye. "As do the others. And don't forget, the Jim Morris has been on the planet's surface for hours now. I'm sure he has everything under control."

"R-i-ght," the captain said, and Lasty didn't understand why he would think that was humorous. "Although I'm sure he has everything under control, I've half a mind to send one of the shuttles anyway."

"That's always an option," Lasty admitted. "But if you wait until we're in orbit, we can give them a soft launch that will give them reentry with much less chance of detection. We know the Egelv did a hard probe a short time ago, but it doesn't appear they got a fix on Claw." He felt funny, giving advice to someone so much senior to himself. What was even stranger was that the Human listened, then actually took his advice.

Advice from a Baerd.

He saw Dutter watching him with poorly concealed pride, and his blush grew as he terminated the connection with as much grace and dignity as he could muster.

He placed his lower right hand on her lower left, and she smiled at him.

◆ ◆ ◆ ◆ ◆

Glowing Mist

Siph Carni pursed her lips in irritation as she glanced at her instruments. She'd caught a few traces of evidence that some small ship, probably a shuttle, was being used over North America. But she couldn't find it! Stealth technology left detectable traces, if you knew what to look for.

But they were good, very good. She had proof of movement, but not enough to plot any sort of flight pattern.

She had even convinced Cromar Try they should do a hard scan across the entire continent. Of course their ship would light up on anybody else's scanners like a star going supernova, but it should give them what they wanted.

All she got for that trouble was confirmation of a presence near the Morris house they had already been to. By the time the data had been sorted and read, the unknown ship was no longer in the area.

Cromar Try refused to do another hard scan. It was too risky. If there was a hostile ship anywhere in the system, they would be watching after the first time. Detection would be unavoidable.

So, she filtered through the flood of data she could get via passive scanning and tried to trace the quarry's path.

She couldn't shake the feeling she was missing something obvious. But what?

Costa tried to focus on the phone conversation and ignore the two people sitting in his office. The Director and Shelly Trent sat across his desk, flipping through files. They didn't even try to pretend they weren't listening as he got an update from Ann Arbor.

"Now listen," he said, trying not to look at them for their reaction. "Are they armed? Then arrest them for concealed weapons. I don't care if they do have permits. By the time that gets sorted out...what? Right there in the hospital?" He struggled to control his features. "How? Well, what about his house? Just one man? Why don't you...oh. I'm going to put you on hold for a moment."

He looked at the Director.

"Ron Hoffman, Yvette Stephanian, Janice Wooley, and the Riahi girl are all at the hospital. They've got about six armed guards stationed in and around the girl's room. They also have their lawyers present. They're saying the girl is still too groggy to give any testimony, and the doctor refuses to allow her to be moved."

"What happened when your men tried to arrest the guards?" Shelly asked.

"The lawyers argued the permits are legal, and that the guards are necessary, and they have court orders." Costa held up his hand as she started to ask the obvious. "Why not arrest them anyway?" Costa shook his head. "This is the real beauty of the situation. The judges that signed the court orders are there, in the hospital, in the friggin' hallway outside her door."

"The judges are there?" Sheila Trent showed disbelief.

"The judges and local authorities. The hospital is part of the University of Michigan, and it dominates the local government. They're basically saying our paperwork is bogus." He smiled wryly. "And they're right, of course."

"Are you telling me local bumpkins are interfering with FBI agents trying to do their job?" Shelly Trent's voice was rising in pitch, he noticed in amusement. "They've pulled weapons?"

"I'm telling you that unless we're willing to have our agents open fire in a hospital, they can't get the guards out of the way. At the moment we're badly outnumbered." Costa looked at the Director, ignoring the aide for the moment. "Did I mention the press are there in force?"

"And at the house?" The Director's voice was quiet, which didn't fool Costa a bit.

"There's one man there from the Hoffman Service, with a restraining order. And camera crews from every network. They're filming anything and everything that happens. We arrested the first guard, but his replacement was there before we even got him in the car, with the media. Everything we take is being recorded and inventoried." Costa shrugged. "There's really nothing to be gained there anyway. "It's the people we need, right now."

"Do whatever it takes. Get them out of there." Shelly Trent's voice was shaking with fury. "The hell with the media or the judges."

"No." The Director didn't even bother to look at her. "While they're in the hospital, we'll have to wait. They can't stay there forever, though."

He looked at Costa. "So, where is this Jim Morris?"

San Francisco, California

Groundhog peered through the night vision telescope at the warehouse on the next wharf. It and the three freighters tied up next to it were the center of a flurry of action.

One of those ships are going to depart in a few hours, Groundhog decided. And it's going to have two women aboard that aren't listed on any manifest. I talked to Morris hours ago. A Lear jet could have made the trip by now. And if I'm right, the actor has something far speedier than a jet at his command.

Groundhog had watched the rental van drive up over an hour ago. It had gone directly inside, and Groundhog had debated the next course of action, when there was some sort of movement on one of the upper floors.

Groundhog checked the schematics of the four story building on his laptop. The top floor on this side was laid out as office space. It only took one careful scan through the night vision binoculars to see, Kimberly and Kiri, pretty as you please, looking a little the worse for wear.

The two women were marched to a sofa and sat down. Guards stood on both sides and behind them, which seemed overkill for two women.

The reason became obvious as Sho Toshida entered the room. He went straight to stand before the two women, and his security chief, Takeda Nagashino, joined him.

A very dangerous man, Groundhog decided. It would be interesting to see him and Morris go at it.

But where was Morris?

Ann Arbor, Michigan

People jostled Afsaneh as she tried to walk down the long white corridor. Someone shoved by her and she stumbled. Then another man shoved her the other way. She tried to get to one of the walls, but swift, walking bodies kept getting between her and her goal.

And they seemed taller than a moment ago. She thought she saw a familiar face through the throngs of people.

"Daddy? Daddy? Is that you? Help me! I can't get through all these people!"

One of the passing giants turned and sneered. "Daddy? Daddy? Help me, help me!" His voice rose in pitch to a mocking high falsetto. She glared at him, and to her horror, his features began to change.

His forehead grew thick, and all vestiges of hair disappeared. His nose thickened into a bearlike snout, and the skin all over his body hardened and became overlapping layers of armored muscle.

She backed away from the transforming monster right into another.

All around her, people were morphing into huge rhino-bears, black panthers, and even giant lobsters. She tried to find a way through them, and glimpsed her father's features through the crowd for a moment.

She stopped in consternation as his face also began to change! His jet-black hair lengthened and became blond. His thick moustache shortened and extended to a close-cropped beard, also blond. The dark-brown eyes brightened into glittering light-green.

"Daddy? Jim? Father?" Afsaneh found herself crawling along the

floor between the legs of monsters, trying to get to the constantly chang-ing, yet still comforting figure across the hall.

But she couldn't seem to get there. The more she crawled, the farther away they got. And...they were hurt! Jim/Father had a horrific scar stretching from above his left eyebrow down past his eye, to the tip of his left ear.

And Daddy was bleeding, real bad.

"Daddy!?" Afsaneh opened her eyes. The glare off the white walls and ceiling made her squint. She blinked several times, trying to make her eyes stronger.

"Afsy, honey, are you okay?" Afsaneh tried to turn her head at the familiar voice on her left. Was that Yvette with tears pouring down her cheeks? And Janice was standing behind her, hands on her lover's shoulders, also crying.

The room was full of people, but other than the two women, she didn't know any of them. There seemed to be about six men in suits at the foot of her bed. At first she thought they were all together, but then she dimly realized two of them were trying to keep between her and the others.

A young, pretty, black nurse reached down on her right side and pushed a button. She smiled reassuringly at Afsaneh. Did she know this woman? She became aware that Yvette was still speaking.

"Afsy, can you understand me?" Afsaneh nodded slightly, and won-dered why there was so much resistance. Her head felt like it weighed a million pounds. She tried to reach up with her left hand, but it wouldn't move. Her puzzled expression must have told Yvette what she was thinking, because the short woman began speaking rapidly.

"Don't try to move, Afsaneh. You've been hurt. Your left arm and right leg are both broken, and you got hit on the head pretty hard. Do you remember the Jade Viking. The cruise ship?"

Afsaneh stared at her. Had she been dreaming all those strange thoughts that kept running around in her head? One of the suits pushed his way forward.

"Ms. Stephanian, step back please. Right now. Do not talk to the girl, please." He tried to pull her away, but Janice took hold of his hand and twisted it. The man gasped in pain and found himself face to face with Janice, scant inches between them.

"Don't you know how to treat a lady?" Janice said through clenched teeth. Afsaneh tried to focus, but she was so tired. Boy, was Janice pissed. She couldn't remember ever seeing the woman so angry. "You don't just manhandle people," Janice continued. "Especially when they're at the hospital bedside of someone they love."

"Then...it was a dream?" Afsaneh looked around the faces, searching for the ones she wanted to see so desperately.

"The cruise ship wasn't a dream," Yvette spoke quickly, giving her a determined look Afsaneh had trouble interpreting.

"That is quite enough." The man shook himself free of Janice's grasp, glaring at the two women. "One more word from you, Ms. Stephanian, and I'll have you arrested for obstruction of justice. And you for assault of a federal officer." This last was directed at Janice.

He turned and gave Afsaneh a placating look. "Miss, I know this must be very confusing to you. My name is Paul Orinsky. I'm with the FBI." He was trying to be friendly, but Afsaneh didn't like him. "I need to ask you some questions about your trip on the Jade Viking."

"You need to back away from my patient." A short, balding man she assumed was a doctor had somehow managed to insinuate himself between the federal agent and Afsaneh. "She can't answer questions right now. You'll all have to leave this room immediately. My patient needs rest."

"She can have all the rest she wants, after I speak with her." Agent Orinsky obviously wasn't used to being argued with by civilians. "If you try and stop me, I'll have her moved out of here."

"No, you won't." The doctor glared at Orinsky. "She's my patient, and she can't be moved. She's just had surgery on her skull, you idiot."

"You won't be responsible," Orinsky said in what he probably thought was a reassuring tone.

"No, I won't. Because she's not going anywhere."

"I'm afraid it's out of your hands, Doctor." Orinsky turned to his men, but whirled back around at the doctor's next words.

"I don't think so. Nurse Weeks, call security. We have armed men making threats here, and I want them removed, arrested if necessary."

"Yes, Doctor." The cute black nurse grinned at Afsaneh and reached for the phone on the bedside table.

"You leave that phone where it is," one of the other agents snarled, stepping forward. Then he found himself blocked off by one of the two guards. Four more slipped into the room and were at the elbows of the other FBI agents before they even knew they were there.

"This is ridiculous!" The doctor clapped his hands for emphasis. "This girl can't be moved and that's that! She's not going anywhere, Agent Orinsky. You can question her later. All you're doing now is causing her stress and leaving yourself open to an extremely expensive lawsuit. You can wait outside."

"I'm sleepy," Afsaneh said, thinking she should make her voice weak. To her surprise, it came out that way without her even trying. "I'm so...tired." The room of people began shifting to a very strange perspective, as if viewed through a camera lens.

"Wait outside." The doctor got Agent Orinsky started towards the door, and his men followed sullenly. Yvette gave Afsaneh a big grin that seemed to distort into a strange caricature of her former self. Her expression changed to one of chagrin as the doctor continued. "You too, ladies. I mean it." Yvette's objection was halted before it left her lips as he raised a hand to forstall any argument.

Afsaneh tried to wave her reassurance, but Yvette was rapidly shrinking into the distance, and probably didn't hear the question Afsaneh tried to get out just before she gave in to the darkness.

"What about Daddy?"

❖ ❖ ❖ ❖ ❖

CHAPTER TWENTY-SIX

San Francisco, California

Jim Morris stared in consternation at the crowded San Francisco shoreline. So many piers! For all he knew, Sukuru could have a dozen different locations; warehouses, office buildings, hotels, the possibilities were endless.

"Is Vicki back on line?" That would solve a number of problems, but Claw was no help.

"No."

"If we only had Kimberly's frequency," Jim said, staring at the screen in discouragement. The shuttle's night vision made the display as clear as if it were daytime, and the detail was phenomenal. But unless she happened to be standing outside, it didn't help. "We could trace her down, even if she was unconscious."

"I do have both Kimberly Martin and Kiri Oshiba's frequencies," Claw said. Jim stared around the bridge in irritation, which grew at the computers next words. "But we can not effect a trace at this time."

"Why not?" Jim kept his voice down with an effort.

"If the Egelv are anywhere within direct sight and scanning, even passive scanning, they will detect us. I am no match for an Egelv ship."

"What about transmitting?" Jim wasn't ready to concede the point yet.

"We can transmit and receive with reasonable confidence." Jim sighed with relief. "However, unless they can describe their position, it would seem of marginal value."

"Shows what you know," Jim muttered.

"Actually, I know..."

He raised a hand in concession. "Okay, you know bunches of stuff." Jim peered at the screen. "If nothing else, it will reassure Kimberly and Kiri to know that help is on the way."

"But at this point, we only have the resources of this shuttle and yourself."

Jim smiled grimly. "I guess we'll just have to make do. Let me talk to both their frequencies."

"Go ahead."

Jim wet his lips nervously. How did they suddenly get so dry? "Kimberly? Kiri? Can either of you hear me?"

He waited, but there was no response. As he listened, he continued to scan the harbor. Commercial wharves and warehouses stretched along the shore as far as he could see in either direction. Dozens of freighters and tankers were docked in the nearby area. There was no way to pick out the facilities Sukuru had acquired from Spencer Corp.

He gave a few of them a cursory look, even though he knew he wouldn't see any sign of the two women. He kept calling to Kimberly, hoping to hear something.

"I am picking up some sort of humming on Kiri Oshiba's wave length." Jim felt a flash of hope. Maybe they couldn't speak or something.

"Kiri, if you can hear me but can't talk, cough twice," Jim said. His eye caught something and he brought the viewer back to a pair of wharves that had three ships docked. Two looked like they were being prepared to depart. Hatches over the cargo bays were being fastened down, and the fuel and electric lines connecting the ship to shore were being withdrawn.

But what caught his attention was the corporate logo that emblazoned the bows of all three ships.

Sukuru!

As that fact sunk in, he heard a soft cough. Then it repeated. One of the women was responding to his request!

"Can you tell where their signal's coming from?" he asked excitedly. "Can we use their broadcast to pinpoint their location?"

"To a certain extent," Claw said, but cautioned. "The signal is too diffused to be more specific without revealing our own location."

"Show me what you can," Jim ordered. His screen split and the left half had a map display of the Bay area. The shuttle showed as a little blue smudge just off shore. A misty yellow pie wedge extended westward, enveloping the three ships and the mass of buildings behind them.

"Can we detect heat images without showing up on somebody else's screen?" Jim shifted the viewer angle from the ships to the buildings. His attention centered on the biggest, a four story warehouse. The windows implied that offices and lounges apparently occupied the entire top floor. "What about this building here?"

The two sides of the screen closed in on the building in question. The right side shifted to a heat scanning mode and splotches of red appeared. One room on the top floor seemed to have a heavier concentration of people. Was one of them his wife?

"Can you tell if any of them is Kimberly or Kiri?" Jim stared at the screen in frustration. He wasn't surprised when Claw said she couldn't identify the individual heat patterns.

The red blobs representing people were moving around fairly regularly. If the women were prisoners, they were probably being held in one spot, hopefully together.

Several pairs weren't moving around, but without more information, it was impossible to do more than guess which might be the women. Jim stood and went to the locker he'd put his weapons in.

"I have to be doing something," he said, trying to contain his impatience. He loaded the pump shotgun, hesitated, then put a final shell in the chamber to give him one more shot. Reloading was not going to be much of an option, he suspected. As he began loading his revolver, he thought about his wife, so near, probably wondering what he was doing. "Give me a sign, a description, something!" he said, louder than he'd intended.

"I see three ships." He stiffened as Kimberly spoke clearly. "Which one are we going on?"

"Yes!" Jim jumped back to his console. "Claw, can you narrow down the possibilities?"

"No more than we already have," came the immediate response.

"Scan for her transceiver, then." Jim pulled his scabbarded sword over his shoulder, then the holster for the shotgun.

"That will reveal our position to the Egelv. I can not..."

"You will do as I say, right now!" Jim barely kept his voice below a shout as he quickly strapped his holster to his hip. He rejected the short sword and throwing knives as impractical. This would be a smash and grab operation. He cut Claw's argument short. "I said now!"

The screen flickered, too fast for Jim to discern what happened. Then Claw showed it again, slowing the process down. The screen shifted color schemes and two figures glowed brighter than the others, then went back to normal. The two figures remained a different shade than their captors.

"I performed a millisecond scan, just long enough to identify their location. There is a possibility the Egelv may not trace such a quick signal. I would urge we leave the area as soon as possible, however."

"Sounds like a plan," Jim agreed. "Now tell me, can any of our weapons take the front wall off that building without harming the people inside or the integrity of the structure?"

"Yes, I can adjust my disrupter to do that. It will be visible to anyone scanning this area, however," Claw warned.

"In for a penny, in for a pound," Jim grinned. "Now here's what we're going to do..."

Glowing Mist

"I've got something," Siph Carni leaned forward. "There was an Ananab energy source utilized briefly." She looked at her instruments. "...in the San Francisco Bay area."

"Let's go. Fastest non-detectable speed available." Cromar Try lifted a hand. "I know it's slower. But I don't know who this is, or if they have friends. How long?"

"Just over nine minutes," Siph Carni said in disgust. "We could be there in...two minutes."

"Nine will do. They won't get far." Cromar Try looked around the bridge, feeling a sense of unease he couldn't place. The two humans sat in their seats, behaving themselves. Jo Coran was firing up the weapons systems. Du Brimar was still sulking, pointedly not offering any opinions or advice.

Cromar Try discreetly used his command security system to monitor Du Brimar's screen. To his amusement, his second in command was only using part of his screen to show the tactical overview of the North American continent. One corner was showing one of the human 'movies' they had seized earlier.

It had been Du Brimar that had pointed out the best place to wait for a revealing energy signal was high over the center of the continent, in an orbit that gave direct sight access to the entire land mass. Cromar Try had assumed he was studying data, or researching, or something a little more productive than watching movies made by primitives.

The screen abruptly shifted to a close-up of the west coast, and Du Brimar spoke for the first time in hours. "I just picked up a disruptor blast display of limited duration. I should be able to pinpoint fairly accurately..."

"Yes, I think I've got it, too. Definitely near this bay area...uh, San Francisco. We should have him, whoever he is." Siph Carni glanced over at Cromar Try, and she had an uncharacteristically worried look on her face. "I may also have another energy signature. Possibly a second shuttle. Same destination as ours."

Cromar Try was glad he'd ordered a cautious approach. A second shuttle? Or something else? He watched the west coastline come into clear view and begin growing on the screen.

They would know, soon enough.

Jade Viking

Captain Tachibana stood behind Inam, looking over her shoulder at the controls, as if staring at them would reveal some hidden bit of information. Around them, Jade Viking showed signs of coming to life. The bridge was now nominally functional, but everything was still being manually directed by the techs at their stations.

Jade Wolverine's computer, Irene, had assured him that Vicki would be back, hopefully her old self. So far, that hadn't happened. The individual computers that combined to make up her central nervous system were almost all back on line. But each had to be directed to perform its function.

Radio reception was working, and the shuttle Claw had sent several updates on her current mission. So far, neither ships had responded. Their orbit kept them stationary over the Pacific, with the North American west coast barely within their direct line of sight. If the Egelv were looking for Jim, they would probably be over the center of the country somewhere. This position should be undetectable to anything short of a direct hard scan. There had been one earlier, but fortunately, it

393

was aimed at the surface.

"They should almost be there," Inam commented. "The shuttle will be over San Francisco Bay in five minutes, according to the flight plan."

"Hmm," Tachibana said. "Tell Kabu to prepare a landing party, well-armed, to take one of our shuttles down to assist Jim Morris, should he find the women."

"Yes, Sir."

"Oh, and give me Commander Lasty, aboard the 'Wolverine." Tachibana kept his smile concealed as he watched the blush of pleasure sweep across the Baerd's features. He wouldn't have believed he could differentiate between types of blushes on aliens, but he could.

Even the Baerd that didn't approve of Lasty and Dutter as a couple were proud of his accomplishments. None of their race had ever risen to the rank of Commander aboard a non-Baerd ship.

He saw Inam stiffen in surprise. Before he could ask, she shifted channels so what she was picking up could be heard by the entire bridge.

"...either of you hear me?" Tachibana rubbed his chin thoughtfully. That was Jim's voice. Inam leaned forward, obviously listening to something he wasn't.

"Sir, they've activated Kimberly Martin and Kiri Oshiba's transceivers. I'm picking up a humming, I think." They heard Jim give the women instructions, then froze as they heard two distinct coughs. Smiles spread across faces all over the bridge. "He's found them!"

"Give me Jade Wolverine," Tachibana ordered. He knew Jim wouldn't hesitate to march into the lion's den, and they needed to send help immediately. He stepped over to stand behind the Baerd as Lasty came on Inam's screen. If he felt surprise to see Captain Tachibana looking over her shoulder, addressing her console, he hid it well.

"Yes, Captain?"

"I'm sending a shuttle with Kabu and some armed men down to assist Jim. Did you plan on anything of that sort?"

Lasty looked embarrassed, but the color never deepened past pink. "Actually, Angela Dawson launched with two men in Fang three minutes ago."

"Damn!" Tachibana swore, and both the Baerd, and for that matter, the rest of the bridge crew all stared at him in shock. None of them had ever heard him curse. "Send Kabu and his team, ASAP," he instructed.

"Maximum effort given to stealth approach. And find out from Irene if we can speed up our time-table on reactivating Vicki."

Captain Tachibana put his hands behind his back as he strode to the main screen and stared at it pointblank.

"We'll need every ace in our hand before this day is over." He saw Claw and two dots that had to be the women appear briefly on the screen as Jim's shuttle sent a quick hard probe. "And keep a close watch for the Egelv. If we saw it, they probably did, too."

San Francisco, California

Sho Toshida waited as his man opened the door for him, then swept into the room as if he owned it. Which, of course, he did. Through the windows in the far wall, he could see the lights of the harbor, and what he assumed was Oakland, across the bay.

All this he ignored. The occupants of the room were his first interest. He had met both women once previously, just before the Jade Viking launched on what would be its final voyage.

They had both looked considerably better then.

He was mildly surprised to see that neither of them were bound. But from what he'd seen of Takeda Nagashino, they were probably too cowed to try anything.

The security man could be very...intimidating.

Nagashino broke off from a conversation he was having with one of his men and came forward to greet him.

"Toshida-san, so glad you have arrived. As you see, we have the cargo, hardly the worse for wear." Both men spoke in Japanese.

"Very good, Nagashino-san." Toshida looked at the two women. Both were barefooted and wore casual clothes that had seen better days. But they glared at him, still unbroken. "Did they give you any trouble?"

Nagashino told him about his method to keep them quiet and subdued. Toshida was impressed, despite himself. The security chief was ruthless and unconcerned about how others might view his methods.

Toshida liked that in a lieutenant. He would make good use of this man. He walked over to the women. There was a guard on either side, both armed. He noted that one of them was that idiot Takuan. What was wrong with his face? His eyes were both blackened, his nose swollen and bruised. Was it broken, again?

The women rose to their feet as he approached. He raised a hand as they were about to speak, presumably to complain about their treatment. "No, no ladies." He gave them a triumphant grin. "You know the penalty for talking. It's still in effect."

They looked at each other in dismay. Obviously, they'd thought his arrival would mean some improvement in their situation. But he rather liked them feeling humiliated.

"I can't count on you to help with the return of my ship, so we'll see what other benefits you can provide." He grew tired of them, and turned away. "My uncle is looking forward to speaking with you," he said over his shoulder.

A man handed him a clipboard with a manifest for the ship they would be taking to Japan. As he perused it, he noticed both women were still standing. He was about to tell them to sit when Kimberly surprised him by speaking.

"I see three ships," she said. "Which one are we going on?"

Toshida smiled thinly as Nagashino stiffened. Well, what would come off now? He wouldn't mind seeing more of both women. Kiri was a beautiful young woman, hardly more than a girl.

And Kimberly Martin? Most Westerners were built like cows, but not her. She had a lithe figure that was tantalizing, and he suspected she was a natural blond. He'd always had a taste for the exotic...

Takuan's head suddenly shoot upright. To Toshida's irritation, the man began stammering in excitement. "She's talking! It must be those things we had!"

What was he clamoring about now? What things? Seeing a white woman in her underwear shouldn't excite him this much. His glare didn't stop the man's stuttering.

"She's signaling!" Takuan took a step closer to Kimberly Martin. "Her..."

Before he could complete the sentence, Kimberly Martin surprised them all by taking a swift step forward and punching Takuan in the face with a right fist.

Toshida didn't know whether to laugh or be angry as he watched Takuan fall backwards, clutching his face, screaming in agony. At the same time, the woman held her hand, swearing at the pain. She's lucky she didn't break it, punching like that to the head, he thought, bemused.

One of the other guards took a step forward, raising his pistol. They were all shocked when Kiri Oshiba shouted and dived between Kimberly Martin and the guard. He fired twice, and the Japanese actress took both shots in the chest. She fell to the floor, and Kimberly cried out and knelt over her.

Kimberly forgot the pain in her hand as she saw Kiri take the two shots meant for her. Her friend staggered backward and fell to the floor, her body twisting in midair to land face down. Kimberly knelt next to her, and hesitantly put her hand on Kiri's shoulder.

Do I dare turn her over, Kimberly thought. Think, Martin. Gunshot wounds, bleeding, shock, what do I do? She can't be dead! I've never had a friend like her. Never been this open with anyone, not even Jim.

This can't be real, she thought numbly. Kiri turned her head to look up. She said something Kimberly couldn't make out, then seemed to sag within herself. A sob escaped Kimberly's lips as she saw Kiri's eyes roll back in her head.

Kimberly gently lay her friend back on the carpeted floor. As she stood, the body at her feet seemed miles away, and a roaring began to build in her ears. She turned around to face Toshida, and knew she was about to die.

Her face felt like it was carved of stone as she took a step forward. A voice spoke from miles away, and she dimly realized it was Jim. It took an eternity for his words to sink in.

"Stay down, ladies."

Kimberly blinked and stopped walking. She ignored the guard who had raised his pistol again. The meaning of Jim's words finally sunk in. She threw herself to the floor, trying to cover Kiri's inert body.

Toshida shook his head. These silly girls were making this so much more difficult than it had to be. Then out of the right corner of his eye he saw things get much more difficult.

397

The outer wall with all the windows vanished. At least a major portion of it did. At the same time, there was a whoosh of displaced air, and a figure appeared out of nowhere.

Toshida gasped and took an instinctive step backwards as the figure walked forward into the light of the room, seemingly suspended in mid-air.

Jim Morris stopped in the newly created entrance. Toshida numbly noticed he held a sawed off shotgun at the ready. The American actor looked around the room coldly, then spoke in a low, menacing voice, in Japanese.

"The first person to move, dies. I'm here for Kimberly Martin and Kiri Oshiba. God help you all if they've been hurt in any way."

Toshida finally found his voice at the same time one of his men went for his gun. "Shoot him! He's only one man!"

Even as he spoke, the shotgun roared. The sound of his words hadn't even died as a guard was propelled backwards into the sofa next to Toshida. His head and shoulders were bright red with blood, and his features had vanished.

At that point, Toshida began to put serious consideration into his own safety and dived behind the sofa as gunfire exploded throughout the room.

CHAPTER TWENTY-SEVEN

As she saw the guard bring his gun up to bear on Kimberly, Kiri reacted without thinking. She dived between them and felt two blows strike her body hard. Then she was lying face down, unable to move. The floor pressed against her cheek, but she couldn't really feel it. Then she was rolled over onto her back, staring at the dingy grey ceiling tiles.

Kimberly's face came into view, a shocked expression on her face. Tears were streaming down both cheeks, and Kiri wanted to reach up and wipe them away, but she couldn't move. She tried to speak, but her voice came out in a tiny whisper. "Don't cry, love."

Kiri tried to say more, but her mouth wouldn't work. In fact, she felt numb. Was she cold? From a great distance, she heard Jim say 'stay down ladies'. It was a little late for that warning, Kiri thought, just before the darkness claimed her.

Jim saw the Sukuru guard go for his gun and didn't hesitate. He fired the shotgun from his hip and pumped another shell into the chamber. The guard catapulted backwards, as if shot from a cannon. Jim sent two more rounds into the cluster of guards to his right, then more to the left, just in case.

He was careful to keep the shots high, so as not to risk hitting the women. The sound of Kimberly sobbing came from near the far wall, and he strode forward purposefully, fearing what he would find. Fury wrapped itself around him, blackness narrowing his vision from both sides.

A movement to the right was rewarded with the last two shells in his gun. As he reached to reload, a guard flung himself forward, shouting defiantly in Japanese.

Jim brought the shotgun up to block the descending sword. The sound of steel meeting steel rang out as the blade hit his barrel. He swept the gleaming shaft of death to his right and kicked up savagely with his left foot, hitting the man squarely in the face.

A bullet flew by his ear, and Jim dived to the left, coming to a halt behind a large desk. He got two shells loaded, and held the shotgun up above the cover and fired. The recoil almost tore the weapon out of his hands, and he swore in irritation at himself.

He knew better than that. He was slightly mollified by the screams of pain that resulted, but his right shoulder felt like he'd dislocated it. He set aside the pain and spoke quietly.

"Kimberly, Kiri, stay down. Whatever you do, don't stand up!" As he talked, he reloaded, listening for the sound of the next rush. He didn't have to wait long. Bullets careened off the desktop and he heard the sound of footsteps running.

Jim dived to the left, rolling as he tried to find more cover. He came to a rest against the wall and fired, pumped, fired again. He couldn't tell if he hit anybody, but the sounds of pursuit stopped.

"Jim Morris." He didn't recognize the voice. "We have you trapped. Throw your weapons down and surrender. There is no need for you to die...today." He noticed the slight hesitation before the last word, and smiled mirthlessly. "By the way, excellent entrance. Very dynamic, very...theatrical."

Jim peered through the dimly lite room, trying to find his enemies. This was not a good situation. He had counted on surprise to win the day, and it just hadn't been enough. So be it, he decided. If he had to die this day, he would take these bastards with him.

But would it save the women? Through his dark mood, he realized it might not be enough. There had to be another way. But what?

As if in answer to his thoughts, Angela Dawson spoke through his transceiver. "Keep your head down, Captain."

Then the ceiling disappeared.

"Cool," Jim breathed, impressed even though it was the same method he'd used. He heard the sound of a machine-gun, then there was wild firing in every direction. "Damn", he said as a several shots hit the wall just above him.

Jim scrambled across the floor towards where he reckoned Kimberly and Kiri to be. He wasn't particularly surprised when he saw Sean and Ellis drop into the room, firing all the while. He was surprised to see Kabu and several other familiar faces come bounding into the opening he'd made his entrance through.

"Secure the entrances!" Now that was Angela, Jim thought. My kind of gal. Take charge, save your boss, kill the bad guys.

He saw her then, near where the women should be. He stared as Takuan rose behind her, and tried to bring his shotgun to bear. He needn't have bothered.

Angela must have radar, he thought as, almost casually, she turned and fired once. The shot from her pistol took half his face away, and Takuan went spinning against the wall and down to the floor.

"Friend!" Jim said as he rose to his feet. She nodded without really looking. He saw what had her attention a few steps later, Kimberly and Kiri.

Kimberly sat against the wall, holding Kiri in her arms as she would a small child. She sobbed uncontrollably and pressed Kiri's face to her chest, stroking the long black tresses with one shaking hand.

Angela crouched next to them and held Kiri's wrist for a moment. A look of relief came over her features, and she quickly holstered her pistol and began to pry Kiri loose from Kimberly's grasp.

"Ms. Martin, she's alive. Let her breathe." Angela repeated the words gently as she pulled the still form free.

"Kimberly?" Jim said hesitantly, kneeling by her. His wife looked up at him, sorrow in her eyes. He doubted she'd heard a word Angela had said. She was trying to form words, and they finally fought their way through her lips.

"She saved my life. She dived in front of me." Kimberly's voiced cleared slightly. "She took the shots meant for me. I was supposed to die, not her." Fresh tears formed and he took her in his arms and hugged her close. "She was my friend. My best..." She couldn't continue. He looked over her head at a grinning Angela. who held up a dart with one hand.

"She was shot with a tranquilizer, sir. Let's get out of here." Angela stood, holding Kiri cradled in her arms. "Fang, bring the force field up to the edge of the building, this floor." She looked at Jim uncertainly. "Is there somewhere nearby we can go to regroup?"

"I have a cabin at Lake Tahoe," Jim said, looking around. The Sukuru people had all fled into the next series of rooms, and Kabu and his men were having no difficulty keeping them pinned down. He had trouble controlling the urge to go after them.

There was a lull in the firing, and the sound of sirens grew louder. Jim helped Kimberly take a step, and Ellis was on her other side, holding her arm. He nodded his thanks to the young man, then called out in a grim voice.

"We are leaving now. You would be well advised to never bother us again. This is your only warning. Come near my people again, you answer to me."

The mocking voice from earlier came from the other room. "We will meet again, Jim Morris. Of that you can be certain."

Jim smiled thinly, then ignored him. "Kabu, send someone with Angela that will recognize the cabin at Tahoe. We'll meet there. Ellis, you come with me."

He looked down at Kimberly's face. She was watching Angela and Sean run out the window on what looked like empty air. But it supported them until they abruptly disappeared.

The sound of sirens were almost right outside, and Jim decided that their leaving would be a very good thing. "Come on, Honey. Let's go."

"Kiri?" He'd never heard Kimberly so forlorn and wondered what the two women had gone through before he got there. The thought made him start to turn back towards where the Sukuru people were holed up. Then reason reasserted itself. They would probably give him a reason to kill them later. He could wait.

"Kiri is safe with Angela. We're going to meet them now." Kimberly didn't seem to be able to walk very well, and he swung her up into his arms. "Ellis, take point. Let's go."

Three minutes later, they were aboard Claw, watching the bullet-ridden warehouse and the cluster of police cars and fire trucks shrink in the distance.

◆ ◆ ◆ ◆ ◆

"Wow, what a mess," Du Brimar commented, looking at the demolished building on the screen. "How did they do so much damage and still get away so fast?"

"Who said they got away," Jo Coran said smugly. "I have a clear reading of the path they took. Follow?"

"Follow." Cromar Try didn't look up from his own screen as he agreed. His tan, brown forehead was furled with concentration, and Matt wondered what he was looking at. The captain turned to his mate. "How many do you track?"

"I have two distinctly different signatures," Siph Carni admitted. "One of them much more sophisticated than the other."

"And?" Cromar Try encouraged her. "Can you tell me why one ship would have two different types of shuttle aboard?"

"One could have been acquired after the ship was commissioned," Du Brimar cut in, and they both gave him an irritated look he didn't seem to notice. "Or, perhaps the Humans have been tinkering with one, trying to improve it."

"That doesn't make sense," Siph Carni countered. "The one signature is clearly Ananab. The more sophisticated is a mixture of Ananab, Tryr, and I don't know what. But it's very nearly on a level with our own technology."

"Oh come now." Du Brimar gave her an incredulous look. "You're not seriously saying that shuttle is as good as Egelv?"

"Not as good, but close." Siph Carni looked stubborn. "Very close. We have evidence these Humans like to tinker with things."

"And they tinkered with an Ananab shuttle, improving it exponentially? In less than a quarter of a cycle?" Du Brimar shook his head. "I don't think so. I think the Ananab bought a rebuilt Hshtahni, or maybe a Hechk'tar shuttle."

Matt watched as the four Egelv exchanged worried looks. Hmm, I don't know who these Hstah...uh, whatever, are, but I think I'm beginning to like them already, he thought.

"They're landing near that lake," Jo Coran said, pointing to her screen. "Yes, they're definitely stopping at that structure near the water."

Du Brimar barely glanced at his screen as he checked something. "Right. Jim Morris, has a vacation cabin on Lake Tahoe, right, Matt?" He gave Matt a teasing grin. "Oh, yeah, you don't want to be as helpful anymore, do you?"

"Bring us in over them," Cromar Try said, meeting his mates eyes.

They stared at each other for a long moment, then both nodded, as if in reassurance. "Prepare to stun the two shuttles and the building area."

"What are you going to do?" Matt asked, his voice thick with nervousness.

"Well, if Jim Morris is down there, I can't think of a better specimen to take back to Egelva. In any case, we can get straight answers from these people. No more hearsay or guessing." Cromar Try frowned. "We can also get a look at that shuttle. That's one mystery I would like to put to rest."

"Specimen?" Teresa spoke for the first time in hours. Her voice was quiet, but Matt heard alarms go off in his head. That is one pissed-off woman, he thought. "More lab samples for your studies?" Her tone rose in both pitch and volume. Oh yeah, Matt thought. Very angry.

Cromar Try sighed and swivelled his seat to face her.

"I know you don't like to think of yourselves in that light," he said, his voice almost gentle. "Either of you. But yes, like lab samples." He didn't try to sugarcoat anything. "Like it or not, you Humans are at the mercy of races such as ourselves, or the Hstahni. You're an intriguing race, but unfortunately for you, clearly inferior."

His sympathetic smile didn't lighten the words any. "But not inferior enough to ignore. I'm sorry."

"You will be." Matt spoke without thinking, but didn't back down. "What you should do, is drop us off and leave now, while you can."

The rest of the Egelv were too shocked by his boldness to speak at first, then Du Brimar rose angrily to his feet. Cromar Try raised a hand, stopping his first officer.

You have no idea, Matt thought. But somehow... He glanced over at Teresa and saw resolve matching his own.

"If you are going to get more 'specimens', will you let us go?" Teresa asked. Matt watched Cromar Try's face as he decided what to answer. In the end, he just swung his chair back to forward without speaking.

I guess that answers that question, Matt thought.

For the next few minutes, the bridge was very quiet.

Jade Viking

"I am fully functional," Vicki said.

The bridge erupted in cheers, and Tachibana sagged in his seat. Inam turned to him and nodded. "All systems back on line, interacting normally, Sir."

"It's good to have you back, Vicki." Tachibana smiled at the idea of welcoming back a computer.

"It is good to be back, Captain Tachibana." If he didn't know better, he would swear he could hear relief in her voice. "Jade Wolverine has just notified me of a detected Egelv ship."

"Where?" Tachibana was all business again. "Can we see it?"

"Irene pointed out the telltale signs," Vicki admitted. "My sensors are inferior to hers, but we are sharing data and I have it on-screen now."

The screen shifted to show the Earth from what looked like several miles up. He recognized the San Francisco Bay area, then the view shifted eastward to a large lake. A tiny black rectangle appeared on the eastern shoreline. It was quickly followed by one red and two orange dots, beached to the side of the black spot.

"The black mark represents the cabin of Jim Morris. The other dots are the shuttles. This is the Egelv ship." A much larger green splotch appeared, covering all the spots. "It is hovering approximately eight hundred feet above the surface."

"What are they doing?" Captain Tachibana twisted and turned in his seat, wishing he could be down there.

"We suspect they are about to use a beam similar to the one used to capture Jade Viking originally." Vicki said. Tachibana shot upright in his chair, then relaxed a little at her next words. "The shuttles are providing a shield that should block most or all of its effects."

"What can we do?" Tachibana asked. He couldn't just sit here and wait, could he?

"We've been in communication with Claw and Fang, and there is a plan. In the meantime, we can only wait," Vicki said.

"We can't have both ships just sit by, doing nothing," Tachibana began to argue.

"Jade Wolverine is in a descending flight plan, using passive means to avoid detection." Vicki hesitated, what was for her, probably an eternity. "Should it come to a ship-to-ship battle, they will be our first offense. We will provide any backup or assistance we can from this orbit."

"We can't just stay up here." Tachibana was stubborn, but Vicki was quick to set him right.

"Captain Tachibana, you will please recall this ship can not enter the atmosphere. Our options are quite limited."

405

Captain Tachibana groaned and slouched down in dismay and embarrassment. "I knew that, too."

"It's easy to forget," Vicki said kindly.

❖ ❖ ❖ ❖ ❖

CHAPTER TWENTY-EIGHT

San Francisco, California

Karl Costa stared out the shattered window. No, not shattered. More like taken, framework and all. Hell, and let's not forget part of the wall, and most of the roof while we're at it.

What happened here? Sukuru had been less than helpful. One of their vice-presidents, Sho Toshida was here. Costa would have thought the man would be furious, demanding that the culprits be apprehended immediately. After all, there were eight dead bodies to account for.

Instead, Toshida seemed more...bemused than anything else. He basically ignored the casualties. He was far more interested in the wall, or what was left of it.

Costa reached out and hesitantly touched the smooth edge. There was no sign of tearing, or breaking. It was as if the building was made of soft butter, and a huge knife had come through, cutting out big swathes. He could understand Toshida's fascination.

"Beatty," he called without looking around. Footsteps hurried over. "Anything in the statements at all?"

"Not likely," Patrick Beatty grumbled. "If you can believe this, the only men who were in this room are the eight dead. The rest were in other parts of the building, and by the time they got here, whatever caused all this was gone."

"What about the wounded?" Costa asked, suspecting he already knew the answer. He was right.

"Ricochets, or friendly fire. No one saw who shot them." Beatty shook his head. "This is awful coincidental."

Costa looked at him, and raised an eyebrow questioningly. "Oh?"

Beatty frowned. "Yes, Sir. I find it peculiar that Sukuru is involved in another unexplainable incident. And everybody has memeory or attention lapses to excuse their ignorance."

Costa looked at his young agent, bemused. Could Beatty be pulling his leg? He looked absolutely serious. "Gosh, Patrick. I think you may have something there. See what you can dredge up, why don't you?" He kept his face clear of any hint of humor. "Where's the forensics expert?"

"She's on the roof," Beatty called over his shoulder as he hurried away.

Costa walked over and stood beneath the large opening in the ceiling. "Diane? You up there?"

"Right here," came a voice right behind him, and he about jumped out of his clothes. Costa kept the irritation off his face as he turned and scrutinized his 'expert'.

Diane Craybas was tall, at least five foot ten, with long, thick, dark hair. She did little to it, parting it in the middle and letting it fall straight down her back. Even though she faced him, he knew it almost reached her waist.

"What can you tell me about this?" he demanded. "Was this done from inside or out? With what type of weapon or tool? Is it...?"

"Whoa, one question at a time." Craybas looked at her notes with a frown. "First, I'm pretty sure these openings were made from the outside..."

"How?"

"How do I know?"

"No," Costa said, trying to contain his impatience. "How were they made?"

"No idea," Craybas answered, making no attempt to mask her own irritation. "Look, Sir. This can go either quickly or very slowly."

Costa didn't like being put on the defensive, but Craybas was one of the best. If only she didn't know it..."I'm sorry. Please go on."

"Certainly," she said, smiling slightly. "As I was saying, I'm certain these holes were made from the outside in." As if to forestall another interruption, she hurried on. "The openings are slightly larger on the inside edge than they are on the outside. This implies that any type of laser or other beam would fan outward the farther it got from the source."

She stopped and looked at him, as if expecting an argument, or more questions. When he said nothing, she continued, a little more enthusiastically. "I don't know if it was a beam, laser, or what. Even if it was cut with some incredibly sharp implement, such a hole usually shows the same characteristics. But I don't think it was cut, at least not with any kind of sharp tool."

Costa limited himself to an "Oh?"

"Right." Craybas stepped to the wall and gingerly ran her hand along the edge of the hole. "Whatever made this opening literally cut down to the molecular level." She turned and for the first time he saw wonder on her face. "Under laboratory conditions, on a microscopic level with computerized controls, we could probably be as precise with a laser. But it would take months if not years to make this big a cut."

Diane Craybas wrinkled her nose and pointed upward. "And that hole is even bigger than this one. According to the time frame of events, this happened in a matter of minutes, or less."

"So..." Costa watched her carefully to see if questions were permitted now. Evidently, they were. "What would it take to do this?"

"I have no idea," she said, looking him squarely in the face. "Nothing we have, or know about. It also appears that the method of cutting was precise enough to only cut the walls and ceiling. Whatever it was, it didn't extend into the room to any extent. Furniture just inside the wall was untouched."

"If it was some very sharp blade, it would only cut to the length of the blade," Costa pointed out. He should have known better.

"So, someone stood just outside the wall, then just over the roof, and sliced out big circular hunks." Craybas made a show of looking around. "What did they stand on? More importantly, where are the pieces of wall and roof that got cut out?"

"Can you tell me anything at all?" Costa was resigned to the fact that she wasn't working up to a solution. She was as stumped as he was.

"Yes," she said, and he waited. She began packing up her equipment and notes. He sighed and gave in.

"What can you tell me?" he asked, fighting to keep sarcasm from his voice.

"I can tell you that nothing we know of can make these holes," Diane Craybas said primly, then shook her head. "And I can tell you I need a drink."

That's the best idea I've heard today, Karl Costa decided.

Groundhog replayed the events at the warehouse again and again, although it wasn't necessary. What he'd seen was burned into his brain, even beyond his eidetic memory. He knew there would be extra-terrestrial technology. He knew Jim Morris would be showing up, and that he probably had some tricks up his sleeve.

But knowing in theory is nothing like knowing by seeing.

What could Morris have used to open that wall? And then he appeared in midair and walked into the room. Afterwards, he and his friends left the same way, by stepping out into midair...and vanishing.

By now, they're probably all back in Michigan. And he had another cross country red-eye flight in front of him.

But he was getting closer. A key person here, a spy there. It was taking longer than he thought it would, but there was finally an ear inside the Jade Viking closed club.

Groundhog smiled.

And that was only the beginning

Lake Tahoe, Nevada

"Wait." Jim stopped at the foot of the ramp that led into Fang. Ellis and Kimberly turned to him with questioning looks on their faces. The moonlight was bright enough to see the dried tears on his wife's cheeks. In fact, with the reflection off the water, it seemed almost as light as day.

It was more than bright enough to see the exhaustion that Kimberly was trying to hide. She'd insisted she could walk, but he saw the dismay as she looked at something as simple as a simple ramp.

Kimberly was a strong person that took pride in her strengths and self-control. She was embarrassed at her earlier collapse. The news that

Kiri had been shot with a tranquilizer gun had only sent her into a new bout of crying, this time in relief.

The days of captivity and all that crying had taken their toll, and she could barely keep from staggering. But she still insisted she could walk.

"I'm fine," she mumbled, but her slurred words betrayed her.

"I know," Jim said, smiling down at her. "But this is one of my ship's shuttles. And a man's ship is like his home."

She looked up at him, perplexed.

"There's a custom I've been looking forward to." He put one arm around her waist and effortlessly swung her up into his arms. "And that's carrying my bride across the threshold."

Kimberly was an wreck, both emotionally and physically, but she was still with the picture enough to see through him. And to see he was preserving her dignity in front of the others. She reached out with her left arm, got a fistful of his hair that fell down over his collar, and lay her head against his shoulder.

"Giddy up, lover of mine. Knock yourself out." Kimberly sighed and he felt her body relax. She spoke the next words so quietly he could barely hear her. "I love you, Jim."

"I love you, too," he started to say, then realized she was already asleep. He carried her inside, and people made room for her on a couch in the lounge. "God, I missed you," he said quietly.

"Update?" he asked as he hurried to the bridge.

"All three shuttles are in position, and almost everyone is in Fang. The Egelv ship is approaching."

"Vicki!" Jim found himself grinning as he settled into the pilot's chair. "Glad to have you back!"

"I am 'glad' to be back, Jim Morris." She sounds a little confused, Jim thought. Probably wondering about the 'glad' part. Time for that later, when they were sitting around a fire with drinks in hand.

Sean appeared at his side, holding out Jim's shotgun. "You dropped this in San Francisco," he said, dropping his eyes. "I thought you might need it."

My god, he sounds embarrassed, or shy or something, Jim marveled. Wonders will never cease, I might actually grow to like this boy.

His thoughts were interrupted by the lights dimming. "What's up?" He found himself whispering and grinned.

"The Egelv ship has just disabled both of the other shuttles," Fang answered softly in his ear transceiver.

"Disabled how?" Jim chewed his lip.

"With an overwhelmingly strong energy pulse designed to send the computers and engines into shutdown." Fang's voice actually sounded a little strained. "No shuttle has a strong enough shield to block such a pulse. Fortunately, this shuttle was protected by all three of our shields. However, it will take approximately eighteen minutes to reboot the other systems. In addition, the Egelv have just delivered an attack with a stun beam over the entire immediate area."

"So," Jim said, rubbing his hands together and grinning at Sean, and Kabu behind him. "We have them just where we want them."

❖ ❖ ❖ ❖ ❖

"Finally," Du Brimar said, rubbing his hands together. He beamed at Matt. "Time to meet the celebrity. Do you think he'll give me his autograph?"

Matt turned away to hide the despair that had to be showing on his face. Teresa sat next to him, stonily staring at the small screen in front of her. From the set of her jaw, Matt decided this was not a good to time to look to her for support.

He saw Siph Carni watching him with open sympathy. She gave Du Brimar an irritated look. "You have the empathy of a lower life form," she told him, showing an unremarkable lack of tact herself.

Matt focused on his own screen and watched as they approached the shore of the large lake below. A cabin grew in the display until they could see it clearly. There were a few people scurrying around the yard, and as he watched, he saw one blink out of sight. Moments later, someone else appeared in nearly the same spot, as if by magic.

Teresa leaned over and did something to his controls and the picture split in two. The left still showed the cabin, but the right side had a map display of the shoreline. There were two blurry smears to the left of the cabin. He tapped one of them with a fingertip and looked at her questioningly.

"Those are the shuttles, still cloaked." Her brow furled in concentration. "One seems to have a more sophisticated cloaking device than the other. I guess they are from two different sources."

Jo Coran snorted. "That is because the Ananab are a scavenger race.

Any ship of theirs might have four shuttles of three different origins. Their drive systems and computers are a nightmare of crossbreeding and patching."

"And those are their good points!" Du Brimar laughed as his long, tan fingers raced over his console. He glanced up from his instruments long enough to grin at Matt. "Boy, are they in for a surprise."

"What are you going to do?" Matt asked, glancing around at the four somber Egelv faces. Actually, it was three. Du Brimar, as usual, was enjoying himself. The Egelv made one last adjustment, winked at him, then looked at Cromar Try questioningly. The captain gave Matt the closest thing to an apologetic expression he could muster, then nodded to his first officer.

"One massive pulse to take down their shields, then a wide dispersal nerve beam, and..." Du Brimar barely suppressed a giggle, and Cromar Try shot him an irritated glare. He ignored it. "...simply stunning results!"

As Matt watched the screen in fascinated horror, both shuttles became visible to the naked eye. Several tiny figures collapsed where they stood. The picture grew as the Egelv ship came to a halt hovering a few hundred feet above the water.

"Anything different with P'Tassum?" Cromar Try asked Siph Carni. She shook her head as her screen split into numerous little boxes. "Exactly the same," she muttered, barely looking away from what had captured her attention.

Matt strained his eyes to see her screen. She was looking at one of the shuttles below. Even Matt could see both were drastically different from one another.

"I've never seen that design..." Her voice was barely legible as she leaned forward. The screen quickly dumped the other displays and she zoomed in to get a close-up look at the object of her interest.

"Can we land, please?" Cromar Try wasn't doing a very good job of keeping the irritation out of his voice. Siph Carni nodded almost unconsciously, and motioned with her hand. The ship dropped down and came to a rest in the shallow waters in front of the rustic cabin and disabled shuttles.

Matt noticed Du Brimar and Jo Coran were leaving the bridge and he tried to be unobtrusive as he followed. He felt Teresa's eyes on him but didn't think the other two Egelv even noticed his departure.

He caught up to the others as they were reaching the hatch.

Somewhere, they had both picked up sidearms. Du Brimar nodded congenially, but Jo Coran's eyes narrowed as she watched him join them.

"One last jaunt, then?" Du Brimar gave him his usual flashy grin as he opened the hatch. Jo Coran frowned.

"Does he need to go on this mission?" Her voice contained suspicion and Matt was careful to keep his face blank. He deliberately hesitated and even took a step back towards the ship's interior as he looked uncertainly between the two of them.

Du Brimar saved him, as he thought the cocky Egelv would. "Oh, let him come. At times he's a brilliant conversationalist. And who knows, maybe he'll be of some use picking faces out of the crowd."

Jo Coran wasn't buying it, but for the moment, she let it pass. The ramp reached almost to the shore, and since there was a wide dock, they didn't even have to get their feet wet.

Matt looked around curiously as they reached the beach. Even he could tell that the shuttle on the left was older and less sophisticated. The one on the right was more streamlined, and looked much newer. He froze, and felt his eyes widening.

The second shuttle had writing and artwork near its bow. Nothing exceptional with that, except it was in English!

Fang was scrolled over the symbol of growling jaws. Under that was a simple name in small letters.

Jade Wolverine.

It was a human ship! As he stared, he noticed its landing struts were extended much further than the other shuttle. It had to be at least twenty feet higher off the ground.

Why would they make it so awkward to enter and exit? They could have parked much lower. There was plenty of room beneath.

In fact, Matt realized, you could probably put another entire shuttle... oh! He saw that Du Brimar was oblivious to all this. He wanted nothing more than to search the house for Jim Morris.

But Jo Coran had stopped walking and was staring at the precariously parked shuttle with confusion. It hadn't occurred to her yet what was wrong with the picture, but she was close.

Matt decided to remove himself from the equation and intentionally tripped in the loose sand. He fell forward and didn't move.

Du Brimar turned and laughed at him. "This is your planet Matt. I would think you'd be a little more agile."

Jo Coran turned away from the shuttle and stared at Matt. Her eyes widened in shock, and her mouth opened to speak.

Then all hell broke loose.

Cromar Try was watching a montage of views on his screen. He had the overview angle, close-ups of both shuttles, the house, and the landing party. He frowned as he saw the Human on the screen.

"I don't think it was wise to let Matt go with them," he commented to his mate. She didn't answer, and he glanced over at her curiously.

Siph Carni was tapping her fingers on the panel in front of her in frustration. "What is it?" she muttered. "What is it?"

"What is what?" Cromar Try didn't even attempt to figure out what was bothering her. He'd learned better than that over the many years they'd been together. "What are you saying?"

"There is something I'm missing. Something I've seen, but can't recognize." Siph Carni leaned forward to rest her chin on her clenched fists, elbows supported by the armrests. It was a very un-Egelv-like pose. In fact, Cromar Try mused, it looked very Human in nature.

"You don't recognize the shuttle?"

She shook her head impatiently. "No, no! Well, yes, but that's not it. Something has been eating away at the back of my brain for several days now. But wh...?" She slapped one armchair with a clenched fist. "That's it!"

Siph Carni make a quick adjustment and the picture of P'Tassum hanging dead in space appeared. She made several more adjustments, then leaned back in triumph. "I thought so!"

"What?" Cromar Try didn't like the sound of this.

"Look at the printout readings on that ship. It shows four shuttles, all on board when we disabled their computer." She turned and looked at Cromar Try. "There's no way an Ananab ship of that type is going to have more than four shuttles."

"So neither of these are from that ship?" Cromar Try began to straighten up in alarm. Siph Carni pointed at the shuttle on the left.

"No, that one is definitely from P'Tassum."

"Then they were able to abandon ship with one or more of the shuttles," Cromar Try was relieved. At first, he thought she was telling him there were more ships in this system. "What about the other shuttle?"

"No, no." Siph Carni did a split on her screen and the P'Tassum now showed on both sides. She waved at the display in disgust. "That is the P'Tassum twenty minutes after we killed it. This is the P'Tassum... twenty minutes ago." She turned to look at him. "Both displays show four shuttles on board."

"So..." Cromar Try stared at the screen, trying to understand, then he got it.

"We've been tricked." Siph Carni began checking the data unfurling across her screens. "I believe the more recent pictures are of a probe pretending to be P'Tassum."

"Then...where is that ship?" Alarms began ringing and Siph Carni gasped and changed her display.

"What is it?" Cromar Try asked, dreading the answer before he heard it.

"Someone just stunned most of the inside of our ship." Siph Carni snarled, making an adjustment on her controls. "At the moment, we are the only people conscious on board."

"Impossible." Cromar Try sat back down in his own seat and slaved his controls to hers. "No Ananab stun beam can penetrate our hull, even without our shields up."

"They fired through our open hatch," Siph Carni said, her teeth gritted together. "I've raised shields and extended them to include the landing party. It's a good thing they had their defenses on automatic, or they'd be out, too. By the...!" She looked at him in frustration. "There's an inhibiting field extended over the area. No disruptors or stun beams will work here until we find and disable it."

"Who...?" Cromar Try let the words die as he saw one of his screens show a Human walk around the side of the cabin to confront Du Brimar and Jo Coran. He shook his head in dismay. "We've been incredibly careless. They were expecting us. What else could go wrong?"

Within moments, he was wishing he'd never asked.

Jim Morris handed the shotgun back to Sean. "Watch it for me. If we don't look too threatening, maybe this won't come to a fight."

"I think it's a little late for that," Sean said darkly. Behind him, Ellis nodded in agreement.

"Well, we'll just have to see," Jim said vaguely and opened the hatch far enough to drop out to the ground. He walked around the corner of the cabin and down to the beach. "Fang, the stun ray?"

"Fired through their open hatch. Most of the crew should be unconscious." He almost thought he heard irritation in the shuttle's voice. "The two Egelv that have disembarked were not affected, however. They have personal shields activated."

He knew there were snipers watching from the concealed shuttle wedged beneath Claw, but he didn't know what the Egelv were capable of, or how they were armed.

But he still had a few aces up his sleeve, and his father's revolver on his hip. "Activate the inhibiting field."

"Yes, Jim Morris."

Jim stopped short as he got his first look at the Egelv. There were two, one male, one female. They were tall, probably McGregor's height, but much more slender.

Their skin was about the color his got when he had a very good tan, but his hair never bleached out that much. It was long and straight, hanging down over their shoulders, and white.

Almost an albino white, he decided. Combine their hair with Baerd skin, we wouldn't even be able to see them. He smiled at the thought. They both wore blue loose-fitting shirts and slacks with what looked like ordinary brown boots.

They seemed content to wait him out, so Jim decided to take the bull by the horns. "Who are you? Why did you attack us?"

The male alien laughed and shook his head, causing the long white hair to flow around his shoulders madly. It also allowed Jim to see the long, pointed ears. He concentrated on what the man was saying.

"Why? Because we wish to. Or because we can." Jim noticed the other alien, the female, wasn't sharing his enjoyment of the moment. "I am Du Brimar, and this is Jo Coran. You may call me...Du Brimar." The alien giggled at his own joke. Was he insane, or drunk?

"I'm Jim Morris, and you're trespassing." Jim didn't smile. "In the broadest and most specific sense of the words." This elicited another giggle, and Jim looked at the female questioningly. She looked all business. He glanced past them and was surprised to see a human lying on the ground. Young, probably around twenty. What was he doing with them? "And you are?" he asked, encouragingly.

"He, is ours," The alien called Du Brimar said, all signs of good humor gone. "And now, so are you. Thank you for making it easy for us. You are the reason we came, after all. The infamous Jim Morris, Tryr

417

and Ananab killer."

"It wouldn't be that hard to add Egelv to the list," Jim said tightly.

"Oh yes it would." The Egelv started to raise his hand, and Jim went into a crouch and began reaching for his revolver.

Several things happened very rapidly, at that point. Shots rang out, but the bullets never reached their mark. There was an invisible barrier that caused them to ricochet wildly. Jim swore and ducked as a bullet whizzed by his ear. Simultaneously, the young man threw himself against the Egelv, evidently trying to disarm him.

Du Brimar shouted in fury and knocked his assailant to the side. He then quickly fired something at Jim.

Jim flinched, then relaxed. The inhibiting field must be up and working, he thought with relief. I wonder if he just stunned me or killed me. Another shot careened nearby and he shouted to Kabu and the others. "Hold your fire!"

He heard Du Brimar speaking with fury in his voice.

"No lower life form touches my person, unless I permit it," he snarled. The Egelv twisted his wrists, and both hands glowed a light blue. He reached for the transgressor, who rolled away, looking fearful as he tried to avoid the touch.

Jim leaped forward, forgetting about the shield for a moment. To his surprise, it didn't stop him, and he almost fell down. He recovered his footing, and reached the Egelv just as he was about to grab Jim's would be savior.

He gave the Egelv a boot in the rear that sent him sprawling into the dirt. With his right hand, Jim pulled the kid to his feet and shoved him towards the cabin.

He saw the female Egelv reaching for him with a blue glowing hand and kicked out, catching her in the midsection. She collapsed backward, falling to a sitting position. She tried to take a breath and a look of amazement, and then of fear, came to her face as she couldn't.

By this time, Du Brimar was back on his feet, his face contorted with anger. "I will kill you both for this!" The blue tint around his hands deepened in hue and he lunged forward.

Jim dropped to one hand and did a sweep that Du Brimar saw coming, but was too slow to avoid. He hit the beach hard, but was alert enough to try and grab Jim's leg with one hand.

Jim rolled backward to his feet and went into a stance. He glanced at Jo Coran and saw she was still sitting down, gasping as she finally

418

got oxygen into her lungs. He watched Du Brimar climb to his feet, his hands a brilliantly glittering dark blue.

"Oh good. We get to see the real Jim Morris in action." Du Brimar's grin held no humor and the glow extended up his arms to his elbows. It seemed to lighten slightly as the area it covered broadened. Du Brimar stopped and cocked his head. He shook it angrily. "I am doing my duty!" he shouted to no one. Jim raised an eyebrow, then realized the Egelv must be talking to his ship. Speaking of which...

"Irene?"

"Yes, Jim Morris," came the soft reply in his ear. He sighed in relief.

"What is this blue weapon? Is it fatal?"

"At it's highest intensity, it could be." Irene sounded uncertain. "There is not much information about Egelv personal weapons. I can tell you it both attacks the nervous system and damages skin tissue. The closest equivalent you would recognize would be getting struck by lightning and burned by a stove at the same time."

"Wonderful," Jim muttered to himself. He decided to make one more attempt to reason with the aliens.

"Du Brimar, Jo Coran, listen to me. And if you can hear me on board the ship, you really need to hear this." He watched as the two Egelv glared at him and Du Brimar took another step towards him. "Understand me. We don't want to fight you. We'd much rather be friends. But no one is going to push us around."

"I'm not going to push you around," Du Brimar's voice grated. "I'm going to kill you. But you will suffer first." With that, he threw himself at Jim.

Jim blocked one outstretched arm with his right forearm. He gasped at the sudden agony, but carried through with first, a kick to the groin, then with the other foot to where he hoped Egelv had kidneys. From Du Brimar's reaction, he rather thought they did.

While the Egelv tried to stay on his feet, Jim backed away a few steps and rubbed his arm trying to relieve the pain. It didn't seem to work. When he tried to raise it, he couldn't suppress a moan.

He almost didn't see the charging Egelv until it was too late. Du Brimar's expression was contorted with rage as he tried to grab Jim by the face.

Jim used the same arm to sweep the extended hands to the side and gasped as the agony renewed itself. He snapped out with his left hand, catching the tip of his assailant's chin. The blow wasn't hard enough to hurt the Egelv much, but it recharged his fury.

Jim tried to dance out of the long arms reach. A fingertip brushed his right elbow and he almost passed out from the pain. But he kept out of reach, his right arm now dangling useless at his side.

"I could use some ideas here," he managed to gasp out. "Irene?"

"If you could weaken the integrity of his power source, the water in the lake might cause his weapon to short out." Jim didn't think Irene sounded very confident. "I could intervene and try to penetrate their shields."

"No!" Jim dodged another attack and moved down to the water's edge where the sand was firmer. "I want to avoid a shooting war, if at all possible."

"You are done avoiding anything!" Du Brimar lunged at him and he kicked the tall alien in the bicep. Du Brimar got a startled expression on his face that turned to pain. The blue spread up his arms to the shoulders, but Jim noticed it seemed to be a lighter shade.

He can extend the field, but it gets weaker, Jim thought exultantly. He dived past Du Brimar and came to his feet attacking. One foot hit high on the shoulder, and he got one quick backhand across the face in. Then he was rolling away, his numb right arm making it awkward to be as smooth as he would have liked.

But Du Brimar glared at him, his face splotchy red from Jim's slap. The blue spread to cover the head and shoulders. But it was definitely lighter now.

Jim grinned at him without humor. He shocked the Egelv by stepping directly forward almost within reach. Before Du Brimar could take advantage, Jim dropped to the ground and kicked upwards into the other mans' stomach.

The force of the blow lifted the Egelv completely off his feet, and he flew backwards to land in the shallow lake water. Steam and electric discharges filled the air, but Du Brimar rose to his feet with the blue field intact. It now covered his complete abdomen.

"A little water isn't enough to affect Egelv technology," he said with a tight grin. He stepped to the side and put one foot up onto the dock.

Jim didn't even hesitate. He leaped forward kicking up towards Du Brimar's head. The Egelv raised a hand in defense, but it was a feint. Jim's right foot smashed down on the extended leg, crushing the knee-cap from the side.

Du Brimar screamed in an unholy pitch no Human could ever duplicate. Then he did it again as Jim never paused, spun, and used the same foot to kick the other knee, also from the inside. The Egelv collapsed backwards into the water, trying to hold both legs with both hands as he rolled from side to side.

Jim turned as Jo Coran rose to her feet and took a step forward. He shook his head. "You don't want to do this. You will have to leave."

"We will do as we wish. I am not so stupid as to try and defeat you this way." Jo Coran spoke coldly. Jim looked at her with interest. "We will disable your shielded shuttle and remove the inhibiting field. Even if you have P'TASSUM still functional, our ship is more than a match for anything made by the Ananab. We will take you aboard, one way or another. Unless you wish to be responsible for the deaths of many of your friends, you will surrender. P'Tassum can not enter the atmosphere, and by itself can do little to help your situation."

"Who said we only had one ship," Jim said. He flashed her a grin that showed lots of teeth, but little humor. "Irene? Come."

There was a sonic boom and Jade Wolverine appeared out of nowhere, hovering a thousand feet above the cabin, all weapons aimed at the parked Egelv ship. The Egelv stared in shock at the unfamiliar design.

Jim got her attention back in a hurry. "If your ship tries to lift off before we resolve this, every weapon we have will open fire. And you are at the bottom of a gravity well."

As if on cue, all three shuttles unstealthed and their weapons centered on the Egelv ship. Jo Coran grimaced and began mumbling inaudibly, obviously communicating with her ship. Du Brimar, on the other hand, was beyond reason. He was shouting at empty air, shrieking as he held his knees, the blue glow gone.

The young man came over to stand next to Jim. He hesitated a moment, then introduced himself.

"Hi, I'm Matt Stickel." He looked very self-conscious as they shook hands. "I've, uh, seen all your movies," he blurted out.

Jim kept the pain off his face as he tried to massage feeling back into his right arm, and nodded towards the Egelv. "How'd you get hooked up with these?"

"They snatched us from a cruise ship in Turkey." Matt said. He watched Du Brimar, and Jim could have sworn he saw sadness in the young man's eyes. "Sound familiar?"

"Just a little," Jim muttered, then picked up the reference. "Did you say 'we'?"

Matt nodded. "A Spanish woman, Teresa Elizari, was with me. She's on board right now." He nodded towards the Egelv ship.

"Hmmm, a Basque, eh?" Matt looked surprised, but nodded and Jim rubbed his chin thoughtfully. They weren't out of this by a long shot, yet. He came to a decision, but before he could act, Jo Coran turned to face them.

"Jim Morris, we will take our leave. This matter can be settled another day." An antigrav raft floated out the hatch and across the water towards Du Brimar.

"Nobody goes anywhere until a few matters are straightened out," Jim said flatly. "Do Egelv understand the concept 'honor'? Of giving your word in promise?"

"Of course we do." Jo Coran glared at him. "We promise not to attack you or your people this day."

"Hmm," Jim said, shaking his head regretfully. "I don't think that's going to do it."

"What do you mean?" Her voice was almost a snarl, and Matt stirred uncomfortably beside Jim. "Don't press your luck, Human."

"Don't press yours," Jim countered. "We have all the advantage here. You will abide by our terms, or the shooting starts."

"Terms?" Jo Coran's eyes were round in shock. This was clearly a new role for her. Her voice grew quiet, which bothered Jim even more. "What terms?"

"First, you have a Human female on board. She is to be released at once." Jo Coran glared at Matt, who took a step backwards, then seemed to gain resolve and stood his ground.

"Second, you will take no more prisoners, or 'specimens' as you probably call them, from this world." Jim was gratified to see what might have been embarrassment flash across her face.

"Third, you will leave this system at once. If you ever return to Earth in any capacity other than emissary of peace, I guarantee it will be your last trip."

Jo Coran raised her head in defiance. "I will do whatever and go where ever my duty sends me."

The two locked stares.

Finally, Jim nodded. "Fine. You and your ship depart at once. If you ever return, it's at your own risk, and you know the consequences."

Jo Coran stood tightlipped for a few moments, then nodded. "Agreed."

"And remember," Jim said, his voice edged with determination. "No picking up any more souvenirs on your way out."

"Agreed. But we will keep the female." Jo Coran smiled vindictively at him. "We will not surrender her."

"Then this battle is not over," Jim said, drawing his revolver with his left hand and aiming it at her. The barrel was in a direct line with her eyes. "You will go nowhere until we have the girl."

"You will not fire." Jo Coran straightened from the unconscious Du Brimar. He had evidently passed out from the pain. "You Earth people have these 'codes of honor' you live by. I am a woman, and he is defenseless."

"And I have had all I'm taking from arrogant aliens trying to push me around," Jim said and shifted his aim to Du Brimar and cocked the hammer. "Further, I don't like this guy one bit. My arm still hurts, so give me a reason."

"Stop!" The voice thundered over the water from the open hatch of the Egelv ship. They turned to see an older male standing in the entrance, his arms gesturing vigorously. "Enough of this! We will release the female and leave. You have my word."

"And who are you?" Jim asked, his weapon never wavering.

"I am Cromar Try, captain of this vessel." He had a dignity Du Brimar had shown no sign of, and Jim was impressed by his courage to put himself within reach of the enemy.

"Deal," he agreed finally. "Let's do it." Behind him, he heard Matt give a sigh of relief as Jim holstered his pistol, carefully lowering the hammer back into safety.

◆ ◆ ◆ ◆ ◆

Teresa Elizari stood up. Siph Carni seemed to be at a loss for words.

She turned to leave, then stopped as she remembered something. She turned back and went to Du Brimar's work station. She gathered up the video tapes strewn around the console.

"What are you doing? Leave those." Irritation showed in Siph Carni's voice as she stood.

"These are stolen property," Teresa said primly. "Are the Egelv now petty thieves as well as kidnappers?"

423

The Egelv stared at her with frustration written all over her face. Then a light seemed to go out of her eyes. "Just get out," Siph Carni said in a dull voice.

Twenty minutes later, the humans watched the Egelv ship disappear into the sky, Jade Wolverine following, with 'Viking waiting upstairs to provide backup if necessary.

Jim shook hands with Teresa after she and Matt finished ecstatic hugs. "Pleased to meet you," he said in flawless Spanish. The woman smiled, looking surprised at his accent.

A familiar voice made Jim turn before she could respond. Kiri stood at the foot of the steps, Angela Dawson beside her, carrying an AK-47. The young Japanese looked a little unsteady on her feet, but her irrepressible sense of humor had already returned.

"Did I miss anything?"

◆ ◆ ◆ ◆ ◆

CHAPTER TWENTY-NINE

Kimberly opened her eyes and stared at an unfamiliar ceiling. How many times in the last few weeks have I had this experience, she thought as she tried to remember where she was.

Then it came back to her with a rush and she sat up in panic.

Someone stood with their back to her, staring out the window. It was a familiar form, but the dim moonlight kept her from identifying who it was.

"Kiri?" she asked, then knew better.

Jim turned to face her, his face still shadowed. "No, not Kiri," he answered in a quiet voice. As if to forestall any more questions, he hurried on. "She's resting in one of the other rooms. She was shot with tranquilizers, not real bullets. She's fine."

Kimberly sat watching her husband as he hesitantly stepped to the side of the bed. He's scared, she realized with a growing sense of wonder. He doesn't know where he stands with me, after our fight. I bet he thinks Kiri and I... She felt her face go red and was thankful for the early morning darkness.

At least I think it's early morning, she thought. Has he been standing there all night? She slid over to make room for him next to her and patted the bed encouragingly.

As he sat, she got a good look at his face for the first time. The scar was healing, but it definitely wasn't going away, she acknowledged with a touch of sadness. And he'd been so damn good looking, too. Not that he was ugly, now, she hurried to add to herself.

She took a closer look and frowned at what she saw beneath the scar. To say he looked troubled was totally inadequate. It went far beyond that.

"What is it, Jim?" she asked, placing a hand on his arm in concern. "Are you okay?"

"As always." His lips twisting ever so slightly as he spoke. "Never a dull moment."

"Quit putting on a face, Jim." She almost didn't recognize her voice, then realized why. It was her 'courtroom' tone, and she hadn't used it in a long time. "This is Kimberly, your wife, remember? What's wrong?"

"It's been...difficult since you left," he admitted, his voice a little thick with emotion. "There was so much that wasn't settled. Then Afsaneh and I haven't been getting along too good lately, and she almost got killed..."

"What happened?" Kimberly gasped, and was startled by her immediate and genuine concern.

"It's a long story," Jim began, but she cut him off. Words weren't what was needed right now for either of them.

"She's okay, right?" He nodded. "We've got all day to talk, Jim." She picked up his hand and kissed it, then held it to her cheek. "Right now, just hold me, and tell me you still love me."

"Still love you?" Jim looked at her incredulously. "Was there ever any doubt?"

"No, but after spending so much 'premium' time with Kiri, I need to reassert my heterosexuality," Kimberly smiled to show she was kidding, but an edge crept into her voice as she continued. "Of course, you could have warned me..."

"Not my business." Jim shook his head, giving her a crooked grin. "You're a big girl."

"That's not all I am," Kimberly said, and drew him to her.

Unnoticed by either of them, the gloomy shadows shifted, then changed to the soft glowing of dawn as the night fled before the early morning sun.

Ann Arbor, Michigan

"Have a nice day!" Afsaneh grinned at the departing backs of the frustrated FBI agents as they filed from the room. Yvette frowned at her, but Janice was studiously inspecting the ceiling, the corner of her mouth twitching. "How'd I do?"

"I thought you did just fine," Dawn Williams assured her. Yvette gave the pretty, black nurse a sharp look which was totally ignored. "I think you might have a future in public relations." Janice snickered.

Dr. Tinsley swept into the room and picked up her chart. As he scanned the data, he nodded in approval.

"You're doing very well, young lady." I think we might send you home in a few days."

"Today would be great." Afsaneh gave him one of her most endearing smiles, which went to waste since he didn't look up from the charts.

"Tomorrow or the next would be better." Dr. Tinsley did look up then, but his expression offered no hope of a change of mind. "If you behave today, get plenty of rest, eat your meals, take your medicine..."

"Do my homework, clean my room, brush my teeth..." Afsaneh chanted, counting the items off on the fingers of her left hand. She stopped and shrugged in resignation. "You remind me of some people I know."

"How's your memory?" Tinsley gave her a shrewd look that made her suspect he could see right through her. "Anything?"

Afsaneh shook her head, knowing better than to make a joke of it. The doctor was on their side, but that didn't mean he approved of lying to the FBI. And after all, he wasn't one of them. For that matter, despite her show of friendship and support, neither was Dawn Williams.

"I'm afraid I've still got a big blank spot in my memory, Doctor." Afsaneh suppressed a yawn. "If I can't check out now, I guess I'll try and get some sleep.

"Good idea." Dr. Tinsley nodded his approval, and gave Dawn a questioning glance. "Nurse?"

Dawn got a guilty look on her face, and hurriedly patted Afsaneh on the leg. "Got to go, Hon. I'm behind on my chores. Talk to you later." Then she quickly left behind the doctor.

"Something about her," Yvette muttered, watching them leave. "I don't know what it is."

"I like her," Janice said, giving Afsaneh a wink.

"You like anything that wears a skirt," Yvette said darkly, pulling the covers up a little on Afsaneh's bed. Afsaneh didn't laugh. She'd seen the routine before. Their union was far stronger than any hetero marriage she'd ever seen. Not that she'd seen all that many, she admitted.

Her eyes seemed heavy, but she wasn't really sleepy. She'd just said that to get the good doctor off her back. Yvette and Janice went on talking, and she closed her eyes for a moment. Their voices gradually faded into a droning sound. She thought about how good it would be to sleep in her own room again. The bed was much more comfortable, and she missed her stereo. And her video player, and her teddy bear, Polaris.

She doubted she'd get any sleep, but it felt good to rest her eyes.

"We'll be landing in three minutes, Captain," Lasty said. He made an adjustment to his controls and the big screen showed the landscape below change from water to land as Lake Michigan was left behind. "Beginning to slow for our sheathed approach."

"Good." Jim smiled wryly at his first officer. "We don't want to shake up the old neighborhood with sonic booms now, do we?"

Jim closed his eyes for a moment, mixed feelings at war within him. 'Wolverine and Viking had escorted the Egelv long enough to be sure they were really leaving. Captain Tachibana said he would stay in constant contact while he verified their exit from the solar system. Lasty had then brought 'Wolverine back to Tahoe to pick up the two shuttles. Kimberly and Kiri were safely aboard, having coffee with Angela in the lounge. And he had just talked with Yvette, found out that Afsaneh was recovering nicely, and was sleeping.

Life should have been good. But as if to refute that, he'd found out both Sasama and Iori were dead, probably killed by the same Sukuru thugs that kidnaped Kimberly and Kiri. He'd liked them both, and Sasama had worked with him almost as long as Kabu and Kiri.

The FBI was less likely to be gullible or easily satisfied with dead bodies becoming part of the equation. Further, there was the matter of Matt Stickel and Teresa Elizari. Inserting them back into their lives wouldn't be simple.

His reverie was interrupted by Irene. "I am picking up four life signs at your residence, Jim Morris. One of them is Ron Hoffman. I believe the other three are his employees."

Jim nodded his head in resignation. Until he dealt with the FBI, guards were the only way to guarantee privacy in his own home. They were also watching Afsaneh. He didn't think Sukuru would try anything right away, but there was no point in being careless. It also kept the FBI from taking her to a more "convenient" location for questioning.

"There are also two Human males in a ground vehicle parked across the road," Irene continued. "If you wish to make a covert landing, we will need to reduce speed."

Jim frowned. If it wasn't one thing, it was another. "Will they be able to see us if we land behind the house and keep the ship cloaked?"

"No."

"Do it, Lasty." Jim watched the Baerd make adjustments, murmuring to Irene softly as the house came into view on the big screen. He was glad to see no hesitation or sign of uncertainty. Lasty had gained a lot of self-confidence over the past few weeks.

A learning time for everyone, Jim thought dourly. He stood as the ship settled gently to the ground. He would get everyone settled inside, then he was going to have a nice quiet visit with his daughter.

A nice quiet visit with his daughter, indeed. Jim scowled as he sat in Claw's co-pilot seat and watched Angela Dawson operate the controls as if she'd been doing it all her life. More like a circus! He'd fully intended to go alone, but Kimberly insisted that she had to see how bad the injuries were.

Fine. Kimberly and he could slip in and out without anyone the wiser. Then Kiri found out they were going, and there was no denying her. Understandable, considering Afsaneh was practically her little sister. Three would be okay.

Uh, uh, said Angela Dawson. If you're going, I'm going, she said. Since Jim was taking Claw, Irene thought it was a good idea.

For security reasons.

"Security?" Jim tried to find a spot to focus on to address Irene. He finally settled for glaring at Angela. She didn't flinch a bit. In fact, she pulled out her service revolver expressively, then made it disappear back out of sight.

"I have a license for this, remember?" Angela gestured at him and the other two women. "None of you can legally carry a weapon."

Jim made a face and pointedly raised his hands. He hated to brag, but this was ridiculous. "Technically, that's not true."

"None the less," Angela answered in a tone that didn't offer any room for discussion.

Jim tried to stare her down, then scratched his head with resignation. "Isn't there one female, anywhere in the universe, that I can win an argument with?" he asked plaintively.

And it hadn't stopped there. Ron Hoffman said he might as well come along, since he was due to head back to Fort Worth in a few hours. But when Ellis and Sean began to make noises, Jim put his foot down.

"I'm beginning to like you boys," he said evenly. "Don't push your luck."

They immediately backed down. They'd already lost one argument with him that afternoon about sleeping quarters. It hadn't taken them long to familiarize themselves with the house, and the guest room next to Afsaneh's bedroom had immediately attracted them. They had both rebelled when Jim told them they would be staying on board the 'Wolverine.

"Sorry, guys. But at the moment, you're both considered missing. We can't have you being spotted here in the house. Anyway, tomorrow's a school day."

"Excuse me?" For once, Ellis had been the one to speak out first. "School day? What are you talking about?"

"You've got a lot to learn about the ship, and plenty of other things. I've got Irene and Dutter making up a course plan for all of you."

"I already know how to operate my station," Sean pointed out, an edge in his voice.

"Sure you do." Jim grinned at him. "But do you have the slightest idea how it works? How to fix your instruments if there's a malfunction? What type of government the Hshtahni have?"

Sean and Ellis glanced at each other in despair. The other young crewmen seemed to accept the logic, but Jim could see these two would take a little longer coming around. He suspected at least one other crewman, currently listed as injured, would be even harder to convince.

Sounds like a job for her new mother, Jim thought, careful to keep any hint of that idea off his face.

The shuttle came to a gentle halt barely a foot from the roof of the hospital. A quick check showed nobody there. Jim used Irene to check in with Yvette. She and Janice were both visiting Afsaneh and Janice came up to open the fire door.

"Come here often?" she asked, grinning.

"Shaddap," Jim muttered. Janice's grin grew bigger. He knew she loved riding him when he was in one of his 'martyr' moods. He began walking briskly towards the elevator, making her hurry to keep up. "FBI?"

"Just one at the room, outside the door." Janice sounded a little out of breath and Jim suppressed a grin. "We've been giving him drinks for the last couple of hours. His bladder should be about ready to give."

"Just one?" Jim was surprised. That seemed awfully low key. The elevator arrived while they waited for the others to catch up.

Janice shrugged her shoulders. "They know Afsaneh can't go home for a few more days. I think they're a little shorthanded. Wait here," she said as they left the elevator and came to a corner of the corridor near their destination. She walked on and Jim watched her through a circular mirror at the intersection.

Janice walked up to the door and put a hand on the knob, then hesitated. She looked at the man in the dark suit that stood next to it.

"Do you know where the johns are?" Janice grimaced and glanced around. "I've gotta pee like a race horse."

The guard winced and pointed down the corridor in the other direction. "About halfway down, on the left." He watched her scurry away, then looked at the other man watching the door.

One of Hoffman's men, Jim decided. The security man laughed and gestured. "Go on," he said with sympathy in his voice. "There's nothing happening here."

The FBI agent looked doubtful, then pained. "Just for a moment," he finally said, giving one last look up and down the hallway.

Thirty seconds later, Jim and his entourage were inside Afsaneh's room, having a tearful reunion.

"Try to keep it quiet," Ron Hoffman said, standing by the door. "We don't need that guard peeking inside to find out what all the ruckus is."

Angela turned the volume up on the television and Ron nodded appreciatively. A moment later, Janice slipped into the room. She winked at Jim. "Guard is back at his station, sir!" She gave him a mock salute to accent her words. "And none the wiser."

"Well, that's something going right," Jim grumbled. He gave Yvette a hug as Kimberly and Kiri fussed over Afsaneh. He was relieved to see her color had returned to her face, and she was acting closer to her old self again. He sighed as he looked at the remains of her beautiful head of hair that showed around the bandages.

"I called Hugh Bishop, and he's getting the judge, just in case," Yvette whispered. "I don't expect any more visits tonight, but I think we should play it safe."

"Whatever," Jim said vaguely. "We're not staying too long."

"Oh?" For some reason, Yvette seemed to be getting quite a kick out of something. "I figured you would stay for a while, catch up on news, maybe watch some television."

"Yeah, right." Jim snorted at her sense of humor. She knew he had little use for America's most popular form of entertainment. He stepped over to the side of Afsaneh's bed. "How you feeling, Punkin?"

"Much better, Father." Afsaneh was glowing with excitement. "I was just telling Kiri and Mom how I drove that FBI agent crazy today when he tried to question me again. I don't think he has much of a sense of humor," she added, trying, but failing, to look serious.

Jim noticed Yvette signaling Kimberly, and started to say something when he saw Angela stiffen and step close to the door to listen. His attention was split as he moved over to join her.

"Haven't you told him about 'it' yet?" Yvette whispered, pointing at the television. Jim was curious, but then he heard the sound of arguing out in the corridor.

"What day is it?" Kiri asked, looking at Kimberly with a pained expression on her face. As Jim watched them and listened to the voices outside, he was disconcerted to see all four women turn and look at him.

"What?" he said, forgetting about the noise outside for a moment. He saw Kimberly look at her watch and wince.

"Am I missing something?" Afsaneh chipped in. "What's the secret?"

"What indeed?" Jim asked, giving Kimberly his most determined questioning look.

"You didn't tell him?" Yvette asked incredulously, and Janice began giggling.

Kimberly gestured helplessly. "We've been kind of busy," Kiri pointed out.

"Excuse me." Jim was amazed at how calm his voice sounded. "What are we..." His attention snapped back to the door and a moment later it opened. Four men in dark suits walked in. They froze when they saw Jim. The senior looking agent barely hesitated.

"Jim Morris?" Jim nodded, masking his irritation. "You're under arrest."

"I don't think so," he retorted, his eyes narrowing at the overweight older man. "Who the hell are you?"

"My name is Karl Costa, senior agent on this case." The smaller man didn't back down an inch. "You evaded my men several days ago in

432

this very building. You're not doing it again. Come with me please." His eyes moved around the room and lighted up when they saw Kimberly and Kiri. "Excellent. Both of you, too. In fact, all of you. You're all under arrest."

"Do you have a warrant?" Anyone knowing Jim well would have flinched at the seemingly mild tone in his voice. Costa didn't budge an inch.

"I don't need a warrant." Costa's lips tightened and his eyes narrowed. "I'm a federal agent, and you are a material witness in a kidnaping and murder case."

"I don't think so," Jim repeated, shaking his head. "If you want to question me, fine. But you're not taking me anywhere."

"You're coming with us." One of the other agents, a very young one at that, stepped forward and pulled out a taser. The young man's look of determination changed, first to confusion, then horror.

Jim made a show of examining the weapon he now held. He couldn't blame the poor guy's chagrin. He hadn't even gotten it raised before Jim stepped forward and pulled it out of his hand. A pinch of the wrist with one hand allowed Jim to take it from the unresisting fingers with the other.

"Give it back!" Costa snapped the words out as he and the other two men started for their guns. They froze at the words spoken behind them.

"Don't move. Leave your weapons holstered. Do not turn around."

Angela grinned and winked at Jim . She'd stepped behind the opening door when they'd entered and hadn't even been noticed. She knew better than to draw her own revolver, he saw. Good. As long as they didn't call her bluff, she controlled the situation.

It wasn't her fault if they thought she had the drop on them.

"You're just making this worse," Costa said through gritted teeth. "You can't go around threatening federal officers."

"Look, Mr. Costa," Jim said quickly, trying to draw attention away from the weapon issue. "We can talk all you want. But not in some federal building. I have no intention of disappearing again. I'm afraid I don't have any memory of the time I was missing..."

"Right, you and most of the others..." Costa was actually snarling now. Jim regretted making an enemy of the man, but there were few other options he could think of. "Are you sure you're not of the group that collectively remembers being kidnaped by aliens?"

"Oh sure," Jim said, rolling his eyes. "That's it. I was kidnaped by aliens. Bugeyed monsters, if you will." He tried to make his voice more conciliatory. "Look, I'm sure there's a logical explanation..."

He was interrupted by Janice, using her thickest drawl.

"That's right. And if you two will shut up for a moment, we can all see what it is."

Jim and Costa both stared at her. She just gave them a big toothy grin and pointed at the television. Kiri was turning the sound up.

"...'Escape From Miami' isn't the only science fiction movie being released this month. Tonight, ET brings you the first exclusive clips from the new Jim Morris film, 'Defiant Fists of Earth'. But first..."

Jim felt his jaw drop and quickly recovered his composure before the FBI agent noticed. He looked at Kimberly, who gave him a tentative smile, even as she answered Costa's first question.

"Yes, it's true, we were doing the finishing touches on the film on the cruise. In fact, we had a viewing on board the second night. Not the entire film, of course, just a sampling."

"You didn't say anything about this before," Costa pointed out, his voice grim. "This is the first time I've heard anything about this. I did mention that some people had conflicting stories..."

"You were serious about that?" Jim watched Kiri ad-lib nervously. He didn't consider it one of her strong suits, but he was relieved to see she wasn't overdoing it. "Our movie had nothing to do with whatever happened to us on the ship. At least, as far as I know. I don't know about Kimberly, but it never occurred to me that you were taking any story about alien abductions seriously."

"It does sound pretty silly," Kimberly agreed.

Jim decided it was time for him to contribute his share.

"Mr. Costa, I have no idea what on earth happened to me from that second night until just the last few days when I found myself near here with Afsaneh. She was hurt pretty bad, so I brought her here, then tried to figure out what had happened." Jim tried to look convincing. "I'm just as confused as you, but it's hard to believe I was kidnapped by aliens."

"What happened to your face," Costa challenged. "Something got hold of you pretty good. Quite a few witnesses said it was a big black panther that stands almost seven feet tall."

"Well then, they know more about it than I do," Jim snapped, feeling irrationally defensive about the grotesque scar.

"I don't..." Whatever Costa was about to say got cut off as Afsaneh interrupted.

"Ssssh! It's starting," Afsaneh said, watching the television intently. Costa glowered, but kept quiet as the show began the segment dealing with the movie.

"Anyone who's ever seen a Jim Morris action movie knows what to expect. Lots of villains in black, usually ninjas. A beautiful woman waiting to be rescued, more often than not, Kiri Oshiba. And, of course, lots of fantastic fights and moving lips that don't always match the dialogue."

Jim grimaced. That was one of his pet peeves and he'd nearly eliminated dubbing in his last few movies. But it always got mentioned, at some point or another.

"This month, we'll be treated to what may well be the first of many Jim Morris action science fiction films. 'Defiant Fists of Earth' opens in what has to be, for Jim, a record number of movie houses across the nation. Diane?"

Jim looked at Kimberly, but she kept her eyes on the television, her cheeks and neck reddening as she felt his gaze.

"Thank you, Perry. As you can see, Jim hasn't lost any of his moves..." The screen showed Jim punching an unseen opponent, fists and feet sometimes meeting black fur, other times thick grayish-brown hide. Behind him was a large picture window that showed a myriad of stars The view switched to an approach of Earth itself, with a dull roaring in the background, obviously intended to be spaceship engines.

The picture changed again, this time showing Kabu shooting an arrow. A shrill screaming sound follows, than a thud and Kabu is seen flying over a guardrail.

"Cool," Afsaneh breathed, and Jim looked at her in surprise. She was staring at the preview, mesmerized.

"But from what I can tell, Perry, this movie has a lot more to it than anything Jim Morris has ever done before. We only saw clips, but they were impressive, and personally I can't wait to see the whole thing! I had an opportunity to talk with Jim's favorite movie flame, Kiri Oshiba. And, to spice things up even more, Jim's new flame, Wall Street lawyer Kimberly Martin. Of course the director, Frederick Farmer, and producer Jerry Weinstein were there, too. And they were very excited about this project."

"Any truth to the rumors about Jim Morris and Kimberly Martin being married, Diane?"

Jim controlled his breathing with an effort. He knew he couldn't expect to have a lot of privacy as long as he was in the movies, but...this? He glanced around the room. Everyone seemed hypnotized by the show, even the FBI agents. He noticed Kimberly's neck was even redder now, and Kiri had a hand stuffed over her mouth, rocking back and forth as she tried to contain her laughter. But she studiously kept her eyes away from him.

Jim buried a groan deep inside. This couldn't get much worse, could it?

Sure it could.

"Perry, I'm afraid it's true. One of Hollywood's most eligible, sexy bachelors is out of circulation. As Kiri told me during a brief moment Kimberly wasn't present, it was love at first sight. A whirlwind overnight romance, followed by a wedding performed on the high seas by none other than the ship's captain. Kimberly was very noncommittal, and wouldn't confirm anything, but Kiri explained that was because Jim and Kimberly wanted to start a family soon, and would keep their private life as far from the public as possible."

The picture switched on Kimberly and Kiri sitting on a couch, laughing and chatting with the hostess of the show. The camera zeroed in on Kimberly and her face filled the screen.

"Oh, my God!" Kimberly exclaimed in horror. "You told them I was going to be a baby factory? And look at me! I'd been driving all day, non-stop from New York. Look at the bags under my eyes!"

"I told you so," Kiri sang out, then ducked her head at the glares she got from both Jim and Kimberly. "Hey, this is great publicity for the movie," she protested, her voice wilting under their withering looks.

"Speaking of which...?" Jim started to say, then abruptly shut his mouth. He'd been about to blurt out his indignation about not knowing anything about any change in the movie. Not exactly brilliant with the FBI standing around hanging on every word.

He saw the younger FBI man he'd disarmed earlier trying to say something to Costa, but was waved to silence. Costa obviously could tell a gold mine of uninhibited chatter when he saw it. Jim drew his attention back to the picture tube with an effort.

"Although we haven't seen a clear picture of the aliens yet, undisclosed sources tell me they're simply spectacular, Diane."

"That's what I'm told, Perry," the woman gushed. "But I think the human elements of the story are what will make this movie the best we've seen from Jim Morris and company to date."

"You may be right, Diane. One of the more intriguing elements of this story surrounds the cruise ship Jade Viking. For those of you viewers who..."

Jim quickly spoke. "Mr. Costa, I can't explain..."

"What Jim is trying to say, Mr. Costa," Kimberly cut in and Jim stared at her in astonishment. "...is that we can't explain the memory lapses we suffered, but it seems like a lot of passengers and even crewmen of the ship that went to the preview kept that memory and perhaps lost sight of its origin. If it was one of the last occurrences before whatever befell us, it would gain strength and believability in some people's minds."

Jim forgot he was angry at being interrupted as he listened to her very convincing presentation. So, obviously, was Karl Costa. He seemed to hang on her every word.

"...and I'm sure you noticed, none of the passengers connected to the movie were victims of this mass...hallucination. That was because we were all so familiar with it, it didn't dominate our memories that evening when...whatever happened, happened," she finished lamely.

Costa stood motionless for a moment, as if to make sure she was finished. Jim discreetly handed the taser back to the young agent who looked at it in surprise, then holstered it.

"Ms. Martin, or should I call you Mrs. Morris?" Costa didn't wait for her answer. "I've heard you're an excellent lawyer, and I must admit, I believe it. You can talk...like no one I've ever listened to. And if I was in a jury, I'd believe you, completely." He beamed at her, but the humor didn't extend to his eyes, or his words.

"As it is, I'm an FBI agent. And I think you're lying through your teeth." He gave her a flinty smile. "And...I also don't think I can prove it right now. But I will get to the bottom of this, you can count on it."

"Now wait just a min..." Jim began, and was startled when he was interrupted for the second time in as many minutes.

"Put it in a sock, Mr. Morris." Costa's face lost all vestiges of good humor, and Jim raised his eyebrows in surprise. "We're still investigating two homicides, those of Sasama Sakakibara and Iori Kojiro. They were linked to one of your cars registered in California, and their bodies were found here in Ann Arbor, where you were first seen."

Jim felt tears well up in his eyes as the thought of his two friends left dead in a dumpster. He balled his fists as the despair changed to an anger that threatened to consume him.

His movement didn't escape Costa's attention. "Don't even think it, Mr. Morris. You're an actor, and you fight on a stage or in front of a camera. I'm an FBI agent, and I live, and fight, in the real world. Nobody yells 'cut!' when it gets rough."

Jim was speechless. The outrageousness of what he'd just heard...it took a supreme effort to carefully form his next words.

"Listen up. I'm only going to say this once, but for your sake, I'll try and use small words." He could sense the entire room was frozen with shock. Costa's men were probably remembering some of his movies, wondering if he really was as good as he seemed. And all Jim's people had to be wondering if he was about to kill this idiot.

"First, Sasama and Iori were my friends. If I ever find their killers, you will be able to connect me to a homicide, maybe more than one. But the last time I saw them was aboard the Jade Viking, and they were both alive and healthy." He could hear the quiver in his own voice and hated the sign of weakness.

Costa didn't back down, and Jim realized he was about to do something very stupid as the man opened his mouth to speak. Jim blinked and his clarity of vision was suddenly astounding. He could see every muscle in Costa's lips as he began to form the first words that would lead to his unconsciousness.

"Agent Costa."

The words snapped across the room like a whip, and both men froze in shock. Judge Maines stood in the doorway, Hugh Bishop peering over one shoulder from behind him.

"Do you have some sort of warrant that I signed during a seizure? Or perhaps in my sleep?" The judge took two steps forward, and Bishop and Dr. Tinsley crowded in behind him, not wanting to miss the fun. "I certainly don't remember signing anything of the sort. And this is my jurisdiction in federal court, and Judge Hansen's in circuit. I just spoke with him. He doesn't remember signing any papers either."

Costa opened his mouth, obviously thought better of whatever he was about to say, and closed it again. He had the look of a man who wished he were somewhere far away. Judge Maines didn't give him time to think.

"Well? What do you have to say?" His mild tone belied the biting interrogation.

"Sir," Costa spoke slowly, evidently determined to control his words. "I would like, no, I need to question this man, and this woman, whom I

438

believe to be Officer Angela Dawson, another missing person from the passenger list of the Jade Viking."

"Is that it?" Judge Maines demanded. He was a very tall man and loomed high over the agent as he spoke.

Costa swallowed hard. "I would also like to speak again with Kimberly Martin, Kiri Oshiba, and Afsaneh Riahi, preferably in separate sessions." He'd lost the winds out of his sails and probably knew it, but Jim had to admit he made an attempt to recover his aplomb. "I feel these interviews are crucial to my investigation, and that my authority is being circumvented."

"Your authority, your authority being circumvented?" The judge glanced at the two men behind him. Costa's head seemed to sink deeper between his shoulders with each use of the word 'authority'. "Well, we wouldn't want the FBI to feel they were losing authority, would we?"

Judge Maines straightened his tie as if considering things. "Fine. The Doctor here tells me visiting hours are over, it's late, and I have a dinner engagement."

He glared at Costa as if challenging him to say anything about his dinner having priority over FBI matters. Thankfully, Costa had the sense to keep his mouth shut. When no one said anything, the judge continued in a milder manner.

"Tomorrow morning, nine a.m., in my chambers. We'll make sure all our little duckies are in a row." Jim was startled when the judge abruptly whirled to face him. "I want to see you at ten o'clock, same place, is that clear?"

Jim nodded quickly, suppressing the urge to smile. The judge didn't even slow down to wait for his answer. "Ms. Martin, Ms. Oshiba, Ms. Dawson, you will make yourselves available at one in the afternoon, for whatever reasonable period of time Mr. Costa needs you, understood?"

All three women nodded meekly. Jim could see Kimberly was bemused by this 'provincial' use of authority by the judge. Kiri appeared to be having trouble controlling her laughter, and Angela was impassive as ever.

"As far as Azfanseh Riahi goes....," Jim winced and wasn't surprised when the interruption came.

"Your honor, that's Afsaneh." She gave the judge her most endearing smile. When he just looked at her without answering, she tried to clarify things. "You said my name wrong. Uh, it's, um, Afsaneh, your Honor." The last words were barely legible as she wilted under his scrutiny.

He gave her a final piercing look, then continued as if nothing had happened. "She is a minor, and has the right to the presence of legal guardian, as well as counsel. Dr. Tinsley has consented to her being questioned tomorrow after dinner by yourself and one aide during visiting hours."

He rubbed his hands together briskly. "Any questions? Comments? Good. Tomorrow then." And he was gone.

Jim watched Costa exhale heavily and gesture to his men. They silently followed him from the room.

Everyone stood or sat in shock until Afsaneh finally broke the silence. "I thought that went pretty well, don't you?"

Groundhog was weary, but not too tired to appreciate the humor of what he'd just listened to. The meeting at the hospital had been hilarious and it was fun visualizing Costa lecturing Morris on the 'real' world.

And that judge! He was priceless. A throwback to the middle of the last century, and small town politics.

Groundhog decided to head back to Jim's house, then noticed the judge getting into a limo parked by the front entrance. It was headed in the same direction as Groundhog, so it was easy to swing in behind, staying a comfortable distance back, even in the heavy traffic flow.

As the two cars continued on in the same direction, a suspicion began to grow in Groundhog's head. They were confirmed when the limo pulled into a driveway. The lights to the house were barely visible through the heavily wooded lot.

Groundhog kept driving. After all, it wouldn't do for the posted FBI agents to notice that the same car drove by at intervals, slowing down each time in front of their stakeout.

Jim sank into the big recliner with a sigh. He wished he could have spent more time with Afsaneh, but with that crowd it was a zoo. She was coming home in a day or two anyway.

He'd sent 'Wolverine to Turkey with careful instructions to Lasty and Angela on how to release Matt and Teresa. If he'd learned nothing else from all this, it was that everyone needed to keep their own spot in their lives open, if possible.

It wouldn't be easy for the two of them to explain their curious memory lapse and disappearance. But at least they would be showing up around the same place they vanished from. Both had been outfitted with new translator patches, compliments of Irene. If they wanted, they could return as soon as circumstances permitted. Jim liked and respected them both and hoped to see them again.

The first non Jade Viking members of Humanity's best hope for the future, Jim mused to himself. He glanced at his watch, then hurriedly roused himself.

"Kiri, can you call Akira's Restaurant and place an order for delivery?" Jim stood with a groan. He hadn't gotten much sleep last night. "Tell them we need a 'D' as in 'delta' order, and to put it on my account."

Kiri and Kimberly stepped into the living room and Kiri bowed deeply. "Ah, so, Master Morris. I shall do thy bidding, oh great one." She ducked the pillow and ran down the hallway, laughing.

"You're ordering out for Japanese food?" Kimberly smiled at him. "Sounds yummy. 'D' order?"

"In the old days, we used to order from them once or twice a week. Delta is a pretty big order, everything from sushi to Teriyaki chicken and sake," Jim admitted, then he looked at her with concern. "You do like Japanese food, don't you?"

"Of course," Kimberly laughed. "Especially sushi."

"Yeah." Jim grinned as they both heard the sound of a car coming up the drive. He waved the startled guard off and winked at his wife. "You cook it up, it tastes a lot like fish."

"Not that old joke," Kimberly protested. "That isn't the food already is it?"

"You wish," Jim said. "As if even Akira's could deliver that fast. No, it's our dinner guests." He used the remote control to open the garage door, and when the sound of the car turned off, closed it again.

"Dinner guests?" Kimberly stared at him, perplexed as she went to the door to the garage with him. "Who's coming to dinner?"

Jim just smiled and opened the door.

"Come in, your Honor."

❖ ❖ ❖ ❖ ❖

"...and that's about it, in a condensed nutshell," Jim said, downing

441

another tiny cup of sake. He tried to refill it from the ornate decanter in front of him, but it was empty. He looked at Kiri hopefully, but she shook her head and upended her own decanter. It too, was dry.

"Jim, if I hadn't known you for...you're not pulling my leg, are you?" Judge Stan Maines ran his fingers through prematurely gray hair as he considered the matter. The judge was twenty years older than Jim, but had worked for the firm that handled all of Jim and Hakim's legal matters. The same firm in which Hugh Bishop was now a senior partner.

"Everything I've told you is absolutely true," Jim assured him, glancing at the other two men to reinforce his statement. Judge Harold Hansen's jurisdiction was county, and he was a few years younger than Maines, but took his job just as seriously. It had taken all of Hugh Bishop's persuasive skills to get them to do everything they'd done on trust alone.

Now that they'd heard the whole story, they looked even less enthusiastic. For that matter, Hugh Bishop had a 'slightly green around the gills' aspect himself. It did sound ludicrous, Jim admitted to himself.

He wished Jade Wolverine would return. One quick tour of the bridge and a look at Lasty and Dutter would convince them like no amount of talking. But it would be hours before they got back. He'd insisted a watch be kept on Matt and Teresa until they were in safe hands.

But maybe there was another way to convince the three men. "Claw, are you up to another flight?"

"I am in a constant state of readiness, Jim Morris." The looks on the men's faces as they watched him apparently talk to himself was priceless.

"Please power up. We'll be right out." Jim winked at Kimberly and Kiri, then gave the men his trademark cocky grin. The two judges and the lawyer exchanged nervous looks. "How would you like to go for a ride?"

◆ ◆ ◆ ◆ ◆

442

CHAPTER THIRTY

Hshtah

Commodore Tka didn't like Lord Qatahkh's palace chambers any more than when he'd last been here. And this time he knew exactly what the dangers were.

Given a choice, he'd be on the Trhktah, making best possible speed for Tryr Prime. He'd already met with a group of Clan Tryhk elders, and his report to them had been bad enough.

They'd met his ship en route. When Tka refused to give a detailed accounting over the radio, the other ship synchronized courses and came alongside.

The invitation to board their ship to give his report had not been unexpected. What had been unexpected, at least for them, was when he politely declined. The elders had been furious and insisted he relieve himself of duty at once. Captain Tzi was to take control of the ship at once and bring Tka over himself.

Captain Tzi, also very politely, declined the opportunity for early flag command. Talk with my brother, he said.

Tka suggested that they board his ship, and eventually they gave in. Several hours later they departed, shaken. There was no more talk of relieving him of command. With little delay, the other ship split off on a high speed course for Tryr Prime, leaving him to finish his duty by reporting to Lord Qatahkh.

If Tka survived that meeting, he was to proceed as quickly as possible to the home planet. He was to be very careful what he reported to the Hshtahni. Tka could empathize with the elders. The Reigna were a story to tell cubs at night. No adult Tryr really believed in them. But there were always rumors, and old stories passed down through the generations.

Once in a while, there would be a mysterious death, usually by poison. Tka remembered a story about a Tryr Clan leader and his brothers being found with their throats torn out.

The Reigna, everyone said in muted whispers. Clan Tqk never fully recovered from that bloodbath, and eventually was assimilated by another clan.

Tka resisted the urge to glance from side to side as he walked down the long corridor. There was certainly plenty of room in these cavernous halls for small invisible assassins.

If the Reigna even suspected he'd viewed their dead, they would silence him without the slightest hesitation. And he was certain they were present. He nervously licked his chops and flexed his paws, causing the claws to extend, then retract. Get that out of your system before you approach the lord, he told himself grimly. Extending your claws in an audience with the Hstahni could get you killed as fast as anything.

"Commodore Tka."

Tka searched the shadowed indentations on both sides of the huge hallway, and almost missed the Hshstahni until he turned his massive head, revealing his glowing eyes.

"Lord Qatahkh." Tka straightened from his bow, resisting the urge to look around for invisible assassins.

"So, you survived."

"Was there ever a doubt?" Tka was startled.

"To date, you and your crew are the only survivors of contact with the Humans." Lord Qatahkh said dryly. "What did you do differently?"

"We didn't approach them demanding surrender," Tka said slowly, mulling that angle. It hadn't occurred to him, but it was true. "We were met by one ship, with the impression there were more sheathed. They seemed open to contact, but their defenses were prepared."

"So you chose not to fight," the Hshtahni said, his tone not revealing his thoughts.

"You told me information was your primary need, and trying to retake the station was secondary, unless we felt certain of success."

"You didn't think your six ships could be certain of success?"

Tka almost stopped breathing. This was a question with almost no safe response. "Lord, I have the utmost confidence in my squadron, but they were prepared, with an unknown number of ships, and a fight

444

would get us no more information than we already had." There was no reaction from the Hshtahni, and Tka hurried to continue. "I decided to offer a one day truce, dock and meet with the Humans."

"Go on."

"I entered the station with a party of six, and we were met by heavily armed Humans, outnumbering us at least three or four to one." Tka took a deep breath. "They had an inhibiting field throughout the station, which I must admit, tempted me."

"And?" Lord Qatahkh was still unreadable.

"The Humans use projectile weapons, as insane as that seems. And they were wary." It sounded weak, even to Tka. "Evidently, there were survivors from the last attack that then tried to escape their captivity, causing a number of casualties before they were all killed."

"All the prisoners?"

Tka had the Hshstahni's full attention now, and recognized the danger. "Yes, some Tryr and Srotag fought their way out of the holding chambers, killing some Humans before they died. Then, the remainder of the prisoners that were still in the holding cell were executed.

"So they have the remains?" Lord Qatahkh's eyes were rising, and Tka worked to control his breathing as the Hshtahni rose to his feet.

"Yes," Tka said slowly. "But not as such."

"Explain." The guttural tone wasn't as neutral as it had been.

"The station increased the gravity inside the holding cell to four hundred times norm." Even Tka had turned his head away when he saw the results on recordings the Humans had shown him. "Telling where one body ended and the next began was...problematic."

"I see." Lord Qatahkh seemed to settle back on his haunches. "So, you met with the Humans, heard their stories, and...?"

Tka hastened to continue. "We told them that the station was in Hshtahni controlled space, and resistance would be futile." He remembered something. "For some reason, when I said that, it caused much mirth. I'm not sure why. They were polite, respectful, but not interested in surrender or submission. I must admit, their lack of fear was impressive."

"And you met the one they call Jim Morris?" Tka was startled. How would word of him have spread back here?

"No. Either he was on one of their ships, or kept out of sight while we were there." Tka thought about it. "Or, perhaps, he was killed in one of the battles. But I think not. His death would shake their confidence."

"Why? He is just one being? Is there a reason his name has surfaced on a number of planets since the Ananab began this farce?"

"He is an impressive warrior," Tka admitted. "Humans are smaller than Tryr, and don't have some of our natural equipment for battle. But I saw documentation of him defeating multiple Tryr in unarmed combat."

"How?" He had the lord's full attention now. "And can you be sure that the evidence wasn't forged?"

"Absolutely sure, no," Tka admitted. "But I saw personal evidence of some of the abilities of the other Humans, and they all acknowledged that he was their best. And the footage I saw was...compelling." He met the Hshtahni's gaze. "I am sending you recordings from our encounter. One battle in particular..." He felt his voice trail off, remembering the Human ripping a Tryr heart out of a chest. He pulled himself together.

"Should I start planning another campaign, my Lord?" Tka sincerely hoped he wouldn't be any part of another attempt to retake the station. He liked the Humans he'd met, and knew any successful assault would only occur with heavy casualties, on both sides.

"No." Lord Qatahkh moved his massive skull from side to side, as if to clear his own head. "The time of Qutay is near, and we will take no action until after. I will discuss this with my Hshtahni brothers, and these Humans will be dealt with, decisively, in perhaps half a full cycle." He settled back into the reclining pose he'd had when Tka had entered.

"You may go."

Seattle, Washington

Karl Costa took a breath between words and wasn't surprised when Shelly Trent interrupted him yet another time.

"So all you really have to report is that you have nothing new to tell us?" Ms. Trent smiled at him with no trace of warmth and he stared back at her. After a few moments, she shifted in her seat as his gaze lingered on. "Well? What are you staring at?"

"I have no idea," Costa admitted, ignoring the sudden choking sound his immediate superior Daniel Blake was making. "I was just trying to decide when reporting to you became part of my job description."

"That's quite enough." The Director spoke quietly, but all attention in the room became fixed on his every word. "Mr. Costa, your job requirements are whatever I say they are."

"Yes, Sir," Costa said. He could feel Trent's smirk without bothering to look. He was only slightly mollified as the Director continued.

"In any case, this is not a time for pointing fingers. Mr. Costa has been hampered by several unforeseen circumstances, not the least of which is the United States Constitution." The Director casually waved a hand to the man sitting to his left. So far, the man hadn't said a word and Costa had almost forgotten he was there. He was medium height, average weight, short brown hair, dressed in 'company colors'; light shirt under dark suit and tie. Practically invisible, Costa thought without humor. "This is Mr. Sim. He will begin a new line of investigation. Mr. Costa, I will expect your final report on my desk tomorrow."

Karl Costa knew a dismissal when he heard one, and did his best to keep his face clear of any expression as he stood, nodded to the Director, then Blake and Sim. He ignored Shelly Trent. "Yes, Sir. I'll get right on it."

He felt their eyes on his back as he walked from the room. Beatty was waiting in the next room and fell in step beside him. Costa shook his head as Beatty started to question him, and neither man spoke until they were outside the building, walking through a courtyard back to their own office building. Then Costa began to swear steadily in a low even tone. His young assistant nodded his head in rhythm, very familiar with the routine.

He caught Beatty by surprise when without warning he shifted from profanity to instructions. "I want you to find out everything you can on a senior agent named Sim. Oh, and I'll need your final report on this case this afternoon, by five if possible."

"By five," Beatty repeated slowly. "That's only a few hours from now."

"I know." Costa knew he was being petty, but it beat shooting up a post office. "That's why I'm telling you now instead of later." He felt better already.

He got Groundhog on the first try.

"I need anything you can find about an agent named Sim. He's in his forties, about six feet..."

"I know who he is," Groundhog interrupted. "This isn't going to cost you a thing."

Costa blinked at that. Nothing was ever free with Groundhog. "David Sim is a senior agent in one of your hidden divisions. I doubt you've even heard of it." Groundhog's voice was cold. "I'm going to cut this short so you can go call your little puppy Beatty off his search before he gets you both killed or worse."

"I'm a bureau office senior agent. I'm not going to just disappear." Costa spoke in a confident tone, and wished he felt as sure as his voice sounded.

"Karl, this man has unlimited power, and answers to one person, your Director. His department makes people disappear all the time. This is all I'm going to say. I will not be available for any work for the next six months, so don't try to call. Think about what I've said."

Costa blinked as the phone line went dead. Groundhog had never used his surname before. He hung up the phone slowly as his mind raced. Maybe it was time to bail out of all this. Alien kidnappers, space-ships, futuristic weapons that cut on the molecular level, ultra-secret agencies that didn't operate with the same checks and balances he did, it was just too much.

He gave himself a shake and began walking briskly back to his office. Time to go find Beatty and call him off, at least for the moment. He came to a sudden halt at the entrance to his building as he recognized Sim standing next to the door.

"Yes?" he said, stalling for time to think. Sim didn't give him any.

"Prepare your final report." The voice was low, almost bland, but the words shocked him. "Your man Beatty is suffering technical difficulties at the moment. I assume he was acting on your orders. I'm not going to take any action at this point as long as you desist. Stick with your designated duties, better yet, take a vacation. A long one."

"Are you threatening me?" Costa felt rage begin to take control of him, then noticed he was bracketed by two large men he didn't recognize.

Sim gave him a cynical smile. "I don't expect to have to speak to you again."

With that, Sim turned on his heel and walked off down the street, his two men keeping pace slightly behind him. Costa tried to wet his lips, but his mouth was bone dry.

Karl Costa wasn't a man that frightened easily. But he was honest enough to admit that what had just happened scared the crap out of him.

"Maybe I am getting too old for all this," he muttered as he went to find Beatty. His floor had developed a power shortage problem, and Beatty was busy at his desk, organizing his notes, starting a first draft by hand.

Costa told him to forget the Sim chore and the lights came on. His mouth went dry all over again. He went to his office and found himself drawn to the window. Looking down, he saw one of Sim's goons standing across the street, watching. He turned and started walking, and Costa lost him in the lunchtime traffic crowding the sidewalks.

For the first time Karl Costa could remember, he felt...old. "I hope Jim Morris and those aliens, if there really are aliens, kick your ass," he whispered, then went to begin drawing up his final report.

Ann Arbor

Matt Stickel set his suitcase down next to the piano and glanced out the windows where he'd been directed. He could see the pool, water emptied out, cover in place for the impending winter. Even the tiki hut clubhouse on the far side of the pool was closed up, windows shuttered.

"They're out there, I swear," Janice grinned at him. "Jim told me you were coming. Just go out behind the gazebo, you'll see. I'd leave your jacket on. It's gettin' cool out there."

Matt fought down the nervousness. It had been a wild few weeks since Jade Wolverine had dropped him and Teresa off in Turkey. The Turkish authorities had been tough, though not so difficult as the U.S. officials he'd finally been released to.

Neither the Turks nor the Americans had been satisfied with his memory loss story. From what little he'd found out, Teresa hadn't fared much better with her own Spanish questioners. But they had both stuck to their stories and eventually been released.

If Matt thought the government was a hard sell, they were nothing compared to his parents. Both were typical of their environment, born and raised in a small town, satisfied to stay there. But both expected him to stick it out in college, get a degree, then hopefully return to the home town, get a good job, settle down.

When he told them he wanted to drop out of school for a while and work for a company based out of Ann Arbor, they exploded. Dropping out at the beginning of his sophomore year was bad enough, but who would he be working for? Where would he live?

Questions he didn't have good answers for. He'd intentionally kept everything very vague, promising to call them soon.

He was torn from his reverie as he rounded the corner of the building and saw Jim Morris squared off against two opponents. They were standing on hard-packed dirt, allowing good footing, but not so hard you couldn't fall on it.

Or be thrown down on it.

Jim stood barefoot in the center of the space. Ignoring the brisk fall weather, he wore shorts and his usual sleeveless sweatshirt.

And a blindfold.

Two young men circled around him cautiously. Matt remembered them from the crew of the 'Wolverine. The big black guy's name was Ellis. He was at least four or five inches taller than Jim, and already heavily muscled like a mature man. His black skin glistened with sweat, and Matt was amused to see a fair amount of dirt clinging to the sweats he wore.

The thin lanky white guy was Sean, and Matt remembered he didn't care much for him. He was dressed the same as Ellis, heavy sweatshirt and pants. Both wore sneakers.

At the moment, Sean was stepping as lightly as he could to his left, trying to catch Jim from an unexpected direction. Matt noticed the actor showed no sign of knowing where either of the two were.

Sean made a quick wave to Ellis, and the big man stepped in close and tried a front kick. Matt watched in fascination as Jim casually blocked the kick with one hand and, at the very last possible moment, dodged Sean's attack from behind. Sean had obviously planned on Ellis' assault masking the sounds of his own, because he was unprepared when he didn't connect, and Jim countered.

Sean hit the dirt hard, but kept rolling til he was clear and back on his feet. During this time, Jim blocked Ellis, kicked him in the stomach, then used a judo throw to send him flying across the ground.

Then all three men were circling again, Sean and Ellis looking for an opening, Jim listening.

"Whoa," Matt said, impressed.

"Who are you?" Matt jumped at the sound of the voice beside him. He hadn't even noticed anyone else, he'd been so caught up with the intricate dance of the fighters. Then he was wondering what on Earth could have kept him from noticing the heavily bundled girl sitting in the electric wheelchair mere feet away.

"What?" Matt tried to recover his dignity as he recognized her from the pictures in her bedroom he'd seen not that long ago in the company of Egelvs. "Oh, uh, I'm Matt, Matt Stickel."

"So, Matt Matt Stickel, who are you?" Matt tore his eyes away from hers with an effort. The pictures hadn't done justice to the piercing blueness, accented by her pale white skin. And he remembered her long, thick jet-black hair framing her face in most of them. He looked at the bandanna she had wrapped around her head.

Belatedly, he noticed the heavy cast on her right leg, and that her left arm was in a sling. It also had a cast showing from beneath the sleeve of the huge sweater she wore. *What the hell had happened to her, anyway?*

"Hello, Earth to Matt-Matt, come in, wherever you are." He flushed as he heard her sardonic tone. "Paging Matt-Matt."

"I'm here to see your father," he said, and made a show of looking over to where Jim was successfully blocking another attack. "He's pretty amazing. I've never seen anything like this."

"You know me?" The young girl looked at him intently. "We haven't met."

"I've just heard of you and seen your pictures. I'm afraid I can't remember your name exactly. Alphons...?" He decided trying to guess her name from memory was a no-win scenario. "No, I don't remember."

"What pictures did you see?" She didn't let up on him. *Was she always so inquisitive?*

"The ones in your bedroom," Matt began, then winced and tried to change the subject. "Did you get your tapes back?"

"Oh, you were one of the burglars that broke in and stole all that stuff from my room?" She gave him a cool look. "Who said Jim was my father?"

Matt felt like reeling from her continuous shifting of gears. He ignored the burglar comment. "You've got his eyes."

"I've got my mother's eyes." She grimaced and started to reach beneath the blanket spread across her lap. She stopped and a slight tinge of color came to her cheeks.

Her cast itches, Matt thought, carefully keeping the grin from his face as he answered her.

"You may have your mother's eye color, if they're blue. But you definitely have his eyes."

"My mother is dead." She stared at him, as if to will him to look away. Her hand started to move again and she caught herself with a visible effort. "My name is Afsaneh Riahi. I still haven't got my video player back yet. And one of the tapes is still missing. Teresa returned the others you took."

"I didn't take anything," Matt protested. "I was a prisoner of the Egelv. They took your stuff, not me."

"Let's break for the day."

Matt turned at the sound of Jim's voice, and couldn't hide his smile as he heard Afsaneh rustling beneath her blanket and give an involuntary sigh of relief. Jim pulled off the blindfold and casually waved at him.

As the three fighters walked over, Matt couldn't resist a quick retaliation. "Feel better?" he whispered.

"Bastard," she hissed, making a show of rearranging her blanket to cover her legs.

"Matt, I see you've met Afsaneh." Matt shook hands with the actor, hiding the awe he felt. He got a distinctly cooler greeting from Sean and Ellis.

"Yes, we were just discussing burglaries and itchy casts." He heard her quick intake of breath and carefully avoided looking at her. Jim's lips moved a little, as if trying to hide amusement. Sean cocked his head, as if trying to decide if Matt was mocking her. Ellis just looked back and forth between the two of them. Matt hurried to continue. "Janice told me to come out here."

"Do you always do what women tell you to," Afsaneh began and Matt started as Jim swung his arm around his shoulders, aiming him at the house.

"Well Matt, let's get you up to the house and settled in. After dinner we'll take a look at your options." Jim glanced back at his daughter. "You know, Afsaneh, Matt tackled one of the Egelv as he was about to

452

shoot me with a disruptor. Very brave thing to do."

Matt met her eyes as he turned away with Jim Morris. She gave him a speculative look that showed nothing of her thoughts.

Then he was listening to Jim explain why he was fighting blind-folded. *Invisible alien assassins? What was he getting into?*

◆ ◆ ◆ ◆ ◆

Sean turned to Afsaneh as Jim and Matt disappeared into the house. "There was a suppression field up. That disruptor wouldn't have done a thing."

Afsaneh operated the toggle switch that directed her wheelchair. She thought about it as she turned around. "Did he know about the field?"

"Who cares?" Sean shrugged. "He's just some geek, happened to be in the right place at the right time."

"Or the wrong place at the wrong time," Ellis pointed out. "And he may have been one of the last people to see Prause alive."

Afsaneh caught her breath at that. They'd only found out a few days ago that the body of Howard Prause had been found at Black's Beach near San Diego. The teacher's body had been mutilated so badly it had taken dental records to be sure of his identity. His stripped body had been thrown from a cliff overlooking the nude beach, but had gotten caught up in some of the underbrush and not found immediately.

Ellis spoke, his voice a low rumble. "I can't say I liked that little dude much. But nobody deserves to die like that."

"Damn straight," Sean agreed, venom in his voice. "I'd like to get my hands on whoever did that to him. He was a jerk, but he was our jerk. Chula Vista hangs tight with their own."

"It had to be those Sukuru dudes," Ellis said, holding the door for Afsaneh's wheelchair. "You know, I think I might go back, do the show-up thing, let my mama know I'm okay. I could talk to a few of the studs in the 'hood, too. We could use more guns. Our side's kinda light."

This last was said as they joined Jim and Matt in the family room. Jim looked up and shook his head. "Ellis, if you think some of your friends might work out for us, fine. But don't get them just to be extra guards. We don't need people who are satisfied to just be hired guns. We want people who will learn, and try to make something of themselves while doing good work at the same time."

"Well, sure," Ellis nodded slowly. "But isn't that all you've got me and Sean here for? We're security, and that's about it."

"And at the same time, you've learned more technical knowledge both about the ships, and the universe out there, than you'd learned in your whole life up to this point."

"That wouldn't take much," Sean joked, nudging his friend.

"I do want to reappear, if you can spare me for a few weeks, sir." Afsaneh felt sad. Once his mother got hold of him, they might never tear him away. Despite what she'd told Jim, she and Ellis weren't romantically involved, but she liked talking to him. She felt that he had grown comfortable talking with her, letting his shy guard down more than once.

"Of course, Ellis." She watched Jim reassure Ellis, then Sean about wanting them both to see their people, make sure that they wanted to stay on the course they'd chosen, then come back, their places safe and waiting for them.

Afsaneh used the moment to observe the new kid. He looked a little older than Sean or Ellis. He certainly was different from them both. And irritating. She couldn't believe he'd embarrassed her with that comment about scratching herself. Let him wear a cast for weeks, months even, and see how he felt.

She decided Matt-Matt Stickel needed a little humbling. And she was just the one to do it.

The doorbell rang and Janice swept into the room. "Sounds like our dinner at the door."

"Oh?" Jim did that thing where he raised his eyebrow that Afsaneh loved so much. "And what would that be?"

"With this crowd?" Janice pointed at the boys expressively. "Pizza, what else?"

"Cool," Jim said, nodding his agreement.

Afsaneh kept watching Matt until he felt her gaze and glanced at her curiously. She knew boys, and the power of sympathy. She gave him a timid smile, then winced as she moved her arm to a more comfortable position. She saw his expression change from cautious to concerned and almost snickered.

Gotcha, boy. There'll be a reckoning, when I'm ready. You're at my mercy. She finished her shifting in her wheelchair, and allowed her breath to come out in a long quiet sigh that everyone else in the room missed, except Matt. His brow furled and he started to rise as if to help her, then settled back in his seat with a confused look on his face.

Matt Matt Stickel, you are toast.

Station Osaka

Governor Lang looked at the clipboard computer in his hand and sighed at the figures it showed. Things were running short, all over the station. The Hoag and Baerd had made discreet comments and run projections, but the bottom line was, if Osaka didn't get some sort of shipment very soon, everyone would be very hungry, indeed.

He sighed and set the clipboard down on his console. He didn't really need a console, but it looked good and felt comforting to have something near his command post that had a function. It also was good for holding his coffee cup.

Except they were out of coffee.

A hand touched his shoulder lightly. He knew without looking who it was, and covered her hand with his own, grateful for the contact. They stayed like that for a while.

Suyo gently disengaged her hand and sat in her seat next to him. She had become like a strong bulkhead to him, lending him her strength. He wasn't quite sure what role he filled in her life, but she seemed happy.

Their affection towards each other had grown over the weeks they'd worked together. It was far more than a work relationship, but so far, neither had made any move to take it further.

It was as if neither of them wished to jeopardize what they already shared. Lang was more than happy to let things proceed at their own natural speed. Heaven knew he had plenty of other things to keep him occupied.

As if on cue with that thought, Suyo spoke. "I've reviewed the notes and records from the first two weeks, and I think our school is going to be a success."

Lang nodded his agreement. School had seemed such an obvious idea until they began considering what should be studied. What was important to learn? Languages seemed a waste, with the convenience of the translators. History? Which history? Social studies? Human, Baerd, Hoag, all the above?

Sure, basic math still followed familiar rules, but there was so much more to know now than any of them could teach. Science was a wide open field, with no mentors to look to.

Except Pearl. And Samantha, Vicki, when she returned from Earth. And Connie, as Danny, rather, Captain DelaRosa, called the computer of his newly converted Ananab warship, Jade Conquistador.

The computers made good teachers. They were understanding, efficient, and of course, knew their material perfectly.

Sometimes he wondered if people, Human or otherwise, were really needed to run Station Osaka, 'Samurai, or any of the other ships.

More to the point, he wondered if the computers ever thought about whether their ships needed to be manned or not. That security virus had made them incredibly sophisticated minds that could learn, and use logical progressions to simulate imagination and initiative.

But was it just simulation?

Jason Lang hated to think what might happen if Vicki, or Pearl, or any of the rest decided Jim didn't really need the rest of humanity to survive.

"I have an energy signature contact at maximum range," Baerd Technician Rvel said, his voice tense. Lang exchanged worried looks with Suyo, then tried to make his voice sound unconcerned.

"Oh, I suppose that's the 'Viking, finally bringing us some fresh fruit and extra rolls of toilet paper."

"A cow would be nice." A male Human voice spoke quietly from somewhere across the room. Muffled laughter followed the words, and Lang had to smile.

Yes, a nice thick steak would be totally acceptable, right now.

Rvel spoke again, both relief and surprise in his voice. "Pearl confirms, it's the Jade Viking. Incoming message."

"Over the main speakers, if you please," Lang said, praying he was guessing right again.

"Greetings and salutations, Station Osaka." Lang smiled as he recognized Captain Tachibana's voice. "This is Jade Viking, bearing fresh foods, fresh ideas, and our first shipment of export goods."

Suyo nudged him, and Lang looked at her questioningly. "The girl," she said quietly, and Lang nodded.

"Viking, old girl." He kept his voice light, dreading what he might hear in a moment. "Did you cross paths with Mr. Morris and his ward in their...yacht, by any chance?"

There was a moment's silence, then the wonderful sound of Tachibana laughing came over the speakers.

"Yes, we've met Irene and are suitably impressed. And Afsaneh is going to be fine." When the cheering settled down, he continued as if without pause. "Although I do pity the people around her during her convalescence." Laughter broke out, but it was quickly interrupted by the sound of Technician Rvel's voice.

"I have another energy signature at extreme range, definitely not from Earth."

There was an uncomfortable silence, and Lang finally cleared his voice and spoke. "Perhaps you shouldn't tarry too long, 'Viking. We have another ship approaching."

"I understand," Captain Tachibana said, his voice grave.

Before he could continue, Rvel raised his right two hands in clenched fists. "Yes! It's a Trixmae ship!" He looked around the bridge in sudden embarrassment and his skin began its inevitable race to scarlet. "It's a Trixmae ship," he said in a quieter voice.

"No, no, Mr. Rvel," Captain Lang waved his hand expansively, and beamed around the room at everyone he could spy. "You're absolutely right in your reaction. That is good news for all of us."

Lang smiled at Suyo. She smiled back and nodded her approval.

Six hours later, Jade Viking docked. Lang and Suyo walked down to greet them, along with several hundred other humans. 'Viking was docked next to 'Conquistador, and Captain DelaRosa met him in the corridor as the hatches were being unsealed.

"It's a great day, sir."

Lang smiled fondly at his ex-First Officer. Danny DelaRosa had grown up a lot in the last few months. "It certainly is, Danny," he agreed, then they both turned to greet Captain Tachibana as he came through the hatch. "Hiroaki, you don't know how good it is to see you."

"I can imagine," Tachibana said dryly. "There's someone I'd like you to meet."

Their attention turned to the diminutive young woman that had accompanied him through the hatch.

"Governor Lang, Captain DelaRosa, Suyo Takashi, I'd like you to meet Teresa Elizari. On Earth she was a lawyer."

"Actually, I still am." Lang liked the soft contralto of her voice, and judging from his body language, Danny liked that and a lot more. She continued. "A lawyer, that is."

"She has her own alien abduction story to tell."

"I'd love to hear all about it." Lang watched with amusement as Danny somehow cut Teresa out from the crowd. "You're from Spain, right?"

Lang looked at Hiroaki and Suyo with amusement, shaking his head. Then he remembered.

"Hiroaki, how has young Craig progressed?"

Captain Tachibana gave him a stern glare that fooled no one. "If you mean Commander Randall, he is handling himself quite well." Then he nodded. "I think he's ready."

"Ready for what?" Suyo looked back and forth between them.

"Captain Tachibana has our most senior officer, and we have a ship needing a captain," Jason said, smiling at her. "We think he's ready for his promotion, and to meet with his new ship, Jade Zulu."

Suyo clapped her hands, startling both men. "He's getting Zooey? I'm so happy for him."

Jason blinked, and then winced.

Zooey?

Osaka, Japan

Sho Toshida straightened from his bow, careful to show no emotion.

His uncle sat behind his desk, face impassive. Two of his personal retainers flanked him, their backs against the wall near the corners of the room. They were close enough to respond to any threat, yet their distance gave the illusion of privacy.

Sho didn't even know their names, but he'd never seen his uncle without the presence of one or both of them.

Some day he would command the same loyalty from his men, if he lived through the next few minutes. Failure was a bitter dish to set upon the table of one's Obayun, even if you were his favorite nephew.

"Uncle." The word came out hoarsely, and Sho resisted the urge to clear his throat. "Uncle, I have failed you. We had the Martin woman, and we lost her."

"Her and the actress." Injo Toshida spoke softly, voice neutral in tone. "And attracted the attention of the authorities while destroying one of my new American warehouses."

"Repairs have already begun on the roof of the building, and I was planning another attempt on the Martin woman when you called for my return." Sho tried to keep any anger or defiance from his voice. "But yes, I failed."

Sho bowed his head and looked at the floor stonily. "How can I make up for my failure?"

"Sit, nephew."

Sho Toshida looked up, startled. His uncle nodded to the chair that hadn't been there a moment ago. Sho sank gratefully into the seat.

"If you were anyone else, I would demand fingers," the old man said quietly. "Or more." Sho swallowed hard. "But I know you. And I know how hard it was to do the right thing just now. You're very proud. It's a trait you share with your father."

Sho winced as he realized that as yet, he'd done nothing to avenge his father's death. "I would like to go back to America and try and correct my errors."

"Soon, soon enough." His uncle glanced at some papers on the desk in front of him. "First I would know more about the technology that was used against us."

"So would I," Sho muttered darkly. He sighed and met the Obayun's eyes. "It gives them a fantastic edge, since we know almost nothing about their capabilities. That teacher was nearly useless as a source of information..."

"I'm surprised he wouldn't tell you more," Injo Toshida said, picking up a paper and peering at it.

"Oh, he told us anything he could." Sho snorted. "He sang almost immediately. Unfortunately, he knew little of use."

"Perhaps next time, you will recognize that fact sooner, thus not wasting the resource with so little result." Sho stung under the reproach, but tried to keep his feelings concealed. He felt his uncle's eyes watching him shrewdly, and knew he hid nothing from the old man.

"Jim Morris is far more dangerous than we suspected." Sho picked his words carefully. "If he were removed from the equation, it might weaken the resolve of the others."

Injo Toshida shook his head firmly. "You had your chance at him. I can't afford to lose you in an unnecessary fight. For the moment, you will remain here, with me. There is much for you to learn about our business."

The Obayun tossed the paper back on his desk. "I would like a complete list of all the passengers and crew of the Jade Viking, their relatives and businesses, and have them put under surveillance."

Sho Toshida stared at his uncle in dismay. "Uncl...Sir, it will be huge! The cost of such an operation will be..." He tried to visualise the potential cost, and failed. "...immense," he finished weakly as his elder gave him a stern look. "Yes, Sir, I will begin at once."

The Obayun nodded his approval and smiled without humor.

"Good." Injo Toshida tapped the stack of papers on his desk thoughtfully. "I think you may be right, nephew. It might be a good idea to make an example of this actor, Jim Morris."

Sho straightened in his seat with excitement, but the older man raised a hand, forstalling his obvious request. "No, you will remain here. We will make one attempt, and not up close. It would be better if certain people understood we can strike from any distance. We will need to find a suitable event or location."

Sho Toshida jumped at the chance to present the plan he'd been formulating. "Uncle, I think I have just the thing..." he said, and began to describe his idea. After a few moments, his uncle smiled and nodded his approval.

◆ ◆ ◆ ◆ ◆

CHAPTER THIRTY-ONE

San Francisco, California

Jim looked back and forth between the two ties. Neither particularly appealed to him, but he'd been told in no uncertain terms that he would wear a tie tonight.

When in doubt, procrastinate. "Irene, connect me with Kimberly, please."

"Go ahead, Jim Morris."

"Kimberly, how long before you get here?"

"Coming down the elevator now, Jim. Irene just let us off on the roof." He smiled at the sound of her voice. It had been weeks since he'd seen her. "I've got Matt in tow, and the others are on the way. They should be here in a few minutes."

"Excellent." Jim resisted the urge to rub his hands together in anticipation. "Afsaneh? You about ready?" He realized the inanity of the question even as he asked it. "Not that outfit, something more discreet."

"You haven't even seen what I'm putting on!" she protested, peering through the partly open door to her bedroom at doorknob height. She was able to get around with crutches, but still used wheelchairs a lot. The hip-high cast on her left leg wouldn't be coming off for weeks yet. God only knew what she planned to wear tonight.

"Let's just say I'm psychic," Jim said in a dry voice. He held the ties up, questioningly. She sniffed at one, then nodded her approval at the other before rolling back into her domain.

He looked at her choice doubtfully, then held them up again, catching his reflection in the big glass picture windows that looked out over San Francisco. The scar that ran from above his left eye down to his ear drew his attention, and he stepped closer to see it better. It was almost healed, but would never completely disappear without plastic surgery. The same thing went for the chunk of earlobe that was missing.

The sound of the lock turning in the front door brought him back from his somber contemplation.

Kimberly swept into the room. Matt Stickel was close behind, but Jim barely noticed him. Kimberly wore a long beige flowing dress that just hovered above the floor. She had a short black jacket wrapped around her shoulders that she took off as she came into his arms. He had just enough time to see the dress was strapless before he was holding her.

Jim belatedly remembered that Matt was still standing near the door, uncertain what he should do. Jim smiled at the young man as they shook hands. Kimberly picked up her jacket, then relieved Matt of his load of clothes on hangers.

"I suspect you're at the 'not that dress, young lady' stage of getting ready, am I right?" Jim grinned at Kimberly's question and nodded. "Well, I brought her a few choices that should be acceptable to both of you."

"You brought some of your own dresses?" Jim choose his words carefully, knowing Afsaneh was listening. "You realize you may never get them back?" he said with a warning tone.

"That's alright," Kimberly said, giving him a smug look, as if knowing more than he. "I'm not going to have much use for these for a while anyway." She smirked. "You'll just have to buy me new ones, I guess."

"Um, okay." Jim saw Matt was trying to hide a grin, and went to the bar against the wall to hide his confusion. "Can I fix you a drink? Champagne?"

"Better make it fruit juice," Kimberly said lightly, pausing half-turned towards Afsaneh's door. "I'm afraid I'm off alcohol for most of the next year."

"Okay, we've got orange juice, cranberry..." Jim automatically turned to the kitchen, then froze and his voice trailed off. He whirled and found himself staring into his wife's eyes. Kimberly looked unchar-acteristically shy as she waited for his reaction, one hand playing with her hair, teeth lightly biting her lower lip.

"You're...?" Jim began, then stopped, afraid he'd misunderstood her.

"Pregnant?" Kimberly finished the sentence for him. "Is that the word you're looking for?"

"With child." Afsaneh's voice came from the next room in a sonorous tone. "Expecting, knocked up, gravid, in a family way, a loaf in the oven, gestating..."

"Shaddap!" Jim and Kimberly yelled in unison, and exchanged sheepish grins. Kimberly gave him a tender look.

"Yes."

Then they were embracing again, forgotten dresses and ties falling to the floor. Jim wanted to hold her close, but was afraid he would hurt the young life she was carrying inside her.

"Hey," she said as his arms held her stiffly. "Right now, the baby is about the size of a..." She stopped, as if realizing she didn't know how big the embryo was. "Well, anyway, you don't have to treat me like porcelain yet."

Jim laughed and was aware of Matt muttering as he sidled around them. "I'll go get that juice..."

Several decades or seconds later, Jim and Kimberly broke from a rather passionate kiss that left him a little breathless. "Boy or girl," he asked, then remembered the McGregor twins and grinned again. "Or both?"

"Heaven forbid," Kimberly shuddered. "No, one at a time will do just fine." She looked up at him, a question in her eyes. "I didn't let Irene tell me which sex because I wasn't sure you would want to know ahead of time."

Jim shrugged. "I don't see any point in waiting, do you?" He felt a lopsided grin twisting his face. "It just causes confusion on colors for the clothes and stuff. And I refuse to call my unborn child 'it'!"

Kimberly laughed and he was relieved to see she seemed to agree with him. "Shall we ask?" she said in a teasing voice. "How about it, Irene? Are we having a boy or a girl?"

"A girl," came the answer. Jim and Kimberly stood holding hands, looking at each other.

"Well?!? Did she answer? What did she say?" Afsaneh popped her towel-wrapped head out the door, giving a cautious look around the room, probably to locate Matt, who was still in the kitchen. Her shoulders were bare. "Tell me!"

"Know how to drive a young girl crazy?" Kimberly asked, and Jim cocked his head, then got it. He laughed out loud, and Kimberly joined him as Afsaneh kept insisting they tell her.

After a few moments, she sniffed at them. "That's not funny," she said archly, then her will disintegrated. "Tell me-e-e!" she pleaded.

Jim finally gave in. "Good," she said, trying to act haughty to regain her dignity. "Little boys are such hellions."

"Now there's the pot calling the kettle black," Jim said, reluctantly letting Kimberly pull away from his grasp. His daughter stuck her tongue out at him, and disappeared out of sight.

Jim sighed, then jumped as Kimberly pinched his butt as she picked up the dresses and ties. She smiled at him sweetly, then with two fingers, disdainfully draped the tie Afsaneh had chosen over her shoulder.

"I'll just take this so you don't accidently wear it," she said dryly as she handed him the other. "I'll be helping Afsaneh, if you need me. Oh, Kiri and the others will be here in a few minutes." She gave him one last smile before going into Afsaneh's bedroom.

Jim sighed and decided he was ready for that drink. "That's okay dear, I'll just have your champagne. No sense letting it go to waste."

Jim realized Matt was still hiding in the kitchen. "Matt, how about you? Anything to drink?"

"I'll have what you're having, Sir," Matt said, reappearing with Kimberly's juice.

Jim gave him a droll look. Got a picture ID, he started to ask, then remembered what the young man had gone through the last few months.

"You like champagne, Matt?" he asked and reached for the fluted glasses. He eyed them skeptically, then brought out two large wine goblets. He filled them both to the brim and handed one to the young man, taking the juice in exchange.

After several healthy sips, Jim took a step towards the bedroom door, intending to give his wife her juice. Both men jumped as it closed abruptly. He glared at Matt, who suddenly developed an interest looking out the window at the San Francisco skyline.

Jim set the juice down as the doorbell rang, but before he could answer it, Kiri swept into the suite, Angela Dawson in tow.

The Japanese actress had a short, wispy white dress that seemed to tantalize the viewer without ever actually revealing anything. On her petite form, it only enhanced her pixyish nature.

Angela Dawson looked relaxed in her long dark-grey dress and loosely hanging black jacket. It almost hid the fact that her shoulders and muscular arms rivaled Jim's own. He kept the smile from his face as he noticed she wore practical flats rather than the high heels Kiri favored. He also noticed the jacket did a credible job of hiding the service revolver under her left arm.

It occurred to Jim that he hadn't seen one of them without the other nearby since...? Hmm, maybe Kiri was getting over her crush on Kimberly. He still hadn't heard the last about not telling Kimberly that Kiri was gay. Protests that it was none of his business had fallen flat on deafened ears.

Kiri flowed into Jim's arms and gave him a fierce hug. "You're looking good, round-eyes Papa-san!" At Jim's look of astonishment, she grinned. "Your daughter has a big mouth." Angela was more sedate as she exchanged handshakes with both men.

Matt played at host and offered the women drinks. Angela pointedly looked at the half-empty glass the young man held. "Are you driving tonight, Mr. Stickel?"

"Um..." Jim watched in amusement. Matt seemed to have just remembered that not only was he underage to drink alcohol in this state, but that Angela was, until recently, a California state trooper. He was saved by the appearance of Kimberly and Afsaneh from the bedroom.

"Ta da!" Kimberly called out as she pushed Afsaneh in what she called her 'old-fashioned' manual wheelchair to the center of the room. Jim stared, only vaguely aware that the others were doing the same.

Afsaneh still had both her casts, and had opted not to struggle with crutches this evening. A wheelchair left a vain young lady with limited apparel options for an opening night ceremony. But with Kimberly's help, Afsaneh had once again exceeded expectations.

Loose-fitting, shiny black slacks de-emphasized the bulky cast on her leg, and the matching corsair-style silk blouse with baggy sleeves and wide collar did the same for the one on her arm. The top two buttons were open, allowing a hint of cleavage to show.

"Janice let out the leg and arm to allow for the casts," Kimberly said, looking very pleased with herself. Jim nodded, wondering if Afsaneh was wearing a bra. He couldn't quite tell, but decided to trust his wife's judgment and good taste.

What really surprised Jim was that Afsaneh had opted to relinquish the bandannas and scarfs she'd worn nonstop since leaving the hospital. Her hair was a uniform half inch and Jim was glad to see her scar was

465

practically invisible now.

Instead of a scarf, she wore a plain headband of beaten silver. Her earrings were dangling silver cutlasses with tiny brilliant sapphires mounted in the handles. Her necklace was a ring of sapphires, also mounted in silver, with a single, larger sword, the tip of the blade just reaching the space between the upper curves of her breasts.

Jim could only nod approval and moan the loss of his sanity for the rest of her single life. Which reminded him. "Hey," he said quietly to Matt. "Quit staring."

"Yes sir," Matt said, his eyes not leaving Afsaneh's features. Jim glanced at Kimberly and she smiled back at him in open amusement over Kiri's shoulder as she hugged her friend. His wife's eyes flicked over at Matt, then back to Jim. One eyebrow rose in a questioning arch.

Jim noticed Matt hadn't moved, and gave him a nudge. "Quit staring at my wife."

"I'm not staring at your wif..." Matt stopped short, and looked around in embarrassment. He picked up the keys to the limo from the coffee table, rattling them. "I guess we're ready?"

"I'll drive," Angela Dawson said in a dry voice, and took the keys from him.

Jim turned his head to hide his amusement as Matt looked lost without a use for his hands, but had to give the kid credit for thinking on his feet. Matt quickly moved over behind Afsaneh and took the handles of her wheelchair. She twisted her head around as he began pushing her across the room.

"You know how to drive this thing?" she asked plaintively as everyone moved to leave. He shrugged and she held up a hand as they passed the coffee table. "Hold it."

He stopped, and Jim saw regret appear on Matt's face for just a moment. Then Afsaneh picked up the half empty glass of Matt's champagne and drained it before Jim could protest.

Afsaneh looked into Jim's glare and made a pitiful attempt at a smile, placing her hand on her leg cast and wincing. It didn't fool Jim a bit, and she knew it, a beguiling grin appearing as he shook his head in resignation.

Jim dug into his pocket and, leaning over her, hissed. "Both of you, before you get into the limo," and tossed a roll of breath mints on her lap. Taking his amused wife's arm, he turned and almost laughed as he heard his daughter's imperious voice.

"Let's go, driver." Jim heard a strangled sound that had to be Matt, but kept his eyes forward. The kid had no idea what he was in for.

Egelvna

Cromar Try could feel his mate, Siph Carni, matching his stride, but didn't turn his head to look at her. He knew that every single movement he made was being scrutinized.

Ahead of them, lofty doors began to swing inward. They were tall enough that a creature twice his own height could have entered without having to bow its head.

Four Egelv stood in the opening, resplendent in brilliant red uniforms representing the Emperor's colors. All of them were armed in the old traditional way, broadsword at their side.

Although Cromar Try knew the weapons were only for show, he also knew all four were experts in their use. He himself had dabbled with a blade or two, over the years, but these guards practiced constantly, as if they might be called upon to defend the Emperor.

The walls contained the true defenses. Indeed, the Palace itself was the primary defense.

The Palace, from its computer air defense system right down to the operation of the toilets, was run by a program that placed the safety of the Emperor, then his family as the highest priority.

Energy repression fields were easy to build, so neither the guards, nor the Palace itself relied solely on energy weapons, even though the Palace commanded enough power to collapse most such fields.

His mind snapped back to the present as they approached the audience stand. Cromar Try had gambled and given a very sketchy accounting, insisting the bulk of the report be made in person, to the emperor himself. If it was decided he was showboating, or trying to build up the importance of his news, it could be very bad for both he and his mate. The emperor was not known for patience. But if Cromar Try stuck to proper channels, he would lose his command, at the very least..

Zinfar Aqa was wearing the tunic of office, a yellow so brilliant it rivaled the sun itself. The Emperor was over a hundred cycles old, barely past middle age, and it was said he kept in excellent shape. His long, ivory hair fell over his shoulders, without a hint of dullness. His glaring, brown face was unlined by age. He sat on an elevated throne, gazing down on them, his expression unreadable.

Cromar Try felt like the young child, guilty of some minor transgression, that had stood before his father countless cycles ago. Except this time, it could cost him far more than loss of recreation time.

He waited, knowing better than to speak first. After several eternities, the Emperor stirred.

"Cromar Try, I believe you were sent to retrieve something stolen from me."

"You sent me to find Ty Musa and the missing program," Cromar Try said, choosing his words with care. Beside him, Siph Carni stirred, as if to say 'watch out'. He ignored her and continued. "We saw no sign of Ty Musa, but we did find the program, and since it had been initiated, we tried to destroy it."

"Tried...?" Zinfar Aqa made the word stretch out in an agonizing manner. "And...?"

"We failed," Cromar Try admitted, and the group of advisors seated off to the side swayed and the sound of excited muttering carried to the throne.

"Quiet." The emperor spoke softly, but there was instant silence. Zinfar Aqa glanced at his Grand Vizier, his expression unreadable. Then his eyes returned to Cromar Try and bore deep into him. "You failed."

"I did," Cromar Try acknowledged, and took a deep breath. This was it, the only chance he would get. "However, I did find something else..."

A very long time later, Cromar Try and Siph Carni left the palace, paused at the foot of the long steps, and looked at each other.

"Whew," was all he could say, and she could only nod her agreement.

San Francisco, California

"Whew." Matt made his breathing slow down as he dabbed at his eyes, trying to make it look like he was scratching his nose. His left arm ached where Afsaneh gripped it too tight. Her breath came in quick little gasps, and her shoulders shook with emotion. Farther down the row, he could hear Kimberly, Kiri, and god only knew who else sobbing, and the murmurs of those trying to comfort them.

That was one hell of a movie, was all Matt could think. How could you pack so much into two short hours?

The lights in the theatre came up and Matt saw a lot of very confused people. It was clear that few of them had expected a movie with substance. They had sat down, popcorn and drinks in hand, anticipating lots of action, little plot, even less meaningful dialogue.

What they had expected was a typical Jim Morris action movie, in space, with hokey aliens and modest special effects. It had been none of that. True, the action was as good as ever. If anything, even more realistic than usual. But since when could Jim Morris, Kiri Oshiba, even the huge, unfamiliar cast of extras all act!

And where had they gotten the budget for those special effects?

People were subdued, and the silence in the theatre was eerie. Both women and men were wiping away tears, a little embarrassed by their reactions until they saw how widespread it was. Then a murmuring began to build, and it grew and a few cheers sounded, as if testing the water.

One person started clapping, up near the front, then more joined in, until the room was echoing with applause, everyone on their feet.

Frederick Farmer stood up in front of Afsaneh, and smiled at her in reassurance. Then he looked at Jim sitting next to her, in exasperation.

"Vicki is a genius!" he announced, then grimaced. "And I hate her!" he said, his expression belying his words. The older man cocked his head, then laughed. "No, Irene, I don't mean that, and please don't tell her I said it. I'm just jealous," he admitted with a sigh.

"Let's get out of here," Jim Morris said, his voice husky with emotion.

Matt started to stand, but Afsaneh still held his arm tight. He pulled it gently, not wanting to lose the connection, no matter how unrelated to him it was.

Afsaneh looked down uncomprehending at her grip on him, then snatched her hand away and wouldn't meet his eyes. Matt lined up her wheelchair so she could get into it with a minimum of effort. She brushed his helping hand away, and twisted around until she was seated. "Let's go," she said, echoing Jim's words.

Matt looked around as he pulled her chair into the aisle. Both Sean and Ellis were watching him, their faces expressionless.

As they made their way out of the theatre, people pressed around Jim and Kiri to offer their praise, ignoring everyone else in the party.

The rest of us might as well be invisible, Matt decided, as a young woman pushed past Kimberly to ask Jim a question.

As they left the theatre, a mob closed around them. Jim and the rest of the cast and crew seemed to take it all in stride, but it made Matt nervous. He glanced around, trying to find a clear path for Afsaneh to the cars.

An Asian man caught his attention, only because he seemed to be the only person present working hard to not notice Jim Morris and company. He casually looked around the crowd, his eyes sweeping through Jim and Kimberly, then his hand reached under his jacket.

Matt's mouth opened, but no words would come fast enough. Then he almost collapsed in relief when all that was pulled out was a cellular phone.

"What's with you, Matt?" Afsaneh sounded irritated and he realized he'd stopped dead in his tracks. He wet his lips to answer, then saw the Asian push a single button and turn and glance upward down the street.

Matt looked up too, and saw nothing but a city of dark, towering office buildings. Puzzled, he looked back just in time to lock gazes with the man. The other's eyes widened and he hurried away.

Matt shot another stare upward, barely registering Afsaneh's strident voice complaining. Then he looked ahead just as Jim Morris turned to see what was bothering his daughter. Matt tried to say something, and Jim's expression became alert very fast. Matt was finally able to get the words out as he jerked Afsaneh's wheelchair to the left, moving forward to throw himself across her lap. He kept pushing with his legs to get her farther away.

"Irene, the roofs! Irene...!" It was all he got out before the pavement behind him splintered, then something crashed through the big windows of the theatre house, sending shattered glass flying inward.

There was a second impact of steel against concrete, then the top story of a building exploded four blocks away.

Matt whipped around to see people panicking everywhere. Women screamed, and so did men. Car doors slammed and engines roared. Inside the theatre, pandemonium reigned.

No one else in Jim's party had moved an inch, except Angela, who had her weapon drawn, and was scanning the crowd. And Jim, who had grabbed Kimberly and yanked her to the side the same time Matt had tackled Afsaneh.

Speaking of which, he looked down to see her staring at him in shock. Her mouth opened, but words wouldn't come out.

"Are you both okay?" Jim was at his side, and Kimberly and Kiri were kneeling next to Afsaneh. Matt could only nod his head, too shaken to speak. "Irene?" Jim listened, then nodded. "She got him. There was only one." He looked at Matt again, and multiple emotions flashed across his features. "Thank you," he said, visibly struggling for control of his voice. Matt could only nod again.

"I owe you," Jim said, then turned away as Matt shook his head in protest.

Matt looked down at Afsaneh. She was holding her broken arm with her good hand, pain on her face as she stared at the ground.

"Are you okay?" he asked. "Did I hurt you? I didn't mean..."

Afsaneh nodded without looking up. She seemed to be fighting to hold back tears. Kiri knelt in front of her, staring at her face intently. She stood and moved around behind the chair.

"I'll take it," she said, her voice allowing no argument. Angela moved to stand on the left side of the chair, and Matt could only nod as he started to back away, depressed at the dismissal.

"No, no, stay here, on her right. Shield her from the crowd." Kiri smiled at him with sympathy, her own face wet with tears.

"Oh," was all Matt could say. As he took his place, he glanced over at Angela, who gave him a grim nod of approval.

"That first shot would have gone clean through Jim and probably gotten Ms. Riahi as well," Angela said, her deep voice firm and steady. "You did good."

Afsaneh's shoulders began to shake, and Matt resisted the urge to put his hand on them to comfort her.

Jim passed in front of them, motioning for them to follow.

"We're getting out of here." Jim had inserted Kimberly between Sean and Ellis, thereby freeing him for action, if necessary.

The three limos were pulled up over the curb in a semi-circle, and within moments, everyone was loaded, and the small procession was roaring eastward. They passed a flurry of police cars and fire trucks, headed toward the theatre. Jim turned around in the front seat and gave them a reassuring smile.

"We've got a rendezvous with Irene a couple blocks away."

471

"What about the cops?" Matt asked, then looked at Angela with guilt. She was driving the limo. "Uh, no offense, Ms. Dawson."

"None taken, Mr. Stickel." Her eyes met his through the rear view mirror for a moment, and he thought he saw a hint of humor in them. Then she was all business again, steering the lumbering vehicle through thinning traffic as they got to the industrial park that was their destination. "I imagine if they have any questions, they know how to find us."

Ten minutes later, they were aboard 'Wolverine, racing eastward into the night.

◆ ◆ ◆ ◆ ◆

Lake Tahoe, Nevada

Groundhog adjusted the binoculars and the three story cabin came into focus. The party seemed to be progressing well enough. Numerous cars, vans, buses even, filled the long driveway from the main road. There were also a few boats pulled up to the small pier and boathouse, testimony to the hardiness of some of the friends of Jim Morris. You didn't just casually venture out onto Lake Tahoe in late November.

Every light in the building seemed to be on, and most of the curtains and shutters were wide open, allowing Groundhog to see the people milling around inside.

Groundhog turned away to consider the accessories stacked neatly on either side of the tripod that held the powerful binoculars. He couldn't be certain what the spaceship was capable of detecting, and it wasn't worth the risk.

Jim Morris walked past one of the windows of the main family room, and Groundhog quickly shifted to the next window as he came into view. He seemed to have recovered his usual good humor, judging from the laughter his comments drew from the group of people that gathered around him.

Groundhog decided it was time to check on the owners of this fine house he was borrowing. They were both laying in their own bed, unconscious, thanks to the powerful sedating gas that had been pumped into their bedroom early this morning.

With any luck, Groundhog would be long gone before morning, and the elderly couple would awaken, unaware that it was a full day later than they thought. When it came to their attention that they had missed a full day, they might chalk it up to their age and approaching senility. Perhaps they wouldn't even mention it to anyone, embarrassed that they couldn't remember what day of the week it was.

Groundhog wanted to be able to use this perch again. Killing the inhabitants, or allowing them to realize they'd been drugged and kept prisoner for twenty-four hours would prohibit that.

On the other hand, if they became suspicious, accidents did happen.

Noting that they were still out cold, Groundhog returned to the window. A quick pan of the area found the Oshiba actress down near the boathouse in the arms of the black woman that had recently begun traveling with her. Watching them kiss didn't interest him, and his scan continued.

There was much to observe and learn from Jim Morris and company.

Osaka, Japan

Sho Toshida kept his expression passive and unreadable as he watched his uncle being told of the failed attempt on Jim Morris.. Let his uncle feel the frustration of trying to deal with these Americans.

This would only strengthen his position in the long run.

Lake Tahoe, Nevada,

Jim loosened his tie and sighed in relief. Safe at home for almost an hour now, several comfortable drinks into the night, a room full of friends, and he'd actually forgotten he had the damn thing on!

He started to take it off, but caught Kimberly watching with disapproval. He winced, then gave her his best puppy eyes look, but she just shook her head and pointed at her high heels.

Take them off, Jim mouthed silently across the room. She gave him a sour look and reached around behind her. He heard a sharp crack, and almost broke into laughter as he realized she'd snapped her bra strap hiding just below the modest back hem.

He grinned and gestured outward expressively with his hands as if to say, let 'em flop! Her look just got more disgusted, and she reached down and caught a handful of panty hose.

He wiggled his eyebrows like a dirty old man and pantomimed pulling them down to the beat of the stripper's theme song. Kimberly let her mouth open slightly and gave him a sardonic stare, narrowing her eyes. Then they widened in innocence, and she glanced around the room.

Jim looked to the left and found Frederick Farmer and Jerry Weinstein staring at him in amusement. Jim tried to look casual and turned the other way.

Yvette Stephanian and Janice Wooley were also watching with interest. He tried to stare them down, but with Janice it was useless. She popped her gum and wisecracked, "You got some kind of itch there, Jim Boy?"

He gave up on that front and shifted his stare back across the room. Every direction, grinning people were watching him, waiting for the next chapter to unfold.

Jim stood up and cleared his throat. "Where is my drink, anyway?"

Before he could take a step, Kabu spoke up. "Uh, your hand, boss?"

Jim looked down to see he held a half-filled glass of champagne already. "Well," he said and drained it. "Now I need a refill."

He fled the room, followed by the sound of laughter.

Jim went to the kitchen to get a fresh bottle. Passing the den, he heard Linda Hoffman's voice. "Y'all shoulda seen what that clever man, Jim Morris was jes' doin'..." He winced and sped up his pace.

Moments later, he had a new bottle open and was refilling his glass. Enjoying the first sip, he decided to try the porch for a while. He quietly closed the side-door behind him and took a deep breath of the crisp winter air.

The moon shone across Lake Tahoe, and in the distance, he could see the Tahoe Queen making its way slowly home from the Squaw Valley side. He'd rode the old riverboat many times, and wished he was on it now. The porch wrapped around the side and back of the cabin, and he began to make his way to get a better view of the lake, when he heard the voices.

He recognized Sean Jackson's and stopped.

"We want to talk to you, man." The cocky young sounded like he was trying to be ominous. "You been hanging around with the boss's

474

kid, trying to make her your property, maybe?"

"No." Jim heard Matt answer softly. "I work for Ms. Martin, who's married to her father. It means I see her from time to time, that's all."

"You seemed awful territorial tonight, driven' her chair, sitting next to her, riding in the same limo." It sounded to Jim like Sean was trying to provoke Matt, and he was tempted to cut it short, but couldn't resist waiting to hear Matt's response.

"Look, I got no claim, and I'm not looking for any with her. She's under age, and quite frankly, she scares the hell out of me. I think she's dangerous." Jim smothered a laugh as he heard Ellis speak for the first time.

"You got that right, man." The big black kid's voice became reproving. "Yo, Sean, cut 'em some slack, will ya? He's just doing what you or I would."

Jim's eyes misted up as the voice grew more somber.

"Really, Matt, you did good, tonight. She's special to both of us, and you got my thanks. I owe you." Ellis was utterly serious, and Jim found himself nodding his agreement.

"Well, yeah." Sean sounded reluctant to give even grudging praise, but he did. "I guess it was cool you handled that okay." Then his old tone returned. "But I still think you're a dork."

"Sean!" Ellis sounded irate.

"No, that's okay, Ellis." Matt's voice was even, and he didn't sound even a little intimidated. "Sean has a right to his own opinion. He thinks I'm a dork, that's cool. Hell, I think he's a dick, but hey, what you gonna do?"

Jim smothered a snort and ducked back into the kitchen as he heard steps approach the corner of the building. He heard Sean protesting, and he grabbed another glass from the counter, then acted like he was just coming out of the cabin.

"Chill, Sean. Hell, I think you're a dick, too! But hey, you're our dick, right?" They came into view, and Jim almost lost his blank look when he saw Ellis beaming from ear to ear.

They both gave him a cautious look that turned to relief when they obviously decided he hadn't heard anything.

"Good evening, sir." Sean said in a straight voice, then snickered a little. Ellis elbowed him. "Ow, quit it, man!"

"Good evening, Mr. Morris," Ellis said in his most respectful voice, and Jim knew it was sincere. This was a good kid.

"Good evening, boys," he said , nodding as he passed them.

"You hear that?" Sean whispered, but Jim could hear him clearly. "He called you boy!"

Jim heard Ellis give his friend a reproving whack on the shoulder. "He called me 'boy' because he's got a daughter nearly my age. You he called boy 'cause you're a dick." They both broke into laughter. "And if you ever call me boy, you'll be looking for your head for days afterwards."

"As if! Come on, right n..." Their voices disappeared into the house and Jim repressed his grin and turned the corner. Matt had obviously heard the exchange and he wasn't surprised to see Jim. When he saw the extra glass, he did raise an eyebrow.

"Sshh," Jim warned and poured him a full glass. "You never know when the wrong people are watching."

"Or listening," Matt said, giving him a challenging stare.

"Or listening," Jim agreed amiably. He raised his glass. "To a safe harbor, if only for the night."

"Safe harbor," Matt responded and drank.

Angela Dawson's voice boomed out of the dark. "You check that boy's ID?"

Jim cracked up at Matt's pained expression. "Relax Matt, you're not driving tonight." He raised his voice. "And you, in the cheap seats, go back to your oriental food!"

"Hey!" Kiri's voice protested. "I resemble that remark!"

Her giggling grew more distant as the two women moved around behind the boathouse. Jim refilled their glasses, then sat down on the bench that ran the length of the porch. Matt looked around, then pulled a folding chair around and settled on it's edge. He met Jim's appraising look head on.

"Getting a lot of that?" Jim asked, motioning after Sean and Ellis.

Matt shrugged, giving Jim a cynical look. "Let's just say the two things I've learned the most about in my martial arts sessions so far are taking a punch and how to fall."

"Not bad things to pick up," Jim said in a neutral voice. "Other things will come, eventually."

"Hmm," was all Matt said.

"Kimberly speaks highly of you." Jim smiled as Matt perked up. "She's says you're a fast learner. Do you like working with us?"

"Yeah, sure," Matt said, brightening at the more pleasant topic.

"I'm just doing go-fer stuff for her, but it's interesting. The week in the Bahamas while we set up Jade Inc. wasn't bad either. This island she bought from the Columbians, I don't understand about, but what else is new?" He gave a self-deprecating smile.

"We bought the island from Columbia?" This was news to Jim, but Kimberly and her committee composed of her, Eric Miles, and Ron Hoffman had been rather reticent about what they were doing. "Hmm, well anyway, I'm glad you enjoy it."

They sat in comfortable silence for a few minutes, then Jim topped their glasses off again. He held the empty bottle up to peer through it, and sighed in regret. Setting it down, he leaned back and gave Matt a nod of encouragement. "Okay, let's get down to it. How did you know what was going to happen on the street?"

Matt told him about the oriental man he'd observed, and the snap conclusion he'd made. Jim frowned, irritated that he hadn't seen the man as well. Damn it, he was getting careless, when he could least afford it.

"That was good work." He suppressed a smile as Matt brightened at the compliment. "I don't suppose we would've had a chance to chase him down, with all the confusion."

"He'd already started walking away," Matt said, nodding his agreement. "Then when the shots were fired, everybody else was running in the same direction."

"Did he look Japanese or Chinese?" Jim almost laughed at Matt's expression. The young man obviously wasn't too clear on how to tell the difference. At least he hadn't said that they all looked alike. "Never mind, I think I know who was responsible."

Jim felt his eyes harden and features stiffen. One more thing for Sukuru to answer for. He forced himself to set that issue aside for the moment, and smiled at Matt with genuine warmth.

"You did good tonight, Matt." Jim finished his drink and looked at the empty glass with regret. He heard a familiar sound from the other end of the porch and leaned forward to speak quietly. "I owe you, don't ever forget that. Those shots would have gone right through me and hit Afsaneh." Jim nodded towards the boathouse. "Never mind what she says, if you want another drink, don't be shy. You'll be bunking here tonight, somewhere or other. Probably one of the rollout couches in the family room. So relax and enjoy the evening, you've earned it."

Jim leaned a little closer, and lowered his voice even more. "I just want you to remember two things." He spoke so quietly Matt had to lean forward as well to make out the words. "First, alcohol slows the healing process for broken bones."

Matt's eyes widened, as if he was wondering if Jim was implying he would soon have some broken bones of his own. Then understanding came to his face, and Jim nodded and stood up to go inside.

"Uh, you said two things, sir," Matt said, also standing.

Jim nodded and kept his voice light. "She just turned sixteen." Then he went in the back door to brave the crowd of the family room once more.

◆ ◆ ◆ ◆ ◆

"That wasn't very subtle," Afsaneh said, rolling into view. "I guess he heard me come out the kitchen door, huh?"

"Not much gets by him," Matt admitted, watching her wheel forward. He sat back down so they would be at the same eye level. She had a blanket over her lap and a light-blue ski jacket for warmth. He looked at her cropped head. "Isn't your head cold?"

Afsaneh blushed at the reference to her shorn hair and tried to cow him with a glare. Matt just smiled and waited her out. There was nothing like a few drinks to vanquish your fears and insecurities, he mused.

She finally relented and pulled another bottle of champagne and two glasses from beneath her blanket. "I brought two glasses. I didn't know you already had one."

"That's okay." Matt grinned at her. "This one's empty. Must be defective."

He watched, impressed as she braced the bottle between her legs, and deftly opened the bottle without spilling a drop, easing the cork out with a loud hissing release of the gasses.

"You're pretty good at that, and with a broken arm."

"Years of experience." Afsaneh handed him the glasses, then filled them both to the brim. She seemed to have trouble deciding what to say as she took one back.

"Well, to a..." Matt began, thinking to ease her tension, but she interrupted him.

"Wait, let me say this," she said. She looked at the glass of bubbles for almost a full minute before she raised her eyes to meet his.

"I appreciate what you did at the theatre tonight." She stopped, as if finished, and Matt began to shrug, but then she started again. "You probably saved either Jim's, or my life tonight, maybe both of us." She sighed and the air came out noisily. "And you were very understanding, when I was upset. You were very sweet." She took a big drink from her glass, her eyes lowered. "Thank you."

Matt nodded and took a healthy swig himself, then gave her a crooked grin. "I'll bet that was tough to say."

Afsaneh gave him a measured look. "You have no idea," she admitted, her eyes never leaving his. They both took another drink, draining their glasses, eyes locked.

Matt finally broke the contact, making a show of discovering his glass was empty. He was glad he was seated, because he suspected his knees wouldn't support him at the moment.

Afsaneh's mouth twisted in a slight smile, and she began to offer him a refill.

"Hey, how's it going, kids?" Kiri came in the back porch door, brushing her hair back with one hand. She was pulling Angela along with the other. They both had a disheveled look about them, and their eyes were bright.

Matt worked his lips to keep a smile from appearing as Kiri snagged the bottle from Afsaneh's grasp, and poured him a refill. Both women had glasses of their own, and she filled them as full as they would go, then turned to Afsaneh. "Another, Afsy?"

Afsaneh frowned as only a few drops came out. "Hey, no fair!"

Angela looked more relaxed than Matt had ever seen her, and she patted Afsaneh on the shoulder with sympathy. "Honey, life ain't fair when you're only sixteen."

The two women exchanged looks as they sipped from their glasses. "Maybe we should get another bottle," Kiri suggested. "After all, we did finish theirs off."

"Why not?" Angela motioned with her free arm, and they took off for the kitchen. "We'll get another bottle, kids."

"Yeah, and go to what bedroom with it," Afsaneh muttered in disgust. "And hey, I'm almost seventeen, going on eighteen!" she called after them. The sound of laughter drifted back to them, and Afsaneh turned to Matt. "You know they're not coming back."

Matt nodded and took a tiny sip. She rolled a little closer, and he sighed and handed her his glass. "You heard what Mr. Morris said about alcohol slowing bones healing?"

479

"I heard." Afsaneh took a sip, and her lips turned upward into a grin. "You know I never listen, don't you?"

"The thought had entered my mind," Matt admitted. He was surprised when she handed him the glass back after a second sip.

"Thank you," he said, and took another drink himself.

"Hmm," she answered, seeming to be trying to come to a decision. She gave him a measuring look. "I don't quite know what to make of you, Matt."

"There's no mystery," he answered, shrugging. "What you see is what you get."

"Right," she said in a dry voice. "Well, I still don't know. You have to understand I like to be in control. And tonight I was helpless, and scared." She was choosing her words very carefully. "I hate being scared, and I've been frightened and helpless for what seems like an eternity. I hate it." Air escaped through her mouth noisily. "Tonight you were the poster child for my fear and helplessness. But you're practically Kimberly's right-hand man, and Jim likes you."

"Isn't that a good thing?" Matt asked quietly, thinking about being a symbol of fear and helplessness, and not liking it a bit.

"I don't know," Afsaneh admitted, and held her hand out for the glass. "But for tonight, friends?"

Matt looked at the young girl with the mesmerizing blue eyes, looking so small in her wheelchair, and kept the pain he felt clear of his face. She had a power over him, such a power that it made him ache. He forced a smile to appear, willing it to be genuine.

"Friends," he said, and watched as she drained his glass.

Everyone was laughing and enjoying themselves and Kimberly felt envy. Right now she would kill for a glass of that champagne being swilled down like there was no tomorrow. And of course, her husband was right in the middle of it all. She could hear his voice and laughter coming from the kitchen.

How many bottles did Jim keep on hand, anyway? In case of emergency, he'd said. She almost wished she were a different person, it would be fun to see Jim's face when she said if she was going for nine months without booze, he was going to do the same!

But, she sighed to herself, she wasn't that type. At least, not in the first trimester. *Come on, Martin, distract yourself.* She saw Ron and Linda Hoffman across the room, talking with two of Afsaneh's friends, Evie Brown and Doyle Franks. She'd listened to Evie play guitar and sing a little while ago, with Doyle providing backup harmonies, and thought they were pretty good. The group noticed her watching, and Linda gave her a warm smile, which she returned.

"Kimberly, I think all the pins are lining up for us." Eric Miles appeared at her side, rubbing his hands together expressively. "We got it, you know."

"Yeah, we did," Kimberly agreed. She noticed he was being discreetly followed by his bodyguard, Kevin Williams. He looked more like a businessman, although his tuxedo was off the rack, rather than fitted, like Eric's. He had short light-brown haired, was clean shaven, a six footer, probably around two hundred pounds of physical fitness.

Pre-Jim, he would have caught my eye, she admitted. He did seem to take his job seriously. Everyone on the premises were survivors of the Jade Viking, friends, or more, but he dutifully followed Miles around, watching the room.

"Jade Inc. is official. And we have the permits to import into the United States, Europe, Japan and China pending..." Kimberly looked around, suddenly concerned. "Is everybody here cleared?"

"Nobody here but friends, Kimberly." Miles waved an arm expansively around the room. "Most of these folks have been helping what we're talkin' about, one way or another."

"You're right," Kimberly admitted. "Ron and Linda were instrumental in getting us import licenses, setting up the deals, you moved the money as needed..."

"You persuaded the Columbians to sell Cin Agua outright," Miles reminded her.

"I believe bribe is the word you meant to use," Kimberly laughed a little ruefully.

"My wife, bribing?" Jim appeared at her shoulder. "What's this I hear about our buying an island?"

Kimberly let him kiss her gently on the lips, then pushed him back a little, wanting to talk about this very subject. "We need a home base. A sovereign base. The Columbians sold us an island, five miles long, three miles at it's widest point, and we got them to relinquish all claims to sovereignty. Jade has a homeland."

"You really think the bribed officials will stay bribed?" Jim look cynical. "Getting other countries to recognize that might be tough."

"We only need a few months to get settled in, then it won't matter what the Columbians or anyone else thinks," Kimberly said, sounding more confident than she felt.

"Us against the world?" Jim's eyes looked sad to her. She agreed with him in sentiment, but that thought was interrupted by the arrival of Kiri and Angela.

"Well, family of round-eyes, Yvette and Janice were telling me we're now dealing in all kinds of interesting things." She smirked, and hooked arms with Kimberly. "Just think. You could have used one of our newest imports that is already catching on. Luna Latex has a wide variety of products already, but..." She leered and winked suggestively at Kimberly, which caused Angela to shake her head. "...Rings of Saturn condoms could change your lives!" She looked a little confused. "Well, could have..."

Kimberly shook her fist good-naturedly at her friend. Then Yvette and Janice came tearing down the stairs.

"We've got it! We just got the first reviews coming over the net!" Yvette raised a triumphant fist in the air and pumped it for emphasis. "They loved it!"

"True shock would have to be what we're hearing," Janice said, stretching her drawl out for effect. "'Defiant Fists of Earth' got an enthusiastic thumbs up from the critics!"

Yvette held up the piece of paper and read out loud. "Definitely the finest hour for the acting careers of veterans Jim Morris and Kiri Oshiba. Displaying a broader expanse of emotions than any of their previous endeavors. An exponential improvement in their skills."

Kimberly looked over at Jim and Kiri, expecting to see approval. To her surprise, Jim looked sad, and Kiri very thoughtful. True, it hadn't exactly been acting...

"Incredible special effects, with the singular exception of the aliens, which were in marked contrast to the rest of the movie. Obviously a concession to the limits of the budget, they lacked imagination and realism." Yvette slapped the papers against a thigh as she pantomimed shooting herself in the head. "Just when we think they might be learning their jobs, these critics reassert their stupidity," she said wryly.

"Well, ah think we're doin' pretty well all around, gals," Linda Hoffman wrapped her arms around the waists of Janice and Yvette. Kimberly watched Jim's reaction as they not only accepted the intimate gesture, but both sank in closer to her. He blinked and looked as puzzled as she thought she would ever see him.

Kiri saw it too, and their eyes met, and Kimberly grinned and pointed with her head. As one, they move in on either side of the three woman, making a chain of five.

"Sisterhood, gotta love it," Janice crooned.

"Ah do," Linda crowed right back, and they shared an expressive, messy kiss on the lips. Kiri and Kimberly pulled the line of women into a circle, wrapping their arms around each other's waists, and they began dancing, if you could call it that, weaving back and forth.

Please, let no one have their cell phones handy for pictures, Kimberly prayed. Kiri grinned at her, and Kimberly impulsively gave her a big wet kiss, also on the lips.

"Have some tequila, have some tequilia..." they began to sing, but couldn't keep the dance going, and the circle broke up, all of them shrieking in laughter.

She saw Jim staring at her, and grinned at him.

Sisterhood, he mouthed questioningly as he was dragged back into the kitchen by Kiri with Janice, Angela and Yvette dutifully following. Kimberly chuckled at his expression and flexed a foot, trying to relieve the tortured muscles of her calves. God, how she hated high heels!

She saw the party would be going on for hours, and decided it was time to get pro-active in her pursuit of pleasure. Frederick looked as if he'd be in the same spot for a while, so she gave him some quiet instructions.

◆ ◆ ◆ ◆ ◆

When Jim was finally able to get out of the kitchen, he looked around for Kimberly, but didn't see her. He'd decided it was time to spend some premium time with his wife, and he had bottles of champagne, seltzer, and two clean glasses just for that purpose.

He noticed Frederick seated over next to the fireplace, and the director motioned to him. Jim walked over and swore as he tripped over something that had been left right in front of the steps leading upstairs.

"Afsan..." he began, then realized the shoes belonged to Kimberly. Frederick was whistling under his breath, as if to some personal tune, and he pointed up the steps.

"If you're looking for your wife...?" he asked, a twinkle in his eye.

"Thanks," Jim said, wondering what the joke was. He picked up the shoes, juggling the bottles and glasses to do so. Someone was going to break their neck, leaving shoes in the middle of the floor like that.

He climbed the steps, his eyes widening when they cleared the final step of the flight. Another flight led to the third floor, and there was a beige bra on the first step. He looked at it for a minute. Of course, he didn't know it was Kimberly's bra, but it looked about the right size, and it was the color of the dress she was wearing.

Jim snagged it as he passed, and his pace quickened on the second flight. Even though by now he half expected it, the panty hose with one leg pointing down the hall still surprised him. He wondered if she'd stood at the top, looking down as she'd taken them off, and he began to breathe harder.

He could see a pile of something in front of their bedroom door, and it came as no shock when it turned out to be the beige dress.

Jim smiled as he tapped on the door with his knuckles. "Hello, anybody home?"

"Not just any body," came the soft reply from inside.

"You got that right," Jim said under his breath, then called out. "So, what's that body wearing, anyway?

"A smile."

Jim grinned and slipped inside the darkened room, locking the door behind him. The indirect moonlight through the window provided plenty of light for him to see Kimberly sitting up in the bed, covers pulled up, only leaving her head and bare shoulders visible.

"You're going to catch a cold, sleeping like that," Jim said, setting the various bits of clothing and glassware on top of the dresser. He leaned over the bed and kissed her. She reached up and took a handful of hair, pulling him down on top of her.

"Who said anything about sleeping?" she asked, her voice sounding thick.

His answer was delayed for some time. When they both finally paused for a moment, Jim began unbuttoning his shirt. As Kimberly helped him with his tie, the covers slid down to reveal her naked breasts.

"Hmm," Jim said, somehow managing to brush his arm along one of her nipples in an agonizingly slow manner as he took off his shirt. "My, those certainly do get hard, don't they?"

"Bastard," Kimberly managed to say, tossing his tie off to the side. It landed draped across a lampshade. He could just see her expression

484

as she glared at him in mock fury. "Pour us something before you get carried away, would you please?"

"Me get carried away?" Jim grinned and complied, handing her a tall fluted glass filled with seltzer water. "Just think of it as thin champagne. So, tell me more about this island."

"Don't change the subject," she replied tartly. "We can talk about that tomorrow. Get your pants off and get your butt into bed." She took a sip from the glass and made a face.

"Are you sure we can do this?" Jim asked, taking his time removing his shoes and socks, then slowly unfastening his belt. "I wouldn't want to do anything to endanger the pregnancy..."

"Listen, mister," Kimberly said, lifting the covers and looking underneath. She smiled at him and wiggled her eyebrows expressively. "I figure we got a limited time for wild, carefree, hedonistic, passionate, imaginative, uninhibited sex before I'm too far along. If you're not interested...?"

"Oh, I think you could say you've caught my attention," Jim laughed, pulling his pants off, just leaving the mini-briefs. He hesitated. Something was not quite right, but he couldn't for the life of him say what.

Kimberly looked at him in askance as he adjusted the blinds on the window. "Hey, the moonlight is romantic. You're not getting paranoid, are you?"

Jim shrugged, at a loss to explain, but left them slightly open, angled upward to allow dim, reflected light off Lake Tahoe. He finished undressing and slid under the covers. Kimberly came into his arms and one leg hooked over his bare hip, pulling them close together.

"I'm not getting paranoid," Jim said, keeping his voice level with difficulty. "I just don't feel like killing a paparazzi tonight."

She laughed and took hold of his hair again. For a moment, their eyes met, barely visible, then she pulled at him, and they were too close for sight.

And, for the night at least, they lived happily ever after.

CPSIA information can be obtained at www.ICGtesting.com
Printed in the USA
LVOW04s0129310115

425077LV00008BA/162/P